THE PRODIGAL SON

THE PRODIGAL SON

Kate Sedley

Severn House Large Print
London & New York

This first large print edition published in Great Britain 2007 by
SEVERN HOUSE LARGE PRINT BOOKS LTD of
9-15 High Street, Sutton, Surrey, SM1 1DF.
First world regular print edition published 2006 by
Severn House Publishers, London and New York.
This first large print edition published in the USA 2007 by
SEVERN HOUSE PUBLISHERS INC., of
595 Madison Avenue, New York, NY 10022.

British Library Cataloguing in Publication Data

Sedley, Kate
    The prodigal son. - Large print ed. - (Roger the Chapman
    mysteries)
    1. Roger the Chapman (Fictitious character) - Fiction
    2. Peddlers and peddling - England - Fiction 3. Great
    Britain - History - Edward IV, 1461-1483 - Fiction
    4. Detective and mystery stories 5. Large type books
    I. Title
    823.9'14[F]

    ISBN-13: 978-0-7278-7623-2

Printed and bound in Great Britain by
MPG Books Ltd, Bodmin, Cornwall.

One

I first saw the strange young man whilst sipping a beaker of my favourite ale (the cheapest), sitting in a corner of the Green Lattis. Mind you, there was nothing unusual about seeing a stranger in Bristol at the beginning of August: it was the time of Saint James's fair.

The priory had originally been granted a nine-day charter for this annual event, but over the years its time had gradually lengthened, first to a fortnight, then to three weeks until, in this year of Our Lord, 1480, it seemed to the inhabitants' blunted senses to have been prolonged indefinitely. Although it was held outside the city walls, drunken brawls and dusk-to-dawn revelry meant sleepless nights for those of us who dwelt within earshot of the priory; and the house in Small Street, where I lived with my wife and three children, reverberated constantly to the shouts and cries of the hundreds of traders who converged on Bristol from all over the kingdom. It was the boast of the prior that Saint James's fair had become one of the most popular in the land.

By day, the city, and particularly Bristol's

many alehouses and taverns, echoed with the strange and – to our west country ears – uncouth accents of certain parts of England that were as foreign to us as those of France or Brittany or the Low Countries. In fact, we had greater difficulty understanding our fellow countrymen from the unknown north and the borders of Scotland than we did the sailors from across the Narrow Sea, who disembarked from the ships that tied up daily along the Bristol backs and wharves.

So, as I said, seeing a stranger that sunny August morning in the Green Lattis was no more surprising than observing an ant on an anthill, and I probably wouldn't have spared him a second glance, had I not been seized by the sudden conviction that I recognized him. Well, perhaps not that, but his face was some-how familiar to me. I had either met him before somewhere, or he reminded me of someone I knew or had once known. Not that his looks were in any way remarkable. It was a small face under a thatch of dark hair, with a pair of equally dark, very bright blue eyes set a little too far apart, a sharp, inquisitive nose and a wide, thin mouth that seemed to be constantly on the verge of smiling. He was not old; certainly younger than myself, and I therefore judged him to be in his early twenties. (At this time, I was approaching my twenty-eighth birthday.) There was some-thing of the Celt in his appearance. A Welsh-man, I thought, until he spoke. Then I could hear the soft, lilting cadences of southern

Ireland.

After that, I lost interest. The only Irishmen with whom I was acquainted wouldn't show themselves openly in a respectable inn like the Lattis, but be tucked away in Marsh Street – Little Ireland as it was known – carrying on their nefarious and totally illegal trade of slaving. (Officially, selling your unwanted relatives into captivity in Ireland had been unknown in Bristol for several centuries. Unofficially, it lined a lot of people's pockets, including those of the great and the good. Especially those of the great and the good.) Needless to say, and as all readers of my previous chronicles will know without being told, my past and infrequent dealings with these gentlemen had been purely in the line of duty, whilst pursuing one of my investigations.

At present, after a short but successful visit to London in the late spring to solve a murder for my friend and patron, Richard, Duke of Gloucester, I had reverted to my proper trade of chapman, much to the relief of Adela, my long-suffering wife. With three voracious mouths besides our own to feed, and a dog who considered it beneath his dignity to provide himself with sustenance from amongst the vermin infesting the city streets, a steady supply of money was essential. High summer, of course, was the time to be striding along the open roads, free of family responsibilities; to be walking narrow, crooked paths or wide rutted highways; to be spending moon-washed nights sleeping in little, sweet-smelling copses, shaggy with leaves. Instead, my attempts at sleep were being rendered hideous by heat, noise and, as often as not, the nocturnal tantrums of my two-year-old son, Adam. But after being absent earlier in the year, I felt in duty bound to ply my trade nearer to home, in the villages and hamlets around the city.

Today, however, I had been restocking my depleted pack from the local market and from the ships at anchor along the banks of the rivers Frome and Avon. I had returned home for my dinner at ten o'clock, but been driven out again, not so much by Adela – who was always willing to allow me a short rest after meals – but by the antics of Nicholas and Elizabeth, my five-year-old stepson and my first-marriage daughter. Closer than two peas in a pod, and with the same predilection for rowdy games, they had, today, been running up and downstairs screaming and shouting at the tops of their voices. (And if you are wondering how a poor chapman came to be living in a two-storeyed house in Small Street, I refer you again to my previous works.)

I was feeling so fraught on leaving the house that a draught of ale in a quiet corner of the Green Lattis had become not merely desirable, but essential if I were to do any work for the remainder of the day. And it was while I was downing the contents of my second beaker that I spotted the stranger.

There were a lot of people in the Lattis that

morning, and this stranger seemed intent on speaking to as many of them as possible, wandering from bench to bench and obviously asking some question; a question to which he was getting no satisfactory answer, judging by the number of shaking heads, pursed lips and expressions of regret on people's faces. It was as he approached my corner that I heard the Irish lilt in his voice, yet at the same time, oddly, I thought I also recognized an underlying west country burr. This, together with the growing conviction that I had met him somewhere before, a long time ago, made me follow his progress around the taproom with the greatest interest.

As though suddenly conscious of my eyes boring into his back, he swung abruptly in my direction and returned my stare with an intensity I found unnerving. Hurriedly, I looked away, swallowing the rest of my ale and, at the same time, fumbling with the pack at my feet, preparatory to leaving. My dog, Hercules, a small mongrel with big ideas, whom Adela had insisted I bring with me, sat up and barked.

'He's a nice little dog,' the stranger remarked, sitting down on the bench beside me, where there just happened to be an empty space.

'He thinks so.'

The Irishman laughed, showing a mouthful of extremely good teeth. Then he hesitated, as though uncertain how to continue, a reticence I hadn't noticed in his dealings with the

9

other customers.

'You're making some enquiries,' I prompted. 'At least, that's my impression.'

The young man nodded. 'That's right. My brother – my younger brother – joined the crew of Master Jay's carvel when it anchored in Waterford harbour about three weeks ago. I was hoping to glean some news of its return, or at least to hear that it had been sighted somewhere by one of the ships putting in to port today. But it seems there's been no word. You wouldn't happen to know anything, I suppose?'

'No, I'm afraid not.' My companion looked crestfallen and I tried to cheer him. 'Three weeks isn't so long, is it? Not when you're searching for something no one is sure really exists.'

It was in fact nearly four weeks since most of Bristol had turned out to give a rousing send-off to one of their own, John Jay, together with his master mariner, the Welshman, Thomas Lloyd, and their crew on a voyage of discovery to find the Isle of Brazil, which, in those days, everyone believed lay somewhere off the west coast of Ireland. Mind you, as far as I could gather, most of the stories concerning the existence of this island were hearsay; and as a mere land-lubber, I considered it foolhardy in the extreme to go sailing off into the blue without knowing exactly what it was I was looking for. But what did I know? I wasn't even a Bristolian, as I was constantly being reminded. I

10

wasn't born with the tang of the sea (or the rivers Frome and Avon – something altogether different, I can tell you) in my nostrils. I came from inland Wells, at the foot of the Mendips.

'I suppose not,' the stranger conceded. 'It was foolish of me to expect any news just yet. But my mother's worried. Colin's her baby. He's only just twenty. She didn't want him to join the ship in the first place. Did everything she could to dissuade him. But John was always mad for adventure, even as a tiny boy. I'm his elder by three years, but he was always the one who got me into trouble when we were young, not, as you might expect, the other way around.'

'Did your father have nothing to say in the matter?'

My companion shook his head. 'Matthew O'Neill is our stepfather. He'll offer advice, but he won't interfere in our lives. He says that's up to our mother.'

'You're not an Irishman by birth, then,' I hazarded. It was a guess, but that faint, underlying west country intonation and the increasing certainty that he and I had met before, made it a possibility.

He smiled. 'No. My name's John Wedmore, and that's where I was born, like my – my father, Ralph, before me.' He gave me a quick, sideways glance, as though afraid I might have noticed that slight hesitation, but I played the innocent and smiled blandly. 'I grew up on my grandparents' sheep farm.

But I'm boring you.'

'Not at all,' I protested politely, far more interested than I was prepared to let on. 'Your own father died?' I made it a question.

'Ten years ago this month. I was thirteen, Colin nearly eleven. The following year, my mother met and married Matthew O'Neill while he was on pilgrimage to Glastonbury, and we went to live with him in Ireland. He's a farmer, like my mother's first husband, except he doesn't raise sheep. Cattle, horses, pigs ... Southern Ireland's pasture is as rich as that of Somerset and Devon. Richer, probably.' He spoke with simple pride, a man happy in his adopted land.

Hercules jogged my right knee with his cold, wet nose, leaving a dirty damp patch on my breeches and reminding me that we had been stationary long enough. Outside, the sun was shining and it was time to be on our way again. But I was reluctant to leave. Two things intrigued me. First, why had this stranger, this John Wedmore, thought it worthwhile to give me his life's history? With no one else in the Lattis had he exchanged more than a few words. He had asked his question, received an answer and moved on, ignoring any attempt to detain him in idle chatter. But with me, he had sat himself down and plunged into conversation. All right, I know I'm nosy. Enough people have told me so for me to accept that it must be true (even if I prefer to call it being interested in my fellow men. And women, of course. That goes

12

without saying).

Second, I had noted – without, however, showing any sign of doing so – his curious reference to 'my mother's first husband'. An odd way, to say the least, of referring to his father.

Hercules gave me another prod, then tried to scramble into my lap, thus ensuring that he could no longer be ignored. If I wasn't careful, he would perform his favourite trick and cock his leg against one of mine; and I had no desire to stink of dog pee for the rest of the day. I rose and offered the stranger my hand.

'I must go,' I said, adding truthfully, 'I've enjoyed our talk. I hope you soon get news of your brother.'

He clasped my hand, holding it for perhaps a little too long, and I had the distinct impression that he was on the verge of telling me something important. But if he had been, he suddenly changed his mind.

'Of the ship and all its crew,' he amended, adding with a slight smile, 'You're not from Bristol, are you? At a guess, I'd say you were born in or around Wells.' My surprise must have been obvious and he laughed. 'Not all west country people speak alike, whatever foreigners might think. My mother comes from there, and I recognize the accent. Her name before her marriage was Ann Acton. Perhaps you might have heard of her? Or of the family?'

Regretfully, I shook my head. Cudgel my brains as I might, I could recall no one of the name of Acton.

'No, I'm sorry.'

He grimaced wryly. 'There's no need to be. I doubt that there's anyone of the name left nowadays. To be honest, Mother never talks of her family, and I've never met a single member of it ... You'd better go. That hound of yours is giving you the evil eye. I don't think his intentions towards you are honourable.'

I grinned. 'You're right. He has a very obnoxious habit when annoyed.' I held out my hand for the second time. 'I'll wish you good-day, then, Master Wedmore.'

If I didn't exactly forget the stranger, there was enough going on during the next few days for me to push him to the back of my mind.

I was at last managing to get more sleep at nights as Saint James's fair drew to a close; but by day, all roads leading from the city were choked with the carts and pack horses of the departing merchants and stallholders. I pleaded the impossibility of selling anything in the countryside at present given such competition; for none of the travellers was averse to making detours into the villages and communities they passed, in order to make a little extra money. (Although, heaven knew, they must have made sufficient money to tide themselves and their families through the harshest of winters and the bleakest of springs in the greatest comfort imaginable, in

14

spite of the depredations of cut-purses and pickpockets, who must also now be looking forward to a life of unparalleled luxury.)

Adela, however, woman-like, refused to accept this eminently sound piece of reasoning and accused me, point-blank, of laziness. Me! A hard-working husband and father ever striving to do his best for his nearest and dearest. I was hurt, and said so. She told me not to be such a hypocrite; and what started as a half-friendly spat might easily have turned into a full-scale domestic war had Adam not chosen that particular moment to tumble downstairs. He wasn't really hurt, but throughout his life, Adam has always been able to turn a very small molehill into a very large mountain by making the greatest possible noise about everything. And this occasion was no exception. His shrieks, cries and groans brought everyone, including Hercules, to his assistance, and it was some time before he could be mollified. And of course it was just my luck that he was still sobbing pathetically on Adela's lap when Margaret Walker, my quondam mother-in-law and Adela's cousin, decided to pay us a visit from her home in Redcliffe.

'That child is allowed too much freedom,' she opined, at the same time eyeing up and down a rather bedraggled Nicholas and Elizabeth. 'They all are, if you want my opinion. Those two look as if they've been playing on the Avon mud-banks.'

They probably had, but both Adela and I

denied the accusation hotly, once more close and united in defence of our offspring. I even went so far as to pat Adam's curly head, and was promptly thumped for my pains by the ungrateful little sweetheart.

Margaret turned on me. 'Why aren't you working on such a fine day?'

I repeated my excuses, which were dismissed with even more scorn than that shown by my wife, but Adela was always loyal – one of her many virtues – and would allow no one to criticize me except herself.

'Why have you come, cousin?' she asked quietly.

Margaret bridled with indignation at the suggestion that her visit might have any other motive than to see her granddaughter, Elizabeth, and how we all went on. But she obviously had various titbits of news she was anxious to impart, amongst others that there was growing anxiety and unease in the city concerning the disappearance of John Jay's ship somewhere in the Atlantic Ocean.

'There's been no positive sighting of it for some time now. And to make matters worse, Maria Watkins informs me that John Jay has died during this past week.'

'John Jay?' I queried, bemused. 'How can anyone know that if he's at sea?'

Margaret sighed, as one dealing with an ignoramus.

'Not that John Jay. His half-brother. The one who married the Botoner girl. They're both sons of John Jay the elder.' I frowned. It seemed to me that the Jay family had singularly little imagination when it came to naming children. Margaret went on, 'I suppose your ignorance is forgivable. You weren't born in the city, after all.'

But mention of the missing carvel had recalled the stranger to mind and set me off on my own train of thought, so that I missed the beginning of her second item of news.

'...insists he's called John Wedmore and comes from Ireland. It leaves poor Dick Manifold in a dilemma, not knowing who to believe.'

'John Wedmore?' I interrupted, startled by what seemed like thought reading on Margaret's part. 'What's happened to him?'

Adam had stopped crying and was falling asleep in Adela's arms, snuffling and dribbling in a most unattractive manner. The other two had grown bored with adult conversation and vanished about their own secret business.

'What ... Who are we talking about, Mother-in-law?' She still liked me to call her that from time to time, even though it was getting on for six years since Lillis, my first wife and her daughter, had died giving birth to Elizabeth.

On this occasion, however, it failed to propitiate her or to improve her temper.

'If you'd pay more attention to what I'm saying, instead of going off into some reverie of your own, you would know that I'm speaking of a young Irishman called John Wedmore – at least, he claims his name is John Wedmore, and he certainly sounds Irish – who's apparently here to make enquiries about his brother, who joined the crew of Jay's carvel in Waterford.'

'Yes. I met him in the Green Lattis a few days ago. He was asking everyone in the alehouse about the ship then. So, what has he to do with Sergeant Manifold? Has he been arrested? It's not a crime, is it, to ask after a missing vessel?'

Margaret turned triumphantly to my wife. 'There you are! I said he was in a dream world of his own. I wonder sometimes how you put up with him.'

'Oh, he has his good points.' Adela gave me a slow, intimate smile that brought me out in goose bumps. Unfortunately, Margaret saw it too.

'That'll do,' she said sharply. 'Keep that sort of thing for where it belongs.' She slewed round on her stool to face me more directly. 'Yesterday, a woman arrived at the fair...'

'But everyone's packing up and going home now,' I objected crassly.

'There are still plenty of traders who haven't left yet,' Margaret snapped. 'Don't interrupt. Her name's Audrea Bellknapp and she's lady of some manor or another, near Wells. It appears she suddenly decided to restock her supply of woollen cloth for the winter, and swears by that stuff they weave up north ... Though why good Bristol red cloth isn't good enough for her is beyond my comprehension.'

18

I didn't reply. I was too busy marvelling, as I always do, at my former mother-in-law's knowledge of anything and everything that goes on in this city almost before it happens. Nothing is ever kept secret for long from Margaret and her two cronies, Maria Watkins and Bess Simnel. The good God alone knows how they obtain their information in so short a time (and I doubt if even He really understands it). Furthermore, they're very rarely wrong about anything, and I'd believe their version of events rather than anyone else's.

'Go on,' I urged.

Seeing that she had at last captured my undivided attention, Margaret mellowed slightly and became more confidential, leaning forward on her stool and tapping my knee in a significant manner.

'Well, while she was haggling over some rolls of cloth with one of the stallholders from Yorkshire, together with her steward and her receiver...'

'Her what?'

'Just what I said when Bess Simnel told me, but Bess has a third cousin who was once a tiring woman to a lady of means. In rich houses, it seems the officer who looks after the control of expenditure is called the receiver.' An odd title, I reflected, for someone regulating the household finances. One could only trust it wasn't prophetic. Margaret continued, 'Where was I? Oh, yes! This Dame Bellknapp was just about to strike a bargain with this fellow from up north, when she suddenly cries out, "Stop that man! That's John Jericho!"'

'John Jericho?'

'The Irishman! The one calling himself John Wedmore. "He's a thief and a murderer!" she says. And sends the receiver to make sure the fellow doesn't get away while the steward goes to find an officer of the law – in this case, as luck would have it, Sergeant Manifold.'

Margaret gave me a sidelong glance, knowing that there was no love lost between the sergeant and myself, Richard Manifold having once had aspirations to Adela's hand. But on this occasion, I simply commented, 'So what happened next?'

'Well, the Irishman denied the accusation, of course. Any man of sense would. But this woman, this Dame Bellknapp, was adamant that some years ago, he had been her page. She claimed that he had robbed her and murdered the wife of her steward, who had disturbed him during the robbery. Indeed, according to Dick Manifold, she called on both her receiver and, in particular, her steward to uphold her accusation. But neither man was prepared to say more than that there was a likeness – a pronounced likeness, the receiver said – to the page, John Jericho.'

'So what was the outcome?' asked Adela, shifting Adam's weight from one arm to the other. He was now sound asleep and making soft plopping noises. His nose was running. His mother wiped it clean on the

20

edge of her apron.

'I believe the Irishman is at present in custody in the bridewell while those in authority try to sort out the rights and wrongs of the matter.'

'Typical!' I ranted bitterly. 'If some poor sod of a butcher or baker had made an accusation like that, with so little evidence to support it, he'd have been sent on his way with a boot up his arse.'

Margaret's skinny bosom swelled. 'There is no need for offensive language, Roger, especially in front of the child.' The child snorted in his sleep and blew two bubbles down his nostrils. Charming! 'Nevertheless,' my former mother-in-law admitted, 'you're probably correct. Maria Watkins informs me that this Dame Bellknapp has some sort of kinship with the mayor, and His Worship feels the young man should be held in custody until the matter is satisfactorily cleared up.'

'And how is that going to happen?' Adela asked in her quiet way. 'If it's just this woman's word against the Irishman's, how can anything be proved one way or the other? If her servants don't back her up...'

'Oh, they will, given enough time and sufficient inducement,' I declared viciously. 'Either this poor wretch will be left to rot in prison, or he'll find himself dangling from the end of a rope. And all because this Dame Whatever-her-name is, is second cousin four times removed to our mayor.'

'Calm down, Roger,' my wife advised me.

21

'All this bile will upset your digestion.' She regarded me anxiously as I began pulling on my boots. 'Where are you going?'

'To the bridewell to have a word with Richard Manifold.'

'Don't be ridiculous!' Margaret snapped. 'This is none of your business.'

Adela added her mite. 'Margaret's right, sweetheart. Leave well alone. Don't get involved with what doesn't concern you. To please me,' she added.

I met her large, dark eyes, so full of love and concern, and experienced the same familiar shock at how much I loved her. I always did whenever I paused long enough to give the matter serious thought; which wasn't as often as it should have been, I have to admit.

'What's this Irishman to you, anyway,' Margaret demanded angrily, 'that you should go to his assistance?'

'I told you. I met him in the Green Lattis and had a talk with him. And he's not Irish by birth. He and his brother are originally from Wedmore, his father's village. And his mother is from Wells.'

Margaret shot up straight on her stool. 'Ha!' she cried.

'What do you mean, "Ha!"?'

'You say he's from around these parts. From Wedmore. Maybe Dame Bellknapp is right about him, after all. Maybe he is this page. And his name is John, as well.'

'That's nothing,' I snapped back. 'You'd find half a dozen Johns even in a place as small as Wedmore.'

I couldn't help wondering why I felt so protective of this young man on the strength of a brief conversation which had taken place a few days ago. Perhaps it was because of that sense of having known him at some time in the past.

'Please, Roger,' Adela insisted, 'don't get involved in this.'

'You need to be out on the road with your pack,' Margaret scolded. 'Your family can't live on fresh air.'

It was a consideration, certainly, but I knew it wasn't Adela's. She was only afraid that I might put myself in danger again.

'All right,' I conceded grudgingly. Adela smiled. It was reward enough. 'As you say, this affair has nothing to do with me.'

I should have known better than to tempt fate in that way. The words were barely out of my mouth when there was a loud, officious knocking on our street door.

Two

I answered the door, Adela still having Adam on her lap, asleep. It was Richard Manifold.

I groaned. 'What do you want?'

Not the most welcoming of remarks, but what he had grown to expect from me. There was an armed truce between us, but we would never be the best of friends.

'I need to talk to you,' he said. 'Can I come in?'

I stood aside reluctantly. 'If you must. We're in the kitchen.' I saw no good reason to open up the parlour. The number of free meals he ate in our house, he was practically one of the family.

He followed me along the stone-flagged passageway to the door at the foot of the stairs, pulling up short on the threshold, momentarily disconcerted by Margaret Walker's presence.

'Ah, Sergeant, have you come to arrest him again?' that dame asked with her usual acerbity, then laughed so uproariously at her own joke that she woke Adam, who began to snivel. Adela gave her a reproachful glance.

Without being asked, Richard Manifold seated himself on the stool I had previously been occupying and smiled warmly at my wife. I wished he wouldn't do that. To add insult to injury, Adela, who was busy trying to soothe our son, instructed me to bring him a cup of ale.

'You look so hot, Dick. It will cool you down.'

Controlling the meaner side of my nature with a commendable effort, I went to the ale barrel in a corner of the kitchen and returned with one of the children's horn beakers, placing it on the table with exaggerated care, so that its contents didn't slop. Adela eyed me warily. She knew that when I was at my most courteous, I was most annoyed. It was my turn to smile, which did nothing to reassure her.

'So,' I said, propping myself against the wall and glaring at our guest, 'what do you want with me, Richard?'

'I'm hoping you'll come back to the bridewell with me. We've a fellow in custody there who insists on speaking to you.'

'I don't know anyone in the bridewell just at present,' I protested. 'And why would anyone wish to speak to me? I'm not a lawyer.'

'No.' Richard sniggered offensively, then attempted unsuccessfully to disguise it as a cough. 'It's the Irishman who's been taken into custody.' He glanced at Margaret Walker. 'I'm certain you've heard about it. The fellow's been in the bridewell for nearly twenty-four hours. Enough time, I'm sure, for the good dames of Redcliffe to have winkled out all there is to know about the affair.'

Margaret tried to look affronted, but succeeded only in looking smug. 'Why would he want to speak to Roger?' she demanded.

The sergeant shrugged, equally perplexed. 'Perhaps he's deranged.' It was his turn to enjoy a joke at my expense. 'He does, however, and as, strictly speaking, he's not been charged with anything as yet, I couldn't see it would hurt to do as he asked.' Richard turned back to me. 'Will you come?'

I agreed with alacrity. I was already wearing my boots, but didn't mention that, but for Adela's dissuasion, I had been about to go and see him. I was in a hurry now to get our uninvited guest out of the way before Margaret divulged the information concerning John Wedmore that I had so recently given her.

Fortunately Adela, as she so often did, discerned my purpose, and rising from her stool, dumped Adam unceremoniously on her cousin's knees. Our son immediately expressed his outrage by lashing out with his fists and roaring at the top of his voice. (He has always had powerful lungs.) While Margaret was making efforts to calm him, I ushered Richard Manifold out of the house.

The bridewell is a gloomy place, tucked into a curve of the city wall close by the Needless Gate; and even though the August day was bright with sunshine, the air inside struck chill against my flesh and made me shiver. I had rescued a friend from there only the previous year, and wouldn't have wished my worst enemy to be confined within its damp and dripping walls.

John Wedmore had a room – if so cramped a space could be dignified by such a description – to himself, just to the right of the entrance and separated from the common cell by a thin partition that might afford him privacy, but did nothing to muffle the cries and groans of his fellow prisoners. A stone ledge, running the length of the outer wall and piled with straw, served as both bed and seat. A tiny, barred window gave insufficient light to do anything without a constantly burning taper; a rush candle whose fragile radiance did nothing at all to alleviate the gloom.

The Irishman – for so I continued to think of him, even though it was not strictly true – was sitting with his head in his hands, but he glanced up quickly as I entered. I heard the key rattle in the lock behind me, and Richard Manifold said, 'Yell when you're ready, Roger. One of the turnkeys will be somewhere about.' On which not-so-reassuring note – the turnkeys being notorious for sloping off to the nearest alehouse whenever the fancy took them – I found myself a prisoner in this depressing little cell.

John Wedmore sprang to his feet and stood staring at me, almost as if I were a ghost.

'You came,' he said, offering a trembling hand. 'I didn't think you would.'

I realized that he was shaking all over and

pushed him back on the bench. 'Sit down, lad. You can barely stand.' I seated myself beside him. 'Yes, of course I came. Did you think I was the sort to leave a fellow human being in distress without seeing what I could do about it?'

He drew a gasping breath. 'No, not really. But as far as you knew, I've no particular claim on you, and you might have been busy.'

'As far as I knew?' I queried suspiciously. 'Why do you say that?'

There was a moment's pregnant silence. Then he muttered in a kind of strangled whisper, 'Because I'm your brother.'

The silence stretched, seemingly endless, before I managed to croak, 'My brother?'

But I knew it was the truth. I knew at last who it was he reminded me of. From the dregs of memory, there floated to the surface a face almost identical to my companion's. My father's.

My father, Roger Stonecarver, had died a month after my fourth birthday, following a fall from scaffolding while repairing the ceiling of Wells Cathedral nave. If anyone had asked me before that moment, I would have said I didn't remember him. But suddenly, I could see him as clearly in my mind's eye as I could see the young man sitting next to me; the same small face, the same needle-sharp blue eyes, same dark hair and thin, wiry body. Oh yes! John Wedmore was my father's son, all right.

'Your half-brother,' he amended. When I didn't answer immediately, he went on timidly, 'I assure you that it's true. My mother told me so, and she wouldn't lie. Why should she? She had nothing to gain by it. She...'

'You've no need to go on,' I said quietly. 'I believe you. I remember him. You're his spitting image.'

'Am I?' he asked eagerly, leaning towards me, his nervousness forgotten. 'I never saw him, of course. He'd been dead eight months when I was born. My mother said he didn't even know of my existence. She hadn't had a chance to tell him ... You don't favour him, then?'

I shook my head. 'No. I look like my mother. Big and fair.' Memories, like a half-remembered dream, were coming back to me; things long buried and forgotten. Although not quite forgotten and not buried quite deeply enough. I had a sudden vivid recollection of finding my mother with tears running silently down her cheeks, while she stood at the table in our cottage, preparing a meal. Childlike, when confronted by an adult's distress, I had started crying, too. She had gathered me up in her arms and rocked me to and fro until I was soothed. Later that day, curled up on my straw mattress in a corner of our single room, I had heard my parents arguing violently outside, but I had been too young to relate the two incidents. I reckoned that I was about three years old at the time, possibly already four, so it would have been shortly before my father was killed. His adultery with this young man's mother must have been the cause.

'You're blaming me.' John Wedmore's voice interrupted my thoughts. 'It's natural, I suppose. But, truly, it's not my fault. I didn't ask to be born.'

'What?' I blinked stupidly at him, trying to adjust my mind, first to the notion of my father having been unfaithful to my mother, and secondly to the idea of having a brother. All right, half-brother. But I had grown so used to the fact that I was alone in the world, apart, of course, from Adela and the children, that I couldn't immediately accept the shackles of another blood tie.

'I said you blame me for being alive. I daresay I'd feel the same if I were you.'

I turned to look at him. He was slumped forward dejectedly, his bony hands and wrists dangling between his knees. He was the picture of misery, and in spite of myself, my heart was wrung. I didn't dare stop to question if this was a deliberate ploy on his part – Adela always vowed that I was much too cynical – but flung an arm about his shoulders and gave them a squeeze.

'Of course I don't blame you,' I assured him with a little too much fervour to sound completely sincere. 'How could I?'

'You didn't take much convincing.' I could tell he was worried.

'I told you. You're extraordinarily like him. When I first saw you in the Green Lattis the

30

other day, I was certain that we'd met before somewhere.'

He drew a deep breath. 'I have to confess I knew who you were as soon as I heard your name mentioned. I made some enquiries about you. And got some surprising answers. It seems you're not just a chapman. You have a reputation for solving mysteries. So when this happened' – he made a comprehensive gesture to indicate our bleak surroundings – 'I wondered ... well, I wondered...'

'If I'd help you,' I supplied, when he seemed unable to continue. He nodded mutely. 'But I must be sure,' I went on, 'that what you've told me so far is the truth. You didn't come here on purpose to find me? You came to Bristol in search of news of your brother?'

'Colin. Yes. My other half-brother,' he corrected me with a wry smile.

'Your—? Oh, yes, of course.' I understood now the reference to 'my mother's husband' that he had made the other day. 'Ralph Wedmore was really your stepfather.'

'Yes, although I didn't realize it at the time. It wasn't until she married Matthew O'Neill and we were living in Ireland that my mother told me the truth.'

'It must have come as a shock.'

'Yes ... and no. It explained a lot of things. It explained why my fa— why Ralph had always preferred Colin to me; why my Wedmore grandparents disliked me, and made it plain that they did so; why I never had anything to do with my mother's people, the

31

Actons, even though some of them lived at no great distance. Nevertheless, you're right, it was a shock. I'd always thought of myself as a Wedmore, and discovering at the age of sixteen that I wasn't, gave me a strange feeling of ... of not belonging.'

I could understand that. Prince or pauper, people need to know who they are. 'Go on,' I encouraged him. 'You seem to have been made aware of my existence.'

'Yes. Of course my mother knew all about you and your mother. And she told me she'd always asked any visitor to the farm about you both. She knew that you'd entered Glastonbury Abbey as a postulant. And she heard that Mistress Stonecarver had died just before Christmas the year that the Earl of Warwick invaded and put King Henry back on the throne. Then, a month or so later I think it must have been, someone told her you'd left the abbey without taking your vows and turned pedlar. That was around the time of the battle at Tewkesbury, and also around the time that she met my stepfather. After that, everything happened in a hurry and Colin and I went to Ireland to live. I didn't even know you were in Bristol when I came here. It was only by chance someone mentioned a chapman called Roger. So, like I said, I started asking questions and from the replies I received, I came to the conclusion that you were the man. My half-brother, I mean. Even so, I don't suppose I'd have claimed kinship if this hadn't happened.'

'Or if I hadn't had a reputation for solving mysteries. Why not?'

He shrugged his thin shoulders. 'Why would you want to be saddled with an unknown younger half-brother?' He gave the ghost of a grin. 'They can be a damn nuisance, as I know only too well.'

That made me laugh. I found my initial, instinctive hostility turning to liking as I saw in him traits of character that I recognized in myself. I had always known that my cynical view of the world must have come from my father: my mother had been far too simple and devout a soul to see life with a jaundiced eye.

I settled my buttocks more comfortably – or as comfortably as possible – on the stone bench. 'Tell me all you can about this Dame Bellknapp,' I invited.

'That's just the point.' He threw out his hands in despair. 'I can't tell you anything about her. I don't know her. I've never seen her before in my life.'

'Then tell me what happened yesterday.'

'What can I say...? Well, to begin with, I'd realized it was useless hanging around Bristol any longer. I could wait for days ... weeks ... and there might be no more news of John Jay and his crew than there is today. Which is to say, nothing. And if I stayed away too long, my poor mother would also begin to worry about me. So, I decided to go home. There was an Irish ship tied up at Welsh Back that was sailing for Waterford this morning, on the early tide.' His voice caught momentarily in his throat and I could see that he was near to tears. 'It's gone now,' he went on gamely, mastering his emotion.

'So?' I prompted.

'So I arranged my passage with the captain and then I went to the fair to find a present for my mother. I knew most of the traders and stallholders had packed up and gone by that time, but there were still enough of them left to make a visit worthwhile.' He drew a deep breath. 'I was just haggling over the cost of a gilt chain – the rogue who was trying to sell it to me wanted twice what it was worth – when I heard this woman shouting, "Stop that man! That's John Jericho!" Of course, I looked around like everyone else, to see who it was that she was talking about. Then to my utter astonishment, I realized she was pointing straight at me. The next thing I knew, one of the two men with her – her servants I guessed them to be – was holding me with one of my arms up my back and one of his arms clamped round my neck. The second man had gone haring off, and returned a few minutes later with a sheriff's officer, this Sergeant Manifold. Meanwhile, the woman was ranting on about how I was a robber and a murderer and should be arrested immediately. I think if she'd had her way, I'd have been strung up there and then on the nearest gallows.'

'What about her two household officers?' I asked, although, thanks to Margaret Walker, I already knew the answer. 'Did they recognize you?'

'They both agreed there was a likeness. The man who was holding me said there was a great likeness, but the other man, the one she called George and introduced to Sergeant Manifold as her steward, wasn't nearly so sure. Something of a likeness was what he said, and reminded his mistress that the murder and robbery took place six years ago. A long time, as he pointed out.'

'But it didn't satisfy this Dame Bellknapp. Is that her name?'

'I think so. I wasn't paying close attention. I think, though, it would have been enough for the sergeant – after all, it was just her word against mine with no one really prepared to back her up – had she not claimed kinship with a certain John Foster, who lives in Small Street. Apparently, he was once sheriff of Bristol and is thought almost certain to be the next mayor.'

Not the present holder of the office, then. Margaret Walker's information had at least proved faulty on that score, which pleased me. Everything else she had told me had proved to be distressingly accurate.

'I know Alderman Foster,' I said. 'Well, not to speak to, but he's a neighbour of mine. A salt merchant, and although he doesn't live in one of the bigger houses in Small Street, he's reputed to be a very wealthy man. A man of considerable influence, too, among the city fathers.'

35

'Oh, I can confirm that,' my half-brother told me bitterly. 'As soon as his name was mentioned, Sergeant Manifold's attitude towards me underwent a change. He instructed those two henchmen of his—'

'Jack Gload and Pete Littleman,' I interrupted with an involuntary laugh. 'That pair of incompetents.'

'I don't know what they're called, and I don't care,' my companion snapped. 'I only know I found myself clapped up here, in the bridewell, while the sergeant went off to consult with his superiors. And the result is that I seem destined to be imprisoned here indefinitely while those in authority try to decide which one of us – this woman or me – is telling the truth. And in the end, of course, they'll take her word against mine, because she's bound to bribe or blackmail her servants into supporting her.'

If he was waiting for me to contradict him, he was doomed to disappointment, because he was right. That's the way the world turns, always has done, always will do, and there's nothing anyone can do about it. Well ... maybe. Sometimes.

'What do you know about the crime you're being accused of?' I asked after a moment's silence.

My companion shrugged. 'Six years ago, there was a robbery at this woman's house ... near Wells.' He added defiantly, 'I was in Ireland six years ago. I explained that. We went there very shortly after my mother

36

married my stepfather.'

'And you never came back?'

'No. Never. Not until last week. And I shan't be returning, either, if I get out of here alive.' He shivered suddenly, and his voice broke.

'Oh, we'll get you out of here,' I said bracingly, and, had he but known it, with far more confidence than I was actually feeling.

He turned to me eagerly. 'You'll help me, then?'

I regarded him mockingly. 'Isn't that why you wanted to see me? To ask for my assistance?'

'Are you angry?'

'No, of course not.' Was I being quite truthful? But he was my father's son. I was sure about that. And if I couldn't help my own kith and kin, what right had I to be helping other people? Besides, any mystery intrigued me. Moreover, I could see as plainly as John could – and it was time to start thinking of him by his baptismal name – that there would most likely be a miscarriage of justice unless someone did something to prove his story true. Of course, I could go to Ireland, seek out his mother and anyone else willing to swear that he had been at home there at the time of this murder. But what good would it do? It was the truth that was needed, and what mother isn't prepared to perjure herself in the cause of her son's life? As for other witnesses, could their memories be relied upon after such a length of time? And in my experience, most communities, particularly rural ones, will close ranks to protect one of their own. Matthew O'Neill was undoubtedly that, and his stepsons would therefore be regarded in much the same light.

So, if I ruled out crossing the sea to Ireland, what was my next step? Obviously, to find out more about this Dame Bellknapp and her history, and as she was related to my neighbour, John Foster, I should have to risk a rebuff from the former sheriff and mayor-elect and pay him a visit. He might know something worth the telling; although distant relatives, if they had any sense, usually remained just that.

I got to my feet and reached down to press my half-brother's hand with my own. 'I'll do what I can,' I promised, and shouted for the turnkey to let me out.

Luck was with me. The young maidservant who answered the door informed me that Alderman Foster was at home, and if I liked to step inside, she would see if he was willing to receive me.

As I had told my half-brother, this was not the largest or grandest house that Small Street had to offer, but the hall's elaborately carved stone fireplace, the painted and gilded ceiling beams, upper window panes made of glass, not horn, a corner cupboard displaying a quantity of pewter and fine silverware, a spruce coffer spread with green velvet cushions and a branched candelabra, holding five wax candles, all spoke of a wealth and comfort that Adela and I would never achieve. Most of our neighbours resented the fact that such a raggle-taggle bunch as my family had come to live amongst them at all, and I was more than half prepared to be told that Alderman Foster was unable to receive me. But five minutes later, he appeared, smiling affably and brushing his hands together.

'Salt!' he exclaimed with a laugh. 'I've been down in my cellars, Master – er—?'

'Chapman. Roger Chapman,' I murmured. 'A neighbour of yours.'

'Ah, yes, I know! You have three small children and a dog.' I groaned inwardly. We were notorious, even Hercules. But, miraculously, the alderman didn't seem to mind. 'I only have two children, a son, Richard, and a daughter, Agnes, but they are all a gift from God.' I wasn't so sure about that, but kept a still tongue in my head. 'So, how may I be of service, Master Chapman? I must apologize for having kept you waiting, but, as I said, I've been down in my cellars, checking my latest consignment of salt, received yesterday from the Rhineland.' His eyes lit with a sudden enthusiasm. 'Have you ever visited the Rhineland, my dear sir? Have you ever seen the city of Cologne? Or its marvellous, wondrous cathedral?' I denied all knowledge of both and was informed sadly that I had missed one of the miracles of the world. 'However,' my host continued, 'I daresay you haven't come to hear me ramble on. What can I do for you?'

And he waved me to an armchair at one side of the fireplace, while he seated himself in another, opposite.

I perched awkwardly on the edge of the hard, carved seat, more embarrassed by his condescension than I would have been had he snubbed me, and explained what I wanted. When I had finished, without admitting to my personal interest in the case, John Foster rubbed his chin thoughtfully.

'A history of the Bellknapps, eh? I heard what had happened, of course. Sergeant Manifold informed me of the incident and asked my opinion of what should be done. What could I say? Audrea Bellknapp's a distant kinswoman of mine, and although we don't see much of one another as a general rule, she always visits me and my wife whenever she's in the city, as she did on this occasion, before going on to the fair. As far as I know, she's a sober, upright and honest woman who wouldn't accuse a man falsely. She must genuinely believe this young man to be who she thinks he is.'

'Neither of the men with her recognized him as this John Jericho.'

'Her steward, George Applegarth and her receiver, Edward Micheldever ... No, they didn't, or so I understand. That is what's exercising Sergeant Manifold's mind. That's why I consulted with my friends.' That meant the mayor and the rest of the Bristol hierarchy. 'But the charge is a serious one. Robbery and murder. It couldn't be ignored.'

'It's your cousin's word against my – against the Irishman's,' I pointed out, sounding more aggressive than I meant to.

John Foster raised his eyebrows, but if he noticed my slip, he gave no sign. He merely shrugged and asked, 'What's your interest in this affair, Master Chapman?'

'I don't like the thought of an innocent man being imprisoned,' I answered with perfect truthfulness.

'If he is innocent, neither do I,' was the swift rejoinder. 'So am I to understand that you are taking up the cudgels in defence of this John Wedmore?' He gave both names an emphasis that it was impossible to ignore.

'John is a very common name,' I said. 'Indeed, it's your own. And although he freely admits to being from these parts originally, the young man swears he was in Ireland six years ago.'

'Do you intend going to Ireland?' the alderman enquired with a faint smile.

'No.' And I gave him my reasons.

His smile grew rueful. 'You believe justice is only for the rich?'

'I think that people with money and influence stand a better chance of it. Yes, of course I do, don't you?'

He didn't answer the question directly, but after a moment, said quietly, 'I'll do what I can to help you in your quest for the truth of this matter. You want a history of the Bell-knapp family. I've already told you, I'm not close to my cousin, but I've probably picked up enough information over the years, during her annual visits to Saint James's fair, to be of some use to you. I stress again that my knowledge is limited, but such as it is, I'll share it with you.'

He arranged himself comfortably, eased his back, cleared his throat and began.

Three

'Audrea Bellknapp is a cousin on my mother's side of the family, several times removed. What her maiden name was, I have no idea and can hardly believe it relevant to anything you might wish to know. Suffice it to say that ever since I can remember she has been first the wife, then the widow of Cornelius Bellknapp of Croxcombe Manor. This, I understand, although I have never visited it, lies a mile or so from Wells, at the foot of the Mendips.

'I have met Cornelius, in the days when he used to accompany his wife to Saint James's fair, and, if I'm honest, I didn't much care for him. A very serious man, strict in his ways and expecting everyone else to be the same; judging people by his own limited perception of right and wrong. A man who lacked – now, how shall I put it? A man who lacked the gift

42

of laughter. Yes, I think that describes him perfectly. But he suited Audrea, who is herself a woman without a sense of humour.

'Cornelius did not, however, get on with the elder of their two sons. According to my cousin, Anthony was nothing but trouble from an early age.' John Foster grimaced sympathetically. 'I imagine the poor young fellow was simply a normal, mischievous little boy, but one who was punished and reprimanded so often for what was nothing more than high spirits that he grew up at loggerheads with both parents, but particularly with his father. Audrea was inclined to blame, at least partially, the boy's nurse, Jenny Applegarth, the wife of her steward, who doted on the child, and was thought to have encouraged his rebellious attitude.'

'Isn't that the woman who was murdered?' I interrupted.

The alderman nodded. 'It is. She was, I believe, stabbed to death while trying to foil a robbery by my cousin's page, this John Jericho you've heard mentioned.'

'The young man Dame Bellknapp accuses Master Wedmore of being.'

'Quite so. But to return to my history. Anthony Bellknapp was some ten or eleven years old – I think I'm right in saying that – on the way to manhood, at any rate – when another son, Simon, was born, and who, for some unfathomable reason, immediately became the darling of both mother and father.' My informant sniffed disparagingly. 'He

43

accompanied his mother to the fair last year and Audrea brought him with her when she paid us a visit. The vagaries of the human heart are hard to define, Master Chapman. I thought him a mean-minded, petulant youth, with little interest in anyone or anything beyond himself and his own interests. However,' the alderman added hurriedly, 'maybe I'm being unfair to him. He wasn't here above an hour, and it's difficult to make a judgement in so short a time.'

'Did Mistress Foster and your children feel the same way about him?'

'My son wasn't present, but ... Yes, yes! I have to admit that my wife and daughter shared my opinion. But again, I digress. Where was I?'

'The birth of Simon Bellknapp.'

'Indeed. Well, his arrival, and the fact that he could do no wrong in his parents' eyes, only made matters worse between Anthony and his father. Eventually, about eight years ago, things came to a head. There was a terrible quarrel between the two, during the course of which it seems Anthony drew his dagger and attacked Cornelius. I gathered from my cousin's account that he did no actual harm to his father, but the assault was serious enough for the young man to be sent packing and told in no uncertain terms never to set foot in the house again.'

'What happened to him?' I asked curiously.

The alderman shrugged. 'No one knows. He's never been seen from that day to this.

Nor has there been any word as to his whereabouts. At the end, when Cornelius was dying – he died the year before last – I think he might have been glad to have some news of his elder son. At least, that was the impression my cousin gave me. And he refused to disinherit Anthony completely. Audrea tells me that everything is left to her until either Simon reaches his eighteenth birthday (when the manor will pass to him entirely) or until Anthony reappears, whichever is the sooner, when everything goes to *him*.' My informant tut-tutted disapprovingly. 'A most foolish way of carrying on, if you want my opinion. It leaves young Simon for the next three years not knowing where he stands; uncertain of his future. Much as I dislike the boy, it's unjust to my way of thinking.' John Foster took a deep breath and stretched his arms above his head. 'So there you are, my dear sir. That's the history of the Bellknapps insofar as I know it. A very incomplete history, I'm sure, but I'm afraid I can do no better.'

'Can you tell me anything about the robbery and murder, sir?'

The alderman shook his head. 'No more than you probably know already. My cousin's young page tried to steal the family silver, was discovered by Jenny Applegarth and he killed her. He disappeared the same night, vanishing without trace. Until, perhaps, now. But if you want more details on that score, you'll have to approach my cousin herself. Or someone of her household.'

'Is she still in Bristol?'

'I doubt it. She's not a woman who approves of inns, and the journey to Croxcombe can easily be achieved in a little over three hours on horseback at this time of year, when the roads are dry and the days longer. I imagine her departure from the city was delayed following her accusation against this unfortunate young fellow – Wedmore? Is that the name? – but, even so, she could still most likely have been home before nightfall. I'd own myself surprised if she were still here, but you could make enquiries. Sergeant Manifold will probably be able to tell you. He must know what arrangements have been made.'

I thanked my host for his time and patience and, although I didn't mention it, his civility. Here, at least, was one resident of Small Street who seemed not to resent having me and mine as his neighbours; and, indeed, he accompanied me to the street door just as if I had been a person of consequence, offering me his hand in farewell.

'I hope you can get at the truth of this affair, my friend. If this young man *is* who my cousin claims him to be, then he deserves to pay the penalty for his crime. I met Jenny Applegarth many years ago, and can tell you that she was a good woman. If, on the other hand, this fellow is *not* the missing page, he must go free. What was it the late Sir John Fortescue said? Better that twenty guilty men should be found innocent than that one innocent man should be found guilty? Something like that. My memory's not all that it should be.'

I thanked him again. He adjured me to visit the beauties of the Rhineland if it were ever in my power to do so, and we parted the best of friends; he, presumably, to continue checking his newly delivered consignment of salt, I in search of Richard Manifold.

I ran him to earth eventually in Redcliffe, where he, Jack Gload and Pete Littleman had been despatched to quell a minor apprentices' riot in one of the weaving sheds. Everything was under control by the time I arrived, and the two ringleaders were being marched away for a spell in the stocks, so he was perfectly willing to stop and chat (particularly as it turned out Adela had just that afternoon invited him to supper). He gave his prisoners into the heavy-handed charge of his henchmen and walked with me down to the wharves where we could look at the ships riding at anchor, the cranes unloading their various cargoes, and where we could admire the bright summer morning, the clouds high and thin, the sharp, salt tang of the sea borne up river on the faintest of breezes, the shadows ruffling the surface of the water in patterns of grey and gold.

'So what did Master Wedmore want with you?' Richard enquired, adding before I could reply, 'As if I couldn't guess! Heard about you, has he? Your wonderful reputation as a solver of mysteries come to his ears?' Even in his present mellow mood he couldn't resist the jibe. 'Wants you to help him, does he?'

I nodded. 'He has asked for my assistance, yes.' I had no intention of mentioning the blood tie between us. For the present that would remain a secret known only to my half-brother, myself and, in due course, Adela. I had never kept anything from her during our married life. If she had any advice, she would give it and I might even follow it. I had the greatest respect for her opinions.

'And what do you intend, then? Is there anything you can do?'

'There might be. I've already called on Alderman Foster to learn something about this Dame Bellknapp. He's a distant kinsman of hers.'

'You've called on John Foster?' Richard was frankly incredulous. 'You had the temerity...?'

'He was extremely pleasant and told me all I wanted to know,' I interrupted. 'Or as much as he could. I'm his neighbour, after all.'

'You're his neighbour on sufferance, because Mistress Ford left you the old Herepath house. However, I've always thought him a tolerant sort of man. One of the richest men in Bristol, for all he lives so modestly. Does a lot of charitable works.' There was a brief silence while we both watched the sunlight dancing on the river; then Richard asked again, 'So what do you intend to do? Why did you want to speak to me?'

'Alderman Foster's of the opinion that Dame Bellknapp would have returned to Wells yesterday if she could. Did she?' My companion nodded. 'In that case,' I went on, 'what about Master Wedmore? What happens to him?'

'It's been agreed that we hold him for thirty days. If, at the end of that time, Dame Bellknapp has not returned to the city with evidence or witnesses to corroborate her accusation against him, then he will be released.'

'Thirty days!' I exclaimed in disgust. 'You're going to keep that poor boy locked up for thirty days while some vindictive old crone browbeats her dependents into backing up her story? If he were—'

Richard sighed wearily. 'I know! I know! If he were the son of a belted earl, or even of a city alderman, it would be different. Of course it would. Grow up, for heaven's sake, Roger! See the world for what it is, not as you think it ought to be. And, furthermore, Dame Bellknapp is not a crone. A little long in the tooth, perhaps – I doubt she'll see forty again – but a handsome woman for all that.'

'I can see she's won you over,' I accused him furiously, and stormed off home without giving him a chance to answer.

I barged into the kitchen, where Adela was seated at the table with Nicholas and Elizabeth, trying to teach them their numbers and letters, took off my boots and threw them across the room. My spirits lifted a little, however, when I realized that my former mother-in-law was no longer present.

Adela relieved the children of their hornbooks, patted them on the head and told them to run along. 'Your father's present mood is unfit for your little eyes and ears.' They needed no second bidding, and after casting me a leery glance, disappeared upstairs, where they were soon to be heard charging around like Hannibal and all his elephants. 'Well? What's the matter?' she demanded.

I told her, calming down as I did so, soothed by her presence and by that rare ability of hers to listen without interrupting. But even when I'd finished, she still said nothing for a full minute, one hand pressed to her mouth, while she assimilated the most important part of my story.

At last she asked, 'And you're certain, sweetheart, that this John Wedmore isn't lying? That he *is* your father's son? Your half-brother?'

'I have no doubt whatsoever. I knew he reminded me of someone the moment he walked into the Green Lattis. He's my father, as I remember him, to the life. And other memories confirm the truth of what he says. He's blood of my blood, I'm sure of it.'

She took a deep, trembling breath. 'Then you must help him. Of course you must. You have no choice in the matter. You ... You don't think he could be who this Dame Bellknapp says he is?'

'He swears he was in Ireland at the time of the murder. I see no reason to disbelieve him, and until I do...' I let the sentence hang.

'In which case,' Adela said quietly, 'if you believe him innocent, then you must do your best to prove him so.'

I sighed, drawing her up into my arms and holding her tightly. 'It'll mean going to Croxcombe Manor,' I said. 'I can't tell how long I might be away. I'll take my pack, of course. The journey will take me the better part of two days; longer if I stop at the intervening villages to do some selling. Here!' I let her go and emptied the contents of my purse on the kitchen table. 'Is that enough to keep you and the children while I'm away?'

Adela counted out the coins and nodded. 'A week perhaps, if I'm careful.' She added reproachfully, 'You haven't been very busy these past few days.'

'I know.' I was contrite. 'I'll take Hercules with me. He'll be one less mouth to feed.'

'Oh, you'll certainly take Hercules with you,' Adela answered cheerfully. 'I had no intention of keeping him here with me. Three children are hard enough work for any woman.'

'A good job it isn't four, then,' I said without thinking.

The moment I'd spoken, I could have bitten out my tongue. How, I asked myself, could I have been so crass, so cruel? It was only a little over four months since our baby daughter had died within a few days of her birth, leaving Adela totally devastated. One glance at her face told me that my mindless remark had done more than reopen a wound still raw and bleeding; it had confirmed her in the belief that, far from sharing her grief, I had been relieved to be spared the extra responsibility of another dependent. Moreover, I had a daughter, Elizabeth. Adela wanted one who was truly her own.

'Sweetheart!' I gasped, trying to take her back into my arms. 'Forgive me! I wasn't thinking.'

'No,' she answered in a flat voice that chilled me to the bone. She didn't repulse my embrace, but endured it in a way that was more indicative of her lacerated feelings than any storm of abuse would have been.

'I'm sorry,' I whispered. 'I didn't mean it.' I kissed her passionately on her unresisting mouth.

She raised one hand and stroked my cheek. 'I know you didn't. It doesn't matter.' But of course we both knew that it did. She gently pushed me away. 'I must prepare the evening meal. Richard's coming to supper.'

'So he told me.' And then, because I knew I was in the wrong, and because I hated myself for having hurt her, I added unkindly, 'I'm sure he'd be only too pleased to advance you any money you might need while I'm gone. And, incidentally, I'd rather you didn't say anything to him about my going to Croxcombe Manor. If he doesn't see me for a week or two, he'll just think I've gone on my travels.'

'I'm not in the habit of discussing our affairs with Sergeant Manifold,' my wife replied coldly, turning away to ladle water from the water-barrel into a pan, which she set to boil on the fire. 'And I certainly shouldn't dream of borrowing money from him. If necessary, I'd go to Margaret.' She watched me pull on my boots again. 'Where are you going now?'

'To the bridewell to tell Master Wedmore ... to tell my brother,' I corrected myself self-consciously, 'not to worry if he doesn't hear from me for a while.'

Adela reached up and took a bunch of dried sage from its nail on the wall before turning to regard me curiously, insult and injury both forgotten in that open-handed, generous way of hers.

'You like having a half-brother,' she said. 'I can tell.'

I grinned sheepishly. 'I'm getting used to the idea,' I admitted. 'If it turned out now that he was lying, and his likeness to my father was nothing more than coincidence, I think I'd feel...'

'Bereft?' Adela suggested.

I nodded.

I set out early the following morning, one of the first to pass through the Redcliffe Gate, taking with me my pack, my cudgel (my trusty 'Plymouth cloak') and my dog.

The latter was full of energy, which was

more than I was, Adela and I having made up our differences overnight in the time-honoured manner, not once, but twice; with the result that although I was a happy man, I was also a tired one. My children had waved me goodbye with their usual indifference, Adam punching me in the belly – admittedly the only part of my anatomy he was able to reach – as a parting reminder that he was growing up and not to be trifled with. (As if I'd dare!) Elizabeth and Nicholas were too used to my departures to regard them as anything other than a normal part of life and therefore wasted no time on unnecessary hugs and kisses. They just reminded me, by the simple expedient of patting my scrip, that they would expect a present or two in it when I returned. That I might, one day, *not* return never crossed their minds, but Adela, as she always did, clung to me and begged me to take care.

As Hercules and I left the walled seclusion of the city behind us, the sun rising steadily to reveal an almost perfect August morning, my spirits revived, and I began to stride out in a manner better suited to the dog's restless energy as he chased imaginary rabbits and rolled in the grass. The sky was almost colourless; inlets, rivers and creeks of palest blue flowed between sandbanks of cloud, while low on the horizon, the light was a dazzling transparency, shimmering with the first, faint warnings of noonday heat. I was where I liked most in the world to be; on the open road, on my own.

54

Well, when I say on my own I don't mean it literally, of course. At that time of year, high summer, the main tracks were crowded; parties of jugglers and mummers travelling from house to house, offering entertainment; itinerant friars, preaching hell and damnation; pilgrims heading for Glastonbury; civic messengers; now and again a royal messenger full of his own importance; family parties going on visits of either duty or pleasure to other members of their kinfolk; and plenty of fellow pedlars taking advantage of the fine weather to be out and about, selling their wares. In fact, if I wanted to be by myself, I was forced into the byways and lesser known tracks, many of which would only be familiar to a native of the area, such as myself.

I may have lost a little custom this way, but not very much. There were plenty of small settlements – mostly charcoal burners and their families – where the womenfolk were glad of needles and thread, a new spoon, either horn or wooden, to replace a broken one, or a good plain buckle for a belt that had seen better days. As for Hercules, he was happy to make friends with every mangy cur who invited him to cock a leg on a favourite tree, or enter into hostilities with any dog sufficiently foolhardy to offer him offence. Altogether, our first day's travel passed in a most satisfactory fashion, keeping us out of the blazing heat and putting enough money in my purse to justify the excursion even in Adela's eyes.

By dusk of that first day, thanks to a ride of some miles in a friendly turf carrier's cart, we had reached the banks of the meandering River Chew, and were directed by a local shepherd to an isolated, but by no means deserted hostelry some few hundred yards south of the main track. The landlord, a jolly, red-faced man by the name of Josiah Litton, welcomed me in, patted Hercules on the head, and, for an eminently reasonable charge, offered me the use for the night of a straw mattress on the stone floor, near the central fire. His only bedchamber, apart from his and his wife's, was at present occupied by a certain Sir Damien Chauntermerle, an important local landowner on his way home after several weeks in London. I was assured that the knight's squire and page would be joining me around the fire to sleep, so I need not be afraid of lacking company. (I groaned inwardly and prayed to the Virgin that neither of my companions snored. It would be bad enough with Hercules wheezing in my ear all night.)

The landlord then bustled about, bringing me a beaker of ale, bread, cheese and some of those small wild scallions, also known as buckrams or bear's garlic. (They are best eaten in spring, when juicy and tender, but even late in the year as this was, they can make a decent meal with cheese if freshly picked.) Sir Damien, it transpired, had supped earlier in his chamber, and the page and squire had gone out to join the groom in the stables for a game or two of hazard.

'Don't suppose they'd object to a fourth,' my host suggested, when I had finished my meal.

Tired as I was, the evening was still far too light to think of sleeping, and I should only be roused when my two companions came to bed. Hercules was happily gnawing on a mutton bone, with which the landlord had thoughtfully provided him, so I decided to take Master Litton's hint, and went out to the stables.

These were a couple of stalls at one side of the inn, the first containing a bony nag, plainly belonging to the premises; which meant that the thoroughbred next door had to be the property of Sir Damien Chauntermerle, even had the fact not been made self-evident by the three men seated amongst the straw, playing at dice.

I introduced myself and was immediately welcomed into the circle with the blunt hope that I had sufficient money to cover my losses. I answered cheerfully that I didn't expect to lose, at which they all laughed so heartily that I insisted on inspecting the dice, suspecting them to be loaded. They had not been tampered with, however, and after several games of raffle and two of hazard, I realized that, in the groom, I was up against a master thrower, whose spin on the dice could produce an almost endless run of sixes. When I had lost more than I could afford, I at last called a halt, a move heartily endorsed by the squire and the, by now, nearly penniless page. The groom just grinned good-naturedly and gathered up his winnings. The rest of us leaned back against the bales of straw and reckoned up our losses, commiserating with each other as we did so.

I nodded towards the horse and the saddle of tooled leather, hung on a nail at the back of the stall. There was also a richly embroidered saddle blanket and some of the harness fittings looked to be of gold.

'A wealthy man, your master,' I commented.

The squire laughed and the other two gave knowing grins.

'He is now,' the former agreed. 'But ten years ago, it was a different story. Poor as a church mouse, was our Sir Damien. Kewstoke Hall was falling into disrepair; the roof was leaking, the rats were gnawing away at the foundations, and those of us who stayed with him did so because our fathers had worked for his all their lives and it was our home as much as his. Still, he's been a good master and not stinted those of us who remained since he became rich.' The other two nodded their approval of his words.

'How did that happen?' I asked. 'And where is Kewstoke Hall?'

'Away to the north-west of here, near the coast. As to the upturn in his fortune, death and remarriage, my lad.' The squire thumped me on the back, reiterating, 'Death and remarriage. His first wife died and he got wedded again, only this time he was careful to marry money and, of course, youth. The first time, when he was young and feckless, was for love. The second time was for security and comfort.'

'Who was the lucky – and presumably rich – young lady?'

'As a matter of fact, the daughter of a widow who lives in these parts. Ursula Bellknapp of Croxcombe Manor.'

'Bellknapp? Of Croxcombe Manor?' I tried not to sound too interested. 'Isn't that somewhere near Wells?'

'Not many miles distant, yes. Sir Damien *was* thinking of paying a visit there before returning home, so he could give Lady Chauntermerle an account of her mother's health, but ... but...'

'He decided against it,' said the page with a giggle.

'They don't get on?' I suggested.

'We-ell, let's just say Dame Bellknapp can be – er – difficult,' the groom smirked, rattling the dice and looking hopefully at the rest of us.

We hastily declined another game and scrambled to our feet, stretching and yawning and generally intimating that it was time for bed.

He called us cowards and spoilsports, but grinned good-naturedly and wished us goodnight. He was bedding down in the stable with his master's precious horse.

The landlord had damped down the fire in

the aleroom, but it was still giving out a comfortable heat. He appeared from his own chamber when he heard us come in, brought the three of us another beaker of ale apiece and waited until, wrapped in our cloaks, we were settled for the night. Hercules opened one bleary eye, gave me a look, then closed it again with a contented sigh.

The inn was stuffy in the August heat and one of the shutters had been opened to reveal the moon, like tarnished silver, rising over the shadowy trees. Somewhere an owl hooted, sharp and clear, against the more muffled drumbeat of advancing hooves...

I sat up abruptly, disturbing my companions.

'Whassa matter...?' the squire demanded indistinctly.

'Listen!' I hissed. 'Someone on horseback, approaching the inn.'

The landlord had also heard it and came out of his chamber, followed by his goodwife, both of them clutching stout-looking staves. I reached for my cudgel just as a voice from outside shouted, 'Ho there, landlord! Travellers! Open up, I say!' There was a loud thumping on the door.

The landlord raised his eyebrows at the rest of us: he couldn't afford to deny genuine trade. We grouped ourselves around him as he cautiously drew back the bolts.

He need not have worried. A perfectly respectable, well-dressed man of about my own age entered and courteously doffed his hat. Beyond the open door, in the moonlight, we could see an equally respectable-looking servant, holding his horse.

The stranger opened his mouth to speak, but before he could utter a word, a shocked voice sounded behind us.

'You! What in the name of God and all His saints are you doing here?'

Four

I swung round to see who had spoken and was confronted by a tall, thin man with a rather small head perched precariously on top of a long, narrow neck. A pair of slightly bulbous brown eyes were, at this moment, wide with alarm and indignation, and the note of accusation in the surprisingly deep voice was unmistakable. The thinning hair was ruffled, as though the speaker had just risen from bed, a fact confirmed by the loose red velvet robe thrown on anyhow over the crumpled nightshift.

'*You!*' he repeated in horrified accents, as though unable to believe the evidence of his own eyes.

'Sir Damien!' the landlord exclaimed apologetically, confirming the gentleman's identity, which I had already guessed. 'I'm sorry that you should have been disturbed. A late night traveller, that's all.'

The knight took no notice, continuing to glare at the new arrival like a rabbit transfixed by the eyes of a snake.

The stranger, whom I judged to be a year or so younger than myself and at least half a head shorter, had taken off his cloak, draping it negligently over one arm, and even in the failing light, I could tell that it was obviously fashioned from good broadcloth and lined with sarcenet. The rest of his clothes, including a pair of fine leather boots and a plume of jaunty feathers in his cap, suggested someone of adequate, if not substantial, means, while his general air and way of speaking indicated a person of breeding.

He, too, had been shocked by this unexpected encounter – he had started violently at the sound of Sir Damien's voice – but he recovered his poise quicker than the older man.

'My dear brother-in-law,' he drawled, 'what a pleasant surprise. I hadn't counted on seeing any of the family until tomorrow at the earliest. My sister is well, I hope?'

Brother-in-law? Sister? This certainly wasn't Simon Bellknapp who, according to Alderman Foster's narrative, could only be fifteen or sixteen years of age. Therefore it had to be the renegade; the missing Anthony.

It was while I was brooding on the unlikelihood of such a coincidence that I realized the worst. God had His finger in the pie again, interfering in my life and manipulating me like one of those wooden puppets on strings that you see at fairs. Of course, as I've said so often before, I had a choice. I always had a choice. I could gather up Hercules and leave the alehouse now and not look back, for I've never felt that God would punish me if I did so: he would leave it up to my conscience. I had abandoned the religious life all those years ago and against my dead mother's wishes, and the Almighty had offered me the chance to serve Him in another capacity, by using my deductive powers to bring the guilty to book. But in this particular instance, He had added an even greater inducement: He had brought me face to face with a brother I hadn't even known I had. I was trapped. I acknowledged it. I was angry and resentful, but already committed. I was intrigued. I couldn't walk away if I tried.

I took a deep breath of acceptance and immediately felt better. The landlord's wife had meanwhile lighted a couple of tapers, and by their frail radiance I studied the stranger more closely. I saw a pleasant, roundish face under a thatch of curly dark hair (the young man had removed his hat) and a mouth with a full, if somewhat pouting underlip. It broke now into a broad grin and the stranger started to chuckle deep in his throat.

'You look just the same, Damien, even after eight years. A little thinner and greyer, perhaps, but otherwise not very much altered. I

63

trust Ursula is in equal good health?'

The knight ignored the question. 'Where have you been all this time?' he demanded furiously, but was interrupted by the landlord asking, 'Master Anthony, is it really you?'

The young man clapped him on the shoulder. 'It's me, Master Litton. Back like a bad penny, as you can see. And your good-wife! As beautiful as ever!' And he planted a smacking kiss on the blushing Mistress Litton's cheek.

'Oh, get on with you! You haven't changed a bit. You always did know how to wind a woman round your little finger. That poor Jenny Applegarth never stood a chance where you were concerned.'

'Ah, my dearest Jenny! How I'm looking forward to seeing her again! How is she?'

There was a moment's silence, then the landlord hurriedly placed an arm about Anthony Bellknapp's shoulders and urged him farther into the aleroom.

'My dear sir, come in! Come in! You need a bed for the night and food. Janet' – he turned to his wife – 'rekindle the fire in the kitchen. There's broth in the pot. I'll tell your man to stable your horse, Master Anthony. Our only spare bedchamber, I'm afraid, is occupied by Sir Damien.' He glanced hopefully at the knight. 'If your worship would care to share your bed...?'

'No I would not,' snapped the older man angrily. 'What I want is an explanation of where that man's been all these years and what's brought him home at last.'

Sir Damien's squire and page had, by this time, tactfully withdrawn to a corner of the room, where they presumably hoped to remain unnoticed, as fascinated by the turn events had taken as I was. I remained in full view of everyone, my own man and answerable to no one. Not that I think Sir Damien was even aware of my presence, so incensed was he by this sudden and unlooked-for return of the prodigal.

The prodigal himself, having once recovered from the shock of meeting his brother-in-law so unexpectedly, seemed to be enjoying the situation. He drew up a stool to the damped-down fire and straddled it.

'What's brought me home, my dear Damien? Why, the news of my father's death, of course, I understand that this – er – unhappy event occurred two years ago, but I was only told of it a month since, and that by pure chance. I've been living in the eastern counties for some considerable time now, and during a recent visit to Cambridge, fell into conversation with a man who also happens to be a native of these parts, although he's not lived here since his boyhood. He corresponds with his sister, however, and knew that my father had died the year before last. He was even able to tell me the terms of the will.' (The sister was plainly the sort of informant every brother would wish to have.) 'Naturally, I settled my affairs in the east and started out for home the very next day. And so here I am, come to claim my inheritance. I can only hope that my mother and brother will be better pleased to see me than you are.' But even as he voiced this pious wish, Anthony Bellknapp glanced at me and pulled a comical grimace.

'Then you're more of a fool than I took you for,' Sir Damien snapped, 'and all I can say is that I'm glad I shan't be present to witness the meeting between you and young Simon. He'll be in a state to cut your throat, so I'd watch out if I were you.'

Anthony laughed openly. 'What you mean, dear brother-in-law, is that you'd like to see him try. No, no! You'd like to see him succeed. Then I'd be dead, he'd be hanged and Ursula would become my father's sole heir.'

'Nothing of the sort,' the knight answered austerely. 'Ursula's dowry was more than adequate.'

The younger man straightened his back and stretched. 'Oh, I know that. But enough is never quite enough, my dear Damien, now is it?'

'I'm returning to bed,' the knight replied. 'I trust you'll have the good manners to be gone before I get up in the morning.' And he mounted the short flight of stairs to the spare bedchamber over the aleroom with a stateliness and outraged dignity it was a joy to behold. At least, I thought so, and, judging by the grin on his face, so did Master Bellknapp.

'What a piece of work he is!' he exclaimed. 'He hasn't changed at all in eight years.'

The landlord followed his wife out to the kitchen, and while they were absent, we were joined by Anthony Bellknapp's servant, who announced that he had watered and fed their two horses and seen them settled for the night. He was a tow-headed lad, whose eastern counties speech fell oddly on my ears, and who smelled powerfully of sweat and bad breath. Nobody else seemed to notice, however, and Sir Damien's squire and page came creeping back to the fire where they were soon in conversation with the young man, whose name, we learned, was Humphrey Attleborough. Anthony Bellknapp leaned forward on his stool, hands dangling between his knees, apparently listening to their idle chatter, but in reality, as I could see by his glazed expression, miles away in his thoughts.

I wondered what he was thinking about, although it took little imagination to guess. He had to be speculating on the nature of his reception at Croxcombe Manor when he arrived there the following day. If he had been entertaining a wild hope that he might be welcomed by mother and brother after his long absence, Sir Damien's attitude must have warned him to expect the worst. And there was yet more grief to come when he discovered that his beloved Jenny Applegarth was dead, brutally murdered. Master Litton's quickness of mind had prevented him learning the truth tonight, but it had only postponed the evil day.

The landlord reappeared, as though summoned by my thoughts, carrying two bowls of broth and the heel of a loaf which he handed to the new arrivals. Then he bade us good-night and withdrew. I once again wrapped myself in my cloak and lay down beside Hercules, suddenly realizing how very tired I was after the exertions of the day, and hoped that the other four would soon follow suit. But I need not have worried. I had been up before dawn and covered, by my reckoning, a good eight miles before being rattled and jolted another eight in the turf carrier's cart over rutted tracks baked hard in the summer heat. The voices of squire and page, master and manservant gradually faded until they were nothing but the echo of my dreams. Hercules snorted and wheezed; then he, too, became part of the distant chorus as I fell deeply and soundlessly asleep.

It might have been the sun streaming in through the open alehouse door that woke me; but I rather fancy it was Master Litton, who 'accidentally' tripped over my long legs as I sprawled beside the cold ashes of yesterday's fire. I sat up with a snort to find that, apart from Hercules and the landlord, I was alone, my companions of the previous evening having all disappeared.

'Where is everyone?' I asked, still drugged with sleep.

'You *were* tired, my lad,' the landlord marvelled. 'There have been comings and goings through here since daybreak, what with five breakfasts to see to, Sir Damien's saddlebags to be packed and hauled downstairs and no one bothering to lower his voice. But you slept through it all like one dead. And that ill-favoured hound of yours.' The intelligent animal lifted his lip and farted loudly just to show his contempt. Master Litton roared with laughter and continued, 'Yes, they've all gone on their way, if not exactly rejoicing, then at least anxious to reach journey's end before nightfall. You're the only one left.'

I scrambled to my feet, noting that the sun was already halfway up the sky and climbing steadily, then staggered outside and held my head under the stable pump until I felt fit enough to face the new day. I combed my hair with one of the combs from my pack, cleaned my teeth with the piece of willow bark I always carried and went back indoors to a meal of oatcakes and (it being Friday) poached fish, which Master Litton assured me was no more than forty-eight hours old, having been purchased fresh from the Abbot of Glastonbury's fishpond the day before yesterday.

'How do I get to Croxcombe Manor from here?' I asked as he placed a beaker of small beer before me and gave Hercules another bone to gnaw on.

'Croxcombe Manor, eh? Well there! If you'd woken betimes, you could have accompanied Master Anthony. But on second thoughts, I'd give the manor a wide berth today, if I were you. Things are going to be pretty lively there,

I reckon, when the prodigal turns up. I don't suppose anyone but George Applegarth will be pleased to see him.'

I swallowed a mouthful of oatcake and asked, 'Why not?'

The landlord cast a quick glance over his shoulder to make certain that Mistress Litton was nowhere about, then sat down opposite me at the table.

'The Bellknapps aren't near neighbours of ours, you understand. On foot it'll take you the best part of the day to get there, especially as you're already late setting out. On horse-back, now, and with an early start, I daresay Master Anthony will arrive by midday. So, as I say, we're not near neighbours, but not so far distant that one doesn't hear things. And the Bellknapp family has been good for gossip in and around Wells these many years, what with Cornelius's feud with the elder boy, Anthony's disappearance and then, of course, the robbery and murder of Jenny Applegarth. And now' – the landlord chuck-led – 'just as matters seem to have settled down, here's the renegade marching back to claim his inheritance and put young Simon's nose well and truly out of joint.' He sighed. 'I'd give my last groat to witness *that* en-counter.'

I said, 'I know a little of the Bellknapps' affairs. A cousin of Dame Audrea is a neigh-bour of mine, in Bristol.' I saw the landlord's look of startled disbelief and hurried on, 'I assure you it is so, unlikely as it may seem.

And to prove I'm telling the truth, I know that Cornelius Bellknapp left everything to his wife until the younger son reaches his eighteenth birthday, when he inherits, but only if the elder brother hasn't returned by then, when everything goes to *him*. And now he has.'

Master Litton nodded, eyeing me with a new and wary respect, as though he wasn't quite sure what to make of me. A pedlar who lived in the same street as a kinsman of Dame Bellknapp was something of a phenomenon, and I could tell he was half inclined to say no more. But curiosity got the better of him and instead of going about his business, he fetched himself a beaker of ale and sat down again.

'So you can understand as well as I do why Master Simon won't be pleased to see his brother, and why I'd like to be a fly on the wall at that meeting.'

'Yes. But you also implied that others in the household won't exactly welcome Anthony with open arms. What about his mother?'

The landlord shrugged. 'Gossip says Dame Bellknapp never had much affection for him, not even when he was small. That's as maybe, and more than I know, but it's certain he didn't get on with his father, and his mother holds his behaviour as partly responsible for her husband's death. Although Master Bellknapp must have felt some remorse for his treatment of Anthony, or he wouldn't have left things as he did when he was dying.'

'You say this George Applegarth is fond of him?'

'Oh, aye! He's Dame Bellknapp's steward and his wife, Jenny, was nurse to both the boys in turn. They've no children of their own and Anthony was like a son to them, the more so because he was neglected by his parents. Yes, George Applegarth, at least, will be delighted by his return.'

I reflected that for a distant neighbour, Master Litton knew a great deal about the Bellknapps, their history and their household. I was not, however, surprised. I had grown up in Wells and knew as well as anyone how far and how swiftly gossip travelled. And what better place than an alehouse – or inn, as I felt sure the landlord would have preferred me to call it – for the telling and hearing of such local tittle-tattle?

'And the rest of Dame Bellknapp's retainers?' I enquired. 'Surely they have nothing against Master Anthony? His return can make no difference to them.'

Again the landlord shrugged and waved his free hand while sipping his ale. 'We-ell, the old chaplain, now, Henry Rokewood, nearing sixty I should guess, he and the older boy never got on. Poor old Sir Henry has a limp and a stammer – had 'em for years – and boys being boys, and a bit cruel sometimes, Master Anthony used to make fun of him. I've seen him do it in the street with everyone looking on and sniggering behind their hands. I've laughed myself, I have to confess, for he was a good mimic. But being the butt of a joke's a different thing altogether, and the chaplain was often near to tears. No, I don't reckon Sir Henry'll be pleased at Master Anthony's return.

'Then there's the chamberlain, Jonathan Slye. His sister has a bastard child, a son. A handsome young fellow, about nine years old. The girl could never be persuaded to name the father, but Jonathan Slye swears it's Anthony.'

And people think that they see life in the towns! 'Go on,' I invited, highly diverted.

'Not much more to tell, really. Rumour has it that Reginald Kilsby – he's the bailiff – has high hopes of marrying Audrea Bellknapp someday. People do say they're already lovers, but that may be just malicious gossip. Dame Bellknapp don't strike me as the sort of woman to marry her bailiff. Bit of fun between the sheets, yes. Marriage, no. But the point is that Reginald Kilsby thinks she might. Simon probably wouldn't raise any objections: his mother can persuade him to almost anything. But Anthony, he could quite well forbid all thought of any such nonsense.'

I grimaced. 'If all you say is true, then you're right. It doesn't seem likely that Anthony Bellknapp is in for the warmest of welcomes when he reaches Croxcombe.'

'No. And furthermore, Edward Micheldever – that's the receiver, a man somewhere about your own age – has not long married a pretty young wife. Anthony's reputation where women were concerned left much to be desired before he disappeared eight years ago. He may have improved with age, of course, but I doubt it. And he didn't mention anything of a wife and family to me during our conversation at breakfast this morning. Didn't talk like a married man either, so I don't reckon he's settled down and got wed.'

'So his arrival really will put the cat among the pigeons?'

'Bound to. Can't but do aught else that I can see. Lord! Lord! There'll be ructions as sure as God's in His heaven and Old Scratch is down below. Here!' The landlord caught up my beaker and his own. 'Let's have another stoup of ale.' He noticed my expression and grinned. 'It's all right. No charge, but don't tell my wife.'

He filled the cups from one of the barrels ranged against one wall, and then, rendered mellow more by the gossip than the beer, resumed his seat. Hercules had abandoned his bone and was stretched out contentedly in front of the cold hearth.

'Do you know anything about the page, this John Jericho?' I asked. 'The lad who was accused of the robbery and the murder of Mistress Applegarth?'

Master Litton rubbed his forehead. 'Nothing much more than that, really. It's a long time ago now. Six years gone. Quite a stir it caused at the time. I remember the family were away when it happened. Master Bell-knapp, Dame Audrea and young Simon,

74

they'd gone on a visit to Sir Damien and Lady Chauntermerle at Kewstoke Hall. Took most of the household with them except for the lower servants, but for some reason, Jenny and George Applegarth must have stayed behind. And the page, of course. Don't know why he didn't go. Must've pretended to be ill. Anyway, he decamped with all the family silver and some of Dame Audrea's jewels that she hadn't packed. Poor Jenny must have disturbed him, so he killed her. Stabbed her through the heart as cool as you please. Disappeared and has never been seen again from that day to this.'

'Did you ever encounter him?'

'Once or twice, when I was in Wells. He was dancing attendance on his mistress.'

'Can you recall what he looked like?'

The landlord screwed up his face. 'Not very well. Small, dark, young. Someone told me later that he claimed he was turned sixteen, but he seemed younger'n that. As I said, it's a long time ago.'

I nodded. 'Was he very long in Dame Audrea's service?'

'Now you're asking me what I've not the smallest notion of. I don't see the Bellknapps all that often; just now and again when I travel to Wells. I just hear the gossip, and I don't suppose anyone would have thought Dame Audrea's getting a new page worthy of mention. It was only when he proved himself such a villain that I even knew his name.'

'A strange name, Jericho,' I commented.

75

'So we all thought. General opinion was that it wasn't his own. Took it from the story of Joshua, we reckoned.'

'I noticed last night that you avoided telling Anthony Bellknapp that Jenny Applegarth was dead.'

'Aye, I did that. Let him hear it from someone else, not me. He'll be heartbroken. I guess he loved her better than anyone else in the world.'

A silence fell between us, broken suddenly by a high-pitched, scolding voice.

'What are you doing there, Josiah, sitting around, swilling ale, like the lazy great lump that you are?' Mistress Litton had arrived, brandishing her broom.

My companion jumped to his feet, looking guilty. 'Just answering a few questions of the chapman's, my dear. He was enquiring about the Bellknapps and the murder.'

The goodwife sniffed, but as it seemed her policy was not to upset a paying customer, she held her temper in check.

'Oh, that!' she said. 'Everyone remembers that.' She nodded at her husband. 'It was the year George Applegarth broke his arm when he fell down the undercroft stairs. It was why he and poor Jenny hadn't accompanied Master and Mistress Bellknapp to Kewstoke Hall.'

'There you are!' the landlord exclaimed. 'That's your answer, Chapman. That's why they'd remained behind.' He regarded his goodwife fondly. 'My Janet has a better

76

memory than I have.'

'Oh, get along with you,' she answered, but her attitude softened towards him. Nevertheless, she glanced significantly at my pack and then at Hercules, indicating that it was high time we were on our way.

I took the hint. It was, in any case, necessary to stir myself if I were to reach Croxcombe Manor at a reasonable hour. I checked with the landlord the directions I had been given yesterday by various people I had met along the road, and he was able to correct some of the misinformation and set my feet on the right track across the Mendips.

'If you follow the main path due south from here, it'll bring you down east o' Wells, which is where you want to be, but the foothills in those parts, around Dinder, are pretty thickly wooded. You might lose your way a bit, but there are plenty of charcoal burners who'll direct you. Not a bad lot if you speak 'em fair, and their womenfolk may be glad of a trifle or two from your pack.'

I paid him and thanked him for all the gossip.

'Well, you can repay me, lad,' he said, 'by calling in on your return journey and letting me know what's happening at the manor, and how matters stand between Anthony and Simon. Will you do that?'

I promised most willingly, but did not add that it might be a few days, perhaps even a week or more, before I came back, depending on how quickly I was able to make any progress in my quest for information concerning the real John Jericho.

I stirred a somnolent Hercules with my toe. 'Come on, boy! Time we were off.'

He was on his feet immediately, shaking himself free of whatever doggy paradise he had been inhabiting in his dreams and barking excitedly. The landlord took my hand warmly in both of his and, to my astonishment, his goodwife kissed me soundly on both cheeks, then blushed a fiery red.

'We'll look for you the day after tomorrow,' she said, 'or maybe the day after that.'

'Maybe.' It *was* possible, if I could find no excuse to remain longer at Croxcombe Manor. 'God be with you both.'

Because of my late start and the fact that I had stopped at a charcoal burner's cottage for food and drink when my stomach began to rumble, the sun, glimpsed now and then between the canopy of trees, was already westering as I plunged deeper into the woods cloaking the lower slopes of Mendip.

I still had not solved the problem of how I could extend my visit to Croxcombe without arousing Dame Audrea's suspicions concerning my true intentions. She was the sort who wouldn't thank a common pedlar for interfering in her affairs, and if she were convinced that my half-brother was indeed this long lost page of hers, then any attempt on my part to persuade her otherwise would be likely to make her even more pig-headed on the subject. Any slight doubt she might entertain would be banished immediately. Therefore, I needed to find a reason to delay my departure until I had 'poked around', as my nearest and dearest would call it, and made some enquiries of my own.

I stopped and looked cautiously all round me. There was no one about. The distant grunting of a wild pig, rooting for truffles, and the twittering of the birds overhead were the only sounds disturbing the afternoon peace.

'All right, Lord,' I said, speaking out loud. 'If You want my assistance in this matter, perhaps You could give me a helping hand.'

Naturally, there was no reply, but I was used to that and proceeded on my way.

Five minutes later, I caught my left foot in a rabbit hole and sprawled my length on the ground. When I tried to get up, I let out a yelp of pain. I had badly twisted my left ankle.

Five

I swore fluently, while Hercules licked my face and stared at me with wide, questioning eyes full of doggy devotion.

'It's all right, lad,' I assured him, reaching for my cudgel and levering myself to my feet. 'The pain will pass in a minute or two.'

I spoke with more optimism than I felt, but even as I did so, I realized that, whatever damage I had done, here was the answer to my prayer. Whether true or feigned, I could plead a twisted ankle as an excuse to beg shelter for at least a night or two – perhaps more – at Croxcombe Manor.

To begin with, the pain was excruciating, particularly traversing rough, heavily wooded ground. Twice, I had to sit down on a fallen log and put my head between my knees to prevent myself from losing consciousness; but after a while the initial agony subsided into a dull, throbbing ache and I was able to hobble along without resting too often. Eventually I staggered into a clearing where yet another charcoal burner was tending his turf-covered fire of coppiced wood. His hut inevitably stood nearby, for the fire has to be kept smouldering for four or five days and needs constant attention every hour or two, both day and night, when charcoal is being formed. (I was enough of a country boy to be familiar with the process.)

He glanced up as I approached, alerted to my presence by the inquisitive sniffing of Hercules around his knees, and rose slowly and stiffly to greet me.

'Thou's hurt thee leg, Chapman,' he observed, not without a modicum of satisfaction; for, from the way he rubbed the small of his back, he seemed to be no stranger to pain himself.

It was difficult to guess his age, his face was so weather-beaten. Yet in spite of its leathery appearance, there was an underlying pallor from his being continuously in the shade of the trees. Somehow, at some time, he had broken his rather prominent nose (or someone had broken it for him) and the rheumy eyes were grey, like the smoke from one of his fires. In spite of the August heat, he wore a woollen hood close about his face, with a badly scorched liripipe, a heavy frieze tunic, and breeches cross-gartered in the ancient Saxon fashion. There was a rough and ready air about him, but he appeared friendly enough.

'I caught my foot in a rabbit hole,' I explained, and nodded towards his hut. 'Could you spare me a drink of water?'

'I c'n do better nor that,' he grunted. 'Does thee fancy some ale?'

I did, of course, and said so, thankfully;

whereupon he relieved me of my pack and beckoned me towards his hut. The sparsely furnished interior – a table, a lamp, a stool and a rough grey blanket covering a bed of bracken – suggested a bachelor existence, for most women will make an effort to soften Spartan surroundings (a jug of wild flowers or a few scraps of brightly coloured fabric of their own weaving).

'You live alone,' I said, not bothering to make it a question.

'Always have done, always will. Sit thee down, then.' And my new acquaintance indicated the stool, adding, 'Don't believe in women. They bugger things up for a man. Th'art married, I can tell.'

'So people keep saying,' I snapped, bending down to rub my afflicted ankle, while Hercules went snuffling after rats, which he seemed to think were making their home among the charcoal burner's bedding.

'Good dog! Good dog!' my companion encouraged him. 'They'm in there somewhere. They do sometimes bite me of a night when I'm asleep. But they be God's creatures, too, I s'pose. They got to live.' With which philosophical utterance, he took a couple of horn beakers from a shelf above the doorway and disappeared outside again. When he came back, he had filled them full and brimming over from a barrel that he presumably kept out of doors where it was cooler. I guessed, also, that he must keep it uncovered, for the ale tasted of smoke and a few other suspicious flavours like old leaves and dead animals. I couldn't help wondering how many woodland creatures, like the late Duke of Clarence in his butt of malmsey, had drowned in drink. I sipped cautiously.

'How'st thy ankle?' the man asked after a momentary silence. 'Thou c'nst remain here the night if thou wishes.'

'I'm hoping to get to Croxcombe Manor. Do you know of it? Is it far?'

He chuckled as though I had said something amusing. 'No, it ain't far. About a furlong or so beyond them trees.' He jerked his head towards the open door and the woods beyond. 'This is Bellknapp land th'art on.'

'You know the family then?' I asked excitedly.

'I know *of* them. Not to speak to, thee understands. I pay my dues for coppicing these woods to Master Kilsby, the bailiff. I don't have no truck with *family*.'

I gave him a knowing wink. (Well, that's what it was meant to be.) 'I daresay you know most of the gossip about them, though.'

'Thou couldst say that.' He finished his ale and smacked his lips with a relish I was far from sharing. I continued to sip heroically, trying to ignore a certain pungent aftertaste that lingered on my tongue.

'All the same, perhaps I can give you some news concerning the Bellknapps that you might not yet have heard,' I said, and proceeded to inform him of my previous evening's encounter with Anthony Bellknapp.

When I'd concluded, he sat staring at me, his mouth wide open, ale coursing down his chin. Gradually, a slow smile broke across his face, eventually becoming a chuckle before flowering into a full-bodied roar of laughter, as he sat on the beaten-earth floor, rocking himself to and fro in a fit of uncontrollable mirth.

'Oh, that does my heart good!' he managed to gasp at last. 'That'll teach Master Simon a lesson! That'll put his nose out of joint, the cocky, bad-mannered little bastard that he is! Oh my! Oh my! Thou's sure, Chapman? Th'art not making it up?'

I shook my head. 'No, on my honour. I'm glad to have afforded you some pleasure in return for your hospitality.' I surreptitiously poured the rest of my ale on to the ground. 'You're not fond of the younger Bellknapp brother, I fear.'

'No one is. Spoilt from his cradle, that one.'

'You've known him a long time?'

'All his miserable life. I've been coppicing these woods nigh on thirty years, although I weren't so old when I started. I was nought but a boy when my father – he were called Hamo Gough, same as me – died and I took over the charcoal burning to support my mother. She's long dead now, God rest her!'

'You know all about the robbery and murder, then, at Croxcombe Manor six years ago?'

There was a sudden lull in the conversation,

and I could sense my new friend's reluctance to proceed. He eyed me warily for several seconds, almost as though he suspected me of knowing more than I was admitting to.

'Oh aye, I remember it,' he finally conceded. 'Everyone in these here parts knows about it. It was the talk of the neighbourhood.'

'The landlord of the alehouse where I stayed last night told me about it,' I said. 'It intrigued me. Did you ever set eyes on the young page who was responsible? What was his name, now? Something strange.'

'John Jericho,' my companion answered gruffly.

'Ah, yes. That's it. An odd name, wouldn't you agree? Do you think it was his own?'

'Never thought anything about it,' my companion answered. There was something defensive in his attitude that I could not understand.

'Did you know him?' I enquired, trying to sound offhand.

'Saw him about when I went to the house to take them wood for the fires.'

'Did you like him?'

'I told thee, I never thought of 'im. No reason to. Didn't push 'imself forward. Quiet little fellow. Not the sort thou'd expect t' murder a woman. No, nor rob anyone, neither.'

'It couldn't possibly have been anyone else?'

The charcoal burner stared at me as if I were mad. 'There weren't ever any doubt

85

about that. If it weren't the page, why did he run away and why hasn't 'e been seen since? Oh, no, 'e done it all right, I'd stake my life on that.'

He spoke with a conviction that puzzled me; a conviction that suggested he might know more than he was telling. Coupled with his previous insistence that he was unfamiliar with this John Jericho, I found it a little odd to say the least. On the other hand, was I allowing my imagination to run away with me, as I was so often accused of doing?

As though suddenly afraid that he had said too much or too little, or simply that his perfectly innocent remarks might have been misconstrued, Hamo Gough jumped to his feet, spilling the dregs of his ale on the ground.

'This won't do,' he muttered. 'Got to attend to my fire. Sit thou there until thee can stand on thy foot again, then thou can be off. If thou stays a while at Croxcombe, maybe I'll be seeing thee now and then.'

It was a clear dismissal and I had no choice but to remove myself and Hercules from his hut. He had offered hospitality to the injured stranger within his gates, but now he wanted me gone. Something had made him uneasy. I just wished that I knew what it was.

I found that my ankle was indeed considerably less painful when I stood up than I had expected, but I wasn't about to admit the fact to anyone. I needed an excuse to stay at Croxcombe Manor for as long as possible, so

I shouldered my pack once more and hobbled out of the hut, leaning heavily on my cudgel. The charcoal burner took his leave of me with, I felt, a distinct air of relief. By the time Hercules and I quit the clearing, he was crouched once again over his fire.

I found Croxcombe Manor quite easily, as Hamo Gough had assured me I should. As the woodland thinned, I came into open pastureland and the foothills of the Mendips sloped away to the Somerset levels around Wells and Glastonbury; blue-rimmed distances hazy with summer heat. A cluster of cottages round a pond, whose glassy surface mirrored my laboured progress, were the only habitations I passed until I reached the manor house surrounded by its moat, its tiled roof immediately indicative of the fact that here lived a family of wealth and substance. The house itself stood at the centre of other buildings, chapel, brewhouse, wash-house, bakehouse, windmill and dovecote. A couple of swans sailed regally on the moat and pigeons disturbed the air with a constant flurry of wings. Geese and poultry pecked for food in the dirt at the back of the house, and as I made my way to the kitchens, I found not only a commodious stable, but also various other enclosures for sheep, pigs and cows. This was, indeed, an inheritance worth having, and I couldn't help wondering, in spite of the increased pain in my left leg, how Simon Bellknapp was bearing up under the blow of his elder brother's unexpected homecoming.

The kitchen door stood wide open, as most do during the summer weather, but whereas the chatter of cook and attendant maids is usually little more than a subdued hum while they are working, on this occasion, the noise was like that of a flock of starlings whose peace had been disturbed by a slingshot in their midst. I didn't need to ask myself why.

I rapped as loudly as I could on the door, but it was not until my third knock that anyone heard me. Then, gradually, silence filled the kitchen as all heads were turned slowly in my direction. The clacking tongues were stilled and the last ragged murmurings died away as one of the maids – a big, red-faced country girl – came forward to greet me.

'It's only a chapman,' she informed the others, and gave me a welcoming grin. 'Come away in, Master. I daresay there's a few things we're all in need of.'

I put on my best limp and most agonized expression. 'As a matter of fact, I've twisted my ankle,' I groaned. 'I tripped over a rabbit hole.'

They were good-hearted girls and immediately all sympathy, one dragging forward a stool for me to sit on, another running to the water-barrel to bring me a drink, a third attending to Hercules, whose imitation of a dog in the final throes of exhaustion never failed to win him 'oohs' and 'aahs' of compassion from any females present. Even the cook left her pastry-making to come and pet him.

'Have you come far?' one of the girls asked me. 'I've not seen you round these parts before.'

'Bristol,' I said, dragging off my pack. 'Here!' I pushed it towards them. 'Have a look inside and see if there's anything you want.'

The cook shook her head. 'We daren't stop at the moment, Chapman. We've supper to prepare and it had better be good. There's enough trouble in the household at present without presenting the mistress and Master Simon with a burnt offering.'

'Or Master Anthony,' one of the girls said with a kind of gasp that was half laughter, half consternation.

So the gentleman had arrived! 'Perhaps the lady of the house, or her maid, would like to inspect the contents of my pack,' I suggested, 'if you haven't time at present. I've a pair of Spanish gloves and a length of Nottingham lace that might interest Dame Bellknapp.'

'You know where you are, then?' the cook queried sharply. 'In spite of coming from Bristol.'

'I was born in Wells,' I said, as though that explained everything. 'Do you think Dame Audrea would be interested in my wares?'

'Normally, yes,' the woman admitted. 'But there's been an upset today and she's other things to think about.' One of the maids giggled and was immediately frowned down. 'That'll do, Betsy. Get on with those vegetables. I shall want them for the pot in a minute.'

I wondered fleetingly why it was that kitchen maids all seemed to be named Betsy or Bess, but asked instead, 'Then could I see the steward? With this ankle, I shall need a bed for tonight at least, maybe longer. If he'd allow me to sleep in a corner of the kitchen, or even the stable, for however long it needs to heal, I'd be grateful.'

There was another giggle, this time from all the girls, who nudged one another as they looked me over approvingly. (In those days I was still a handsome fellow, though I say so myself. Taller than most men and blond, like my Anglo-Saxon mother. My father had owed his appearance to his Welsh ancestry; looks he had passed on to his bastard son, my half-brother.) Nor was the cook immune to my physical charms – all right! I was a conceited oaf, I admit it freely, but it doesn't make it any the less true – and after a moment's consideration, while she pummelled her pastry into submission, she instructed the girl called Betsy to go and find Master Applegarth.

The girl returned after a minute or two to say that the steward had agreed to see me in his room. Admonishing Hercules to remain where he was and to guard my pack, I got to my feet with exaggerated difficulty and followed her out of the kitchen and along a passage to a door at the end. Having knocked, she then lifted the latch and pushed me inside.

I found myself in a decent-sized chamber, furnished with a bed, chair, stool, a plain but stout oak coffer for clothes, two brass candlesticks holding what were obviously the finest wax candles and, on the window seat, several cushions covered in a blue and yellow weave that matched the bed-hangings; a feminine touch that reminded me the steward had once been married to the murdered nurse.

George Applegarth himself was, at first glance, an undistinguished-looking man of middling height, somewhere around his fiftieth year, I reckoned, with thinning hair, originally brown, but now greying, and a long, thin face with a narrow, hawk-like nose and pallid lips. The sort of face, I thought, that could be seen in a crowd and forgotten almost at once – until, that is, I met his eyes. They were grey; not the washed-out blue that sometimes passes for that colour, but a deep, definite slate-grey, and the kindest I had ever met, in which humour, sadness and a love of his fellow man all seemed to mingle.

Seeing my plight, he motioned me to sit down, inviting me to take not the stool, but the carved armchair that had to be his own personal seat. I immediately felt guilty that I was deceiving him as to the severity of my injury, but consoled myself with the thought that it was necessary; that this was not a man who would wish to see an innocent person punished for something he did not do. Just for a moment, I was tempted to take him into my confidence and explain the real reason for my presence at Croxcombe Manor. After all, he had seen my half-brother when he had accompanied Dame Audrea to Bristol, but had so far refused to identify him as the missing John Jericho. But second thoughts prompted caution. If he was close to his mistress, duty might urge him to confide in her.

'Now, Chapman,' he smiled, 'I understand you're looking for a bed for the night.'

'I've injured my ankle, Master Steward, as you see. I was hoping I might rest up here for a day or two. A corner of the kitchen, close to the fire, would suit my dog and me admirably. And we wouldn't make ourselves a nuisance during the day.' I was about to add the words, 'I promise,' but thought better of them. There was no need to lie more than I had to.

'You have a dog?' he queried, suddenly doubtful. 'Does he chase geese or poultry?'

'Not as long as I have him under control.'

The steward smiled faintly. 'And how often is that?'

'He mostly does as I bid him. He's not a bad dog, and will generally come at my call.'

'Mmm ... Very well. I should be reluctant to deny you shelter while you're crippled.' The thin face was full of kindly concern. 'And I feel sure, in the circumstances, that Dame Audrea will have no objection. We often give food and shelter to more than a single pedlar here, at Croxcombe. However, I must confess that today is not the best of days...' His voice tailed off and he drew a deep breath. 'But that's not your concern, and my mistress may well have need of something from your pack. So, yes, you may stay here until your ankle heals. But unless summoned by Dame Audrea, remain in the kitchen quarters.'

I thanked him and rose to go, but as I did so, the door of the room burst unceremoniously open and Anthony Bellknapp strode in.

'George,' he was beginning, then stopped short, staring at me. 'By all that's holy!' he exclaimed. 'Fancy finding you here! You're the chapman I met last night at the alehouse.'

I acknowledged the fact, and was starting to explain my present predicament when we were joined by a youth of about fifteen or sixteen years of age who I immediately recognized from Alderman Foster's description as the younger Bellknapp brother. The same mouth which, in Anthony, curled up at the corners, expressed only anger and discontent in Simon. And from the lines running from nostrils to chin – far too deeply engraved for a boy of his age – I guessed his usual expression to be sulky. But at the moment, it was positively murderous.

'I thought I'd find you here,' he jeered, seizing his brother by the shoulder and forcing him round to face him. 'I thought you'd be looking for friends! Nobody else wants you here, but of course for Jenny's sake, her husband is bound to stand by her darling boy!' He began to shout. 'Why have you come back? *Why?* Why couldn't you have been dead, like we thought you? You bastard!

93

You *bastard*!'

Simon had his brother by the throat, shaking him backwards and forwards, showing surprising tenacity and force for such a slender young man. Indeed, it took all the steward's and Anthony Bellknapp's combined strength, together with whatever small help I was able to give them, to loosen his grip. Anthony fell back gasping, clutching his neck.

When he could at last find his voice, he rasped, 'I've come home to claim my rightful inheritance, and none too soon, by the looks of things. You haven't changed one jot, my dear little brother. Just the same obnoxious brat that you always were.' He had sunk down upon the stool and was breathing heavily, but appeared to have his own temper under control in spite of his mauling. But then, suddenly and with absolutely no warning, he heaved himself to his feet with a roar of anger, grasped the unsuspecting Simon by his upper arms and fairly propelled him out through the door, speeding him on his way with a parting kick.

'You mustn't let him insult you, George,' he said, sinking on to the stool again. 'Nor Jenny.' He took a shuddering breath, his eyes filling with tears as he reached out a hand to the steward. 'George! Sweet Virgin! I've only just been told. About Jenny, I mean. My God, my God! How did it happen? A robbery, Mother says. All the pewter and silver taken, as well as some of her jewels.'

'Yes. Six years ago just past.' George Applegarth was standing very erect, a terrible, lost expression on his face, unconscious of Anthony's outstretched hand. 'I found her,' he went on bleakly. 'Stabbed through the heart, lying in a pool of her own blood.'

'Don't! Oh, don't,' the younger man groaned. 'My dearest Jenny. And the villain who killed her – this page, John Jericho – has never been caught?'

'Not yet. Although...'

'Although...?'

'Dame Audrea thinks she may have found him.'

Anthony was up off his stool in an instant. 'She didn't mention that! Tell me!'

They both seemed to have forgotten my presence, so I sat as still as possible, willing myself to be invisible, hardly daring even to breathe, while the steward recounted the recent events in Bristol, including his own doubts on the matter.

'But why don't you think this man they've arrested is John Jericho?' Anthony demanded in obvious exasperation. 'If Mother's certain...' It was plain that in his anger and horror over his old nurse's murder, he wanted a scapegoat and wanted one fast. Dame Audrea's word would be good enough for him.

But the steward shook his head stubbornly. 'He's not the man, Master Anthony. I agree that he could be young Jericho six years older; small, dark haired, blue eyed. But to my mind, there's something that tells me he

95

isn't.' He held up a hand. 'Don't ask me what, because I can't tell you. I just know that the man in the bridewell at Bristol is not the man who killed my Jenny, whatever the mistress says.'

As though on cue, the door to the steward's room was flung open once again and Dame Audrea entered with an imperious tread, followed by her younger son, wearing his most hard-done-by and aggrieved expression. Dame Bellknapp was not a tall woman, being something under middling height, but her presence was commanding. It would have been impossible to ignore or overlook her, even if she didn't speak; the essence of the woman pervaded every corner of the room. I doubted if she had ever been beautiful – her nose was too large and her chin too pointed – but she had a pair of fine clear blue eyes, dark, well-marked eyebrows and, like her sons, a full-lipped mouth that could, doubtless, express softness, but which, at the moment, was shut like a trap while she surveyed us. When at last it did open, it was to express outrage and disapproval.

'What has been going on here, Master Steward? Simon tells me he was insulted and thrown out of your room. Please explain yourself.'

'Let George alone,' Anthony snapped, getting to his feet once more. 'My precious brother did his best to throttle me. *I* was the one who threw him out. And I'll remind you, Mother, that I'm the master here now. You and Simon will both do well to remember it.'

'We'll see about that,' Dame Audrea returned coldly. Her eyes fell upon me. 'Who's this?'

Before anyone else could answer for me, I dragged myself to my feet, making as great an effort of it as I could without overdoing it, and explained my presence. The lady was not impressed.

'You may certainly sleep in the kitchen for a night or two until your ankle is better,' she said, looking me over as if I were a cockroach she had just discovered in the linen closet. 'We refuse no one in need at Croxcombe. But that is your place, not here in the steward's room, listening to all our family affairs.' She addressed George Applegarth. 'You should know better, Master Steward, than to allow such a thing. I had more confidence in you. Go to the kitchen now, Chapman, and I'll send my woman later to look over your wares.'

I gave her an ironic bow – well, I hoped it was ironic – and began to edge my way towards the door, limping as I went, when I was stopped by a hand on my arm.

'Master Chapman and I are acquainted,' Anthony Bellknapp announced. 'In fact, we are old friends.' The man was an accomplished liar, but I have to confess that I liked him none the less for that. 'He is here,' Anthony continued blandly, 'at my invitation and as my guest. He will be housed and treated accordingly by all of you.'

97

Six

There was a brief silence, during which astonishment was gradually replaced by outrage on the faces of Audrea Bellknapp and her younger son. George Applegarth's expression was more difficult to read, although I thought I saw amusement and a certain flicker of approval light those slate-grey eyes.

'Thank you, Master Bellknapp,' I said gravely. 'You're very gracious.'

Anthony just had time to flash me a grin and a barely concealed wink before the full torrent of his mother's wrath broke over his head.

'How dare you countermand my orders like that? You absent yourself for eight years – eight years, mark you! – without a word as to your whereabouts, leaving us uncertain as to whether you are alive or dead. You return home with no advance warning to disrupt all our lives, and then immediately assume you can usurp the authority which I hold in trust for your brother. Not only that, but you also have the gall to foist your disreputable friend on us' – I realized with a shock that she meant me – 'and then expect us to treat him with the same courtesy as we should use towards one of our guests.'

Dame Audrea paused to draw breath, but Anthony gave her no chance to proceed further. In a voice as coldly furious as her own, he reminded her again that he was now the master of Croxcombe Manor. 'And so that there should be no doubt on that head, on my way here, I took the precaution of calling on lawyer Slocombe and confirming the contents of my father's will. Croxcombe is left to me provided I claim my inheritance before Simon reaches the age of eighteen.' He gave a malicious smile. 'And as I remember perfectly that I was already past my tenth birthday when he was born, and as I am now twenty-five...' He didn't bother to finish the sentence, merely shrugging his shoulders and leaving us to draw the inevitable conclusion for ourselves. Simon Bellknapp was still only fifteen. After a moment Anthony went on, 'I am therefore the master here, my dear mother, and anything I choose to do must, I'm afraid, be acceptable to you and Simon or you can arrange to make your home elsewhere.'

I heard the steward gasp, and had to admit that I was myself taken aback by such plain speaking. Sons, whatever the circumstances or provocation, did not generally treat their mothers in such a forthright and disrespectful fashion. For her part, Dame Audrea, although trembling with anger, recognized that she was, for the moment, beaten, and that it would be beneath her dignity to brawl openly with her son in the presence of her steward

99

and a mere 'disreputable' pedlar. She therefore swung abruptly on her heel in the direction of the door.

'We shall see you then at supper. You, too,
Chapman.' (She turned the word into an
insult.) 'Come, Simon! There's nothing you
can do here.'

'You shouldn't have spoken to your lady
mother like that, Master Anthony,' the steward reproved him as the door of his room
shut with a thud behind Dame Audrea and
her younger son.

Anthony grimaced. 'I'm sorry, George.'
Although I couldn't say that he sounded very
apologetic. 'But I have to make my position
clear. I know my mother. She's a high-
stomached woman. I have no doubt she'll
have had things all her own way since my
father died – and I can tell by your expression
that I'm right. As for that brother of mine, he
needs putting in his place. He's a vicious,
mean-minded brat, spoilt from the moment
of his birth. And dangerous, too. You saw how
he went for me. But for you and the chapman
here, he might well have throttled me.' He
turned towards me, holding out his hand. 'I
owe you something for that, my friend. I'm
holding by what I said. You must count
yourself my personal guest for as long as you
wish to stay here. And you must certainly
remain at Croxcombe until that ankle is
stronger. Now, George, tell me in detail this
terrible story of the robbery and Jenny's
murder.'

★ ★ ★

The steward's account of events that night six years previously differed little in essentials from the version I had pieced together for myself from the various scraps of information that had come my way. John Jericho had entered Dame Audrea's employ some two years before. No one knew much about his past or exactly where he had come from. He had simply wandered into the kitchen at Croxcombe one day, half starved and looking for employment.

'An orphan, he claimed, and no other family.' George Applegarth spread his hands and pulled down the corners of his mouth. 'That was all we ever learned about him, though I felt in my own mind it wasn't the truth. And the name Jericho ... I was always suspicious of that. But for some reason, the mistress took a strong fancy to him and made him her page. The master told her she was being foolish. Mistress Ursula – Lady Chaun-termerle, I should say – when she came on a visit, told her mother the same. Sir Damien, too. But she wouldn't listen.'

'Mother never took anyone's advice about anything,' Anthony interrupted with a laugh. 'If people gave it, it only made her the more determined to go her own way.'

The steward nodded. 'But, of course, two years later, when everyone seemed to be proved right, her bitterness against young Jericho was extreme. He'd made a fool of her, and that she could never forgive. Her hatred of him is unrelenting.'

'This man who is now in the bridewell in Bristol,' I said. 'This man she has accused of being John Jericho, you don't agree with her, Master Steward. Or so I understand.'

He glanced sharply at me. 'Now who do you understand that from?'

'Before I left Bristol, everyone was talking about it. Sergeant Manifold, the arresting officer, is a friend of mine.' (Well, sort of.) 'This man, John Wedmore, declares he was in Ireland at the time of the murder.'

The steward nodded. 'He's not the guilty man,' he said.

'But can you convince Dame Audrea of that?'

'She won't make me testify to the contrary.'

Anthony Bellknapp clapped his old friend on the back. 'Good for you, George. If, that is, you can hold out against her. But unless she's altered greatly during the past eight years, my mother can be a formidable enemy if she doesn't get her own way. You'd do well to take care.'

'And you'd do well to heed your own advice,' the steward retorted with a smile. 'Your return has upset all her plans for the future. She intended to go on ruling this household even after Simon came of age.'

'He might take a wife,' I suggested.

'Only a girl chosen by his mother.' George Applegarth smiled. 'Oh, Simon won't realize it, but the mistress has always been able to twist him around her little finger.'

'Lord, yes!' Anthony agreed. 'That was my misfortune, that I'd never let her. She set my father against me from the moment I lisped my first word of defiance. Otherwise, I believe that he and I might – just might – have been friends. He obviously tried to make some amends to me when he knew he was dying.' My host paused, staring into space as though reflecting on the past, but then continued, 'Anyway, if you can bear it, George, tell me about the night of the murder. Why hadn't you and Jenny accompanied my parents on their visit to my sister?'

The steward shook his head. 'I can't rightly remember now.' He sounded impatient. 'There was some good reason. Jenny wouldn't have gone, in any case. Master Simon was nine by then, and declared himself too old to have a nurse.'

'And why had the page remained behind?'

Once again, George Applegarth made a gesture of dismissal, as though the pain of recollection was almost too much for him to bear. 'Toothache, earache ... some ailment of that nature.'

'But, of course, whatever he said it was, was faked,' Anthony protested. 'He only pretended to be sick in order to stay behind at Croxcombe so he could steal the silver.'

'Yes.' George's voice was barely audible, and I could tell that while he must inevitably relive that night over and over in his mind, he would prefer not to talk about it.

Whether or not my host shared my perception I had no idea, but he persisted with his catechism. 'You didn't hear Jenny get out of bed? She didn't try to wake you?'

'No.' The steward took a deep breath. 'Or if she did try to rouse me, she didn't succeed. I blame myself. Too much ale with my supper. It always makes me sleep like the dead.' He clamped a hand to his mouth as he realized the infelicity of this remark, and made a little mewling sound like an injured cat.

It was not my place to say anything, but I glanced at Anthony in an attempt to convey that it was time to stop this questioning. He continued relentlessly, however, apparently oblivious to the other man's distress in his quest for the facts.

'So you knew nothing of what had happened until the next morning, when you got up and found her dead and the family treasure and John Jericho gone?'

George Applegarth nodded mutely, unable to speak. His face was the colour of parchment and had a waxy sheen to it. I thought he was going to faint, but to my relief, Anthony saw it, too, and bit his lower lip in contrition. He put an arm around the steward's shoulders and, as I struggled out of the armchair where I had been sitting all this while, lowered him into it. George began to shudder.

'My dear old friend, what a crass fool I am! Why in heaven's name didn't you tell me to shut up?' The younger man thumped himself on the forehead with his fist. 'Why am I such an unthinking blockhead? Chapman, why didn't you kick me on the shin? No, no! That's not fair. The fault is mine. *Mea culpa.* George, can you forgive me, bringing it all back like that? If you want to kick my arse, I'll bend over willingly and let you do it.'

That produced a faint smile and a shake of the steward's head. He forced himself to his feet again.

'It's only natural you should be curious, Master Anthony; that you should want to know what happened. It's just that I think I've got over it,' he added apologetically, 'and then when I'm reminded, I discover that I haven't. My dear Jenny ... We'd no child nor chick of our own and she loved you two lads like she was your mother.' He made a determined effort to speak more cheerfully. 'Take no notice of me, my dear boy...' He choked, coughed, then drew back his shoulders, bracing himself to resume his duties. 'Now I must go and oversee the laying of the supper table. Your first meal at home, I want everything to be as you would wish it.'

'Of course you do.' Anthony grinned, still looking a little shamefaced; but his natural resilience – or natural insensitivity? – was already convincing him that George Applegarth could not really be as upset as he had seemed. 'And mind those idiot place-setters put me where I belong, in the centre seat on the dais.' He added grimly, 'I'm bound to have my mother and brother one on each side, I suppose. But the seat of honour is

105

mine.'

The steward bowed his head in acquiescence. 'That is perfectly understood. And now, if you'll excuse me...' He took his wand of office from the corner where it was kept and made for the door. But with his hand on the latch, he paused and turned back. 'Be careful, Master Anthony. You've made enemies by this sudden and unlooked-for return.'

As the door closed behind him, Anthony laughed. 'If George thinks I'm afraid of either Simon or my lady mother, he's getting senile in his old age. Now, come along, Chapman.' He offered me his arm. 'I'll show you to my chamber. The housekeeper should have had it prepared by this time. Then it'll be supper. I don't know about you, but after all this excitement, I'm ravenous.'

Supper was a difficult meal from the moment that Dame Audrea arrived in the hall to find her elder son already installed in her customary place in the centre of the dais; and herself relegated to the seat on his left hand. Simon would have attempted to oust his brother by force had he not been restrained by his mother's frowns and hissed admonitions to behave.

The tensions and undercurrents among family members and retainers were aggravated by the presence of strangers; two monks returning to Glastonbury, a merchant on his way back to Bath, a royal messenger travelling on the King's business which had taken him first into Wales and who was now heading south to Plymouth, and a band of mummers touring the surrounding countryside. All had begged asylum for the night and, according to the rules of hospitality, none had been refused. With the exception of the mummers, who, as mere entertainers, were relegated to one of the lower trestles, the guests sat at the high table, where the strain of making normal conversation soon began to show on the faces of the dame and her younger son. The King's messenger and the Bath merchant were naturally unaware of anything unusual, but the two monks, obviously acquainted with the Croxcombe household, were plainly agog with curiosity.

At Anthony's instruction, I had been seated among the household officers, one or two of whom made plain their resentment of me out of loyalty to their mistress. Chief of these was a red-haired man of roughly my own age, addressed either as Edward or Master Micheldever, and whom I knew from Josiah Litton to be the receiver. And, again drawing on my recollections of what the landlord had told me, I also knew that the young girl beside him must be his recently acquired bride. She was, indeed, extremely pretty with a peach-like skin, eyes of a deep cerulean blue, a rosebud mouth and, when she smiled, a row of tiny, pearly teeth. Altogether too good to be true; and I decided within the first ten minutes of meeting her that, if I were her husband, I wouldn't trust her out of my sight. For all her apparently modest demeanour and lowered lids, I noticed the way her gaze strayed constantly towards the high table, her moist lips parting invitingly every time she encountered Anthony Bellknapp's approving stare. There was going to be trouble there, as Josiah Litton had foreseen.

The man with the thinning grey hair, faded blue eyes and stammering speech sitting opposite me, could only be the chaplain, Henry Rokewood. He, too, kept looking towards the dais with a kind of dreadful fascination, his colourless lips trembling with panic and his stutter growing noticeably worse each time that Anthony glanced in his direction.

To Sir Henry's left sat a burly fair-haired man, almost as broad as he was tall, bull-necked and generally giving the impression of someone you wouldn't want to meet in a dark alley on a moonless night. He might easily have been somebody's bravo, but he wasn't, and the others addressed him respectfully as Master Chamberlain. I racked my brains to remember what the landlord had told me concerning him, and eventually recollected that he had a sister whose bastard son was thought to be the progeny of Anthony Bell-knapp, although the girl had never been persuaded to name him as the father. The chamberlain was called Jonathan Slye.

That left, among the senior members of the household, Reginald Kilsby, bailiff, a tall, well-built man with an air of self-consequence that was almost tangible. He was handsome and knew it, with plentiful dark hair just beginning to grey at the temples, and a pair of fine hazel eyes which he opened to their widest extent whenever he condescended to make free with the pearls of wisdom he was convinced fell from his lips. The proprietorial way in which he smiled at Dame Audrea, and the looks of venom that he darted at her elder son, gave credence to the landlord's assertion that the bailiff entertained hopes of marrying his mistress. I recalled the rumour that he was already her lover and wondered if it were true.

It was a strange meal, with an air of unreality about it, stemming from the fact that there was one burning topic uppermost in everybody's mind, but no one felt able to discuss it in so public a location. Even when George Applegarth, his duties done, joined us, squeezing in alongside me on the bench, the talk was of a desultory nature. Someone ascertained that I came from Bristol and asked about John Jay's missing carvel, but the interest was perfunctory. It was not local enough to concern them in this part of the world. What might be big news in Bristol and Waterford (and other Irish towns) was of little concern in rural Somerset. Young Mistress Micheldever, whose name, she informed me, was Rose – she had by this time discovered that I was worth her attention – asked me if I knew anything of Queen Elizabeth's latest pregnancy, but when I said no, she lapsed once more into a bored silence. I could have told her that I had seen the Queen and other members of the royal family only two or three months earlier, in London, but that would only have involved me in explanations that I would rather avoid. It might have aroused suspicions of my real reason for being at Croxcombe, and I wished to remain a chapman who had twisted his ankle and was waiting for it to mend.

The business of eating and drinking was at last at an end. If the guests had thought it odd that they were offered no entertainment after the meal, they were too polite to comment. They bowed over their hostess's hand, thanked their host and followed the steward as he conducted them to the guest chamber or (in the case of the mummers) to the kitchen. Not sure what to do, and feeling at a loss, I wandered outside to breathe the fresh air of the August evening. It was still hot, and the hazy sunshine lay across lawns and formal flower-beds, byre and fields and distant pasture like the bloom on an overripe plum. Somewhere a bird was singing and there was the bittersweet tang of new-mown grass. I wandered over to the edge of the manor's encircling moat and watched the swans swimming regally up and down, their proud necks arched in two feathered question marks, reminding me that I had a problem to solve.

I found a rough wooden bench, nothing

more than a plank linking two stumps of trees, but in a spot shaded by a willow and where the bank was starred with buttercups and daisies and the small, creamy-white flowers of meadowsweet scented the air like honey. A lady's nook, I guessed, but one equally acceptable to a weary traveller whose ankle was aching uncomfortably and who needed peace and seclusion to gather his wandering thoughts together.

Someone sat down on the bench beside me.

'I thought I saw you come out here, Chapman,' Rose Micheldever announced with all the satisfaction of having run me to earth; and although there was plenty of room on the bench, she wriggled along its length until our shoulders were touching.

Mindful of her jealous husband, I shifted my buttocks another two or three inches to the left. Then I turned my head and observed her as closely as I dared without giving her the wrong idea. She was gazing out over the moat, apparently absorbed, as I had been, in the movements of the swans; but it didn't take me long to to realize that her interest in ornithology was negligible. The flutter of her eyelashes told me that she was presenting her profile for my consideration – and, of course, delectation.

It was a profile well worth regarding, I had to admit. She was just as pretty side-faced as full on, with the small, straight nose above the delicate mouth showing to even greater advantage. As a beauty, she would be a catch for any man, but I thought I had detected a note of patronage, a slight air of condescension, in the receiver's dealings with his wife, and I wondered who she was and where she came from.

'All alone, Mistress, on such a lovely evening?'

As openings go, it was trite and definitely not up to my usual standard. I need not have worried, however. It was the sort of coy banality that she was used to, judging by her answering, provocative giggle.

'Oh, Edward's working,' she said, closing the gap between us as we again rubbed shoulders. (And more than shoulders. I could feel her soft little posterior nestling into mine.) 'He's in the counting-house. He has to enter up his ledger; the number of people entertained today, the extra food consumed, the fodder and stabling for their horses. Tomorrow, he'll record the tally of candles used in the guest-chamber overnight, damage to bedding, if any, what they eat for breakfast. The receiver is a very important member of the household,' she added on a note of pride, before concluding with a sigh, 'but he always seems to be busy.'

I gave my most sympathetic smile. 'That's hard on a bride. I'm assuming you and Master Micheldever haven't long been married?'

'About six months, I think.' She continued with apparent artlessness, 'It seems much longer.'

I say 'apparent' because, with another little

squirm, our posteriors seemed to be making firmer friends than ever. I moved further along the bench again, but I was running out of space.

'Do you come from around here?' I asked, stretching out my legs and supporting myself on my hands, thus managing to keep an arm's width between us.

She giggled. 'Of course. My father, Thomas Bignell, keeps the butcher's stall in Wells.'

That explained her husband's attitude. Rose Micheldever was not only very pretty, but she had probably brought a substantial dowry with her as well. But as an illiterate tradesman's daughter, she wasn't of the same social standing as the man she had married. It might have been a good match for the receiver, but it was an even better one for her and her family, who could now boast a connection, however tenuous, with the Bellknapps of Croxcombe.

'Have you known your husband long?' I probed.

She considered this. 'Since I was about ten years old.' There was a pause, while she did certain calculations on her fingers. 'I think he must have been twenty or thereabouts when he first arrived here. My father always reckons Edward came to Croxcombe Manor the same year as Master Anthony quarrelled with the old master and left home.' She gave a little shiver of excitement. 'Fancy him turning up again after all this time. I can't really believe it. Wait until my parents hear about it.

My mother and her friends won't be able to talk about anything else. And fancy you being a friend of his!'

So that was my attraction for her. And there had I been imagining that it was my physical charms.

'Hardly a friend,' I admitted with foolhardy honesty. 'To be truthful, we only met for the first time last night, in the Litton alehouse. But tell me,' I went on, 'if you were ten in the year that Anthony Bellknapp left home, you must remember the murder, here at Croxcombe, two years later.'

'Of course I do. Nobody talked of anything else for weeks. My mother wouldn't allow me out on my own for months afterwards. Although that was silly. John Jericho was long gone by that time, along with all his plunder.'

'Do you recollect this John Jericho?' I asked.

She pursed her little rosebud mouth. 'I can't say I ever took much notice of him. He used to accompany Dame Audrea to the market and to the cathedral on occasions, but otherwise I didn't see much of him. In those days I never came to the manor. Never dreamed that one day I'd be living here.'

'Can you recall what he looked like?'

Rose shrugged prettily. (Everything she did was pretty. Her mother had trained her well.)

'Not really. I think he was small and dark, but I certainly wouldn't know him again, if I saw him.' She looked round and fixed me with those great blue eyes. 'Edward – that's my husband – says he's turned up again after all these years. Dame Audrea recognized him when she was at Saint James's fair, in Bristol. He's changed his name, of course. Well, he would have done, wouldn't he? And he speaks with an Irish accent. But Edward says that's just to throw people off the scent. He's sure it's John Jericho.'

'I know all about it,' I said. 'People in Bristol are very incensed about the arrest' – well, I was – 'because he hasn't been charged with this crime. There seems to be some doubt about his identity. Neither your husband nor Master Applegarth, who were with Dame Audrea at the fair, seem prepared to back her up.'

'Oh, Edward's sure,' Rose asserted. 'It's just George who isn't. He persuaded Ned at the time not to make a positive what-d'you-call-it? Thingummy...'

'Identification?' I suggested. She nodded. 'Why not? Do you know?'

'George declares this man isn't him. John Jericho, that is. But my Ned's thought it over and he says it is. Two against one. He's going to Bristol again with Dame Audrea next week. At least, he was. I don't know how this business of Master Anthony's return will affect their plans.'

This was bad news. But Rose could be right; the confusion and upheaval attendant upon the prodigal's reappearance was bound to upset even the most fixed of intentions. I wondered cynically what bribe Edward

115

Micheldever had been offered to make him ready to support his mistress's allegations against my brother. By contrast, my respect for the steward grew even greater. Here was that rare man whose integrity and probity were not to be compromised.

Rose had been prattling on while my thoughts wandered, wrapped up as I was in my feelings of contempt for her husband. But something she suddenly blurted out caught my attention.

'What was that? Somebody you know saw John Jericho and someone else abroad the night of the murder? In the woods around here?'

She looked stricken. 'I shouldn't have told you. I don't know what made me say it. I've never uttered a word to anyone else before, not even to Edward.'

'You mentioned a name, Ronan.'

'My brother,' she admitted. 'Ronan's always been fond of a bit of poaching with his mates. Still is. Nothing much,' she added hurriedly. 'A rabbit or two. Maybe a pheasant now and then. It's just for the thrill of it. He gives what he snares to his ackers. His friends,' she corrected herself as she fell into the local vernacular. 'He daren't bring anything home. Father would half kill him. Ronan's been doing it for years and so far he's never been found out.' She clasped her hands together in real perturbation. 'I don't know why I've said anything now. Promise me, please promise me that you won't tell anyone. That you won't

116

mention it to my husband!'

I saw my chance and, meanly, took it. 'I won't say a word if you'll undertake to introduce me to your brother.'

Seven

I was taking advantage of her, and I knew it. Talking to a stranger, she had been betrayed into making a confidence which, with someone she knew, she would have guarded against. She had had no idea of any personal interest on my part in Jenny Applegarth's murder, although I had admitted to Bristol's general concern over the fate of John Wedmore and the lack of a charge against him.

She turned to look at me, her little face sharp with suspicion. 'Why do you want to meet Ronan?'

I searched for a reasonable explanation.

'I like mysteries,' I offered at last, rather lamely. 'I'm curious to know if this young man at present in the Bristol bridewell is truly the John Jericho who disappeared six years ago, or if Dame Audrea and your husband could possibly be mistaken. If your brother did indeed see John Jericho in flight on the night of his escape, there might be something he could tell me, some small piece of information, that could give me a clue to the truth.'

'I don't see how.' Rose was defensive.

I didn't really see how, either, but where murder is involved, I have always worked on the principle that no scrap of information is too trivial for consideration. Ronan Bignell might well have nothing to impart worth the telling, but I knew I couldn't afford to ignore an opportunity so fortuitously dropped into my lap. But persuading his sister to introduce us was going to take all my charm and tact.

I sat up straight again on our rustic seat, removing the barrier of my arm and thus allowing Rose room enough to nestle close once more if she so wished. She didn't wish; in fact, she edged in the opposite direction. She no longer trusted me. In her eyes, I had somehow tricked her into revealing a secret about her brother and was now prepared to use it as blackmail. I had to reassure her.

'Look,' I said urgently, 'of course I won't breathe a word of what you've just told me. I give you my solemn promise. It's just that if I could speak to your brother, I'd be most grateful.'

She hesitated, glancing sideways at me. I assumed my most trustworthy expression with a hint of soulfulness thrown in. Well, that was what I intended, but I probably looked just plain constipated, because Rose burst out laughing.

'All right,' she conceded, her faith in me partially restored. 'Dame Audrea has given me permission to visit my father's shop in Wells tomorrow morning. Edward will be busy, as I told you, and one of the outdoor servants was going to accompany me. But if you offer to be my escort, I don't suppose any objection will be raised.' She eyed my ankle, suddenly doubtful. 'If you can walk so far, that is.'

'Oh, a night's rest will work wonders,' I answered confidently. 'And if you'll be so kind as to moderate your normal fleetness of foot to my stumbling gait, I've no doubt we shall do extremely well.'

'You do sound pompous sometimes,' she giggled.

So much for trying to impress!

'In any case, my dog will hold us up,' I warned her. 'He's unable to pass a rabbit hole without investigation. I must take him with us if you don't mind. At the moment, he's asleep in the kitchen, worn out after our day's exertions. But by tomorrow he will have fully recovered and be raring to go.'

'I like dogs,' Rose assured me. 'I'd like one of my own, but Ned won't let me have one. He says if Dame Audrea lets us have our own cottage, maybe then I can. But at present we just have a room like all the others.'

'Mistress Micheldever!' exclaimed a hearty voice behind us, and I turned my head to see Anthony Bellknapp walking across the grass towards us. His eyes twinkled. 'And my "old" friend, the chapman. I wondered where you'd both got to. You're a sly dog, Roger, monopolizing the only pretty female for miles around.' He sat down on Rose's other side, and I waited for him to make the obvious comment. He did. 'A rose between two thorns,' he announced with all the panache of one making an original remark.

I concealed a smile, but I could see Rose was impressed. But she would have been impressed even if he'd said nothing more than 'good evening'. He was not only a man and passably good looking, he was also surrounded by an aura of romance and mystery; the prodigal son returned out of the blue to claim his inheritance.

'Oh, Master Bellknapp!' she breathed ecstatically. My nose was quite put out of joint.

'Anthony,' he insisted. 'You must call me Anthony. After all, you're my receiver's wife.' He raised one of her hands to his lips and gallantly kissed it; but I didn't need any of my mother's extraordinary powers of the 'sight' to know that, if he had his way, matters weren't going to rest there. I wondered idly just how long it would take him to coax this particular little rosebud into his bed. And within the next half-hour, I could see the same thought gradually dawning on Edward Micheldever as he watched Anthony's attentions to his wife.

Anthony had come to inform us that he had, after all, prevailed upon his mother to ask the mummers to sing for their supper, and to preside over the entertainment. I don't know what pressure he had put on Dame Audrea, or how many harsh words had accompanied the confrontation, but the lady had eventually been recalled to a sense of her obligations as a hostess and agreed to put aside family animosity until after the guests' departure the following morning. On our return to the hall, Rose and I found the trestles and benches stacked along the walls, and only three chairs remaining on the dais. Four stools had been placed for the two monks, the royal messenger and the Bath merchant, who had been haled back from their beds, but everyone else either had to find a seat on the floor or perch uncomfortably on the sideways-ended trestles. Everyone else, that is, with the exception of Rose, who was swept along by Anthony on to the dais where he ordered Simon to give up his chair to her.

The boy naturally refused, whereupon his brother promptly seized him by the scruff of the neck and sent him sprawling on the floor.

'Mistress Micheldever shall be our Queen of Revels,' Anthony announced to the astonished company, while Rose simply looked distressed at the turn events had taken, glancing anxiously towards her husband.

The receiver, glowering furiously, was making for the dais to reclaim his wife when Anthony roared with laughter and imperiously waved him aside.

'Good God, sir! Can't you take a bit of fun? I should think any man would be pleased to see his wife so honoured.' He smiled at Rose. 'Sit down, my dear, sit down! Steward, tell the servers to bring some wine and beakers, and we'll all drink to the Queen of Revels's health. Let the toast be to youth and beauty!'

Simon had by this time picked himself up from the floor and was about to launch himself at his brother when a sharp word from his mother checked him. I wasn't close enough to hear what she said, but it was obvious that Dame Audrea was not prepared to parade the family disarray in public and could only sit out the hours until bedtime with the best grace she could muster. The same applied to Edward Micheldever, who was forced to look on as Rose, still shaken, but with her confidence beginning to return, spent the evening as the not-so-reluctant object of Anthony's attentions.

The mummers were better than I had expected, miming the stories of Abraham and Isaac, Cain and Abel with sufficient skill to capture the attention of an audience whose thoughts had every incentive to stray. (Even the Bath merchant and the King's messenger couldn't help but be intrigued by that other drama enacted on the dais, and had plainly been as agog with curiosity as the brothers from Glastonbury.) This was followed by a juggler who entertained us with a dexterity that kept at least seven or eight coloured balls in the air at once and drew gasps of admiration from the watchers, and the show concluded with a one-man band on his pipe and tabor while the rest of the company danced a vigorous *estampie* from eastern France. By which time, the hour was pretty well advanced, the evening shadows lengthening, the candles, cressets and wall torches flickering low in their holders. A few shreds of daylight still vied with the flames, but Dame Audrea stood up, took a determined leave of her visitors, passing them over to the care of her chamberlain and steward, and retired from the hall.

With her departure, there was a concerted movement as George Applegarth and Jonathan Slye ushered the guests to bed. The cook took charge of the mummers and led them away to the kitchen, while Edward Micheldever, with a face like a thundercloud, leapt on to the dais to reclaim his wife. At the same moment, Simon Bellknapp surprised his brother by stealing up behind him and locking an arm around Anthony's neck with such force that the older man's head cracked loudly against the back of his chair. His grip tightened as Anthony clawed at the strangling arm.

'You bastard!' he shouted. 'I'll kill you! Just see if I don't!'

I would have limped to Anthony's assistance, but was too slow. Several servers and the bailiff were ahead of me, Reginald Kilsby's burly form well to the fore as he tugged Simon's arm free of his brother's throat.

He hissed, 'Don't be such a bloody fool!

You can achieve nothing by this.' I had by now managed to scramble on to the dais myself, and was close enough to catch his following words uttered in almost a whisper. 'Leave it to your mother and me.'

I doubted if anyone else had heard them. They were all making too much noise. Anthony was cursing and swearing and trying to get at his brother but being hampered by both Edward Micheldever and the chaplain, whose high, fluting voice was begging, 'D-d-don't, Ma-Master Anthony. D-don't!'

Anthony's fury bubbled over. 'D-don't?' he mimicked. 'D-don't? You bleating old bellwether, let me go! At once, d'you hear me? That murderous little pimp just tried to kill me! I'm going to wring his neck before the hangman does it for him.'

The chaplain coloured painfully, but, to his credit, he refused to release his grip on Anthony's wrists, while the receiver tightened his hold on the upper arms. At this point, the steward and chamberlain returning to the hall, George Applegarth immediately took charge.

He nodded at Simon. 'Go to your bedchamber, Master, and stay there. Your lady mother has had enough for one day, without you brawling with your brother all night. And the same goes for you, Master Anthony, and all the rest of you.' He turned to a stout woman with an imposing bunch of keys dangling from her belt, and who must, therefore, be the housekeeper. 'Mistress Wychbold and I will lock up and see all safe. Now, go!'

Anthony, his good humour seemingly restored, burst out laughing and clapped the steward on the shoulder.

'George! You're wasted as a mere household officer. You ought to be the one making sheep's eyes at my mother, angling to be her husband. You'd be of far more use and support to her than that great lummox over there.' And he waved a derogatory hand at Reginald Kilsby, who was standing with his arm about Simon's shoulders. 'Oh, you needn't think I haven't noticed, Master Bailiff,' he mocked. 'I'm neither a fool nor blind. I was watching you during supper and after. Well, let me tell you this!' There was an ugly gleam now in Anthony's eyes. 'While I'm master at Croxcombe, I won't be having you for a stepfather, you can make up your mind to that.'

I saw the bailiff's free hand clench at his side, but he said nothing, merely urging Simon towards the door, muttering something in his ear. Anthony turned to me.

'Master Chapman, if you're ready, our bed awaits. With your permission, I'll lead the way.'

With a sigh of relief, after a long day packed with incident, we both shed our clothes, pissed into the chamber-pot and rolled between clean sheets into the comfort of a goose-feather mattress. Anthony's servant, Humphrey, picked up our discarded garments,

125

placing them tidily on the lid of a chest, pulled the bed-curtains and retired to a truckle-bed in one corner of the room. Silence and darkness enveloped us.

Until that moment, I would have sworn that I was too tired to utter a word, or even to prop my eyelids open. But, perversely, I was suddenly wide awake. I turned my head on the pillow and looked at the muffled form beside me. Anthony was lying on his back, and I could see the white of the eye nearest to me. He, too, was awake and staring at the bed canopy overhead.

'Why are you doing it?' I asked. 'Why are you set on antagonizing everyone?' When he didn't answer, I went on, 'All right! I know it's not my business, but I'm the curious type. I should have thought you'd need all the goodwill you can muster.'

Again, it seemed as if he wasn't going to reply, and I was preparing to wriggle on to my side – my right, so as not to aggravate my injured left ankle – when my bedfellow gave a deep-throated chuckle.

'Now, why should you think that? Surely the boot is on the other foot. Everyone at Croxcombe needs *my* goodwill. I'm the master here. They all have to dance to my tune, including my mother and brother. Besides, apart from George Applegarth, I don't have a liking for any of them.'

'Does that include Dame Audrea and Master Simon?' I asked.

'Most certainly.' He also turned his head so

as to look at me. 'You've seen us together, and I'm sure a "curious type" like you will have pieced together something of my family history by this time. There's no love lost between us. Indeed, my mother never had any love for me. She disliked me from birth: I don't know why. But I owe her nothing.'

It being more or less what Alderman Foster had told me, there was really no answer that I could make.

'It just seems a shame,' I protested feebly, 'that now you have at last returned home after all these years, there should be so much discord.' He moved restlessly, so I changed the subject. 'You've been in the eastern counties, I think you said. I've never seen those parts. What's it like?'

'Flat,' was the brusque reply; then, relenting, my companion added, 'It's fen country mostly. I missed the hills and valleys of the west. In all the time I lived there, I only ever met the one west countryman.'

'The one who told you your father had died? I seem to remember you said he has a sister who lives in Bristol.'

'That's right, he has. In fact, he, too, is a native of the city, for all he calls himself William of Worcester. His real name, he told me, is Botoner.' The name was one I had heard mentioned recently, but I couldn't immediately place it. Anthony continued, 'As a matter of fact, when I encountered him, he was on his way to Bristol. First time he'd been back in years, but his brother-in-law died recently and there are family affairs that need his attention. And there was a tale about his brother-in-law's brother. He's missing at sea, I gathered. Looking for some island or other.'

Of course! Margaret Walker had mentioned that John Jay, the one who was dead, had married a woman called Botoner. I gave Anthony a brief history of the Jays. Extremely brief: I knew next to nothing about them.

'What was this William Botoner, or William Worcester, doing so far from home?' I enquired.

'Oh, he's lived in the eastern counties the greater part of his life. In fact, he regards them as his home, far more than Bristol. He's quite an elderly man. Sixty. Sixty-five. He was secretary for years to a Sir John Fastolfe, who was quite an important man, it seems. Fought at Agincourt – Sir John I'm talking about – was made Lieutenant of Normandy, later Governor of Maine and Anjou. But then he was accused of cowardice when he retreated before the forces of the Great Whore, Joan, at Patay, so he returned home and concentrated on his English estates. I think that was when my informant went to work for him. Sir John was a very rich man by that time. Made a lot of money in the war. Mind, Master Worcester reckoned he'd always been pretty well breeched. Property in London, including the Boar's Head tavern and other premises. And he built himself a castle somewhere in Norfolk. Not the sort of thing you and I would have the money for, friend.'

I laughed and agreed. 'Does this William Worcester still work for him?'

'Lord, no! I think Master Worcester said Sir John died more than twenty years ago. But then there was a lot of trouble connected with his will. Litigation with a family called Paston, in which he – Master Worcester, that is – was heavily involved for quite a long time. Don't ask me what it was all about. He did try to explain, but I lost interest, I'm afraid. As you may imagine, I was far more concerned with what he'd told me about my father's death and will, which, of course, was old history to him – over two years old – but was fresh news to me. I knew I had to get home as soon as possible and claim my inheritance. He suggested we rode as far as Bristol together, but I couldn't wait. I didn't want to be hampered by a fellow traveller. Particularly by one who'd let drop that his pet hobby was making notes and measuring the dimensions of every town and village that he passed through.'

'Sweet Virgin! Really? He wasn't pulling your leg?'

'He showed me his notebooks, all scribbled in a kind of dog-Latin that would be murder to understand. He plans to map out the topography of Bristol, so he informed me, during the intervals between sorting out his sister's affairs. Besides, he feels he ought to wait until there's news of this missing ship belonging to her brother-in-law.'

This reminded me with a jolt of John Jay's

lost carvel, and the reason why my half-brother had come to Bristol in the first place. Had it not been for young Colin Wedmore joining the ship at Waterford, John would still be safely at home in Ireland and not imprisoned in the city's bridewell. For a moment, I was tempted to be honest with my bedfellow about why I was at Croxcombe; to confess that my injured ankle was nothing like as bad as I was pretending and to ask his aid. He had been more than kind to me. True, it was for his own perverted ends – but I felt that I owed him the truth.

'Master Bellknapp,' I began, but an enormous, rumbling snore cut me short. Turning my head once again, I saw that Anthony was sound asleep, still lying on his back, mouth agape. Another mighty snore followed the first in quick succession. I sighed. I was in for an unquiet night.

It was worse than I had anticipated. I soon discovered that Humphrey Attleborough also snored in a sort of treble counterpoint to his master's deeper tones. Moreover, Anthony was a restless sleeper, tossing and turning until the bedclothes were in a tangle that it was impossible to unravel. Not that I minded being exposed to the air: it had grown infernally hot inside the cocoon of bed-curtains and feather mattress, and the third time I woke in what seemed less than a few minutes – but was probably an hour or more – I could feel the sweat running down my back and the inside of my thighs. I slid quietly out of bed, parted the curtains and emerged thankfully into the cool of the room beyond. The shutters and casement had been opened slightly by the servant before he had retired to his truckle-bed, and moonlight filtered through, laying long stripes of light and shadow across the floor and across my naked body. I breathed in the scents of the nearby woods and heard the chime of a distant bell, borne faintly on a gentle breeze, ringing the hour of matins and lauds, so I knew it must be those witching hours of the night between twelve and dawn. I pushed the shutters and casement a little wider, taking care to make no noise which might disturb my sleeping companions. For a moment or two, I stared at the lacework pattern of trees and the moon, pinned like a brooch high on their shoulder, before a sudden movement attracted my attention and made me lower my gaze to the moat. Someone was standing beside it, on the near bank, apparently looking up at our bedchamber window; although I could not be sure about this, wrapped as the figure was in that ever useful garment, the all-enveloping cloak and hood. (With a sudden surge of irritation, I wished I had a gold noble for every time in the past few years that I had encountered this mysterious, cloaked man – or woman. It was getting monotonous.) As soon as the figure became aware of my scrutiny, it moved away, but whether its gait was male or female, it was at too great a distance for me to tell. I stared after its retreating back for as long as I could, but gained nothing except the shivers as the sweat dried on my clammy skin. Reluctantly, I half-closed the window again and went back to bed, pondering on who it might have been.

I lay awake for some time, remembering the steward's warning to my sleeping (and still snoring) companion to watch his step, and Anthony's childlike enjoyment in courting trouble by affronting almost everyone he could. But then, ignored as a child, banished as a young man from home and his parents' affection, it was impossible that he should have turned out to be a saint. Indeed, he exhibited a far better character than I would probably have done in similar circumstances...

At this point I must have drifted off to sleep, because the next time I woke, I was conscious of having been dreaming for what seemed quite a long time. I tried to recall some of the dreams in case there was a nugget of gold among the dross, but soon realized they were that jumble of meaningless nonsense that comes after a tiring day and badly digested food, and is the product of a restless mind.

The cacophony of sound had abated a little on both sides of the bed-curtains, but was still enough to prevent me from falling asleep again with my usual ease. So, once more, I slipped out of bed and crossed to the window. It was not yet quite light, but the distant horizon was showing the merest rim of fire, the first, faint harbinger of approaching day. Humphrey Attleborough, with the abandon of youth, was sprawled half on, half off the truckle-bed, the covers pushed back, and displaying a set of manly equipment that might well frighten all but the most stout-hearted of maidens. It was obvious that he, too, was having dreams, but not of my sort. He would be remembering his with pleasure.

A slight sound sent me whirling round to face the door, where I could see that the latch was being very slowly and carefully lifted from the other side. For a second or so, I stood, transfixed. Then, limping slightly, I began to steal stealthily towards the corner where I should be concealed from the intruder's view as he entered.

Unfortunately, Humphrey chose that moment of all others to fall out of bed completely, banging his head on the floor and yelling loudly enough to waken the dead. I tripped over his prostrate form and cannoned into the wall, stubbing one foot against the clothes chest as I did so and striking my head a blow that set my ears ringing and stars dancing before my eyes. Anthony Bellknapp, roused at last, erupted from behind the bed-curtains, demanding in outraged accents to know what in the Devil's name was going on.

By the time we had sorted ourselves out, Humphrey and I had examined our various cuts and bruises and I had explained, not just about the lifting of the latch, but also about the figure I had seen earlier from the bed-chamber window, there wasn't a hope of discovering anyone still outside the door; although, of course, this didn't prevent our looking. Like the idiots we undoubtedly appeared, we all three jostled out into the passageway, staring up and down its length but, naturally, finding no one. The wall torches had long since burned themselves out, and the darkness and silence were almost total.

Not for long, however. Various sounds – raised voices, the opening of doors, the striking of flint on steel – indicated that we had disturbed other members of the household. Dame Audrea's voice, raised in annoyance to ask what was happening, sent Humphrey and me scurrying back into the bedchamber to hide our nakedness under the sheets. And after a moment's hesitation, Anthony joined us, closing the door behind him.

A polite knock heralded the arrival of George Applegarth, dressed sedately in a rubbed brown velvet gown over his nightshift and a candle in its holder held high in one hand.

'Master Anthony, your lady mother wishes to know the meaning of this disturbance.'

Anthony pushed the bed-curtains aside and looked his steward up and down. 'Tell my lady mother,' he drawled insolently, 'to mind her own business. No, on second thoughts' – he giggled – 'tell her we were holding an orgy.'

The steward sighed and raised his eyebrows

at me, inviting a sensible explanation. I thought Anthony would protest at this flouting of his orders, but he merely lay back against the pillows, still grinning, while I told George Applegarth of the night's events. They seemed to upset him.

'I warned you, Master,' he said, addressing Anthony in the scolding tone of an old and privileged retainer, 'to be careful. You've been home less than a day and you've already managed to antagonize all the most important members of the household. Be more conciliatory, do! Or some harm will befall you.' He turned the light of the candle on me. 'Did you get a good look at this cloaked figure? Did you recognize anything about it?'

I shook my head. 'It was standing by the moat. Too far away for me to tell if it were a man or a woman, even. It could have been anyone.'

The steward pursed his lips. 'If it was on this side of the moat, it most likely means that the person is from within the manor. The gates are locked at night and the moat's deep and takes some swimming ... Ah well! I'll report to Dame Audrea that the boy here' – he nodded in Humphrey's direction – 'was riding the night mare and fell out of bed. But I repeat my warning, Master Anthony. Take care. And keep your bedchamber door bolted at night. And you can wipe that silly smile off your face. I mean it when I say that you're in great danger.'

Eight

Morning brought another beautiful day and a feeling that the night's events had been merely the stuff of dreams, part of the ridiculous muddle that had haunted my sleep. But as I lay on my back looking up at the bed-canopy, which, together with the curtains, I now saw depicted the story of Diana and Actaeon, the reality of what had happened began to dawn. I had indeed seen someone staring up at this window, and, later, someone had tried to get into this room. Yet the episode had had its humorous side, and I couldn't avoid a snort of laughter as I pictured three grown men, as naked as the day they were born, struggling to get out of the door all at once, jostling and pushing like overgrown schoolboys. And before that again, the image of myself sent sprawling by the sheer accident of Humphrey Attleborough falling out of bed just at that particular moment contained all the elements of a May Day farce. I let out another snort, while at the same time cursing the ill luck that had prevented us from collaring the would-be intruder.

'What's making you so merry?' enquired

Anthony Bellknapp, raising himself on one elbow and smiling down at me.

I jumped. I hadn't realized that he was awake. I explained and his smile broadened into a grin.

'All the same,' I went on, growing serious, 'you should heed what Steward Applegarth told you. Be careful. Either that, or ... or...'

'Or moderate my behaviour,' he finished for me as I faltered to a stop, suddenly conscious of my position as a guest under his roof.

'Well ... yes.'

He laughed. 'We'll see. And now I must get up or my mother will have usurped my position at the breakfast table and my prerogative of speeding our overnight visitors on their way. The brothers at least will have enough gossip to take back to Glastonbury to keep the entire abbey agog for a month.' He yelled, 'Humphrey!' and threw a pillow at his still snoring henchman. 'Clothes, razor, man! Quickly!'

While the servant, half asleep, pulled on shirt and hose, and went off to the kitchen to fetch hot water and soap, I took the opportunity to ask my host if I might stay a few more days until my ankle had completely mended.

'Stay as long as you like,' was the careless answer. 'You have my permission and that's all that need concern you. I shall give instructions that you are to be treated like any other guest. You can continue to share my bed at night. In fact, I think I shall feel safer if you do.' He eyed me shrewdly. 'I have a suspicion that you're not here just because you've hurt yourself; that you've some purpose in mind. No, no! Don't bother denying it. I'm not accusing you of anything. You don't worry me. I've told you. You can remain at Croxcombe as long as you wish.' As Humphrey reappeared, weighed down by a pail of steaming water, he repeated with even greater emphasis, 'I'm the master here now.'

It was several hours later, when the departing travellers had been sped on their various ways, when not only breakfast, but dinner also had been eaten, and after the chaplain had led us in morning prayers and the household officers had been summoned to Anthony's presence to receive their instructions for the day, that Rose Micheldever sought me out to remind me about our visit to Wells. Not that I needed any reminding, my one reservation again being that I might not be able to walk the three miles there and back without proving a drag on my companion.

'That's all right,' Rose said, smiling. 'Dame Audrea keeps two donkeys for jogging about the countryside, and she's said that I may borrow them. She sometimes does so when I go into Wells. Your dog can run alongside.'

'Does she or your husband know that I'm going with you?'

Rose was evasive. 'They know somebody's going with me, naturally. It wouldn't do for me to ride about on my own.' Her underlip protruded defiantly. 'Edward thinks it's one of the grooms,' she admitted. 'I expect the mistress thinks the same.'

I hesitated, but only briefly. I had no desire to cause trouble either for myself or Rose. On the other hand, I urgently wished to meet her brother and she seemed to have no qualms about the consequences of her invitation. So I went.

As readers of these chronicles already know, beasts of burden and I do not get on well together, but a donkey was a great deal easier to manage than a horse, although its plodding gait meant a slower journey and therefore protracted discomfort. By the time we reached Wells, I was thankful to dismount and stretch my aching legs.

It was many years since I had been in the city itself, and I had forgotten how awe-inspiringly the cathedral's domineering presence diminished the buildings round about. Wells was, as it had always been – and for all I know, always will be – first and foremost the great Church of Saint Andrew. Everything else huddled in its shadow and paled into insignificance. The conduit still brought water into the marketplace from the wells, bubbling up from beneath the earth, that gave the city its name and where, as a young boy, I had gathered with my friends to play fivestones and catch-as-catch-can or to sail stick and leaf 'boats' in the water. The usual clutch of beggars had congregated beneath the porch, where they had taken shelter ever since it was completed earlier in the century, under the auspices of Bishop Beckington. That indefatigable builder had also overseen the row of houses and shops adjacent to the porch, one of which displayed an open counter on which reposed a butcher's block, knife and saw, with joints of meat swinging on metal hooks beneath an awning. Two men, in bloodstained leather aprons, were attending to a regular supply of customers, the sure sign of a prosperous community.

The elder of the pair glanced in our direction with a delighted smile as Rose, without waiting for my assistance, slid from the back of her donkey with a cry of 'Father!'

I have frequently noticed throughout my life that butchers are big, jolly men (well, I suppose you need a sense of humour if you're cutting animals into collops all day long), and Master Bignell was no exception. He had a round, red face with twinkling blue eyes, a mouth that curled upwards at the corners in a perpetual smile, and even his nose seemed to be nothing more than a circular dab in the middle of his other features. I could recognize a certain likeness between father and daughter, and suspected that, later in life, when her present prettiness had faded, Rose would probably grow plump and matronly with only an echo of her former good looks.

The second man, whom I assumed – rightly, as it turned out – to be Ronan Bignell, the person I had come to see, was taller and somewhat leaner than either his father or sister, but with the same friendly, happy disposition; a fact that made him an obvious favourite among the women, and went some way to explaining the popularity of this particular butcher's stall. He greeted Rose affectionately, leaning across to plant a smacking kiss on her cheek, while his sire, abandoning a customer in the middle of serving her, came out from behind the counter to wrap his daughter in an all-embracing hug.

'You're looking well, my girl.' He patted her belly. 'Not increasing yet?' But when she shook her head, he seemed less disappointed than resigned. 'Well, well! These things won't be hurried. Where's Edward? Not with you? And who's this?'

He eyed me with a certain amount of suspicion, and I guessed that he was under no illusion as to his daughter's predilection for men. She had made a good marriage both for herself and her family, and Butcher Bignell wanted nothing to spoil it.

Fortunately, at that precise moment, both men's attention was claimed by Hercules's investigation of one of the carcasses hanging up behind the counter; and by the time I had thwarted the dog's ambition to consume a whole pig for his dinner, smacked him, scolded him – much to his outraged fury – and tucked him safely under one arm, Rose had her answer ready.

'This is Master Chapman, Father. He's a guest of our new master, Anthony Bellknapp.'

If she had expected to create a sensation,

she was not disappointed. The news of Anthony's return had not previously reached the city, and the reaction of everyone within earshot was most gratifying. The elder Bignell staggered back a pace or two and supported himself against the counter, the younger's mouth fell open in amazement, the woman he had been in the process of serving screamed and dropped a basket containing half a dozen eggs, which shattered all over the cobbles, several other customers flatly refused to believe what they were hearing, while yet another went haring off around the market-place, determined to be first with these wholly unexpected and unlooked-for tidings. Before she knew what was happening, Rose found herself at the centre of an eager and excited crowd clamouring for details; so, still clutching a highly indignant Hercules, I eased my way free of the ever-increasing throng – which I could see already included a number of beggars and pickpockets, intent on seizing this golden opportunity to relieve respectable citizens of their pouches and purses – and edged around to where Ronan Bignell was standing behind the counter. I touched him on the shoulder.

I had great difficulty in prising his attention away from his sister even after he became aware of my presence, but finally he demanded irritably, 'What?'

'I'd like to speak to you,' I said apologetically, and was bracing myself for the furious refusal I could see hovering on the tip of his tongue, when he suddenly realized who I was.

'You're the man who came with Rose. You must be staying at Croxcombe Manor.' He took hold of my arm and shook it excitedly. Hercules growled but was ignored. 'You must know all about it.'

It was no use pretending not to know what 'it' referred to, so I admitted reluctantly, 'I – er – yes. I suppose I know something.'

Seeing me as a source of private information which could lead to his being wiser than his neighbours, Ronan Bignell, keeping his grip on my free arm, propelled me out from behind the counter and away from the crowd in the direction of the cathedral. It was not until we were within sight of the Bishop's palace, surrounded by its moat, that he paused and turned to face me. For a moment, I thought he might recognize me from childhood days, then realized that he was too young. I reckoned he couldn't be much more than twenty or twenty-one, which left a gap of seven or eight years between us. He wouldn't remember Roger Stonecarver, although there had to be others in Wells who could.

We sat down beside the moat while Hercules went off about his own business – I wasn't worried: he would always return at my whistle – and I submitted to Ronan's eager questioning. I had made up my mind during our short walk to be perfectly honest with him, so as soon as he fell silent, I told him the truth; my history, or such of it as was relevant, who and what I really was, how and for what reason I came to be at Croxcombe just at the time of Anthony Bellknapp's return, the meeting with my previously unknown half-brother and his imprisonment on Dame Audrea's charge that he was the missing murderer, John Jericho and, finally, my mission to clear his name. As a bonus, I also told him the little I knew of Anthony's history, although I omitted the events of the previous night.

Ronan Bignell listened, fascinated, but when I'd finished, he asked, 'Why, though, do you want to talk to me?'

I explained what Rose had told me and he groaned.

'Women!' he exclaimed bitterly. 'You can't trust 'em, not even your own sister.' He shrugged resignedly. 'But to do her justice, she's never breathed a word to my father, and I don't suppose she ever would. It's true, a couple of my friends and I have always been fond of a bit of poaching. We just like the excitement, and the Croxcombe woods are full of rabbits and hares. Doesn't do any harm to anyone that I can see. We've been doing it for years, ever since we were lads. I let Rob and Dick take whatever we snare. Their parents aren't such law-abiding citizens as mine.'

'And can you remember what you saw the night of Jenny Applegarth's murder?' I prompted him.

He puckered his lips thoughtfully. 'Clearly. What happened after stamped it on my memory for ever. When we heard of the robbery, that poor Jenny Applegarth had been murdered and that the page was missing, along with a fair amount of the family's valuables, well of course I remembered what I'd seen the night before.'

'And that was?'

Ronan Bignell shifted uncomfortably. 'Look, this is a secret,' he said. 'Neither Rob nor Dick nor I have ever told anyone. Well, I told Rose, which I can see now was a mistake, because I ought to have known that sooner or later she'd be bound to tell someone. Mind you, I suppose I can't complain. She has managed to keep silent for six years – as far as I know, that is,' he added with a sudden spurt of anxiety.

'Surely if she had confided in anyone else,' I soothed him, curbing my impatience, 'someone or other would have said something to you by now. Six years ago, Mistress Micheldever was a child, and children, although they have long memories, are interested more in their own affairs. And in fact, she told me very little, merely that you thought you'd seen both John Jericho and another man abroad in the woods on the night of the murder.'

'And how did I come to see them?' he asked, answering his own question. 'Because I was poaching. She told you that.'

'Master Bignell,' I said patiently (or as patiently as I could), 'I don't care about your poaching. It's nothing to me and I certainly have no intention of disclosing the fact to anyone. I've been frank with you about what has brought me to Croxcombe, and I should be very grateful for equal frankness on your part.'

He was still reluctant. 'I don't see how it will prove that this man – this half-brother of yours – isn't John Jericho. In fact, I can't see it will be of any value to you at all, can you?'

I clenched my fists to stop myself from striking him and answered as reasonably as I could, 'Maybe not. But I have no idea what might prove to be of value and what might not just at this moment, so I should appreciate an account of what you and your two friends saw on the night of the murder.'

He fought against telling me for another few seconds, then suddenly gave in.

'I don't know what hour of the night it was. Time didn't worry me in those days. I'd discovered a way of getting in and out of my parents' house without them being any the wiser. Sometimes, when it was summer, as it was then, I didn't get home till dawn. But thinking back, it could have been around midnight. We'd had time enough to snare a couple of good fat rabbits and were on the trail of another, if I remember rightly, somewhere around Hangman's Oak. Do you know the Croxcombe woods, Master Chapman?' I shook my head and he went on, 'There's a sort of clearing there, where the trees thin out towards the edge of the woodland. A young fellow was staggering about, moaning and clutching his head, and then he was sick. One of us, I forget which, said, "He's drunk," and then Dick said, "It's Dame Bellknapp's page, that one with the funny name." And I said, "John Jericho." And the other two agreed.'

'Did you go to his assistance?' I asked, and was answered with an incredulous snort.

'Of course we didn't. We weren't supposed to be there. Naturally, we didn't know anything about the murder then, or we might've tried to apprehend him.'

'What did you think?' I enquired curiously. 'I don't suppose you see many people reeling around the woods drunk, at midnight.'

'I daresay you're right, but I don't imagine that occurred to us at the time.' He laughed. 'All we thought about was not being discovered ourselves. The three of us just sloped off by another path as quietly as we could.'

'You're sure the page was drunk? He couldn't have been ill or – or wounded?'

Ronan Bignell shrugged, trailing his fingers in the water of the moat. 'We did talk it over next day, of course, when the news of the murder came out, and we decided that perhaps he might not have been drunk after all, just horrified and sickened by what he'd done. We even discussed whether or not we ought to tell anyone what we'd witnessed, but, quite honestly, what would have been the point? John Jericho had killed Jenny Applegarth and run away. Everyone knew that, and all we'd seen was him escaping. We didn't know where he'd gone, so we couldn't put the sheriff's men on his track. We'd just have landed ourselves in trouble if we'd owned up to being in the woods after curfew.'

The argument was reasonable enough. John Jericho would have been well on his way by the time news of his crime reached Wells. The three lads had had nothing to gain, but everything to lose by being honest.

I stared thoughtfully at the walls of the Bishop's palace, shimmering in the heat of the August morning. Echoes of the town from beyond Bishop Beckington's arch were borne on a gentle breeze. I glanced up at the side of the cathedral where the painted statues of the saints glowed jewel-bright in their niches.

'When you saw the page,' I asked suddenly, 'did he have anything with him?'

'Anything with him?' My companion was puzzled.

'Yes. The murder, as I understand it, was incidental to the robbery. He'd made off with a considerable amount of plate as well as jewels. Therefore he must have been carrying his spoils in something. Did you see a sack or a knotted cloth lying anywhere around?'

Ronan Bignell began to laugh. 'Do you know, in all these years that's never occurred to me? It's never even crossed my mind. Nor Rob's, nor Dick's that I know of. No, we didn't see any sack, but unfortunately I don't think that tells you anything except that it was darkish in the woods, in spite of it being a moonlit night, and that we were in a panic. We were only concerned that the page didn't see us and report us to Dame Audrea. What I'm saying is that there *might* have been a sack, but if there was, we simply didn't notice it.'

I could see that further questioning on that score was useless. Even if I persuaded him to introduce me to his two friends, Rob and Dick, I doubted they could tell me more. And if they did, it made no odds. There had never been any dispute about the identity of the murderer.

'Rose hinted that you also saw someone else in the woods that night,' I suggested hopefully.

'No, that was the next night. We saw one of the charcoal burners, but as they tend their fires day and night, there was nothing unusual in that. Except, that is, that this one wasn't tending his fire, but standing and surveying the ground around Hangman's Oak as though he were looking for something.'

'Hangman's Oak? That was where you saw the page.'

'But this was a day later and the page had long since disappeared, so there's nothing in that to get excited over.'

'Doesn't it strike you as a coincidence?'

Ronan shook his head. 'No. Why should it?'

There was no really satisfactory answer that I could give him. Nothing logical; it just seemed to me to be of some significance.

'Did you recognize the man?'

'Oh yes! It was that rogue Hamo Gough. We didn't worry too much about him. He's not above doing a bit of poaching himself.'

'You say he was surveying the ground—'

'He seemed to be. I couldn't say for certain.'

'All right. But was that all?'

'What else would he be doing?'

'He wasn't perhaps ... by any chance ... digging?'

'No. Why in heaven's name would he have been doing that?'

I shook my head. 'Just a foolish thought. Forget it.'

Ronan stroked his chin, regarding me thoughtfully. 'It's odd, though, that you should ask me that question. It's brought back something that until this minute I'd completely forgotten. A few days afterwards, I was taking meat from our stall to the manor house kitchen and had taken a short cut through Croxcombe woods when I met Hamo Gough not far from his cottage. And now I come to think about it, he was carrying a spade over one shoulder. It obviously didn't strike me as odd at the time, or it would have stuck in my memory. He can be a surly bastard when he chooses, and my recollection is that he didn't even return my greeting. Then again, he does sometimes go digging for truffles.'

'And that's probably what he was doing,' I agreed glumly.

There was silence between us for a moment or two while we listened abstractedly to the noises of the marketplace and I wondered idly where Rose had gone. To visit her mother and friends and tell them the great news, no doubt.

Ronan, who seemed to have gone into a reverie of his own, said suddenly, 'I know what Rose must have been thinking of when she told you I'd seen someone else in the woods that night. The night of the murder, that is. She's confused it with something Father saw. It was all of six years ago and it's no wonder if things have got a bit muddled in her mind.'

'Master Bignell also saw somebody in Croxcombe woods?'

'Not in the woods, no! I wouldn't have been there if I'd thought there was the smallest risk of encountering *him*. It was some time later, two or three days perhaps, and of course we were all still talking about Jenny Applegarth's murder – well, I suppose it was the main topic of conversation for months – and Father suddenly recalled seeing a man on horseback in the neighbourhood of the house on the night she was killed. He – my father – had ridden over to Shepton to visit a friend and was returning home by the track that runs along the manor's northern boundary. It was dusk and he couldn't see the horseman at all clearly. He remembered that Master Bell-knapp and Dame Audrea were away, visiting their daughter and her husband at Kewstoke

Hall, and that young Simon and most of their household had gone with them. He said he thought of riding after the stranger to warn him that he wouldn't be able to secure a bed for the night as the master and mistress were both absent, and, indeed, he turned aside from the track with that end in view. But by the time he reached the moat gate, the man and his horse had vanished. So he assumed he had mistaken the man's intention, rode on home and thought no more of the incident until a day or so after the murder, when he suddenly wondered if what he'd seen might have some significance.'

'Master Bignell didn't say anything to the sheriff's men?'

'There seemed no point. We all knew who the murderer was and everyone was trying to find him. There were enough posses out to capture ten men – Rob and Dick and I went on two of 'em – but even so, John Jericho outsmarted us all. My own guess is that he lay low by day and travelled by night, but even so, it wouldn't have been easy for him, not on foot with a sack to carry. But he did it. He fooled everyone and hasn't been heard of again from that day to this. At least, that is to say, not unless this half-brother of yours turns out to be him. And if Dame Audrea thinks he is, God help him! She's a woman who knows she's always right.'

'I suppose this business of Anthony Bell-knapp's return might distract her,' I suggested hopefully.

'Don't you believe it,' my companion spluttered. 'She won't be easily deflected from anything she undertakes. She's perfectly capable of carrying on two or three vendettas at once.'

'You don't think, in the light of what your father saw that evening, that John Jericho might not have been Jenny Applegarth's killer? You don't think this stranger, whoever he was, could have had anything to do with it?'

'Lord, no!' Ronan Bignell was scathing. 'Why else would the page have disappeared? What was he doing in Croxcombe woods when we saw him, if not running away? Why did he pretend to have something wrong with him so as to stay at home, instead of accompanying Dame Audrea to Kewstoke Hall?'

'But how do you know – how does anyone know – that he was only pretending? Perhaps his illness was genuine.'

'Well, even if it was, he took advantage of it for his own fell purpose,' Ronan insisted.

I sighed inwardly. Further argument was fruitless in more ways than one. I wasn't here to prove John Jericho innocent of the crime of which he stood accused, but to disprove, somehow or another, that he and my half-brother were one and the same person. And Ronan Bignell's stories, interesting though they were, were of no help on that score whatsoever.

'So this is where you two are hiding,' said Rose's voice, and, turning our heads, we saw her tripping towards us through Bishop Beckington's archway. 'Father's been asking where you've got to, Ronan.' She dimpled at her brother as seductively as she would have smiled at any man. 'You don't mind my having told Master Chapman about what you saw all those years ago, do you? I didn't think it would matter after such a long time.'

'You mean you couldn't resist a handsome face,' her brother retorted, then smiled and pinched her cheek. 'But if I hear of you confiding in anyone else, there'll be trouble. And there'll be trouble, too, with Edward if you don't watch your step, my girl. And don't give me that innocent stare. You know quite well what I mean.'

And as if on cue, another voice, swollen by the echoing archway, boomed out, 'Here you are, Mistress Micheldever. What a dance you've led me. Why didn't you ask *me* to accompany you to Wells?'

It was Anthony Bellknapp.

Nine

I saw Ronan Bignell frown as the newcomer slipped an arm familiarly around Rose's waist, but his disapproval turned to excitement as he recognized Anthony Bellknapp.

It was one thing to be told of the prodigal's return, but quite another to see him in the flesh. That small corner of Ronan's mind that had retained a vestige of disbelief was now forced to accept the truth of my and his sister's story. After eight years without a word, the best part of a decade with no knowledge as to whether he was alive or dead, the elder of the two Bellknapp brothers stood before us, bronzed, fit, his dark brown curls well combed, his blue eyes sparkling with mischief. Well dressed, too, and if his hose and tunic were not the extreme of fashion – and, let's face it, the extreme of male fashion at that time was enough to make your average citizen laugh himself silly – they were made of good cloth and yarn and had been cut by an expert tailor. His riding boots gleamed with the gloss of the best Cordovan leather. Whatever else had, or had not, happened to Anthony during the years of his self-imposed exile, he hadn't starved. In fact, he seemed to have done very well for himself. I wondered idly what he had been up to, and made a mental note to ask him whenever the moment seemed propitious.

Rose hurriedly introduced her brother, and immediately Anthony's manner towards her underwent a change. It became jocular, almost fraternal, as he pinched her blushing cheek and then released her.

'Ronan Bignell! Yes, I do remember you, even though you must still have been a lad at the time I left Croxcombe. Mind you, I wasn't much past my seventeenth birthday myself, when I come to think of it.' He turned back to Rose. 'As I was saying, Mistress Micheldever, you should have waited for me before riding into Wells. I would have mounted you on a decent horse instead of letting you traipse around the countryside on a donkey.'

'I didn't know you were intending to visit the town, sir,' was the demure reply, 'and Master Chapman was anxious to speak to my brother.'

Anthony raised his eyebrows at me in a look of enquiry, but I shook my head, sending what I hoped was a warning glance at Rose.

'Only some queries about old acquaintances of mine.' I thought quickly. 'The Actons.' The name just came into my head, apparently from nowhere, and it took me some seconds before I recollected that it was an Acton who had been my father's mistress and my half-brother's mother.

To my astonishment, Ronan Bignell said promptly, 'Oh, there are no Actons in Wells nowadays, but I know of a couple of that name living out towards Wedmore.'

'Th-thank you,' I stuttered. 'If you'll be good enough to give me more precise directions, I-I'll pay them a visit.'

Anthony Bellknapp's eyebrows rose even higher. He wasn't deceived. 'It's taken you both a long time to establish that fact,' he remarked drily, then let the matter drop. He offered Rose his arm. 'Mistress Micheldever, now that I've found you, allow me to buy you a favour, some trinket or other, from one of the market stalls.'

Rose hesitated, but only for a moment. She obviously guessed that such a gift would be frowned upon by her husband, but she was unable to resist the lure of some free finery to adorn her person. She took the proffered arm, and Ronan and I followed her and Anthony back under the archway into the hubbub of the marketplace, which was now at the height of the morning's trading.

Bakers, butchers and brewers, tinkers, tailors and weavers, shepherds and herdsmen, with animals they were hoping to sell, hot pie vendors yelling the attractions of their wares – 'Pies piping hot! Good meat! No gristle! Come and dine! Come and dine!' – and vintners shouting, 'White wine, red wine to wash the food down. A beakerful free with every one you buy!' made for a crescendo of noise that hurt my ears. I had forgotten how rowdy Wells market could be. It could compete with Bristol's any day of the week.

The sensation created by news of Anthony Bellknapp's return, followed by his actual appearance in their midst, seemed to be evaporating. People continued to stare at him as he moved among the stalls, and to whisper behind their hands, but business had resumed with its customary briskness. Ronan went off to join his father, and to receive, by the look of things, a furious reprimand for his prolonged absence. Meantime, I rescued Hercules from a confrontation with an angry goose, an encounter he was in serious danger of losing. As compensation for being again tucked unceremoniously under my arm, I let him share the meat pie I had bought and was eating.

There was a sudden gap in the surging crowd, and I saw Anthony and Rose standing at a little distance beside a stall that sold jewellery. While I watched, Rose slipped a necklace over her head and admired her reflection in the mirror of polished steel that the stallholder held up to her. Anthony passed some coins across the counter and I inched closer, curious to know what price he was prepared to pay for the possible future pleasure of laying his receiver's wife. For there was no doubt in my mind that that was what he was after; and judging by the smile that Rose bestowed on him, he was already more than halfway to achieving his goal.

Another woman, who until that minute had

been just a part of the milling crowd, suddenly stopped in front of Anthony, blocking
his progress. Her back view, which was as
much as I could see at that moment, in its
plain blue gown and linen coif suggested a
well-fed, well-built country girl, and her
hands, roughened by work and weather, up-
held this impression. Her left was on her hip,
in that stance a woman adopts just before
giving you a piece of her mind (and heaven
help you when she does); the right one
clasped that of a young boy, some nine or ten
years old, who was half turned towards me,
and who bore a striking resemblance to the
Bellknapp family, particularly to Anthony. I
saw the latter's eyes flicker as he, too, recognized it.

I edged closer, easing myself unobtrusively
around the woman to stand next to Rose.

'Anthony!' the woman exclaimed, looking
him up and down. 'So, it's true. You've
returned at last.' She glanced down at the
boy. 'Lucas, this is Master Bellknapp. Anthony, this is my son, Lucas Slye.'

Anthony bowed. 'Dorcas, it's good to see
you again. You ... You haven't married, then?'

'No.' She gave him a challenging smile. 'I
resisted all attempts of family and clergy to
make a respectable woman of me. My son
and I live at home with my parents.'

'A fine lad. He's a credit to you.' Anthony
was making a brave effort to return the smile,
but I could see he wasn't finding it easy. It
was more of a rictus grin.

'Dorcas!' Rose greeted the other woman with a kiss. Then, becoming aware of my presence, she said, 'Master Chapman, this is the sister of Croxcombe's chamberlain, Mistress Slye. And this is her son, Lucas.'

Dorcas Slye, as I had already surmised, had the round, healthy looks of the country girl, with the same blue eyes and short neck of her brother, Jonathan. Her skin was like the bloom on a ripe plum and was completely innocent of the white lead that fashionable women would have considered necessary to tone down its high colour. She was very pretty if you have a taste for the bucolic, which, at some time or another, Anthony Bellknapp plainly had had. There could be no doubt that Lucas was his son, even though Dorcas Slye, if I remembered correctly, had refused to name him as the father. Whether or not the resemblance had struck Rose, I had no idea: somehow I doubted it. There was an underlying innocence about her that belied the sharp, acquisitive gaze and predatory smile. But there could be little question that other people would remark on the similarity now that Anthony, whose features must have grown dim in their recollections over the past eight years, was once more before them. The gossip would flare up again; and although it seemed to be of little moment to Dorcas herself, her family would be bound to resent it. Jonathan Slye, the chamberlain, had probably recognized the danger as soon as he clapped eyes on the prodigal. Anthony Bellknapp's tally of enemies was mounting fast. It was small wonder that George Applegarth had advised him to watch his back.

I became aware that Rose was inviting me to admire her new necklace. 'Coral and jet,' she said happily. 'Jet to ward off evil spirits.'

I wondered if it might also ward off a husband's jealousy, but saw that no such consideration had disturbed Rose's peace of mind. Dorcas Slye was regarding the necklace with a mocking smile, doubtless recalling similar gifts in the past and all too conscious of their consequences. Anthony, too, suddenly looked uncomfortable.

'Master Chapman,' he said, 'do you return with us to Croxcombe? I shall take up Mistress Micheldever behind me on my horse. Ronan Bignell will return the donkey to the manor when he brings the next delivery of meat.'

As I had no intention of following behind them like a humble retainer, I excused myself.

'If you'll allow me continued use of my donkey, I'll ride in the direction of Wedmore and find my friends, the Actons. As I said, Master Bignell will give me more detailed directions.'

Anthony seemed a little taken aback, having quite correctly decided in his own mind that these friends of mine had been a hurried excuse to conceal whatever it was that Ronan and I had really been discussing. But my sudden decision to search out the Actons would

161

both allay his suspicions and might also prove to be of some value to myself. Although what, I couldn't imagine.

Half an hour later, I was jogging along the Wedmore track, on my own at last. Judging by the sun, it was now past noon, and here and there the silver trunks of birch trees rippled like water in the afternoon light. The countryside was looking beautiful. The feathered gold of ragwort caught my eye, white trumpets of bindweed were being crushed beneath the donkey's hooves, and buttercups and golden-eyed daisies spangled the molehills. (The day's eye, how well that little plant is named.) Altogether, it was a brilliant scene, the colours glowing jewel-bright under the sun, and making me glad to be alive.

According to Ronan Bignell, Edgar and Avice Acton scraped a living from a small-holding somewhere to the east of Wedmore, watered by a little tributary of the meandering River Axe. Greatly to my surprise, they weren't difficult to find. Everyone of whom I sought directions seemed to be familiar with their names even if he or she was not acquainted with the couple in person. I gathered that they were an elderly pair who were probably either my half-brother's grandparents or a great-uncle and great-aunt. As it turned out, the latter surmise was correct.

When I eventually came across them, the

two were sitting contentedly outside their cottage, enjoying the sunshine and drinking small beer from horn beakers which were obviously home-made. As I approached, I saw the man take a handful of grain from a bag beside him and throw it into the dirt. With a great clucking and squawking and much flapping of wings, two hens, a goose and a duck went running after it, the duck being at a decided disadvantage because it had to lumber up from the stream that all but encircled the property. In a nearby sty a couple of pigs rootled and snorted; one a heavy-bodied, stumpy-legged creature with drooping, floppy ears, obviously a descendant of the wild boars that had roamed the woodlands for centuries; the other lighter-skinned, longer-limbed, with a pointed snout and bright, intelligent eyes. A Tantony pig as country people called it (or a Saint Anthony pig, if you wanted to give it its full name), the sort of porker most often seen for sale in town and city marketplaces. There were also a sheep, a goat and a cow, turned loose to graze the adjoining meadow.

I approached quietly, the donkey's hooves making no sound on the lush grass, and was about to alert the Actons to my presence when Hercules did it for me, making a headlong rush at the poultry and scattering them in all directions. I slid from Neddy's back, yelling ferociously at him to come to heel and startling the rest of the livestock in the process. After such an entrance, I could hardly have been surprised if the Actions had requested me to leave forthwith, but both husband and wife roared with laughter and Hercules, recognizing a couple of well-wishers, went to sit between them, daring me to touch him.

'Nice li'l dog,' the man said, tickling the miscreant's ears.

'Sometimes,' I agreed, still advancing threateningly. Hercules barked at me and licked his new friend's hand. (That animal can be such a sycophant!) 'Master and Mistress Acton?' I enquired.

They laughed again.

'Don' know about Maister,' the man answered. 'But I'm Edgar Acton and this here is my Goody. What can we do for you, young fellow?'

When you are less than two months off your twenty-eighth birthday, it's not often you're called a young fellow. I beamed and forgot to be cross with Hercules, stooping myself to tickle his ears. He allowed himself to be placated and condescended to lick my hand as well. Meantime, Goody Acton had gone into the cottage and fetched out another stool and beaker of ale, and before I was allowed to explain the reason for my visit, I was pressed to sit down and refresh myself.

'It's a danged hot day!' her husband exclaimed. 'Better fetch some water for that there donkey, my old sweetheart. And for this here dog.'

So it was not until the needs of Hercules

and Neddy had been supplied that I was at last able to tell my story. I began by asking the couple if they were indeed kin to the Anne Acton who had married first her cousin, Ralph Wedmore, and then an Irishman, Matthew O'Neill.

The old man nodded. 'Aye, Anne were my niece. My brother's daughter. Bright, pretty lass, she were. Never could make out why she married Ralph. He were my sister's son, but took after his father's family. Miserable lot the Wedmores. Never had much to do with 'em after Jeanne died.'

'Nor with your great-nephews, Anne's sons?'

'We did try once or twice,' Avice Acton said defensively. 'But it was soon plain we weren't welcome. Anne only had the one lad then. John I think she'd named him. After her father, Edgar's brother.'

'That's right.' The man nodded. 'I believe there were another lad later on, but we never saw him. Both of us had a feeling there was something not quite right about Anne's marriage to Ralph. Something being hidden, if you know what I mean. Ralph and his parents didn't seem to treat the boy like one of their own. Me and Avice, we wondered...'

'Aye, we did wonder.' His wife looked at me, suddenly expectant.

'You were quite right to wonder,' I affirmed, and proceeded to recount the whole story, leaving as little out as possible.

When I had finished, there was a long

silence while the couple digested what I had told them. Finally, Goody Acton heaved a great sigh and Edgar nodded his head.

'That makes sense,' Avice said at last.

Her husband added, 'It do that. Don't get the pig by the tail, mind! Anne weren't a flighty piece. Reckon she must've been uncommon fond o' your father to let herself bear his child.'

'I think my father was probably very fond of her,' I answered in a low voice. 'Looking back, I can see now that it caused my mother a lot of grief. He never knew about the child, of course. I think he must have been killed before your niece could tell him.'

Edgar nodded. 'And now you say John's in gaol, accused o' murder?'

'Wrongly, I feel certain.' And I went again over the circumstances that had landed John Wedmore in the Bristol bridewell. 'He insists that he was in Ireland six years ago, living with his family. His mother and younger brother and stepfather.'

'Do you believe him?' Goody Acton asked, her shrewd old eyes regarding me thoughtfully.

'I have no reason not to. Moreover, he'd be foolish to return to this country, to this part of the world in particular, if he was wanted for murder.'

'Bristol ain't 'xactly this part o' the world,' Edgar objected. ''Tis miles away, over other side o' Mendip. Up country.'

'No great distance to Dame Audrea,' I

166

pointed out, 'with her carriage and her horses. And it was the time of Saint James's fair. If John had ever been in her employ, he'd have remembered that she always visited the city for that, and to see her kinsman in Small Street. He'd surely have calculated there was a chance of meeting her. He'd have waited.'

'Not if he were worried about his brother,' Avice argued. 'All the same, I think you'm most likely right. This Dame Audrea's mistaken him for somebody else. They'm not a violent lot, the Actons.'

'No, we'm allus been reasonable folk,' her husband agreed. 'But the Wedmores! They're a different bucket o' shit.'

'But if the pedlar's telling us the truth,' his wife demurred, 'Anne's eldest ain't a Wedmore. He's a bastard of this young fellow's father.' She turned to me. 'Any history o' violence on your side the family?' I shook my head. 'There you are then. There's been a mistake made, no doubt about it.'

'Maybe! Maybe!' Edgar pursed his lips and sucked at his few remaining teeth. 'But what we can do about it, I dunno. Don' like t' think of Anne's boy wrongfully accused, but like I say, there ain't nothing we can do.'

'You couldn't swear to the fact that six years ago John was in Ireland?' I asked, but without much hope of a positive answer.

They both sighed regretfully.

'We told you,' Avice Acton said, 'we never had much to do with Anne and her family, not when the boys were young. And we got

167

out o' the habit of asking after them when strangers stopped by. We did hear Ralph had died, but not for a year nor more afterwards, by which time Anne had got herself married again to some Irishman or other and gone to live across the water. 'Spect we heard both things together, though after all this while I can't be sure.'

'Do either of you remember anything about the murder at Croxcombe Manor, six years ago?' I enquired desperately. (I had guessed this was a wasted journey before I started out.) 'Did you ever set eyes on the page, John Jericho, during the time he was in Dame Audrea's employ? When you went to Wells, perhaps?'

'Lord love you, I ain't been to Wells since I can't tell when,' Edgar chuckled. 'What do we want to go jauntering around the countryside for? We got everything we need right here. If they want to see us, people come to us.'

'Six years is a great time to remember anything,' his wife said. 'Although, now I come to think of it, something do stir in my mind. Someone – can't rightly recollect who – did tell us there'd been some trouble over to Mendip way. Robbery or some such thing. But whether that were six year or six month ago, I couldn't swear to. One day's pretty much like another, and time don't mean much here, like it does to city folks. We just follow the seasons round.'

I could well believe that. The peace of the place was profound. There was a kind of enchantment in its silence and isolation. Cares and worries were slipping from me; Adela, the children, the need to earn a living suddenly seemed nothing more than a distant dream. I could stay here for the rest of my life, just myself and Hercules, and no one would ever know what had become of me...

I pulled myself together. It was time I was going before the witches and hobgoblins and woodland sprites that inhabit the wilder corners of this land had me in their thrall. I got to my feet and held out my hand to the dog. 'Come along, lad!'

'You're not going!' Avice Acton exclaimed, sounding disappointed. 'We see so few strangers and it's always a pleasure to hear about the outside world.'

'Aye, it is that,' Edgar agreed. 'And once, it seems someone come asking after us in Wedmore. Or, at least, so we were told, though he never turned up here. Lost his way, I s'pose, or was given the wrong directions.'

'Some o' them over t' Wedmore's got turnips for heads!' Avice was scathing of her nearest neighbours. 'We were that gutted when we heard. Nice young lad, too, by all accounts. Asked in the alehouse, and some fool told him we'd moved away. Danged idiot! Others said no and told him how to find us, but like Edgar says, he never came.'

'How long ago was this?' I asked, but neither had the slightest idea, Edgar Acton hazarding anything from one year to ten, his wife offering six weeks, eight months, four years.

Time past; time present; time future; it was all one to the Actons who, within a very short time, would confuse this visit of mine with somebody else's. I thanked them profusely for their hospitality, remounted the donkey, whistled up Hercules and rode back by twisting paths and barely visible, dried-up tracks to the main highway leading from Wells to Wedmore. I was about to turn eastwards to return to Croxcombe, when, on a sudden whim, I decided to continue in a westward direction, looking out, as I did so, for any alehouse that stood near the road.

This wasn't hard to find, and beside Wedmore's market cross I noticed a promising small tavern that looked a likely place for anyone needing directions from the local population. But I was unlucky. In a crowded taproom, no one recalled a stranger enquiring after Edgar and Avice Acton for the past ten years or more. Yes, of course they would remember! Well, someone would, I could be sure of that. In Wedmore the old people prided themselves on their memories. Why, they could recall when...

The landlord touched me on the arm. 'Try the alehouse a mile or so back, on the Cheddar road,' he advised. 'Little, out o' the way place. No one much goes there, but you never know. If you stay here, you'll end up buying 'em all free ale while you listen to their life histories.'

I thanked him, paid twice the price for the stoup of ale I'd had, and departed while the storm of reminiscence that my question had provoked was at its height.

The afternoon was by now some way advanced, and the distant hills were slabbed with purple and gold as the sun continued its slow descent towards the horizon. It took me a while to locate this second alehouse, so distant did it seem from any haunt of man. And when at last I found it, it was nothing more than a single-storey daub-and-wattle building devoid of human life except for the surly landlord, standing outside his door surveying the glimmering landscape, and a potboy asleep in the sunshine on a rough-hewn bench. I nearly didn't bother to dismount. There was certainly nothing to be learned here.

I was mistaken. For a start, the landlord was not as surly as he looked, and, when approached, seemed glad of the opportunity to chat to a stranger. He woke the potboy, shifted him off the bench with instructions to bring us both some cider and water for Hercules, and invited me to sit down.

'Come far?' he grunted.

'Today, from Wells, but I live in Bristol.'

'Powerful big place, Bristol. I went there once,' he added proudly.

'Big enough,' I acknowledged, 'though not so big as London.'

My companion regarded me with respect. 'You been to Lunnon?'

'Several times. I was there earlier this year.' I didn't admit to being on friendly terms with the Duke of Gloucester. There was no point. It would serve no purpose and he probably wouldn't believe me anyway.

'Cor!' was all he said as the potboy returned with two beakers of cider. 'So what brings you here? Not many folk comes this road. A few local shepherds and cowherds. But me and the boy – 'e's my grandson – we scrape a living o' sorts. I've thought o' movin' on, but where'd we go? No, so long as we'm happy, I reckon that's all that matters.'

'I imagine you don't see many strangers?'

'No. Too far from the beaten track.' He turned his head and gave me a curious stare. 'How d'you come to be here?'

'It was suggested to me by some people in Wedmore. I'm trying to find someone who might remember a young man in these parts some time ago who was looking for Edgar and Avice Acton. I don't suppose you have any such recollection? I can't even tell you exactly when it was.'

I was in for my second surprise.

'Yes, I remember,' the landlord said. 'Mind you, I couldn't say how many years agone it were, but I do recollect 'im.'

'Can you remember what he looked like?'

'Oh, aye. Small, dark lad. Thought 'e were a Welshman to begin with. 'E had that look about 'im. Told 'im where the Actons could be found. What's your interest in 'im?'

'I've been visiting the Actons today. They'd

172

heard about the young man enquiring for them, but it seems he never turned up. They wondered why not.'

The landlord shrugged. 'Must've lost his way. Easy enough done, I reckon.' Like all country folk, he saw no absurdity in discussing events of the past as if they had happened last week.

'You ... You didn't discover the young man's name?' I asked, and he nodded. 'What was it? Can you recall?'

I found myself holding my breath. If the answer was John Wedmore, then it might well be that my half-brother was lying and he had returned to Somerset since his mother's re-marriage. In which case, I could go home to Bristol forthwith.

'What was it?' I repeated.

The landlord grunted. 'A queer name. Something out the Bible. Let me see now. Ar. Got it! John Jericho, that were it.'

Ten

At his words, I felt a sudden surge of relief, but it was short-lived, because I immediately wondered why I should feel that way. It didn't really alter a thing. At least, not what I desperately needed to prove; that John Jericho and my half-brother were two different people. Indeed, in some ways it suggested the opposite, for why would the page have been making enquiries about the Actons?

His description, too, that the landlord had given me – small and dark, like a Welshman – tallied with John Wedmore's appearance. My father, whom he so closely resembled, had often been mistaken, so my mother had told me, for one of our neighbours across the Severn.

I swallowed what was left of my cider, then asked my companion, 'I suppose there's no chance that you can recall more exactly when this was? What year?'

He shook his head. 'Long time agone, I know that.' He puckered his brow and thought hard for several seconds before indicating his grandson, who was asleep again, curled up on the far end of the bench. ''E weren't that old, but 'e were walkin', I do remember that.'

'How old is he now?'

The landlord shrugged. 'Don' rightly know. His parents – my daughter and her husband – left him with me when 'e were just months old and never came back. I never did know what became o' them. Made what enquiries I could, but never got no answers. They just vanished. Somebody did for 'em, I reckon. Outlaws or some such.' He sighed. 'It's a common enough story.'

I nodded sympathetically. Many English roads were still not safe to travel unless you were well armed or were part of a company. I was all right. I was big and strong and always carried a stout cudgel. But even so, as a family man, I wondered sometimes if I took too many risks. I should stick to the highways rather than the byways, as Adela was constantly telling me.

I glanced at the boy, trying to assess for myself how old he was, but failed. He could be anywhere from nine to eleven or even twelve years old, depending on his size in relation to his age.

Regretfully, I rose to my feet and once again whistled to Hercules.

'I must be going,' I said, 'if I'm to get back to Croxcombe in time for supper. Thank you for all your help.'

He seemed disappointed that I was leaving so soon and offered me food, which I politely declined. I mounted the donkey and said my farewells.

Hercules was beginning to flag so I rode slowly. I didn't have much option, in any case. Neddy, too, was showing signs of mutiny at being worked so hard. I don't suppose he had ever previously been asked to go any further than Wells and then return to the manor.

So what, I asked myself, as I once more jogged eastward towards Croxcombe, had I learned? And the honest answer had to be nothing of any moment. I was still unable to prove that Dame Audrea's accusation against my half-brother was a case of mistaken identity, although I had received confirmation of his former history from the Actons. That was something, as up until then, I had had to take his story on trust. But I had nothing that would clear his name. What I needed to discover urgently, if I could, was what had become of the real John Jericho after his murderous spree. And so far, the only sighting of him had been by Ronan Bignell and his friends in Croxcombe woods on the night of the killing, staggering drunkenly around and being sick. After which, he had vanished into thin air.

The donkey had by now slowed to a reluctant amble, allowing me plenty of time to think. So I started where I should have begun, instead of dashing off to Wells with my usual impetuosity, and with no more plan of action than my two-year-old son, Adam, had when he climbed on top of a cupboard without any thought as to how to get down. If I

176

had been John Jericho, carrying a sack of stolen goods, what would I have done? More importantly, where would I have made for?

The obvious answer to the first question, as Ronan Bignell had suggested, was that I would have laid up by day and travelled by night, using the most untrodden paths and least known tracks and risking the chance of being waylaid by robbers and outlaws. But just suppose he had been waylaid, in possession of his spoils! His body might well have been rotting in some unmarked forest grave for the past six years and would never be found ... It was more than a possibility, but I couldn't afford to think like that, not if I were to save my half-brother's neck from a hangman's noose. So, on to the second question. Where would he have made for?

The nearest city where he wasn't known seemed to be the only sensible answer; a place where he could dispose of his spoils to those who could turn plate and jewels into money. But there was a snag to that reasoning. John Jericho had been a young boy and, as far as I could gather, unversed in the ways of crime until he succumbed to a momentary temptation while his master and mistress were away from home. In a strange city, he would have had no idea whom to contact in order to make a clandestine sale. There would have been posses of sheriff's men out looking for him in all directions, and the last thing he would have wished to do would have been to attract attention to himself. A boy with a sack might have been just a lad trying to run away to sea, carrying his belongings, whereas people would have remembered instantly a boy trying to sell what to any discerning person looked like stolen goods...

Run away to sea! Of course! John Jericho would surely have made for the nearest port and made his escape ... to where? To Ireland was the most probable answer. And that meant Bristol, with its undercover slave trade that was supposed to have been wiped out centuries ago, but still throve with the connivance of both Bristolians and Dubliners.

I was in the wrong place. I should be at home making my enquiries. And yet it was highly unlikely that anyone would remember anything after six years. And there were always so many other ships from all parts of the trading world anchored along the Backs or the banks of the Frome that John Jericho could be anywhere. I had to face it. There was as much hope of finding him now as there was of man learning to fly (although some mad fools had tried even that).

I suddenly felt deeply depressed as I realized I was up against an almost insoluble problem. And yet I had to try to find an answer to it. If I could avoid it, I wouldn't let any innocent man go to the gallows, let alone my own flesh and blood, and as I skirted Wells and rode towards Croxcombe, I debated what was the best course to take next. Should I return to Bristol on the offchance that I might pick up a clue to the missing page's

178

whereabouts? Or should I remain where I was as long as I could in the hope of persuading Dame Audrea that she was mistaken in her identification? Perhaps, after all, persuading the steward to persuade *her* might be the better way. Maybe it was time to declare my interest and tell George Applegarth the truth. He was my natural ally. I nodded to myself. I had made up my mind.

'Gee up, Ned,' I adjured the donkey. He rightly ignored me and proceeded at his own stately pace.

As we ambled across the bridge spanning the moat, it was apparent that something was amiss. I could hear a woman crying, loud, noisy sobs bordering on hysteria. Someone else was shouting and there was a flurry of activity that had nothing to do with domestic matters like the laying and serving of supper. (And I was starving.)

Hercules made straight for the kitchens with all the ease and assurance of one certain of his welcome. (That dog had a talent for ingratiating himself with almost anyone.) I conducted Neddy back to the stables and handed him over to a groom, who intimated that it was not his job to look after donkeys and suggested I take the animal to the pad-dock. I did my idiot's smile and ignored him.

'What's the fuss about?' I asked, jerking my head in the direction of the house.

The man shrugged. 'It's been going on all afternoon. So far as I can gather, it started

with a right old set-to between Master Anthony and the receiver. Word has it that
Master Micheldever as good as accused our
new master of having designs on Rose's
virtue.' He snorted derisively. 'That wouldn't
be hard. She even gives me the glad eye, and
as you can see, I'm no beauty. Not that I'm
saying there's any malice in the girl. There
ain't. She's just one of those who can't help
herself. Anyway, where was I?'

'A set-to between the receiver and Master
Bellknapp.'

'Oh, ah! Came to blows apparently. Dame
Audrea and Chaplain tried to separate them
and got a mouthful of abuse from Master
Anthony for their pains. Especially Sir Henry.
Cook told me it was pitiful to see the poor old
fellow lashed by Master's tongue. Stammering idiot, something about not worth his bed
and board, limping old fool who could barely
climb the pulpit stairs and so on and so on.
All this time, Rose – Mistress Micheldever, I
suppose I should say – was having hysterics,
and eventually Master turns on her and yells
at her to hold her noise. Says he can't stand
snivelling women. Mind you, Cook says Rose
was so shocked, because no one had ever
spoken to her that way before, she couldn't
make a sound for about ten minutes or more.
Then Master Simon arrives on the scene with
Bailiff and that leads to more fisticuffs between the brothers, while Master Kilsby, he's
patting Dame Audrea's hand like he's Saint
George and she's the maid being threatened

by the dragon. So Master Anthony, he just knocks Simon aside and lands a hefty punch on Bailiff's nose and the man starts to bleed all down the front of Dame Audrea's gown. She lets out a squawk and clips his ear, telling him to be more careful.' The groom began to laugh immoderately, rocking to and fro on his heels and holding his side. 'Lord! Lord! I wish I'd seen it all! But I'd taken Mistress's horse to the blacksmith to be reshod. Just my luck to miss a scene like that. It's quietened down a lot now.'

Just my luck, too, it seemed. I made my way towards the house and entered the hall, where a couple of servants were righting a trestle table and a bench before hauling them and others into the middle of the floor ready for the evening meal. The housekeeper, Mistress Wychbold, was passing through, hurrying towards the stairs and carrying a bowl of steaming, herb-scented water, several clean cloths draped over one arm, presumably on her way to administer to the afflicted. Rose was still crying somewhere, but the noisy sobs had diminished to a wail and had now almost ceased. The main combatants had vanished, but would no doubt reappear at suppertime, trying, as people do in those circumstances, to look unconcerned or as if they had got the best of the argument.

I decided to go in search of the steward.

He was in his room, and bade me enter when I knocked.

'Ah, Master Chapman!' he exclaimed.

'Come in, come in. I understand from Master Anthony that you rode over to Wedmore in search of some old friends. Were you successful? Did you find them?'

'I did. And have missed some excitement here, so I've been told.'

George Applegarth frowned, his long, thin face puckered in a look of distaste.

'If you think physical violence and the unnecessary abuse of an old man exciting, yes, I suppose you have.'

It was the nearest I had heard him come to expressing disapproval of Anthony Bell-knapp's behaviour.

I raised my eyebrows. 'You regret that the prodigal has returned?'

'No, no! I didn't say that. In many ways I'm very pleased to see him. It's only right that if he's alive, he should get what's due to him. But there's little doubt that his homecoming has had disastrous consequences. He was always...' The steward broke off abruptly, suddenly recollecting to whom he was speaking. I was the stranger within the gates; a common pedlar. He should not be discussing the Bellknapps with me. 'Do you wish to see me? What can I do for you?' He added drily, 'You appear to be walking far more easily than you were doing this morning.'

I smiled and admitted, 'My ankle was never as badly injured as I've been making out.' It was obvious from his slight look of contempt that he had already guessed as much. I hurried on, 'I'd like to talk to you, if you're willing to listen, but only if you'll promise to keep my confidence.'

He hesitated for a moment, running one hand through his thinning grey hair. Then, coming to a decision, he nodded and waved me to the window seat, turning the armchair to face me and sitting down.

'Well?' he asked.

'It's about the young man accused by Dame Audrea of being John Jericho. The man at present held in the Bristol bridewell.'

The steward looked startled. Whatever he had expected me to say, it plainly hadn't been that.

'What about him?'

'Do you think he's the missing page? You don't, do you?' George Applegarth hesitated in a way that made me suddenly uneasy, and I added urgently, 'Sergeant Manifold told me that you didn't.'

The steward, elbows resting on the arms of his chair, put his hands together and looked at me over the tips of his steepled fingers.

'What's this young man to you?' he enquired at length.

'He's my half-brother. The half-brother I've only just discovered that I have.' And I explained the circumstances of my and John Wedmore's meeting.

'And you believe his story?'

'I'm convinced of it. I wouldn't have said that I remembered what my father looked like very clearly – he died when I was four years old – but as soon as John said he was his son,

183

I could recall his features instantly. In fact I'd been trying for days to think who it was John reminded me of. From the first moment of seeing him, he was familiar.'

'And where does Master Wedmore – is that correct? – say he was six years ago, at the time of the murder?'

'In Ireland, near Waterford.' And I repeated my half-brother's past history.

My companion nodded slowly, watching me narrowly but saying nothing, while I grew more uneasy by the second. At last, however, he lowered his hands and spread them wide, like a man discarding secrecy in favour of openness and honesty.

'Your half-brother's innocent,' he said firmly. 'There's not a shred of doubt in my mind about that.'

'But can you convince Dame Audrea?' I asked, leaning forward and almost tumbling off the window seat in my eagerness.

He smiled wryly. 'I don't know. She's an extremely hard woman to convince to the contrary once she's made her mind up about anything.'

'But you must,' I cried, forgetting myself in my concern for my half-brother's welfare. 'Mistress Micheldever has already implied that her husband might be thinking of endorsing Dame Audrea's claim. In return for a suitable bribe, of course,' I added bitterly.

The steward looked grave. 'I'd advise you not to go around making that sort of accusation, Master Chapman. Dame Audrea does not bribe her servants. If Master Receiver thinks that he might do himself some good by pleasing the mistress, that's an entirely different matter, and not for me to comment on.'

'But surely you can't think it right to allow an innocent man to suffer for a crime he didn't commit. And you've just said that you're convinced of my half-brother's innocence.'

George Applegarth grimaced. 'Calm yourself, lad. I'll find a way of persuading Dame Audrea to see sense.'

I regarded him doubtfully. 'Do you think you can?'

He laughed and got to his feet. 'I can but try. Meantime, I see no good reason for you to remain at Croxcombe. Go back to Bristol. Tomorrow. Leave the matter in my hands. What did you think you could achieve by coming here, anyway?'

'I don't know,' I admitted miserably. 'I suppose I was hoping to find out something about the real John Jericho that would prove he couldn't possibly be my half-brother. That he had some distinguishing feature that the other doesn't have.' I sighed. 'Unfortunately, every description of him seems to tally with John's appearance.'

'Well, what else did you expect?' the steward demanded impatiently. 'If they didn't bear some resemblance to one another, Dame Audrea would never have accused your half-brother of being her former page. It stands to reason.'

When he put it like that, I supposed it did, and it made me feel somewhat foolish. But I couldn't have sat still and done nothing, and what else had there been for me to do? All the same, as Master Applegarth had pointed out, I really should now be returning home to Adela and the children. Could I trust him, though, to do his best to change Dame Audrea's mind? Strangely, I had a feeling that I could.

'What do you think became of John Jericho after he ran away?' I asked suddenly, as I, too, stood up, dwarfing the steward with my girth and height.

'I – I don't know,' George Applegarth admitted. 'I...' He shrugged his shoulders.

'You must have thought about it,' I insisted.

'Well ... Yes ... I suppose I have.' He must have noted my cynical expression, because he added apologetically, 'The truth is, I haven't wanted to think about him. After Jenny was killed, I didn't want to think about the murder for a long time. I blame myself for not being there when she needed me most. I'd protected her all our lives, from the time we first met when she was a pretty lass of sixteen.' The grey eyes clouded as he looked back into the past. 'And she *was* a pretty girl; the prettiest I'd ever seen. Oh, she grew stout in middle age, but to me she was always beautiful. I loved her with all my heart.' The simple declaration affected me unbearably and I would have stopped him from saying more, but he was already speaking. 'So, you see, I tried to push the happenings of that night to the back of my mind. But you can accept my solemn word, Chapman, that it would give me no satisfaction to have the wrong man punished for that heinous crime.'

'And you do believe that my half-brother is the wrong man?'

'I feel sure of it.'

'Why? What makes you so certain?' I was arguing against myself now, but I needed reassurance of the steward's good faith.

He shrugged. 'I can't say. I just know in my bones that the man in the Bristol bridewell is not the man who murdered my Jenny.' Seeing my disappointment, he smiled ruefully. 'I'm sorry, I can't say more than that. You were hoping for better.'

I didn't deny it; but as the cook, or one of her minions, was now banging loudly on the back of a skillet with a wooden spoon to announce that supper was ready, and shouting, 'All good folk to table!' I had to take my leave. The steward, too, was suddenly in a hurry to take up his position in the hall and ensure that everything was in order. Whatever the state of warfare in the house at large, George Applegarth would continue to do his duty conscientiously. He was that kind of man.

I thanked him most sincerely for his time and patience, and in return received his promise that he would do his utmost to convince Dame Audrea of John Wedmore's

187

innocence. Then he seized his wand of office and preceded me into the hall.

Fortunately, there were no guests this afternoon (apart from myself) requiring a meal or a night's shelter. I say fortunately, because it was obvious, from the moment I set eyes on the row of sullen faces ranged along the far side of the high table, that however sunny the weather outside, it was going to be exceedingly stormy indoors. As there were no visitors, the officers of the household dined with the family on the dais, and George Applegarth ushered me to a stool at the far right end of the trestle, beside Rose Micheldever. It was plain that she had been crying, but as the receiver's basilisk glance was fixed on me from the moment I sat down, I refrained from speaking to my unhappy young neighbour, let alone commiserating with her. It was while I was returning Edward Micheldever's stare with as much composure as I could muster, that I noticed the central chair, with its beautifully carved arms and red velvet cushion, was occupied not by Anthony, but by Simon Bellknapp. On his right hand sat his mother, Dame Audrea's aristocratic features a stony mask, betraying by not so much as the twitch of an eyebrow or the flutter of an eyelash that she knew this to be an affront to her still absent elder son.

But the steward knew it, and I saw him bend over the back of the chair and mutter something in Simon's ear.

'Nonsense!' was the loud reply. 'I'm the

rightful master here. Tell him, Mother! We intend to have my father's will overset. We shall appeal directly to the King, if necessary. Anthony's not coming back here, thinking he can claim my inheritance. My father intended Croxcombe for me, whatever he wrote in his will.'

All eyes had been fixed on Simon during this outburst, and I, for one, had failed to notice his brother's entrance through the door at the back of the dais. Humphrey Attleborough was with him, and man and master suddenly appeared, one on either side of Simon, each grasping an arm of the chair. At a nod from Anthony, they heaved it up to shoulder height – a considerable feat of strength – and pitched it, together with its occupant, over the table to crash on the floor below. Luckily, it missed the two trestles at which the servants were sitting, and splintered in the space between them.

There was a moment's aghast silence and stillness before Simon let out a shriek. 'You've broken my arm!' Scrambling from the wreckage, he supported the useless member, his left, with his right hand, blood streaming from a cut over his left eye. Aided by one of the horrified servers, who had just entered the hall with the first course, he sank on to the end of the nearest bench, moaning and shaking with pain and fright. Dame Audrea, her face as white as the lace collar of her gown, swung round on her heel and dealt Anthony a blow across one cheek that ripped the skin from the bone. (The clawed setting of one of her rings must have caught him.)

'Get out of this house now, tonight,' she ordered, 'or be prepared to take the consequences.'

Anthony, putting up a hand to staunch the blood trickling down his face, grinned insolently at her.

'What consequences, Mother? I'm the master here and you know it.'

I could tell by her expression of frustrated rage that Dame Audrea did indeed know it. She had spoken at random, so angry, in spite of her display of self-control, that she was barely aware of what she was saying. She clenched her hand as though she would strike again, but then thought better of it and descended from the dais to attend to her afflicted younger son.

Mistress Wychbold, the housekeeper, was before her, sending a couple of maids scurrying to the medicine chest for a bag of powdered comfrey, splints and bandages, while a page was despatched to the kitchen for a bowl of warm water and with a request that someone make up a strong draught of lettuce and poppy juice to ease the patient's pain. The rest of us, supper and our hunger forgotten, stood around quietly while the housekeeper and Dame Audrea skilfully made a poultice of the powdered comfrey and warm water and packed it inside two splints of oak wood, holding everything in place with bandages torn from what looked like an old white

counterpane. Simon, who had lost consciousness during part of this procedure, revived
enough to swallow the lettuce and poppy
juice potion and to allow himself to be led
away to his bedchamber, supported by his
mother on one side and George Applegarth
on the other. He had also recovered sufficiently to turn and hiss at Anthony as he passed
him, 'You'll pay for this. Just see if you don't.
Even if I have to kill you with my own two
hands.'

Dame Audrea said sharply, 'That's enough
of such talk, Simon. You must rest for a week
or so and your arm will soon be as good as
new. I'd trust Matilda Wychbold's skills with
a lot more than a broken limb.'

Anthony suddenly stepped forward, blocking his brother's slow progress.

'Look, Sim' – I guessed this to be a childhood shortening of Simon's name, rusty from
lack of use, judging by the awkward way it sat
on the older man's tongue – 'I'm sorry. I
wasn't thinking. I'd forgotten the dais. It was
stupid, I admit it. But you shouldn't have
usurped my place. You won't be able to alter
Father's will, and if it's legal, which it is, the
King won't help you to overset it.'

He might as well not have spoken. 'I'll get
you for it,' Simon panted, 'and that man of
yours. I'll kill you both.'

'That will do!' his mother snapped and
urged him forward, she and the steward half
carrying, half dragging the injured boy from
the hall. As the door closed behind them,

there was another silence before Anthony gave a loud, forced laugh.

'Well, where's the food, then? Humphrey, find me another chair. Back to your places everyone, the entertainment's over.' He picked up a half-full goblet of wine that Simon had been drinking. 'Mistress Micheldever, your very good health!'

Rose gave a frightened sob and ran out of the hall. Her husband, after giving one murderous glance at Anthony, followed her.

I saw the prodigal's eyes narrow furiously. The Devil had him by the tail now and he was in a dangerous mood.

'Then here's to another fair lady.' He raised the goblet higher. 'The lovely Dorcas Slye and her handsome son.' And he grinned at the outraged chamberlain. But the fool hadn't finished yet. 'T-t-t-to you, Sir Henry, my s-s-stuttering f-f-friend.' He sat down abruptly as Humphrey brought another chair, looking round for further mischief, as though he was unable to stop himself. He wiped away a further trickle of blood from his cheek and looked at the bailiff. 'By the way, Master Kilsby, tomorrow, you may take whatever money is owing to you and go. I no longer need you here. I'll not have you as a stepfather. In fact,' he added loudly, as Dame Audrea came back into the hall, 'I'll not stand for a stepfather at all. Widows should stay widows and honour their husbands' memories. Now, everyone fall to. Your supper's getting cold.'

Eleven

I had forgotten that the next day was Sunday, so I naturally postponed my journey home until the Monday. Travelling on the Sabbath, then as now, was not generally acceptable unless it was a matter of life and death.

The night before, I had again shared Anthony Bellknapp's bed, and had once more taken it upon myself to caution him about his conduct. I had, of course, no right to do so, being a guest and a stranger; but in the curtained intimacy of the four-poster, I felt I might stand a better chance of being attended to than George Applegarth and his necessarily perfunctory warnings. But I was wrong. Anthony merely yawned and told me to mind my own business. He was perfectly justified, and for me to have pursued the subject further would have done no good. Indeed, it could have done positive harm. So I changed tack and informed him that I would be returning to Bristol first thing on Monday morning.

'Hell's teeth! I haven't upset you that much, have I?' he laughed. 'It's just that I won't have people instructing me what and what not to do.'

'You are perfectly entitled to tell me to keep my nose out of your affairs,' I agreed. 'No, no! It's not that. But I've done as much as I can and —' I broke off, realizing that my tongue had run away with me.

Anthony heaved himself up in the bed, arms clasped around his knees, and, turning his head, looked down at me curiously.

'Done as much as you can about what?' he asked, adding, 'You know, I've had an idea there was more to your visit here than met the eye.'

I had told George Applegarth the truth, so I might as well be frank with Anthony. Besides, it suddenly struck me that I could try to enlist his interest in persuading Dame Audrea that she had no case against my half-brother without stronger support than that of Edward Micheldever. In any case, Anthony would probably enjoy putting a spoke in the receiver's wheel. So I explained my personal interest in proving John Wedmore innocent of the charge against him.

'What's more, I fully intend to do it,' I said with greater confidence than I actually felt.

'Great boast, small roast,' my companion grinned in a tone of voice that was bordering on a sneer.

Now I can honestly say that I didn't often blow my own trumpet – in fact, I sometimes went to considerable lengths to keep my past achievements quiet – but there was a condescension in the way he spoke that riled me, and before I could stop myself, I was giving him details of all my past successes in un-ravelling the various mysteries and problems that had come my way (in the course of which I naturally had to touch on the work I had done for the Duke of Gloucester).

'So you see,' I finished, 'I do have some experience of discovering the truth.'

By this time, of course, I was feeling thoroughly ashamed of myself as one so frequently does after deliberately setting out to impress. And succeeding. For Anthony was regarding me with a kind of resentful awe, while his disbelief in what I had told him vied with a conviction that I had not been exaggerating.

'Well,' he remarked eventually, 'I must spread the word tomorrow that we are entertaining a friend of the royal family.' He laughed again, but nastily. 'You will no doubt find that Mistress Micheldever hangs, in future, on your every word. I shall be quite eclipsed in her affections.'

'There's no need for you to say anything of what I've told you to anyone else, especially Rose Micheldever. I have no designs upon her virtue, I assure you. Master Steward knows only a part of the story; that John Wedmore is my half-brother and that I am trying to prove his innocence. He, also, is convinced that John is not the former page. All I ask is for you to try to persuade your mother likewise.'

'I know nothing about the matter,' Anthony answered roughly. 'I wasn't here.'

'I realize that.' I tried to sound humble, an almost impossible task after my recent attack of egomania, which I now deeply regretted. 'But you would have my undying thanks if you would do what you could.'

'That, of course, must be of paramount importance to me.' Then, quite suddenly, he gave me a lopsided grin and abandoned his hostile tone. 'All right, Chapman, I'll do what I can.' His grin grew more pronounced, and I guessed that my conjecture had probably been correct; the prospect of foiling any project of Dame Audrea's filled him with satisfaction.

'Thank you, you're very good.'

'What will you do when you get back to Bristol?' he asked.

I shook my head and admitted I hadn't decided. 'But I'll think of something,' I added sleepily.

Anthony lay down again, heaving himself over on his left side and taking most of the blanket with him.

'I'm sure you will,' he agreed.

I woke very early the following morning, conscious of having slept badly. My bedfellow and Humphrey Attleborough were still snoring noisily, so I got up as quietly as I could, donned shirt and hose and, having crept through the sleeping house, including the kitchen, without arousing anyone save Hercules, I let myself out into the yard and held my head and hands under the pump. Then I wandered across the paddock to the moat, the dog running ahead of me, wagging an ecstatic tail. The damp morning air smelled deliciously of ripening apples and burning wood, and a white mist, ankle deep, ruffled about my feet. The gatekeeper, yawning and stretching, appeared to unlock the moat gate, so, after a while, Hercules and I wandered across the bridge and let ourselves out into the countryside beyond. A few minutes walking in an easterly direction brought us into Croxcombe woods and another minute or so found us in the clearing where Hamo Gough had his dwelling.

There was at present no sign of him, but the door to his hut stood open, so I knocked and peered inside. He wasn't there, either, so I guessed he must be somewhere in the woods, gathering sticks for his fire or looking for truffles. Hercules, with a whimper of excitement, immediately began a search for rats. I hung around for a few minutes in the expectation of Hamo's return, but soon got tired of waiting, and, having winkled an angry dog out from under the bed, made my way further into the dim, cathedral-like gloom of the woods. Suddenly, I could hear someone swearing in a soft, steady flow and what sounded like the thud of a spade hitting hard ground. I picked up Hercules, putting him under my arm and ordering him to be quiet, and inched quietly through the trees until I found myself on the edge of another clearing in the middle of which stood a huge and very ancient oak. Hangman's Oak? It had to be, almost certainly; and not just because the spreading lower branches lent themselves to such grisly work, but also because the charcoal burner was digging furiously at its base.

In between cursing, he muttered from time to time, 'C'mon! C'mon! Thee's here somewhere.' And then, later, as he rested on the spade handle, sweat pouring down his face, 'I don' reckon 'e 'ad time to dig thee up.' And again, 'I were back too quick, and 'e'd gone.' None of which made any sense to me, but I let him dig for a little longer before stepping into view.

'Searching for something, Master Gough?'

At the sound of my voice, he jumped so hard that he hit his foot with the blade of the spade and let out a screech that was half fright, half pain. When at last he could speak, he demanded furiously, 'What thee doing here, Chapman?'

'An early morning walk with my dog,' I replied, all innocence. 'What are you doing?'

'Diggin' for truffles,' he snapped. 'What's it seem like?'

'That far down?' I queried, indicating a hole about a forearm's length deep.

He stared at me for a second or two, nonplussed. Then he grunted, 'Got carried away. Weren't thinkin' what I were doing. Jus' went on diggin'.'

It was a lame explanation, but he knew I couldn't contradict him. I had nothing to accuse him of; but my guess was that my conversation with him, two days previously, concerning the robbery at Croxcombe Manor, had awakened old memories. Ronan Bignell had told me that he and his friends had seen Hamo Gough surveying the ground around Hangman's Oak the night following that of the murder. He hadn't been digging then, but I was willing to bet a substantial amount of money that he had gone back to dig later. And perhaps for several weeks after that. Finding nothing, he would have tired of the exercise in time and given up. But here he was, six years on, his memory jogged, hopes newly reawakened, once more digging around Hangman's Oak.

But for what?

The obvious answer was the Bellknapp treasure, but that raised yet another question. Why? Did he have reason to believe that John Jericho had buried his spoils from the robbery in Croxcombe woods? Had he seen something on the night of the murder? According to Ronan Bignell, the page had been taken ill somewhere in the vicinity of Hangman's Oak. Furthermore, neither the butcher's son nor his friends had any recollection of seeing a sack, which might mean nothing – Ronan had said that it was dark under the trees in spite of it being a moonlit night – or it could mean that the thief, realizing he would be unable to travel further until his indisposition had passed, had already dug a hole and dropped the booty in it...

But what had John Jericho dug a hole with? He had not, presumably, been carrying a spade, so that left his bare hands. This seemed highly unlikely unless the ground had been exceptionally soft, perhaps after heavy rain. Surely he would have done nothing more than cover the sack with leaves and other detritus from the forest floor until he was feeling better. If the charcoal burner had indeed been an observer, he would have known this. Could he, therefore, have spoken to the thief? Had he come across him in the throes of his sickness and offered help? But in that case, was it likely that John Jericho would have told him the truth; that he had stolen from his absent employers and killed Jenny Applegarth? Unless, of course, he had not been ill, but drunk; so drunk that he had been unaware of what he was saying. Perhaps he had given himself false courage to commit the robbery by drinking a quantity of Master Bellknapp's wine. But the depths of drunkenness that a man has to plumb before being unable to recall his words and actions the following day are profound. Surely, in such a case, the page would have been too inebriated even to reach as far as Croxcombe woods. Such a degree of intoxication, however, might explain the murder...

I became conscious of the fact that Hamo Gough, still resting on his spade, was regarding me suspiciously.

'What's going on in that head o' thine, Maister?' he enquired. 'Eh? Eh?'

'Nothing,' I lied, wishing that I could make some sense of the muddled thoughts crowding my brain. I grinned weakly at him.

He threw down the spade and asked, 'Hast eaten?'

'I've not yet breakfasted,' I admitted. 'It's very early, and my hosts weren't stirring when I left the manor. I mean to return there now.'

'I'll give thee summat,' he offered, much to my astonishment. 'A bacon collop and a beaker of ale. That do thee? Thee looks like a young fellow who could eat two breakfasts.'

I guessed that this sudden burst of generosity was just a ploy to distract my attention from his digging, but I accepted nonetheless. I was indeed a fellow who could eat two breakfasts, and always had been; although I was aware, as Adela had lately pointed out more than once, that I was heavier than I had been a year or so previously. Fortunately, my height concealed the unwelcome fact.

Hamo shouldered the spade and preceded me from the Hangman's Oak clearing to the one where his cottage stood. Halfway along the track which connected the two, he paused, head tilted sideways, listening. Then he shrugged and continued walking. His first job on reaching home was to attend to his smouldering, turf-covered fire before producing an ancient skillet and frying the promised bacon collops on top of it. They had a strange, smoky taste that was not unpleasant, but I remembered in time to refuse the proffered beaker of ale, having just seen

Hamo fish a dead rat out of the barrel, confirming my worst suspicions regarding its outdoor location. We sat in the open on this beautiful morning to eat our meal, while Hercules begged for scraps or disappeared inside the hut from time to time after bigger game. (He returned after one of these forays with a decapitated mouse, dropping the headless corpse at my feet and smirking proudly. And if you think dogs can't smirk, you're wrong.)

'Thee ankle's better, by the looks o' it,' the charcoal burner remarked suddenly. 'Art still at the manor? Things is pretty lively there, I daresay, now Anthony Bellknapp's come home again?'

'Lively enough.' I scrambled to my feet and stretched. 'I'm leaving them to it. I'm returning to Bristol tomorrow.'

'Ar.' He followed my example and got up from the grass where we'd been sitting. 'Thee'd best be getting back now, I reckon. Sir Henry'll be preaching his Sunday morning sermon and they'll expect thee to attend that. I'll come to the edge of the woods with 'ee.'

'There's no need for that,' I protested. 'I have my cudgel and I can look after myself.'

'Don't doubt it,' he grunted. 'But I'll come, all the same.'

There was little point in arguing: he seemed to have made up his mind, so I let him go ahead, but kept a firm grip on my stick, wary of his unexpected decision to accompany me.

Hercules, alert as ever to any change in my mood and sensing in his own mysterious way my apprehension, trotted alongside the pair of us, instead of running off about his own business as he would normally have done. And when Hamo suddenly stopped in his tracks, the dog growled warningly. But we need not have worried. The charcoal burner merely repeated his previous performance, cocking his head at an angle and listening.

'What's the matter?' I asked.

He continued in the same way for a few more seconds, then shook his head.

'Jus' thought ... No, it's nowt.' But I could see that he was uneasy.

At the same moment, I, too, imagined that I heard a twig crack somewhere amongst the trees and undergrowth that bordered the path. I stood, straining my ears, and Hercules whined, but there was no further sound. Hamo started to move again, whistling tunelessly as he went, and both the dog and I relaxed.

There was no further incident, and Hamo left us where the path emerged into the open countryside with nothing more than a grunt and a curt nod of his head, vanishing into the trees once more and swiftly disappearing from view. He had got rid of me and my awkward questions at the expense of a slice of bacon and a piece of stale oaten bread. No doubt he felt it was worth the price.

As Hercules and I neared the manor, I saw three figures approaching the moat gate along the road from Wells, and even at a distance, recognized them as Thomas Bignell and his wife and son. I waited beside the moat for them to draw abreast.

'Dame Audrea sent a message yesterday inviting us to breakfast and to hear Sir Henry's sermon,' the butcher said before I could greet them, as if he owed me an explanation for their presence.

'You were up betimes, then,' I said. 'You've had a long walk.'

'It's nothing. We're always up at sunrise,' Ronan put in, 'and Mother likes to see Rose of a Sunday.'

'We all do,' his father added in a tone of reproof, while Mistress Bignell nodded her agreement.

I suspected that today they had been particularly eager to take advantage of the invitation, it being possible, or even probable, that Dame Audrea's message had hinted at some discord between their daughter and son-in-law. And as for the Dame herself, she must surely hope that the appearance of Rose's parents and brother in their midst would have a restraining influence on both Anthony and Edward Micheldever. For my own part, I was delighted to see Thomas Bignell, as it occurred to me that I might be able to question him about the horseman he was reported to have seen on the night of Jenny Applegarth's murder.

But before I could do that, we had to sit through Mass and a somewhat rambling sermon by the chaplain in the Bellknapp family chapel, followed by breakfast (my appetite in no way impaired by this being my second meal of the day, although it was barely past the hour of prime). Anthony incurred his mother's displeasure by being late on both occasions, his arrival each time creating the maximum disturbance. He apologized in a rather sneering way, blaming his tardiness in the first instance on having risen late, and in the second on an urgent visit to the privy. I could tell that he was in a bad mood (I was glad to have avoided him earlier by rising betimes); a mood that was not helped by the appearance at breakfast of Simon, very pale, but smiling bravely, his injured arm ostentatiously reposing in a sling. Dame Audrea fussed around her younger son with a solicitude that seemed to me to be foreign to her nature, a suspicion that was given colour by Anthony's sharp reprimand.

'Sit down, Mother, and stop this charade. You demonstrated precious little concern when I had broken bones as a child.'

Dame Audrea showed heightened colour and her lips thinned to an almost bloodless line, but she made no answer, merely taking her seat and turning with some polite remark to Thomas Bignell, who, with his wife and family, including the receiver, was breakfasting at the top table. Reginald Kilsby was also there, seated at one end, and Dame Audrea made the mistake of glancing in his direction and giving him a small, tight smile. Unfortunately, Anthony saw her and, leaning forward in his chair, addressed the bailiff in a loud voice that carried to all corners of the hall.

'I thought I told you to go, Master Bailiff. You may remain today as it's the Sabbath, but tomorrow, at sunrise, I shall expect you to be on your way. Master Chapman is also leaving us. His ankle, it seems, is mended. So you can bear one another company on the first leg of your respective journeys.' He raised his beaker of ale. 'To you, Mistress Micheldever.'

He then proceeded to complain about the beef and boiled mutton that had been served up, declaring one to be too tough and the other tasteless, and ended by throwing plate and all at the head of a luckless server. He then sent for the cook, and when she came, hot and breathless from the kitchen, gave her a dressing down in front of the assembled company on the poor quality of the food.

'Now I'm back, things will have to change,' he declared. 'I'm used to better.'

The assembled company looked embarrassed, shuffling their feet and muttering uncomfortably. Nor was anyone surprised when the incensed cook tossed her ladle on the floor and told Dame Audrea that she, too, would be off the following day, at first light.

'I've been a loyal servant to you, Mistress, as you well know, and I'm sorry to go. But I'll not stay to be insulted by your son. Lady Chauntermerle has offered me a place at Kewstoke Hall whenever I want it. Someone else can cook your food from now on.'

We were all relieved when the dreadful meal was over and we were able to escape out of doors. The Bignells looked appalled by the scene they had just witnessed, and I saw them standing by the moat, conferring in agitated whispers with Edward Micheldever.

I joined them just in time to overhear the receiver say loudly and clearly, 'It's a pity he ever returned. We all thought he was dead. It's a great pity he isn't.'

Thomas Bignell saw me out of the corner of one eye and hushed his son-in-law imperatively.

'You don't mean that, Edward.'

The receiver had noted my approach at almost the same moment, but refused to be silenced.

'I mean it all right,' he answered truculently. 'The man's a menace.'

I joined the group, trying to look as though I had not the slightest idea of what they had been talking about, but it was no use, not with Rose there. She immediately clutched my arm and begged, 'Roger, you won't repeat what Ned's been saying, will you? Promise me.'

'In the name of God, Rose,' her husband hissed under his breath, 'leave it!'

I judged it best to be frank. 'I won't pretend not to know who you were discussing, but Anthony Bellknapp will not be told of it by me. In any case, I'm returning to Bristol tomorrow morning, as you heard.' Edward Micheldever looked as if he didn't believe my protestation of silence, but that was up to him. I was sincere. I turned to the butcher. 'Master Bignell, I understand that the night Jenny Applegarth was murdered, you saw a stranger, a horseman, riding near the manor. Is there anything you can recall about him that might give even the slightest clue to his identity?'

'Dear God, it was six years and more ago,' Thomas Bignell spluttered. 'And what's it to you, anyway? Why bring that up?'

To my relief, for I was sick of repeating the story, Ronan gave his father a brief history of my interest in the affair; but, unfortunately, this was the first Master Bignell and his wife had been told about the arrest of my half-brother, and the next ten minutes or so were spent in unprofitable exclamations, demands for further details, reproaches to their son-in-law for not informing them of the part that he had played in the drama and speculation as to whether John Wedmore was indeed the missing page. By the time the butcher was ready to give me his attention and answer my question, we had been joined by Anthony Bellknapp, seeking his errant guests.

'What's this little conclave about?' he demanded, not unpleasantly, but with an underlying aggression.

Rose sent me such a pleading glance that she might as well have told Anthony straight out that he had been the subject under discussion, and that nothing good was being said of him. I saw his eyes flicker in the receiver's direction, but Edward Micheldever was muttering something in a low voice to Ronan Bignell and failed to notice either Rose's look at me or Anthony's reaction.

I said quickly, 'We were talking about Jenny Applegarth. Master Bignell, here, saw someone in the vicinity of Croxcombe Manor on the night of her murder and I wondered if he could tell me anything he noticed about the man. But he says it's all too long ago.'

Anthony smiled. 'Ah, yes, of course. You're trying to prove that this John Jericho and the man in gaol in Bristol are two different people. Master Receiver, you, I believe, were with my mother when she had the man apprehended. What do you think? Is he this missing page?'

I challenged Edward Micheldever with an enquiring stare, and he shifted uncomfortably. But he had already made up his mind where his interests lay and nodded vigorously.

'There's no doubt in my mind that he's John Jericho.'

'Master Steward doesn't agree with you,' I snapped.

The receiver shrugged. 'It's two against one,' he pointed out.

'A fair enough argument, you must admit, Chapman.' Anthony clapped me on the back. 'I'm afraid I couldn't offer an opinion even if I saw this man who claims to be your half-brother. I never set eyes on the murderous page. But if they are one and the same,' he added viciously, 'I'd not lift a finger to save the man who killed my darling Jenny. She's the only woman who was ever a mother to me. But why are we all standing out of doors? Master Bignell, you and your wife and son will dine with us, I hope, before setting out again for Wells. I've done penitence to the cook. Grovelled, in fact, and she's agreed to stay. Meantime, let's go inside. It's getting hot again. We'll have some wine to refresh ourselves. Mistress Bignell, allow me to offer you my arm.'

Edward and Rose followed them into the cool of the house, with the butcher and myself bringing up the rear. My mind was in turmoil. If the receiver was determined to back Dame Audrea in her accusation against John Wedmore, it was very unlikely that George Applegarth's disagreement would carry much weight. Two to one, as Anthony had said, would probably be sufficient to condemn him in the minds of a jury. Perhaps I should have to go to Ireland after all. If it did come to a trial, there would have to be some witnesses in his defence, however partial they might be. And what I had discovered was useless. I had failed completely to prove that my half-brother was not John Jericho...

I became aware that the butcher was speaking.

'I'm sorry, Master Bignell,' I apologized. 'I didn't quite hear what you said.'

'It was nothing of much consequence,' he

210

answered. 'It's just that now you've mentioned it – about the night of the murder, I mean – you've got me thinking. Haven't given it so much as a passing thought for years. By the way, who told you I'd seen someone near here that night? Oh, well, never mind. But the fact is...' He paused, screwing up his face in a great effort of concentration. 'The fact is, I get the oddest feeling that there was something vaguely familiar about that horseman.'

Twelve

Unfortuantely, although I pressed Master Bignell to say more, and although Anthony, overhearing our conversation, turned his head to add his entreaties to mine, the butcher was unable to say anything further, or to elucidate what exactly it was that he remembered. He could only repeat that, now he had been forced to recollect the incident, he could recall the faint sense of recognition he had experienced, but which, at the time, he had dismissed as nonsensical.

'And still do,' he concluded robustly. 'He was just a horseman riding by, on his way home after curfew. I'm a fool to have you believe otherwise.'

I was unable to get anything else from him;

and as it became obvious that he wished me to drop the subject, I did so. I couldn't help wondering, though, why he had so suddenly shied away from the subject, but suspected that he might not want to upset his host with further talk of Jenny Applegarth's murder. Anthony's stricken look suggested that talking about it still had the power to distress him.

Once indoors, Edward Micheldever excused himself as having work to finish, and went off to the counting-house, not altogether happily, but plainly confident that Anthony would not dare to pay court to his wife with her parents and brother present. And to some extent, he was right; although Anthony's proposal that we should while away the hours until dinnertime by playing board games, meant that he could seat himself next to Rose, gradually edging his stool nearer to hers as each game progressed.

A servant was despatched to search for the various diversions Anthony remembered from his childhood and eventually returned weighed down with boards and dice and counters which, as bidden, he piled up on the dais table of the great hall, the remainder of the trestles having been cleared to one side while the floor was swept and fresh rushes laid. Master and Mistress Bignell declined taking part, content, they said, to watch the rest of us amusing ourselves, as befitted young people. So Ronan and I sat opposite Anthony and Rose and played 'tables', a game involving as much luck as skill, the throw of the dice largely determining how quickly one couple could clear their opponents' counters from the board. Anthony and Rose won after a certain amount of cheating on the part of our host, a fact that enabled him to squeeze his partner's shoulders and give her a triumphal, but brotherly, peck on the cheek. (I saw Rose glance nervously at her parents, but they seemed to see nothing amiss with this gesture of disinterested affection.)

We then played merrills, a game variously known as three men's morris or, in its more complicated form, nine men's morris, and yet again Ronan and I were defeated. We did, however, manage to win at fox-and-geese, but when we all threw for ourselves at raffle, Anthony won hands down. But as he insisted on playing with his own dice, which he produced from his pocket, I couldn't help wondering if they were loaded. I noticed the same gleam of suspicion in Ronan's eyes, and I thought he was about to say something when a diversion was created by the sudden and breathless arrival of the chaplain.

'M-Master An-Anthony! Playing g-games on th-the Sabbath! N-no! It w-won't d-do, you know!'

'You p-p-p-prosy old f-f-f-fool!' Anthony mocked, looking furious. 'I'm master here now, and I'll do just as I like. And don't you forget it!'

I could see that Sir Henry was trembling and that his knuckles had whitened where his hands were so tightly clasped together, but he bravely stood his ground.

'I-it's n-not r-right,' he said, his stammer becoming more pronounced than ever. 'You sh-should be r-reading the Scriptures.'

Anthony leapt to his feet. 'You stupid old man! Go away and leave me alone!' He seized a heavy wooden box, full of chessmen, and heaved it with all his might at the chaplain. But it missed its target, felling instead the steward who, with two servants, had entered the hall unobserved in order to oversee the preparations for dinner. It caught George Applegarth on his right forearm, knocking him to the ground.

Immediately, Anthony was all contrition, vaulting over the table and jumping from the dais.

'George!' he exclaimed in horror. 'I haven't hurt you, have I? Holy Virgin! You haven't broken that arm again, have you? Can you move it? Tell me you're all right.'

'I'm winded, that's all,' the steward gasped, struggling to sit up. 'I daresay I'll have a bruise as big as a plate, but otherwise there's no harm done that I can tell.'

'Th-that w-was meant for m-me,' the chaplain quavered. 'Y-you m-might have k-killed me.'

Dame Audrea swept into the hall, attracted by the disturbance, demanding to know what was the matter and followed by Simon, still looking extremely pale.

She was promptly informed of the trouble

214

by Sir Henry.

'He won't be satisfied until he's crippled the lot of us!' Simon declared shrilly.

'It certainly would appear so,' Dame Audrea agreed, her patrician features a mask of disdain. She turned on her elder son and said in a low, furious voice, 'Haven't you more pride than to behave like a lout in front of guests? What Master and Mistress Bignell must think of you I shouldn't care to guess.' She glanced over her shoulder at George Applegarth. 'Are you all right, Master Steward?'

He tenderly felt his right arm and then nodded. 'All seems well, Mistress. No bones broken.'

'Well, you're lucky,' Simon snarled. 'Mother, can't you make him go away again? Why doesn't somebody get rid of the bastard? If I had the use of both arms, I'd do it myself.'

The Bignells looked, if it were possible, more shocked than before, and Dame Audrea said hastily, 'That will do, Simon! I'll have none of that wild talk, if you please.' She waved a hand at one of the servants and then indicated the jumble of games on the top table. 'Clear these things away and prepare the hall for dinner. George, I will oversee the laying of the trestles if you wish to retire to your chamber and rest your arm.'

'What a fuss about nothing!' Anthony exclaimed angrily, aware of having lost face in front of Rose, who had retreated to her parents' side, looking frightened. 'George is

215

made of sterner stuff than to complain about a little bruise, aren't you, my friend?' And he embraced George Applegarth's shoulders, giving them an affectionate squeeze.

The steward smiled faintly. 'I've said, I'll do well enough. There's no call for anyone to worry. Now, you two men' – he nodded at the servants – 'get the tables set up. Dame Audrea, if you and Master Simon will just get out of the way...'

Dame Audrea moved towards the Bignells, no doubt with the idea of making light – or as light as she could – of an ugly family scene, but Simon stayed where he was, his features contorted with hatred.

'I meant what I said,' he shouted at his brother. 'In God's Name, I wish someone would kill you!'

No sooner had he spoken than there was a vivid flash of lightning, followed by an ear-splitting clap of thunder. The flames of two candles, standing in a wall niche, were suddenly extinguished. Rose Micheldever gave a little sigh and fainted.

It was one of those summer storms that seemingly comes out of nowhere, is fierce in its intensity while it lasts, but then is gone, leaving the world a cleaner, fresher and greener place.

The clouds must have gathered since we came indoors, and I realized that the hall had indeed been growing darker for some time, unnoticed as we became absorbed in our

216

games. Nor had we been aware of the beat of the rain as it drummed against the sides of the house. The crash of the thunder had scared us all.

There was general consternation as we all moved towards Rose, supported by her father's arm and looking almost as pale as Simon. But whereas he was obviously in genuine pain from his broken arm, it occurred to me that Rose's swoon was more for effect than because she had been genuinely frightened. I didn't doubt that she had sustained a momentary shock, but it was not until Anthony had wrested her from Master Bignell's arms, carried her bodily to the armchair on the dais and forced wine down her throat that her eyes fluttered open and she gave a tremulous smile.

'Wh-where am I?'

Her mother came fussing up on her other side, frowning at the sight of Anthony chafing her daughter's hands and raising one of them to his lips in a tender salute. Unhappily Edward Micheldever saw it, too, as he entered the hall, summoned from the counting-house by a servant who had informed him that his wife was ill.

'Leave her alone, all of you,' he said brusquely, approaching the dais and mounting the steps. But although he included everyone in his displeasure, it was at Anthony that he directed his gaze. 'Let her alone,' he repeated, pulling Rose roughly to her feet. 'If you feel unwell, girl, go and lie down.'

'Oh, what a kind and considerate husband!' Anthony sneered, glancing from the Bignells to Rose and back to the receiver. 'You could surely have done better for your daughter than that oaf, Master Butcher! I only wish I'd been here when she became of marriageable age.'

I heard the steward, standing just behind me, suck in his breath. George Applegarth knew as well as I did the sort of mischief Anthony was up to; the seeds of dissatisfaction he was sowing in the Bignells' minds that the marriage they had arranged for Rose was not, perhaps, as advantageous as they had once thought it. As for Edward Micheldever, his expression indicated only too clearly that he shared Simon's sentiments concerning the ultimate fate of the prodigal. If looks could have killed, Anthony would have dropped dead on the spot.

Rose was dragged reluctantly away by her irate husband, the discontented droop of her rosebud mouth showing that she had over-played her hand, pretending to be worse than she was. Anthony knew it, too, and gave a crack of unseemly laughter as she was bundled through the door leading to the private quarters of the house. He was enjoying himself; and, to my great surprise, just before she disappeared from view, I saw Rose glance back at him in dawning comprehension, as if the scales had suddenly fallen from her eyes.

She did not reappear for dinner, but at ten

o'clock, the rest of us sat down to yet another uncomfortable meal. Our host had been telling nothing less than the truth when he said he had grovelled to the cook and been forgiven, for she had plainly put forth her best efforts with a first course of broiled venison steaks in oyster sauce and a side dish of chicken stuffed with grapes, followed by pears stewed in wine syrup and a sweet curd flan. Had there been only the food to consider, it could have been a highly enjoyable occasion, but too much raw emotion was poisoning the atmosphere to make for good digestion. Dame Audrea and the three Bignells made stilted conversation, trying to pretend that nothing untoward had happened; Simon pushed the meat around his plate and glowered at his elder brother; Edward Micheldever, although showing a hearty appetite, looked sullen; the chaplain was still upset; Bailiff Kilsby, with the threat of imminent dismissal hanging over his head, was silent and morose; while Jonathan Slye, the chamberlain, staring malevolently at Anthony whenever he thought that young man wasn't looking, did little to detract from the general air of gloom. What gaiety there was, was generated by the lower servants, who seemed undisturbed by the quarrels and carryings-on of their betters.

Only Anthony, among those at the top table, appeared to be enjoying himself, eating greedily and occasionally smiling to himself in a way consciously intended to aggravate anyone foolish enough to display an interest in him. As this included everyone except his mother and the steward, both of whom studiously ignored him, he could be said to have achieved his object.

It was still raining, but less heavily than it had been when the storm first broke. Indeed, gleams of sunlight were beginning to pierce the clouds and make patterns among the rushes. One of the servants, under Dame Audrea's direction, pushed the shutters wide again, allowing the air to flow into the hall. As everyone rose from table, the Bignells began to mutter about taking their leave. Anthony made no effort to detain them.

'You must see Rose first,' Dame Audrea said, and offered to conduct them to the Micheldevers' chamber.

Her words were interrupted by the arrival of a lay brother from the cathedral, seeking hospitality. The main track to Wells, he explained, was flooded and a narrow plank bridge across a stream had been washed away by the violence of the recent storm. He himself was on horseback and would be able to continue his journey later, when the waters had subsided a little, by using the ford a mile or so upstream, but he would advise anyone on foot to delay their journey until tomorrow. The man having delivered and been thanked for his warning, George Applegarth conducted him to the kitchens, where a meal would be found for him from the remains of our own.

This news, I could see, left the Bellknapps in a quandary; whether to offer the butcher and his family horses from their stables or invite them to remain at Croxcombe for the night. The two donkeys would hardly be able to carry the three of them, and horseflesh was precious; too precious to entrust to comparative strangers in the dangers of a swollen stream.

I watched these considerations flit across Anthony's face as he silently deliberated the problem, but it seemed to me there was more going on behind that polite façade than was immediately obvious. In the end, he came to a sudden decision.

'You must stay the night, Master Bignell, you and your family. Mother, will you see that the guest chamber is prepared?'

Dame Audrea flushed at this casual command, for all that it was framed in the shape of a question, but Mistress Bignell was too busy expressing their thanks to notice her host's rudeness.

'For you must know, Master Bellknapp, that Thomas has never learned to swim, and has a great dread of water in general, and floods in particular. Why, walking here this morning, he found it quite an ordeal to walk across that narrow bridge, for there's no rail to it, and his balance isn't what it was, is it my dear?'

The butcher reluctantly agreed, although he plainly would have preferred his wife to be less forthright about his limitations. Nevertheless, he, too, thanked the Bellknapps for their proffered hospitality. Only Ronan appeared less than happy with the prospect of a day spent on his best behaviour instead of being able to sneak away for some Sunday fun with his friends.

He had good reason. The day dragged. Rose recovered sufficiently to join her family, walking with them by the moat, attending yet another of the chaplain's sermons, preached in the chapel at midday, or chatting quietly to her mother, sitting on a bench in the sunshine watching the swans. The board games that had passed the time so pleasantly between breakfast and dinner were not suggested again. Indeed, Anthony disappeared for the rest of the day, taking Humphrey Attleborough with him, so I rescued Hercules from the kitchen and took him for another walk in Croxcombe woods in the hope of encountering Hamo Gough once more. But he, also, was making himself scarce. His hut stood empty, the fire smouldered away unattended and there was no sign of him anywhere in the area surrounding Hangman's Oak. The pit he had been digging in the morning had been hastily filled in and the spade left propped against the tree; but although I called several times, the charcoal burner, whether he heard me or not, failed to materialize.

I contemplated the ground around the oak and prodded it with my cudgel, but in spite of the rain, it was too well protected under the trees to have more than a surface softness.

Hercules assisted me to the best of his ability, snuffling and rootling at the base of the tree, scrabbling furiously with his paws until, suddenly tiring of what seemed to be a pointless exercise, he sidled off about his own concerns. Eventually I, too, got bored, stretched my length on the damp woodland floor and was almost immediately asleep...

It was one of those dreams that I experience from time to time, when I'm aware that I am dreaming and can watch myself almost as an onlooker, detached and impersonal. I know the dream is trying to tell me something and that it will be up to my waking self to discover what it is. In this instance, I was back in the hall of Croxcombe Manor, but it was night-time and dark. There was moonlight seeping in around the frames of the shutters and, at first, I thought I was alone. Then I had a growing feeling that someone was there with me; I gradually became conscious of a woman's shadowy figure standing slightly behind me. I couldn't see her face and was unable to turn my head to do so. But in spite of this, I knew who she was without being told. I knew that she was Jenny Applegarth.

She remained motionless for what seemed like an age, before suddenly staggering backwards and falling to the floor, as if she had been struck by some unseen hand. I attempted to go to her aid, although I knew perfectly well that I couldn't move, being chained by the rules of my dream to the spot where I stood. But then the steward was kneeling beside her – in spite of the fact that I had neither seen nor heard him enter the hall – his right arm in a sling. With his left hand, he was shaking her by one shoulder, but as he opened his mouth to speak, the scene dissolved and reformed, becoming George Applegarth's private chamber. Anthony Bellknapp was questioning the steward about Jenny's murder. He was going on and on, while all his questions were parried with a stubborn politeness that hid a deep and inexpressible sadness, seeing which, I stepped forward to intervene ... And was at once wide awake, looking up into the branches of the oak, while Hercules blew hotly in my left ear and licked my face, indicating that he had finished his business and was ready to move on.

'What is it? No more rabbits around here that you haven't scared shitless?' I asked, heaving myself to my feet and all the time trying desperately to hang on to the rags of my dream. But although it took no great effort to recall it in total, I was at a loss how to interpret it, so stored it away in my memory to think about later when Hercules wasn't threatening to trip me up with his silly antics. I seized my cudgel and began walking back along the half-hidden track that led eventually to the edge of Croxcombe woods.

As we approached the clearing where Hamo Gough had his hut, I could see him crouched over his fire, feeding in more twigs and bits of coppiced timber from a basket on the ground, and which he had evidently collected during the course of the day. I was just going to hail him, when another man emerged from the trees opposite, calling his name. In the ordinary course of events, there would have been nothing in this to surprise me: there must have been plenty of people in the neighbourhood who knew the charcoal burner well enough to exchange greetings with him. But what pulled me up short and made me grab Hercules with a terse injunction to be quiet – he always understands when I'm in earnest, and I could feel him quivering with silent excitement under my arm – was the fact that the newcomer was the 'lay brother' from Glastonbury who had warned us all of the effects of the storm on the road to Wells.

He was chuckling over this now with Hamo. 'That storm was a godsend. Although I don't doubt I'd have thought of some other reason if I'd had to. So, who is it's so anxious to keep the Bignells at the manor for the night? And why?'

'None o' thy business,' Hamo grunted. 'Thee's done thy part.' He fished in the greasy pouch hanging from his equally unsavoury belt and produced some coins. I could hear them jingle as he passed them over, dropping them one by one into the other's outstretched palm. 'It's never a good idea,' he added, 'to enquire too closely into Bellknapp affairs.'

'You're right there,' the second man agreed. 'Anyway, thanks for thinking of me. As I said, the storm was a blessing in disguise, and claiming that the footbridge had been washed away was a cunning stroke, even if I say so myself. I suddenly remembered my lad, Dick – he's a friend of Ronan Bignell's – telling me that Thomas can't swim.'

The charcoal burner turned back to his fire. 'Thee owes me a favour, so don't thee forget it.'

'I shan't.' The 'lay brother' led his horse forward from where he had tethered it among the trees, mounted and, picking his careful way, disappeared along the woodland path.

Still clutching Hercules in a warning clasp and moving as silently as I could, I followed a circuitous route back to the main track and set out in the direction of Wells. Some three-quarters of an hour later, I had reached the spot where the plank bridge spanned the admittedly swollen stream, but there was no question of it having been washed away, nor was there much flooding of the stream itself; certainly nothing that would have deterred a person set on reaching home, where hose and shoes could be hung out to dry.

Slowly, I retraced my steps in the direction of Croxcombe, Hercules running happily alongside me. The rain clouds had completely vanished by now, leaving behind a landscape of unrelieved green, heavy and monotonous beneath the unrelenting heat of the afternoon sun. I was in a quandary. I knew that I should warn somebody that the Bignells had been deceived into passing the night at the manor, but who? Which one of its inhabitants had arranged it, and why? Which of them could I trust? Suppose I confided in the wrong person? There seemed to be only one option open to me: I had to inform everyone of what I knew.

Supper was already halfway through by the time I reached the manor again. The Bignells were at the high table in the company of their daughter and son-in-law, Dame Audrea, Anthony and Simon Bellknapp. A place had been kept for me at one of the lower trestles, but I ignored it, marching straight up to the dais where, addressing no one in particular, I told what I had overheard between Hamo Gough and the stranger in Croxcombe woods.

When I had finished, there was a disbelieving silence. It was Thomas Bignell who spoke first.

'That's nonsense!' he exclaimed. 'I recognized the lay brother who brought the news. His son, Dick, is a friend of Ronan's.'

Ronan nodded. 'Master Fossett wouldn't play a trick like that. And anyway, why should he?'

There was a general murmur of agreement. 'You're having a joke with us, Master Chapman,' Anthony accused me, leaning back in his chair and regarding me through narrowed eyes. 'I wonder why.'

'I am not joking,' I protested indignantly. 'I've walked as far as the footbridge and it's still in place. It hasn't been washed away.

Someone in this house had deliberately set out to keep Master and Mistress Bignell at Croxcombe for the night. Don't ask me why! I can't hazard a guess.'

My sincerity was beginning to take effect, and everybody started to glance uneasily at everyone else until Anthony suddenly brought his fist crashing down on the table, rattling the plates and cups.

'Whatever the purpose behind this stupid jest may be – if, that is, friend Roger is *not* enjoying a joke at our expense – then let me beg you, Master Bignell, to take no notice of it. Stay the night as we had planned. Rose and Edward will be pleased to have you here, and in any case the hour is now too advanced to set out for Wells on foot. Rest assured that no harm will come to you under *my* roof.' As he accentuated the word *my*, he smiled mockingly at his mother and brother as if inviting them to challenge his authority. (Simon was about to do so, but I saw Dame Audrea give his sound arm a restraining squeeze.)

The Bignells were looking hesitant, as though not quite sure what to make of it all, and still half inclined to suspect me of making up the story.

'Perhaps...' Mistress Bignell began shyly, nudging her husband gently in the ribs, 'perhaps if, after all, the bridge isn't broken...'

'I won't hear of your leaving,' Anthony said firmly. 'I shall consider myself deeply insulted if you go. My mother, also.'

Dame Audrea had, perforce, to agree. She

had her reputation for hospitality to consider.

'Please stay,' she said graciously to the Bignells. She eyed me with dislike. 'I'm still not altogether convinced that this is not some sort of stupid jest on the pedlar's part, but otherwise, I can only echo my son's assurance that nothing untoward will happen to you under this roof. You will be perfectly safe.'

Thirteen

Sunday evening passed as slowly as the rest of the day, except that there was now an atmosphere of unease and suspicion – although I had to admit to myself that the suspicion was directed mainly at me. For some reason, my story was only half believed, and my suggestion that someone should be despatched to Croxcombe woods to confirm it with Hamo Gough was ignored. Of course, there was one person in the household who would have obstructed the proposal, but there was no cause for him – or her – to raise objections while no move was made by anyone to contact the charcoal burner. When I protested, Anthony, as master of the house, merely shrugged and said he would have a word with Hamo in the morning. But as, by then, I would have started my journey back to Bristol and the Bignells would have returned to Wells, it was small consolation. I doubted if Anthony would bother. As he pointed out to me, whoever had wanted the Bignells to remain the night at the manor, and for whatever purpose, the culprit would hardly make a move against them now.

I sulked; and after evening prayers – conducted by an even more nervous Sir Henry, conscious of Anthony's growing impatience with his stammering speech – I retired out of doors to a bench beneath one of the hall's open windows and angrily discouraged anyone who tried to join me.

'Oh, behave like a child, then!' Rose shouted, rebuffed in her attempt to sit alongside me, and flounced off to walk with her father and Anthony, who were strolling, deep in conversation, beside the moat.

I felt guilty when she had gone: she was so plainly worried by my story, wishing to discuss it with me, that I tried to recall her, but by that time she was out of earshot. Ten minutes or so later, I felt even guiltier when Anthony and Thomas Bignell ambled back into view, once more on their own, obviously having rid themselves of her unwanted presence. I guessed that she might be the subject of their conversation and would therefore have been an embarrassment to them.

I was not alone in this suspicion. Edward Micheldever's voice sounded suddenly just above my head, and I realized he was standing on the other side of the open window, in the hall.

'What plot is that bastard hatching now? Look how busily he's talking to Thomas. He's made a dead set at Rose ever since he clapped eyes on her. I wish to God he'd never come back. I'd like to see him dead!'

'Be quiet,' George Applegarth's voice answered him sternly. 'That's no way to speak of your master. And, whether you like it or not, Ned, by the terms of his father's will, he is the master here. You'd do as well not to forget it. Besides, nothing he can say to your detriment can alter the fact that you're Rose's husband in the sight of God and the Church. Thomas Bignell's a pious man. He won't be swayed by any inducements Anthony Bellknapp offers him. Good God! He isn't the sort to encourage his daughter to become another man's mistress, however rich that man might be. And in any case, Anthony's not as rich as all that. He has a mother and brother to support, even though he might hope to disregard the fact, land to maintain, a large household to run, hospitality to dispense. He's more likely to be on the lookout for a wealthy wife than saddle himself with a demanding mistress. And in the end, Rose's morals are her own, not her father's.'

'Rose doesn't have any morals where men are concerned,' snarled the receiver. 'Haven't you realized that by now, George? A word of encouragement from Thomas and she'd have no qualms whatsoever at becoming Bellknapp's whore. I knew what she was like when I agreed to marry her, but I thought she was safe from temptation here. Apart from Kilsby, there's no one to take a girl's fancy, and Reginald's been too occupied trying to snare Dame Audrea's affections to look elsewhere.'

'I tell you, Thomas wouldn't—'

'My father-in-law has ambitions above his station in life,' was the snapped rejoinder before the steward could finish. 'And if the chapman's story is true – and I'm willing to hazard my last groat that it is – then Anthony has arranged this whole thing. He needs more time to talk the old man round, for I don't deny Thomas would have some qualms about persuading Rose to sell herself for money. I tell you, at some time during today, Anthony has paid Hamo Gough to find a way of keeping the family here overnight. And that's what he's doing now; persuading Thomas to talk Rose into becoming his paramour!'

'I've never heard such arrant nonsense!' the steward spluttered. 'It's midsummer madness with you, my lad, and that's the truth.'

'It's not midsummer and it's not madness, just you wait and see,' the receiver retorted furiously. 'Look how earnestly the pair of them are talking to each other! Linked arms, heads close together ... And as for Anthony not being a rich man, pah! You've seen his clothes, his horse. His damn servant's better attired than I am. Whatever Master Anthony's been doing over in the eastern counties all these years – and I'd be willing to wager my

232

life it's been nothing honest – it's made him money all right.'

A third voice was added to those of the two men already standing by the open hall window.

'Are you talking about that cursed ruffian out there?' demanded the bailiff. 'May he rot in Hell!'

'That's enough!' George Applegarth declared. 'I'll not stay to listen to more of this. I'll admit he's treated you shabbily, Reginald, but God's brought him home to be master over us and we must put up with the consequences. Besides, you'll not lack employment for very long. Sir Damien and Lady Chauntermerle will take you in and give you an honoured place. You've always been a favourite of theirs.'

'I'd rather rule as master here,' was the terse reply. There was a short pause during which the steward must have moved away, for Reginald Kilsby's next remarks were a scathing attack on him. 'That man's lower than a snake the way he crawls on his belly to whichever Bellknapp's king of the dunghill. Until that loathsome creature out there reappeared, it was Simon, as future master of the house, whose word was Holy Writ. Even Audrea' – the lack of title claimed a familiarity with the dame that it was impossible to mistake – 'grows tired of it now and again, but he's such an old and loyal servant and friend that, until now, she'd never have dreamed of dismissing him. But this loyalty of his to Anthony could

233

well be the undoing of him...'

The conversation faded as the bailiff and receiver retreated further into the hall, and then ceased altogether as they went about their business. The figures by the moat also vanished and did not return, so I was left to my thoughts in a gathering dusk that was thick with the scent of meadow flowers and yesterday's scythed grass. Mulling over the receiver's surmise that Anthony had been in touch with Hamo Gough, I recalled my own meeting with the charcoal burner that same morning and the impression I had had of someone following us. I remembered the way in which Hamo had paused, head to one side, listening, and I had myself heard the occasional snap and crack of a twig as though something, or somebody, was lurking in the undergrowth. Could that have been Anthony, waiting for me to be on my way so that he could speak to my companion in private? He would have known the previous day that the Bignells had been invited to spend the Sabbath at Croxcombe Manor.

But speculation was fruitless. I could make a reasonable guess, but that was all. And I was tired. It had been a long day, and I had an even longer one ahead of me on the morrow as I began my journey homewards. Although I was looking forward to seeing Adela (and – yes! – even the children) again more than I could say, I nevertheless felt a sense of defeat that I had failed to discover anything that could clear my half-brother of the charge

Dame Audrea had brought against him. He was still locked up in the Bristol bridewell facing an accusation of murder. It crossed my mind that the one thing I hadn't done was to speak to Dame Audrea herself and try to convince her that she was mistaken. But where were my arguments that would demolish her case? What in fact did I know for certain about this man who had suddenly burst into my life, claiming kinship? I had nothing to go on except an innate conviction that he was indeed my father's son, and honest. Certainly not enough to convince a person as sure of herself as Audrea Bellknapp. With such a woman, my intervention might well make her all the more determined to prove herself right at any cost. No, it was best to leave well alone where my hostess was concerned and put my trust in George Applegarth.

I sat on the bench for a while longer, going over the murder of Jenny Applegarth in my mind, wondering what had become of the real John Jericho after he had fled from Croxcombe on that fatal night, where he had gone, what he had done with his spoils; wondering, too, what it was that Hamo Gough had seen – or thought he had seen – to make him dig around Hangman's Oak in search of something he seemed convinced was buried there. But the problem refused to resolve itself. No sudden flash of inspiration illumined my mind.

I stood up, realizing that the air had grown damp and that my joints were quite stiff with having sat still so long. I went round to the kitchens to say goodnight to Hercules, who was being so pampered by the maids and cook that he could barely condescend to wag his tail at the sight of me. Well, every dog was entitled to his day and his would be over very shortly. The first time Adam tweaked his tail and bawled deafeningly in his ear, he would know that he was home. I told him as much, making his adoring female admirers laugh, and the cook promised me breakfast at whatever hour I decided to set out, even if it were the crack of dawn. I thanked her and she turned back to her preparation of the 'all-night' trays, with their jugs of wine and half loaves of bread, which the servers were busy fetching and carrying round to the various bedchambers, including the one shared by Anthony, Humphrey Attleborough and me. Indeed, Humphrey had been sent to collect our tray, his master, as he explained, being already in bed and impatient for his evening snack.

'You'd better get on in, Chapman,' he advised. 'Master Bellknapp's not in the best of humours.'

I made no comment, guessing that Anthony had failed to persuade Thomas Bignell to use his influence with his daughter. I reflected that, in spite of his winning ways, Anthony was an unprincipled rogue with fewer scruples than most men, which prompted me to ask Humphrey how his master had amassed his fortune.

Humphrey shrugged. 'As far as I know, there is no fortune. He lives by his wits mainly. Games of chance and hazard. Sometimes we're in pocket, sometimes not. I've only been with him three years, but I assume he's always lived the same way. Which is why he needed to come back and claim his inheritance as soon as he learned about it.' He jerked his head. 'I must go or I shall be bawled out for dawdling. Are you coming?'

'In a moment. I'm not at Master Bellknapp's beck and call. I'm away home tomorrow morning, early.'

The servant grimaced. 'You've not stopped long, then. Not three days. Your ankle's mended now, has it?'

'My ankle? Oh ... Yes.' I had forgotten my injury. 'It was only a twist. Nothing serious. By the way, do you happen to know if your master got up early this morning and went to Croxcombe woods?'

Humphrey gave me an odd look. 'He got up early, but it's not my business to ask him what he does or where he's been. Ask him yourself if you want to know.' With which sound advice, he took himself off in the direction of our bedchamber.

I hung around in the kitchen for a few more minutes as a matter of principle and to prove my independence, exchanging goodnights with the cook and the maids. I listened to the former's pithy description of Anthony's character, and how she didn't expect to remain at Croxcombe for very much longer, before taking myself off to bed.

My host was already under the coverlets, but sitting up and drinking some of the wine from the 'all-night' and chewing on a crust of bread. Humphrey, who had stripped and was seated on the edge of his truckle-bed, was also munching. Anthony waved a hand at the tray, which had been placed on a chest beneath the window. 'Help yourself,' he invited, as he had done the previous two nights, but without the same joviality.

Humphrey was right: his mood was surly and he seemed anxious to be left in peace to think his own thoughts. Something had upset him, so I undressed in silence, poured myself wine from what remained in the jug, swallowed it quickly and tumbled into my half of the bed. Just as I was dozing off, however, Anthony asked abruptly, 'You've found out no more, then?'

I forced myself awake. 'I'm sorry,' I mumbled stupidly. 'Found out about what?'

'About this page, John Jericho, of course. You boasted to me what a wonderful solver of mysteries you are, but you don't appear to have got very far with this. And tomorrow you go home ... Well? Have you discovered anything?'

'No,' I admitted, wishing to high heaven that I'd kept my mouth shut concerning my past successes. No good has ever come to me by blowing my own trumpet: it invariably leads to dire humiliation and makes me regret that I didn't hold my tongue. Some people

238

can do it; some people can glorify themselves with impunity, but not me. I've always suspected that God gets annoyed when I take all the credit, most of which should rightly be His. So I just grunted and turned on my side, presenting my back view for Anthony's consideration and almost immediately drifting off to sleep. I thought I heard him laugh in that particularly mocking way of his which reduced poor Sir Henry to a stuttering, quivering jelly, but I couldn't be sure. I was already on the borderline of sleep.

When I opened my eyes again, it was already growing light. The bedchamber shutters were still closed, but haloed with brilliant sunshine. Somewhere a cock was crowing, king of all he surveyed and eager to make the world aware of the fact. I was lying on my back and continued to do so for several minutes, conscious of a dull ache behind my eyes and a throbbing head. If I had experienced these symptoms at home, I would have said – or, most likely, Adela would have said – that I had drunk too much the night before, but although I searched my memory, I could not recall having consumed much wine either at supper or afterwards. Indeed, for the whole of the previous day, I had been unusually abstemious. Perhaps, I thought, cautiously lifting my lids, I was sickening for something. Perhaps God was going to keep me at Croxcombe after all.

I sat up carefully and felt a little better,

glancing across at Humphrey, huddled beneath his blanket and snoring with his customary vigour, then sideways at my sleeping companion. But to my surprise, Anthony's half of the bed was empty. For some reason, he had risen betimes. He might, of course, simply have gone to relieve himself in the garderobe, but we had a piss-pot in the bedchamber so it seemed unlikely. (On Friday, the first night of my three-night stay, we had actually had a contest to see who could pee the farthest distance without missing the pot. I had felt certain I would be the winner, but it was Humphrey who had won.) Oh well, I thought, easing my legs out of bed, I was not his keeper. It was his own house and he could do as he liked.

By the time I had dressed and checked my pack, to be sure that no one had pilfered its contents, I felt less unsteady on my legs, but had a raging thirst. I made my way to the kitchen and drank deeply from the water-barrel, then went outside to wash under the pump. By the time I returned to the kitchen, the cook had appeared and was boiling water for me to shave with.

'Eggs?' she asked, preparing to crack a couple into a pan of spitting fat.

But my stomach rebelled and, as much to my own surprise as hers, I shook my head.

'Bread and cheese will do,' I said, and drank more water. 'Master Bellknapp's up early,' I added.

The woman shrugged indifferently. 'Is he? I

haven't seen him.'

Hercules had come sniffing round me in the hope of scraps, so I offered him cheese which he contemptuously declined. The cook took pity on him and fed him some of yesterday's meat. I watched him wolf it down with a queasy feeling in my insides.

The maids arrived from whatever corner of the house they slept in, rubbing their eyes and yawning, but rousing themselves sufficiently to insist on kissing me goodbye. The cook enquired if they had seen the master anywhere about as he apparently wasn't in his bed, but no one had. One of the girls noticed that I wasn't eating my usual hearty breakfast and asked the reason. When I explained, she volunteered the information that she had been awakened twice in the night by the sound of people moving about, and wondered if there had been anything amiss with the food at supper. The cook was so outraged by this suggestion, however, that the girl hurriedly denied any such possibility and said that she had probably been dreaming.

I was beginning to feel better, so I once more took my leave of the women, generously allowing Hercules to accept all the hugs and kisses and honeyed phrases that I flattered myself were really meant for me. Then, picking up my pack and cudgel, I went out of the back door, past the stables and animal pens, admired, as always, Dame Audrea's formal flower garden and headed for the bridge across the moat, where the keeper was

241

busy unlocking the gate. Suddenly I remembered the Bignells and wondered if they were
all three all right. I presumed they were. No
commotion had announced any great catas-
trophe, and I was more than ever convinced
that Edward Micheldever was probably correct when he accused Anthony of being the
author of the plot; of wanting extra time to
persuade the butcher to use his influence
with his daughter. Thomas was to see the
advantages of Rose becoming the mistress of
a wealthy man...

I paused in my tracks, glancing back at the
manor. There was something not right about
any of this. There was something I was missing. No man, not even one as set up in his
own conceit as Anthony Bellknapp, would
conceive of such a plan. Surely not! And yet,
there was a kind of audacity about him,
something amoral as though he had long ago
ceased to live by anyone's rules except his
own, that made me revise this opinion almost
as soon as it was formed. I had sensed from
our first moment of meeting that he had the
sort of egotism that borders on hubris; and if
the late Cornelius Bellknapp had been as
stiff-necked and proud as his wife, it explained why they and their elder son had never got
on.

But Anthony also had charm when he chose
to exert it, which Dame Audrea, I suspected,
had never possessed, nor probably ever
could. I had fallen under his spell, even while
being made aware that as far as unpleasant-

ness of character went, there was less to choose between him and his younger brother than I had at first imagined. It was obvious, too, that George Applegarth knew Anthony for what he really was, but that he and his wife had always loved and protected him, as the steward was prepared to go on doing for Jenny's sake...

Hercules dashed back along the track to see what had happened to me, then nipped at my boots, jumping up and barking. He didn't approve of all this standing around and thinking. I bent and patted his head.

'All right, lad. I'm coming.'

We entered Croxcombe woods and I made my way to where Hamo Gough had his hut, but once again, both clearing and hut were empty. I had hoped, because of the earliness of the hour, to have caught him tending his fire before he went off, coppicing. But it was not to be; nor had I noticed him in the neighbourhood of Hangman's Oak. I hesitated, wondering if I should wait for his return, then decided against it. Anthony's plots and schemes no longer mattered to me. I was leaving them behind with every step I took. The only people at the manor who concerned me now were Dame Audrea, her receiver and her steward. No doubt I should be seeing all three very soon in Bristol, and my trust was in George Applegarth that he would be able to convince the other two that my half-brother was not the missing page. At least, it was really Dame Audrea that he had to persuade.

Edward Micheldever seemed to me to have no convictions either way: he would simply agree with whatever the Dame decided.

Hercules gave me another nudge and we went on again, but although, by this time, I had overcome my sickness of the early morning and was feeling more like my usual self, there was no spring in my step and my feet dragged. I knew in my heart of hearts that I was doing what I had never done before, abandoning a mystery without having solved it. Without, if I were honest, having done anything much to solve it. As I trudged along, I went over and over the facts in my head, but always coming to the same conclusion. As long as there was no chance – and there was none that I could see – of discovering what had happened to the real John Jericho, I could never prove that John Wedmore was innocent of the accusation made against him. In fact, the whole expedition had been a waste of time and ill thought out, I castigated myself. I should be growing less impulsive, not more, as I approached my twenty-eighth birthday.

All the same, I had been so sure at one point that God had been directing this venture – poking His divine nose into my business, directing me, harassing me as usual – that I had had no doubts that I was doing the right thing. Now I was beginning to wonder if I had overlooked something, some clue that God had given me, but which I had been too stupid to notice. Was I losing the gift that He had blessed me with? And if so, would it be taken away?

Wrapped in these gloomy thoughts, I must have been walking steadily for quite some while, not marking the passing of the hours, but following by instinct the well-worn tracks that had led me through the maze of woodland paths until I suddenly found myself in what seemed to be a familiar spot, by the banks of a gently flowing stream. I rounded a bend and there, standing outside the door of an inn that I immediately recognized, arms akimbo, surveying his domain, was Josiah Litton. He spotted me almost at the same moment as I saw him and beamed all over his face.

'Chapman!' he said. 'You kept your promise to call on us on your way home. Come along in, lad! Come along in!'

The aleroom was quiet, filled only with sunshine and dancing dust motes and the sound of Goody Litton's energetically wielded broom. No one, it appeared, had stayed overnight and I was their first visitor of the day. The goodwife laid aside her broom and grinned, as glad to see me as her husband.

'Josiah! Ale!' she commanded, pulling out a stool from under a table and urging me to sit down. 'You've been to Croxcombe Manor?' she asked and I nodded. 'Good! You've been gone three whole days and nights. We were afraid you'd forgotten us or decided not to return.'

I didn't admit that I had indeed forgotten

them and that my reappearance had been the merest accident.

'I came back as quickly as I could,' I lied.

The landlord put a pitcher of ale and three beakers on the table, settled himself on another stool opposite me, and invited me to begin.

'Anthony reached the manor ahead of you, of course, but not by more than an hour or two if you made good time. You must have witnessed his reception almost from its beginning. Tell us everything.'

So I took him at his word and told him the whole story, including my own involvement in it, my encounters with Hamo Gough, the little I had learned concerning events on the night Jenny Applegarth was murdered, and finished with the previous day's ploy by some unknown person to ensure the Bignells remained at the manor overnight.

'I suppose I should have assured myself that they were alive and well before I left Croxcombe,' I added uneasily. 'Anthony was missing from bed this morning when I woke, and I suspect him of being the person responsible for the hoax.'

Janet Litton, who had been listening intently, hanging on my every word, now gave a decided shake of her head.

'I think you're mistaken, Master Chapman, in laying that trick at Anthony Bellknapp's door. Your reason, or, rather, the jealous husband's reason for thinking Master Bellknapp guilty is impossible to believe. It doesn't make sense that a man would make such intentions known to a girl's own father. Only other men could be so credulous as to think so.'

'But my love,' the landlord argued, 'someone wanted the butcher and his family to stay at Croxcombe for the night, and was prepared to go to great lengths to attain his ends. Master Bellknapp seems to be the only person with any motive.'

'Maybe not,' declared the goodwife shrewdly. 'Didn't you tell us, Chapman, that Master Bignell saw a rider near the manor on the night of Jenny Applegarth's murder? And didn't you also tell us that he had decided, thinking it over after all these years, that the horseman might have been vaguely familiar to him?'

'That's so, yes. What are you suggesting?'

'Perhaps that person overheard the butcher's remarks and doesn't want to risk even the slightest possibility of being identified. And that couldn't be Anthony Bellknapp, for he disappeared years before the murder. The crime has always been laid solely at the door of the page. But suppose someone else had been in league with John Jericho, and that someone is still there, at Croxcombe.'

I stared excitedly at Janet Litton. Her idea might provide the answer to one puzzling aspect of the robbery. How had a young lad of smallish stature, and on foot, managed to carry a heavy bundle of stolen goods clear of the neighbourhood without being apprehended? But an accomplice on horseback could have managed it...

Before I could pursue this line of thought, however, there was the sound of horse's hooves outside and a moment later, Humphrey Attleborough burst through the inn door, his face as white as a sheet.

'My master,' he gasped without waiting for us to ask what was the matter. 'Master Bellknapp! He's dead. Drowned in the moat.'

Fourteen

My first thought was that it was all wrong. It was Thomas Bignell who couldn't swim, who had been tricked into remaining at Croxcombe Manor for the night, whose body – if anybody's – should have been found floating in the moat. Then I pulled myself together, aware we were all three, the landlord, his wife and I, staring at Humphrey Attleborough as though he were some shade or being conjured up by our overwrought imaginations.

But before I could interrogate him, it was necessary to calm him down. Humphrey was shaking like a leaf in a high gale, and it was obvious from the welts on the palms of his hands that he had been clinging on to the horse's reins like a man possessed. Which made me glance through the open door at the sweating animal and recommend to Josiah Litton that the poor beast be seen to before it took a chill. He immediately bustled off while his goodwife hurried to fill a beaker and bring it to Humphrey; indeed, she had the good sense to fill beakers for us all as an antidote to the shock we had sustained. By the time the landlord returned, having stabled the horse and rubbed it down – although not, I suspected, with such care as he would usually have taken – Humphrey was recovering somewhat and appeared in a fit enough state to reply to the dozen or so queries hovering eagerly on my lips.

'When was the body discovered? And who found it?'

The lad swallowed another mouthful of ale, his teeth chattering on the rim of his cup. He answered the second question first.

'I found it. When the master didn't show up for his breakfast, I began to get worried. No one else seemed to care.'

That was understandable. Anthony's absence must have been a relief to almost everyone.

'Who was at breakfast?' I queried.

Humphrey pressed a hand to his forehead. 'I – I can't rightly recall. Dame Audrea and Simon and the Bignells – Master and Mistress Bignell and the son – they were all there, at the high table, I'm sure of that. The dame was enquiring what sort of night they had passed. There were some servants at the lower board, the ones who don't take their meals in the kitchen with the cook, but I can't remember which. I was beginning to worry about Master Bellknapp by that time and was watching the doors into the hall, expecting him to appear at any moment.'

'What about the receiver, the bailiff, the chaplain, were they present?'

'Oh, Sir Henry was. Yes, of course, he said grace before the start of the meal. But as for the others, maybe.' He sounded distressed. 'I really don't recall.'

'Steady.' I laid a hand on Humphrey's arm. 'You'll remember later, when you're calmer. What about the steward?'

'George Applegarth? Yes, now you mention him, he was busying himself around.' Humphrey suddenly grew petulant. 'But what does it matter, where anyone was at breakfast? My master had been in the water for several hours. He was all stiff and blue. His body had caught in a patch of reeds just where the moat curves away to the west in the direction of the woods.'

I was still puzzled. 'But how did he come to drown? I know the moat is fairly wide there and the bank must have been slippery after yesterday's rain, but is he, like Thomas Bignell, unable to swim?'

Humphrey began to shiver again. 'It wouldn't have mattered whether he could swim or not. Someone had hit him a stunning blow to the back of the head. He stood no chance. He might have been dead before he fell in.'

'Murder, then,' breathed Goody Litton, her eyes wide and frightened.

'No chance of an accident in that case,' her husband agreed, trying, not altogether successfully, to suppress the excitement that violent death arouses even in the gentlest of us when it doesn't touch us personally.

My own feeling was one of dismay although not of surprise. There were too many people at Croxcombe Manor who had wished the prodigal dead. Whoever had the thankless task of investigating this sudden death would not find himself short of suspects ... A thought occurred to me; more than a thought, a suspicion.

'What are you doing here?' I demanded, rounding on Humphrey with an angry suddenness that made him jump. I could tell at once by his guilty expression that my suspicion was correct.

'I – I was sent after you.'

'By whom?'

'D-Dame Audrea.'

'Why me?' I asked grimly. 'And who has ridden for the local sergeant-at-law?'

'Dame Audrea doesn't want the law involved.' Of course she didn't, not with the finger of suspicion pointing straight at Simon as the suspect who had the most to gain by his brother's death. But she wanted to know who the murderer was, not only because she was thankful for present deliverance, but also to be wary of him in the future. A person who had found the strength of purpose to kill once, might well find it a second time if the need ever arose. Unless, of course, the murderer was Dame Audrea herself, in which case it was even more desirable for her to keep the law's representative at arm's length.

'So, why have you been sent to find me? How did you manage to track me down?'

I could guess the answer to the first question. I had opened my big mouth so wide that everyone must know by now that I had been employed by no less a personage than the King's brother, the Duke of Gloucester, to solve several murder cases for him, not to mention other mysteries that I had unravelled on my own account. This would teach me not to boast. It was high time I cultivated that much maligned virtue, modesty. As for how Humphrey had managed to find me, he simply said vaguely that he had asked people if they had seen a travelling pedlar with a dog; and because of my unusual height – and because Hercules had chased and frightened half to death three ducks, a sheep and an unknown quantity of chickens – my progress had been marked and remembered. I cursed fluently under my breath.

'Dame Audrea,' he concluded, glancing at me doubtfully, 'wants you to discover the murderer for her.'

I was just about to refuse this request with less than my usual courtesy, when a thought struck me. To do as the dame asked would give me a powerful bargaining counter. I would try to track down Anthony's murderer – and hold my tongue about the result if that was what she wished – and in return she would promise to drop her charge against my half-brother. When I eventually returned to Bristol, she would give me letters exonerating him addressed to the sheriff, the mayor, her kinsman, Alderman Foster, and to anyone else it might concern. So, instead of snapping Humphrey's head off, I smiled benignly at him.

'Naturally, I shall do my very best to assist Dame Audrea and bring the killer of her son to justice.'

'I – I don't think that's – that's what she wants,' Humphrey faltered, confirming my own suspicions in the matter. But then his eyes blazed with righteous indignation. 'But I do! I want to know who murdered Master Bellknapp! Whatever others may think of him, he's been a good master to me. Never a blow, let alone a whipping, and barely a harsh word in all the time I've been with him. I'll see he gets justice!'

I pursed my lips. 'I'd be careful, if I were you, lad, about going against Dame Audrea's wishes. You could end up in the moat as easily as your master. Your late master,' I added significantly.

Humphrey eyed me apprehensively, but said nothing. His silence worried me more than any protestations as to his future intentions would have done, but there were more important things to think about.

'Dinner,' I said, turning to the landlord and his wife. 'It must be getting close to the dinner hour and I've eaten nothing since breakfast. Master Attleborough here probably hasn't eaten at all this morning.' Humphrey shook his head dolefully and I patted his shoulder. 'There you are, then. Food, Master Litton, is what we both need to sustain us before our journey back to Croxcombe Manor.'

Humphrey and I ate our oatcakes, coddled eggs and slices of boiled beef in a secluded corner of the aleroom, which was now filling up fast as workers from the surrounding fields and woodlands ambled in to refresh themselves after an hour or two's hard work. (Foreigners are always complaining that the English don't take work seriously enough, and that we could feed half Europe if only we would put our backs and hearts into our respective jobs instead of lolling about drinking ale and stuffing our faces. But like most of my countrymen, I feel that is the rest of Europe's problem, not ours. Our first duty is to look after ourselves.)

'What happened when you reported finding Master Bellknapp's body?' I asked Humphrey in a low voice. 'What was the reaction of the manor's other inmates?'

'Well, to begin with, only general consternation and wonderment as to how it could have happened, until George Applegarth – he and the receiver had pulled the body free of the weeds and on to the bank – turned him over and we discovered the great bloody contusion on the back of his head. Then, of course, there was uproar. Rose Micheldever had hysterics and even Mistress Bignell screamed. The men, well, I didn't notice them too much, but Master Bignell, he looked sick and scared. I do remember that.'

'And Dame Audrea?'

Humphrey shrugged, but his eyes narrowed malevolently. 'Oh, she behaved as you would expect. She just stood looking at the body for a long time without a flicker of emotion, and then she said, "So! Somebody's taken their revenge at last. I wondered how much longer we would have to wait."'

I nodded, unsurprised. There was something implacable about Dame Audrea. Whatever she felt, whether it was elation or horror – and I suspected that in this case, dismay and fear would also play their part – she would never let it show.

'What happened next?'

'My master's body was carried into the hall and laid on one of the trestles while the dame called all the officers of the household to the top table to consult them. There was a lot of talking and arguing, and while that was going on, I overheard Ronan Bignell telling someone that he and his parents thought they should leave the family to its grief – ha! – and would be on their way. As it's Monday, the butcher's stall should have opened long since: they would be losing precious custom. Unfortunately for them – the Bignells, I mean – Dame Audrea also heard what Ronan was saying and forbade them to go. Then she asked where you were, and seemed astonished to learn that you had already started on your way home. She said you were to be brought back immediately and that I was to ride after you; that you probably couldn't have got far. I said wouldn't it be better if I rode to Wells and fetched the sheriff's officer? But she said no, she didn't wish to involve the law unless it was absolutely necessary; and as we didn't as yet know what had really happened, we didn't know whether it was necessary or not. She thought you might be able to find out the truth.'

'And did the others agree to this proposal?'

'Most of them. They none of them wanted a lawman poking his long snout into the manor's affairs. And with good reason. There was hardly one of 'em that hadn't uttered threats against my master or wished him dead. Or something of the sort.'

'Mind you, there's safety in numbers,' I remarked thoughtfully. 'Whoever tries to discover the truth about Anthony Bellknapp's death is going to have his pick of suspects.' I added, 'You said most of them were willing to accept Dame Audrea's proposition that I should be fetched back to Croxcombe. Who disagreed?'

Humphrey suddenly looked uncomfortable. 'No one disagreed exactly.'

'What then? Exactly?'

'We-ell, Simon, he thought you ought to be brought back, but only because—'

'Because?'

Humphrey squirmed uneasily on his stool and refused to meet my eyes. 'Because,' he admitted at last, 'Simon suggested you might be the murderer yourself.'

I was astounded. 'And what does Master Simon suggest is my motive?'

'I don't think he'd thought about that. He was just out to make mischief.'

'Or,' I said slowly, 'it was an attempt to discredit me because he has more to hide than the rest of them.'

'He does have one arm in a sling,' Humphrey reminded me, finishing his ale.

'His left arm, and he's right-handed.' I leaned my elbows on the table and chewed one of my thumbnails. 'This contusion on the back of Master Bellknapp's head, would it have needed two hands to inflict it?'

Humphrey devoted at least half a minute's consideration to the question before answering.

'No, probably not. It could have been done one-handed with a sufficiently heavy cudgel or stick.' He pushed aside his plate, sighing regretfully. 'I can't eat any more. I haven't the heart. You can finish my beef if you want to.'

I took him at his word – I hate to see good food wasted – and suggested that he go and bring his horse around to the front of the inn while I settled up with the landlord. As we rose to our feet and emerged from our shadowy corner, it was obvious from the sudden hiatus in the general buzz of conversation that Josiah Litton had not been slow to spread the news of Anthony Bellknapp's murder. I wondered how Dame Audrea imagined she could keep the matter quiet when it would be common knowledge in half the surrounding countryside by nightfall. But that was before I recollected the countryman's deeply ingrained suspicion and avoidance of anyone in authority; his ability to clam up closer than an oyster and play the moonstruck fool in the presence of the law. Her elder son's death might be the topic under discussion in many a wayside hovel by this evening, but Dame Audrea need have no fear that any word would reach the ears of those likely to view the matter in a serious light. I realized that after years of living in a city, I had almost stopped thinking like the country boy I really was.

By the time I had paid for our breakfast, Humphrey had returned to the aleroom, ready to leave. He had lost his initial pallor and was looking more like his normal cocky self, so I told him to ride on ahead and announce my return at the manor. (There are few things more undignified than loping along either beside or behind a horse, and being in the inferior position of having to look up at the rider.)

Once I had seen Humphrey on his way, I paused long enough to swallow another beaker of Josiah Litton's excellent ale and to promise him that I would do my best to keep him informed of any developments, before gathering up my pack and winkling out Hercules from the Littons' kitchen, where he was gnawing on a large mutton bone, given to him by Janet. Finally, I took my cudgel from the corner, where I had propped it on entering the inn, and emerged into the sunlight, directing my footsteps back the way I had come.

I had gone only a few paces, when I realized that I was holding my trusty 'Plymouth Cloak' upside down. (Now, you might think that there's not much difference between one end of a stick and the other, but I had done what many people do; the old trick of splitting one end lengthwise for a matter of six inches or so, forcing the wood apart and filling the gap with melted lead. When this hardens, it makes the cudgel a more lethal weapon than before, but it also makes it top-heavy. The end with the lead in it is the end that you have to put to the ground, or the stick takes on a life of its own and bruises you in the chest and shoulder. I had had several one-sided struggles with mine after I had first performed the operation, but forgotten that I'd done it.) With a muttered curse, I reversed the cudgel, but as the weighted end swung in an arc towards the ground, I noticed a dark discolouration near its tip. I arrested its progress and pulled it back to eye level, my heart beating uncomfortably fast. And with good reason. A closer examination of the wood around the leaded end convinced me that it was stained with blood.

I must have covered the next mile in a daze, unaware of my surroundings or where I was going. It was more by luck than judgement that when I did finally pause to take stock of my surroundings, I found myself in a small clearing that I recognized from my outward journey as being not far from the main Wells to Bristol track. With a sense of relief, I sat down on a fallen tree trunk and thought seriously about what my unwelcome discovery might mean.

For a start, it could implicate me in Anthony's murder. Indeed, if I looked at the evidence dispassionately, and if I didn't know better, even I might be inclined to suspect myself. But that, of course, was nonsense. Apart from the fact that I had no motive, I knew I had slept soundly all the previous night, not waking until early this morning to a sensation of feeling sick and more than a little unwell.

So, could anyone have entered our bedchamber during the night, taken the cudgel, used it to kill Anthony and returned it without disturbing Humphrey or myself? And at that point, another idea presented itself. The longer I thought about it, the more it became an absolute certainty. The wine I had drunk before getting into bed had been drugged. It explained the drowsiness that had gripped me almost as soon as my head had touched the pillow; the nausea, headache and pain behind the eyes that had afflicted me for several hours this morning after waking; the heavy, dreamless slumber. I tried to picture again the previous night's scene when I had joined Anthony and Humphrey after saying goodnight to the cook and the kitchen maids. The all-night tray was on the chest beneath the bedroom window. Humphrey was eating, but not drinking. My host, on the other hand, was doing both. So had he, too, been drugged? But what would have been the point of that? If he had slept as soundly as I did he would never have been lured from his bed on whatever pretext the murderer had used.

The next question seemed to be, had Humphrey drunk the wine? He had certainly been snoring away when I quit the bedchamber this morning and had looked white enough when he caught me up at the alehouse to have been suffering the effects of sickness. But that could simply have been shock: he was the person, he claimed, who had discovered Anthony's body.

Or was he the killer? On the face of it, like me, he appeared to have no reason to do away with his master, but there might be some hidden resentment that I didn't know about. He could well have been lying when he sang Anthony's praises as a good and tolerant employer, his apparent desire to see the murderer brought to justice just empty protestations to throw me off the scent...

But why should I suspect Humphrey when

there were so many other people at Crox-combe Manor with far more cogent reasons for wishing Anthony Bellknapp dead? The receiver, consumed with jealousy over Rose; the bailiff, dismissed from his post and robbed of his dream of marrying Dame Audrea; the chaplain, mocked and aped and made to look a fool (for even the worm will eventually turn if goaded too far); Simon, stripped of an inheritance he had thought most certainly his; the Dame herself, who had never liked her elder son and who had no influence over him as she had with her younger; all these people must surely be considered as culprits ahead of Humphrey.

But when could the all-night wine have been drugged? And what with? The latter question was more easily answered than the first. I remembered Mistress Wychbold, the housekeeper, sending one of the maids to make up a lettuce and poppy juice potion when Simon broke his arm. No doubt there was still some of the draught left, standing around in the medicine closet. But who had put it in the wine? Humphrey had fetched the all-night tray from the kitchen and could have done it on his way back to the bedchamber. But that meant that Anthony would have suffered the effects of the drug as well as myself. Dragging him from his bed, through the house and out to the water's edge would almost certainly have created enough distur-bance to rouse someone. Besides, if Anthony was unconscious already, there would have been little point in hitting him on the head before tipping him into the moat. No, it was more probable that my host had arranged an assignation with someone – in which case, might he not also have been responsible for drugging the wine?

The longer I considered the idea, the surer I became that this was what had happened. Anthony could easily have hidden a flask of the lettuce and poppy juice somewhere in the bedchamber, and, as it turned out, he had had plenty of time to put it in the all-night jug before I went to bed. But why? Because he had this nocturnal meeting and wanted to make certain that I didn't wake up to note the length of time that he was absent? Probably. He had taken my cudgel with him for protection, which indicated a suspicion that there might be trouble. Not Mistress Micheldever then; he had not had a rendezvous with the lovely Rose. But, whoever else it was, there had been an argument, a quarrel of some kind, during which my cudgel had been wrested from Anthony's grasp and used to club him on the back of the head...

Hercules thrust a cold, wet nose into my hand and took hold of my sleeve with his teeth, growling ominously. He was tired of waiting and wanted to get on. He had terrified every rabbit within half a mile's radius and was now looking for fresh fields to conquer. I was half inclined to shake him off with a stern word and a kick up his nether end, but then decided he was right. I should get back to Croxcombe and discover the facts before I deluded myself any further that I knew what had happened last night.

But what to do about my cudgel? I had been given the opportunity to extricate myself from any suspected involvement in Anthony's murder, and I should be a fool not to take it. Consequently, I stopped at the next stream I passed and washed the stained, weighted end of the stick in the running water, scrubbing it as clean as I could with a handful of grass and dry bracken. Then I disguised such faint marks as remained by plastering them well with mud scooped up from a patch of earth under the trees that had not yet dried after yesterday's storm. It occurred to me, as I regarded my handiwork, that I had given myself one advantage over the other residents at the manor; only I and the killer knew what the murder weapon had been. I had only to keep my ears open and wait for the murderer to give himself away. And on this optimistic note, Hercules and I set out to cover the last few miles to Croxcombe.

Dame Audrea might have sent Humphrey after me to bring me back, but I couldn't pretend that she was delighted to see me.

'You went off in a great hurry this morning,' she accused me as I was ushered into her private solar by George Applegarth. 'Common courtesy would surely have dictated that you take your leave of me.'

'Madam, I'm sorry,' I apologized, 'it was ill done of me, but I wanted to be on the road as early as possible and had no desire to disturb your rest. But you see that I have returned as you requested. Allow me to condole with you in this hour of your great loss.'

Her lips thinned and the blue eyes snapped angrily. 'Don't be sarcastic with me, Master Chapman. You know very well that my elder son's death is nothing but a relief, both to me and to his brother.'

'That's honest, at least,' I said. 'I trust you'll be equally frank with the sheriff's officer when he comes. There's no policy better than honesty.'

She took a deep breath. 'I've warned you, sirrah, I won't stand for insubordination. If that man of Anthony's delivered his message aright, you are perfectly well aware that I have no intention of involving the law. My son slipped, hit his head on a stone, fell in the moat and drowned.'

'Was there a stone?' I asked.

'No, of course there wasn't! Anthony was hit a stunning blow on the back of the head.'

'What with?' I tried to sound as nonchalant as I could.

'How do I know what with?' she blazed. 'I wasn't there.'

I noticed that she had taken the first opportunity to protest her own innocence. The trouble was, I was half inclined to believe her.

'Lady,' I said, 'I won't pretend not to know

why you've sent for me. Because of the things I've told people, you think I might be able to solve this crime for you without, as you put it, involving the law. So why not leave things as they are? Give out your story of an accident, bury your son and forget that it's a lie. If you don't want to see the murderer punished, why do you wish to know his name?'

She got up abruptly from the window-seat where she had been sitting, and started pacing about the room, hitting her balled right fist into the open palm of her left hand.

'Why should you think that I don't want to see the murderer punished?'

'Because he might be your other son.'

'Nonsense!' she exclaimed harshly. 'Simon has neither the courage nor the strength to kill anyone. Oh, he's a boaster, I'll grant you that, but he's too careful of his own skin to risk the hangman's noose. You look surprised. Do you think me the kind of doting mother who isn't aware of, or won't admit to, her children's shortcomings? I'm not such a fool. But Simon I can manage. I always could, and so could my late husband. But not Anthony. He was a wayward child from the time he was breeched. There was something evil in him that neither of us could touch.'

She was exaggerating, of course, to ease her conscience. Anthony was dead and she was glad that he was gone – life could return to normal – but she had to find excuses for her sense of relief. She wanted to know who his murderer was so that she could avenge her

266

son in her own good time. There was to be no public retribution, but somehow or other, she would see his killer punished.

I asked, 'Are you absolutely certain, lady, that you want me to discover the criminal for you? These revelations often don't come singly. You may feel sure that your younger son is innocent, but the truth could be different.'

She hesitated, then squared her shoulders.

'I'll take that chance,' she said. 'So, Master Chapman, can you make good your former boast, and find this killer for me?'

'I can only try,' I agreed. 'I'll do my best. But on one condition.'

'Condition?' In her mouth it was a dirty word, and she made no attempt to hide her amazement at my temerity. 'What condition?'

'That you drop your charge against my half-brother, John Wedmore, that he is your missing page, John Jericho.'

'Your half-brother? Your half-brother is John Jericho?'

'No,' I said patiently. 'That's what I'm telling you. You've made a mistake. John Wedmore is not the murderer of Jenny Applegarth. Her own husband has failed to identify him as such.'

'Then George is a fool,' she snapped. 'That man now under arrest in the Bristol bridewell is John Jericho. He may be six years older, but I'd know him anywhere. And Edward Micheldever agrees with me.'

'Your receiver would agree with you whatever you decided,' I retorted, 'and you know it.' She did know it. I could tell by the way she avoided my eyes. 'The steward's word is good enough for me.'

Dame Audrea had stopped pacing and come to rest in front of me. We were like two fencers about to cross swords. She raised her eyes to mine.

'Do I understand,' she asked finally, 'that you won't assist me in this matter unless I withdraw my accusation against your ... your half-brother, did you say?' I nodded. She turned and paced the room again. A full minute passed before she paused and returned to her former position. 'Very well.' The words were torn from her with the greatest reluctance. 'But I warn you, pedlar, if you fail to find my son's murderer, I'll have your kinsman's life, notwithstanding George's testimony to the contrary.'

Fifteen

I believed her. She was the kind of woman who kept her word.

'Very well,' I said. 'We understand one another. I'll do my very best to unmask Master Bellknapp's killer, and if I do so to your satisfaction, you'll drop your charge against John Wedmore. If I fail, your accusation will stand.' She nodded. 'In that case, I'll begin my investigation at once by asking you, Dame Audrea, to tell me where you were and what you were doing last night.'

'Me? Are you interrogating *me*?'

Her thin bosom swelled in righteous indignation and she drew herself up to the full extent of her not very imposing height. But in spite of these drawbacks, she could still look formidable. I was a head and more taller than she was, but I nonetheless felt like a small boy who has been shown the cane and told to stand in the corner. I took a deep breath to steady my nerve, and reminded myself that I must not be intimidated.

'Dame Audrea,' I pointed out firmly, 'you are as much under suspicion as anyone else. You cannot pretend that you found your elder son's sudden return a blessing. Indeed, his arrival ruined your best hopes of continuing to rule Croxcombe Manor – as you have no doubt ruled it since the death of your husband – for the rest of your life. Or at least for the foreseeable future. You have as much to gain from his death as anyone. You must, therefore, appreciate that I cannot exonerate you without being convinced that you did not commit this crime. Otherwise, there's no point in my proceeding with the enquiry.'

I thought for a moment that I had gone too far. The over-large nose and pointed chin quivered, the blue eyes snapped in anger. But the expected dismissal did not come. She was, after all, a fair-minded woman and was forced to acknowledge the truth of what I'd said. Grudgingly, she answered, 'I was in bed, of course, and asleep.'

'Can anyone – your maid for example – vouch for that?'

She shrugged. 'The girl has a truckle-bed in my room, certainly, but she sleeps like the dead. I might as well be honest and admit that whenever I get up in the night to use the piss-pot, which I frequently do – at my age that, I believe, is not uncommon – she never wakes. Doesn't even stir. So,' the Dame added ironically, 'whether or not she would know if I'd left the chamber, in order to murder Anthony, is debatable. She would undoubtedly confirm my presence, if she thought that was what I wanted her to say, but you would be none the wiser, my friend, as regards discovering the truth.'

I grimaced. 'Then I shall have to take your word, it seems.'

She relaxed a little. 'I assure you, you may do so. I will be frank, Master Chapman, and admit that Anthony's return after all these years was a bitter blow, not only for me, but also for Simon—'

'And for Master Kilsby?' I interrupted, beginning to recover my confidence.

To my surprise, a faint blush reddened the sallow cheeks. But it was a blush of anger, not embarrassment.

'So people have been gossiping, have they?' She answered her own question. 'Of course they have! How stupid of me to expect otherwise. Then let me say, here and now, that whatever hopes my bailiff may entertain of becoming my second husband, they are doomed to disappointment.'

'Does he know that?'

She thought about it for a second or two before giving a little snort of laughter.

'Probably not. But Reginald is an excellent bailiff and a good companion. I don't wish to lose him in either capacity.'

'Which you could do if he knew your true mind?'

'My daughter, Lady Chauntermerle, has been throwing out lures to him for some time. She and Sir Damien are dissatisfied with the man they have. However, we have strayed from the point.'

'Which is?'

'That, despite my resentment at Anthony's

return, I am not so unnatural a mother as deliberately to murder my own son. Nor would Simon kill his brother.'

I wasn't sure that I believed her on either count. There had been moments during our conversation when I had been almost totally convinced of her innocence, but a lingering doubt remained. And as for Simon, I was extremely dubious about him. All the same, I was inclined to share his mother's conviction that he had neither the strength nor the courage to perform such a deed; that he was a boaster and a coward, too frightened to risk his own skin. But I should gain no more for the present by continuing to question Dame Audrea. She had told me all that she was going to tell me for now – over the years, it was a state of mind I had grown to recognize in people – but she might be persuaded to talk more later.

I thanked her for sparing me her valuable time, and intimated by my manner and way of speaking that I had more or less dismissed any idea that she was Anthony's killer. I also hinted, from the things I didn't say, that I had accepted Simon's innocence. Her manner grew more affable and she even went so far as to express her appreciation of my willingness to return to Croxcombe.

'You will be wanting to pursue your enquiries elsewhere,' she said, waving a gracious hand as an indication that I could go. 'You may continue using Anthony's bed while you remain with us, but you will have to continue sharing the chamber with his manservant. Master Attleborough is keen to leave us, but I thought it safer to refuse him permission for the time being. God alone knows what deep resentment he might possibly have been harbouring against my son.'

'I assure you, Dame Audrea,' I smiled, 'that such an idea had already occurred to me.'

The dame inclined her head in approval. It was obvious that she would much prefer the killer to be an outsider, a stranger like Humphrey, whom she had never set eyes on until four days ago, than any member of her household.

'What will you do next?' she asked as I turned towards the door of the solar.

'I must speak to everyone in turn, although whether any of them will be as honest with me as you have been...' I let the rest of the sentence hang.

If Dame Audrea suspected me of irony, she disguised it very well. Her strong-featured face was expressionless as she wished me good luck. 'And I haven't forgotten our bargain,' she added.

Whether or not she would honour it, remained to be seen.

With my hand on the door latch, I was thrown violently backwards as someone forced his way into the room. One of my feet became hopelessly entangled with the other and I went sprawling amongst the rushes. From this undignified position, I looked up expecting to see Simon Bellknapp, and was astonished to find myself instead staring into the face of Thomas Bignell.

'Master Bignell, please explain this untoward conduct immediately,' hissed Dame Audrea. 'This is my private solar. I didn't even hear you knock, let alone receive permission to enter.'

It said much for the perturbation of the butcher's mind that he paid no attention to her. Indeed, I doubted that he had even noted the reprimand. He leaned down and helped me to my feet.

'Chapman, Humphrey Attleborough has just this minute told me of your return, and why. You are to investigate the murder of Master Bellknapp, is that not so?'

I was still tenderly feeling my person for damage and answered shortly, 'Yes.' Then, finding myself more or less intact, except for a couple of bruised elbows, which had suffered the brunt of my fall, I added, 'At Dame Audrea's request.'

Thomas Bignell suddenly seemed to take in his surroundings and the presence of his hostess.

'Madam! M-my apologies,' he gasped. 'I-I didn't realize that this is your personal chamber. Master Steward told me the chapman was here. He didn't say.'

Dame Audrea frowned. 'Well, now that you are here and have found Master Chapman, what is it you wish to tell him with such urgency?'

The butcher was trapped. He would plainly have preferred to speak to me in private, but there was nothing he could do about it. He had no option but to tell us both.

'It ... it's about Master Bellknapp,' he said uncomfortably, shifting from one foot to the other like a flea hopping amongst the rushes.

'What of Master Bellknapp?' I prodded, when he hesitated.

'Last night ... he ... he asked me to meet him. After everyone had gone to bed.'

'Why?' demanded Dame Audrea.

'Where?' I asked, almost in chorus.

'In the hall,' he replied, choosing to answer me.

Which left me with no alternative but to echo the dame's question, 'Why?'

'He ... he wanted to speak to me.' This was followed by another silence.

'What about?' I almost yelled. 'For God's sake, man! This is like squeezing blood from a stone.'

Master Bignell's discomfort increased. He scratched his head and continued to shuffle his feet until I was ready to do him bodily harm. But at last he managed to blurt out, 'About Rose and ... and Edward. He told me earlier in the evening that he thought Rose was unhappy in her marriage, and that maybe Ned was unkind to her. He said I should speak to Ned, or, if I didn't wish to, he offered to do it for me.'

Dame Audrea snorted in derision. 'He wanted her for himself, you foolish man! He

275

intended to make mischief between you and your son-in-law so that when he eventually managed to lure her away from Master Micheldever, you wouldn't cut her out of your will. You're known to be a very wealthy man.'

'But why, if he'd already said all that to you,' I asked, 'did Master Bellknapp want to meet you again after the rest of us were out of the way?'

'He ... he said there were things he needed to tell me that no one else must overhear.' The butcher coloured faintly. 'Intimate things concerning my daughter's marriage.'

'And you believed him?' I asked scathingly. 'Good God, man! Had your wits gone woolgathering? He'd only known Rose three days! What could he possibly have discovered in that time that nobody else would know?'

Thomas Bignell raised his chin. He resented my tone.

'Rose might well have confided in Master Bellknapp. There's no doubt he had a way with the women. Any fool could tell that. And,' he added even more belligerently, 'people, men and women, often do confide in strangers secrets that it might embarrass them to tell anyone close to them.'

'He has you there, Chapman,' Dame Audrea observed, as I struggled to find an answer to refute this statement. She turned to look at the butcher. 'And did you meet my son in the hall as you had arranged, Master Butcher?'

276

He nodded. 'I thought I should listen to what he had to say. If Ned is mistreating my Rose, I ought to know about it. So, when the house was quiet and it seemed that everyone was asleep, I got up, put on my bed-robe over my night shirt and went downstairs into the hall.'

'Was Master Bellknapp there?' I asked.

'He arrived a few minutes later.'

'And?' I was growing more and more frustrated. Thomas Bignell thought and spoke at the snail's pace of the true countryman. It made me realize again how long it was since I had lived there.

'Well, first, he admitted that he was the person who'd arranged to keep me at Croxcombe overnight. Then he said he thought there was someone still up and about. He felt sure he had heard someone moving, so it was better if we went outside where no one could overhear us. It was a warm night, so we'd take no harm. He said he'd just go out and look around to make certain there was no one there, and when he was satisfied he'd come back and fetch me.'

'And did he? Come back and fetch you?' I wanted to know, suspecting what his answer would be.

The butcher shook his head. 'No, he never returned.'

It was Dame Audrea who eventually broke the silence. 'Did you not wonder what had happened to him?'

'Of course I did. At first, I waited, thinking that perhaps someone had been outside and that Master Bellknapp had been forced to hide until whoever it was went back to bed...'

'No one came in through the hall?' I asked, but the butcher shook his head.

'No one. Nor did I see anyone about when I went to look for Master Bellknapp.'

'When you failed to find my son, what did you think had happened to him?' the dame asked.

I frowned at her, displeased. I felt I was losing control of this enquiry, and I didn't like it.

Thomas Bignell scratched his stomach and looked unhappy. 'I didn't know. I ... I just supposed he'd either changed his mind or had been playing a joke on me. After a while, I went back to bed.'

'You didn't search for Master Bellknapp?' This time, I made certain I was first with the question.

'Oh, I looked around a bit,' the butcher asserted. 'Of course I did. What do you take me for? I wandered about for some time, but I couldn't see him anywhere and it was getting chilly. So, like I said, I returned to bed. I thought Master Bellknapp would explain matters in the morning.'

'Did you walk along the moat at all?'

'Yes, a little way. And round by the stables and the animal pens and Dame Audrea's flower garden, but he was nowhere to be seen. He'd completely vanished.'

'Did you hear or see anything? Did you have any suspicion that someone else was out of doors last night?' I queried.

Thomas Bignell chewed his lower lip. 'I honestly don't know. I was extremely confused by that time. I couldn't work out what game Master Bellknapp was playing with me. If it was true that he really had gone to such lengths to keep me here at Croxcombe overnight, why had he suddenly disappeared without saying a word of what he wanted to tell me? To say truth' – the butcher shuffled his feet awkwardly and avoided Dame Audrea's eyes – 'I was beginning to get nervous. It – it crossed my mind that maybe it was all a ruse to do me some harm.'

'Why on earth would Anthony wish to do you harm?' the dame demanded. 'I'm not denying that he had a vicious streak in him – extremely vicious, as I've already told Master Chapman – but he had no grudge against you, Master Bignell.' Her eyes narrowed. 'On the other hand, did you have any reason to quarrel with him? We only have your word for Anthony's reason for wanting to speak privately with you. It might be that he was trying to warn you not about Master Micheldever's conduct, but about Rose's. I have frequently observed that she is far too familiar with other men; that she encourages their attentions. Maybe my son wished to bring this fact to your notice. Maybe you took exception to what he said and got angry. Angrier than you intended. Perhaps it was you who hit him on the back of the head and pushed him into the moat to drown.'

The butcher was aghast. 'No, no! I assure you! Everything happened exactly as I have described it.' He flushed a deep, dark red as the Dame's strictures on his daughter sank in. 'And my Rose is a good girl! A bit young and flighty as yet, but she'll settle down and be a good wife to Ned, you'll see. You've no cause to blacken her name like that.'

Dame Audrea was plainly unused to being addressed in such a forthright manner, and it was her turn to look deeply affronted. I stepped in quickly to avert a full-blown confrontation between them.

'Lady, it's too soon to be accusing anyone of Master Bellknapp's murder. You've called me back to investigate his death, so I suggest, with your permission, that I get on with doing just that. There are many people in this house who have openly expressed a desire to see your elder son dead, but, so far as I know, Master Bignell is not one of them. However, that doesn't necessarily make him innocent, as you have so rightly pointed out. But at present, I suspect everyone and no one.'

Dame Audrea hesitated, momentarily uncertain whether or not to take umbrage at what she undoubtedly saw as my impertinence, but in the end convinced herself that I had meant no offence and that little else could be expected from an ignorant pedlar. 'Very well,' she agreed. 'You may proceed.'

'And you haven't forgotten our bargain?' I

280

reminded her.

'I never forget bargains,' she snapped. 'My word is my word. But just remember that there are two sides to every bargain. Now, I have household tasks to see to. I shall leave you to your work.'

She swept out – there was no other word for it, the skirt of her gown billowing around her like a wind-filled sail – leaving Master Bignell and myself in possession of the solar.

'I – I've told you the truth, Master Chapman,' the butcher stammered. He put a hand to his forehead. 'Do you think ... I mean, is it possible that Anthony Bellknapp was being murdered while I was waiting for him in the hall?' He turned even paler than he was already. 'Or even while I was outside looking for him?'

There was no point in trying to spare his feelings.

'I'm afraid so,' I said.

He gave a gasp and his knees seemed ready to buckle. He was either genuinely distressed or a brilliant dissimulator. On the whole, I was inclined to the first opinion and to eliminate him from my list of suspects. He had not intended to stay the previous night at Croxcombe and, apparently on Anthony's own confession, had been tricked into remaining. But before I could suggest that the family was allowed to depart and return home to Wells, I needed to speak to both Ronan Bignell and his mother.

They were waiting anxiously outside, seated

on the bench beneath the hall window, and Mistress Bignell rose in some agitation as we approached. She told me, without being asked, that the three of them, her husband, her son and herself, had shared the same bed and that Thomas had confided in them from the start about his nocturnal meeting with Anthony Bellknapp, and the reason for it.

'You didn't advise against it?' I asked.

'Of course not. If Ned Micheldever is being unkind to our Rose, we ought to know about it.'

'If it's true, he'll have me to reckon with,' grunted Ronan.

His mother hushed him. 'To be honest, Chapman, I don't know that I believed Master Bellknapp, but Thomas had to listen to what he had to say, now didn't he? But why it had to be said in such secrecy, I'm sure I don't know.'

Neither did I, and it was something that bothered me more than a little.

'When Master Bignell returned and told you what had happened, what did you think?'

The goodwife shook her head. 'I didn't know what to think. I suppose I thought it some kind of a joke on Master Bellknapp's part. It never entered my head that any harm could have come to him.'

'And your son didn't leave the bedchamber while your husband was away?'

She shook her head. I thanked her and promised to speak to Dame Audrea about permitting the three of them to leave. Then I went back into the hall, where Anthony's shrouded form was laid out on one of the trestle tables. George Applegarth was keeping watch beside it. As I drew near, he raised his eyes to mine and I saw from his puffy lids and the tear stains on his cheeks that he had been crying.

We stared at each other for a long moment across the body. Then, without being asked, the steward pulled back the covering sheet and turned the head to one side so that I could see for myself the bloody contusion at the base of the skull.

'What was it done with, do you think?'

'A very heavy weapon.' His tone was dry, as one answering a foolish question.

'Do you know of such a weapon?'

He shrugged. 'A good-sized tree branch would have been sufficient. Or an iron skillet from the kitchen. Or one of those heavy-based brass pots that Dame Audrea occasionally uses for flowers that she brings into the house. There must be any number of things that could have been used.' He gave me a wintry smile. 'And if you're going to ask me where I was last night and what I was doing, I can only say that I was asleep in my bed. But if you ask me to prove it, I cannot. I have no witness. Nor have had,' he added bitterly, 'since my Jenny died.'

He stayed a moment or two longer, staring down into the dead man's face, before drawing the sheet over it again.

'So' – he raised his head with a challenging

look – 'what have you discovered so far, Master Chapman?'

I informed him of Master Bignell's part in the night's proceedings, and saw him frown.

'You think it an unlikely story?'

The steward grimaced. 'Perhaps. But I see no reason why Master Bignell should make it up, unless...' He did not finish the sentence.

'Not the obvious killer, surely?' I queried. 'There are at least four or five others in this house who have far better reasons for wanting Anthony dead than the butcher and his family.'

George Applegarth smiled faintly. 'Very true. But murder is sometimes done on impulse.'

'I agree. But not, I think, in this case. The Bignells were tricked into remaining at Croxcombe last night, and if Thomas Bignell is to be believed, it was Anthony's doing.'

'And is he to be believed, do you think?'

'That's easily discovered. I shall visit Hamo Gough before supper and ask him who paid him to arrange the deception. There's no reason that I can see, not now that Master Bellknapp's dead, why Hamo shouldn't admit the truth.' I paused, biting my inner lip and frowning.

'Is something bothering you?' the steward asked.

I hesitated, deliberating whether or not to share my doubts with a man whose opinion and judgement I valued; but in the end, I decided against it. It was better to keep my own counsel for the present at least. But I felt in my bones that there was something wrong with Master Bignell's version of events; not in itself, for I was convinced that he had told the truth as far as he knew it. But his wife had unerringly put her finger on the story's weakness when she asked why Anthony Bellknapp had needed to arrange a meeting with Thomas after everyone else was in bed. Whatever he had had to say regarding Rose's marriage to the receiver, could as well have been said during the day, when they had been walking together beside the moat. It didn't make sense. And I felt sure that only when it did, would I be able to discover the identity of the murderer.

Sixteen

It was by now mid-afternoon and I set off to see Hamo Gough without wasting any more time. George Applegarth seemed unaffected by my decision not to confide in him; in fact, if anything, he appeared relieved by my departure, merely remarking that he would get Reginald Kilsby to help him carry Anthony's body into the chapel and place it before the altar, as Dame Audrea had requested. I said I hoped to be back by suppertime, and would he inform the rest of the household members that I would want to speak to them that evening.

I took my cudgel and Hercules and set off, past the huddled shapes of the cottages in the nearby hamlet towards the darker, shapeless mass of Croxcombe woods. A sudden, brief shower of rain, over almost before it had begun, left water droplets sparkling everywhere and the sun gilding the edges of the leaves with haloes of soft, wet light. A few cottagers and coppicers gave me good-day as I passed; and a young man in a green velvet hunting coat and white leather boots, a hawk on his gloved wrist and silver bells on its jesses, raised his riding crop in salutation. A couple of good hounds pranced at his heels, to whose proudly waving tails and mincing ways Hercules took immediate exception, but I managed to grab him before his annoyance blossomed into a full-blown confrontation.

I had not expected Hamo Gough to be at home, and had been prepared to wait until his return, but he was there, crouched over his fire in the act of replacing the squares of turf over the smouldering wood. He straightened up at the sound of my approach – Hercules had spied the scut of a rabbit disappearing into the long grass that fringed the edge of the clearing and was barking like a fiend – and gave me a long, hard look.

'I thought thee'd be round,' he remarked, unsurprised.

'As a matter of fact I was on my way home

to Bristol when Dame Audrea sent after me. You've heard the news of Master Bellknapp's death, then?'

The charcoal burner grunted, indicating the pit at his feet. 'This lot's nearly ready, I reckon. Another day should do it.' He reverted to the subject of Anthony's murder. 'Thee can't keep a thing like that secret.'

'Dame Audrea's hoping to,' I pointed out. 'That's why she's called me back. I have her blessing to ask questions of whomsoever I please.'

He gave a short bark of laughter. 'I weren't meaning the law, Maister. Thee can keep anything from those fools if thee's a mind to. So, hast come to question me?'

'If you're willing.'

'What dost want to know?'

'Well, I know, for instance, that you arranged for someone to call at the manor yesterday and tell Thomas Bignell, his wife and son that they couldn't get home to Wells last night because of a footbridge washed away in the afternoon's storm, so forcing them to remain at Croxcombe. I was in the woods later in the day and overheard your conversation with your fellow conspirator. What I want to know is the name of the person who put you up to it. Was it Anthony Bellknapp?' I wondered if he would tell me the truth, which I already knew.

Hamo Gough pondered for a moment or two, sucking his blackened stumps of teeth, then he shrugged.

287

'No reason not to tell thee now, I s'pose. Ay, it were him. Appeared just after thee'd left, yesterday morning. Thought I'd heard someone prowling about while we were talking. Said 'e wanted to keep Master Bignell at the manor overnight. Could I do summat to make sure it happened.'

'Did he say why?'

'Why what?'

'Why he wanted the butcher to stay at the manor for the night,' I answered impatiently.

'No.'

'Didn't you ask him?'

'No. None o' my business. Besides, if thee doesn't ask, thee doesn't get told, and if it's anything to do with the Bellknapps, it's best not to know. Leastways, I've always found so.'

I sighed. I could tell that there was no more to be got out of Hamo on that score. But I was still curious about his digging activities.

'The night Jenny Applegarth was murdered,' I said, 'did you see anything?'

He was at once on his guard. I could see the wariness in his narrowed eyes and the tensing of his body, like an animal scenting danger.

'What would I have seen?' His tone was belligerent.

'I'm asking you.'

'Then thee can ask away. I'm saying nowt.'

'Does that mean you could tell me something, but won't?'

He shrugged. 'Think what thee likes. No odds to me.'

He compressed his lips and folded his arms

across his chest with a finality that said more than words. But I gave it one more try.

'You keep looking for something around Hangman's Oak. Ronan Bignell and his two friends saw you surveying the ground there the night following the murder, and a few days or so afterwards, Ronan met you carrying a spade.'

'I digs for truffles, don' I?' Hamo spat angrily. 'I told thee. Besides, thee doesn't want t' believe anything those three thieving monkeys tell thee.'

'I've seen you digging near the oak, myself.'

He fairly bounced up and down with rage.

'Truffles! Truffles!' he shouted. 'I digs for truffles!' Hercules, who, up to then, had been minding his own business, objected to the charcoal burner's tone and growled menacingly. Hamo recoiled. 'Keep him off me, dost hear?'

I admonished the dog, who then started barking at me, just to let me know what sort of a lily-livered milksop he thought I was before suddenly spotting a rat scurrying inside the hut through the open doorway. He shot after his quarry like an arrow speeding from a bow and, a moment later, the air was rent by a medley of shrill canine screams and yaps as he attempted to come to grips with his enemy.

I raised my voice a little in order to make myself heard.

'The night of Jenny Applegarth's murder, did you see the page, this John Jericho, reeling around as if he were drunk and being sick?'

'That were six year gone. Why art askin' me about Jenny Applegarth's murder? I thought it were Anthony Bellknapp thou'rt interested in.'

I hesitated. I didn't really know why myself, except for a growing conviction that the two were somehow connected. Yet I didn't see how they could be. But a memory niggled at the back of my mind; there was something I knew I ought to remember.

But the crescendo of noise from within the hut had now reached a pitch it was impossible to ignore and, abandoning our game of question and answer, Hamo and I, by mutual consent, rushed inside just in time to witness the kill as Hercules seized the rat and bit it clean through the neck with his sharp little teeth. He then laid his trophy at my feet with a proud wave of his tail.

Normally, I would have commended his efforts, but on this occasion he had completely demolished the charcoal burner's bed in pursuit of his opponent. The layers of dried bracken and leaves and parched summer grasses that had been carefully built up over the years to make a decent mattress lay scattered over the floor. The smell of mould and decay and long dead seasons, together with the dust of ages, filled the little room. A number of small, bleached-white skeletons indicated that various woodland animals had lived out their lives and met their deaths within the bed, while a nest of baby rats, waiting for the mother who would now never return, was receiving Hercules's best attentions.

Hamo Gough stared about him in dumb fury at the wreck of his sleeping quarters, several times opening and shutting his mouth like a stranded fish, in speechless indignation. I decided it was politic to leave before he could express his anger with his fists. And although I could easily have beaten him if it came to a fight, my heart would not have been in it. I wished him a brief good-day, whistled to Hercules and prepared to go. As I did so, I tripped over the grey blanket that had been Hamo's covering, but now lay, a torn and sorry mess, among the debris of the mattress. I stooped to retrieve it – it, at least, was not past salvaging – but realized as I did so that it was not really a blanket, as I had formerly assumed, but a cloak. And its original colour had been pale blue, not grey, although it had weathered to its present shade probably over a period of years exposed to the strong sunlight that poured in through the open door of the hut during the summer months.

But the thing that really arrested my attention was a shield embroidered in faded scarlet silk on what proved, when the garment was held the right way up, to be the left shoulder of the cloak. Inside the outline of the shield was a bell, oversewn in satin stitch to form, when new, a solid block of colour. It suddenly dawned on me that I had seen this badge many times in the past three days since arriving at Croxcombe Manor: it was the badge of the Bellknapp family and adorned the livery of their servants. I shook out the cloak and held it up with both hands. It had not been made for a tall man, nor one of any great girth. Nor, I suspected, had it been worn for a very long time. Six years, perhaps?

The cloak was rudely snatched from me, and I spun round to find Hamo Gough looking positively murderous.

'Get out!' he roared. 'Thee and that bloody dog o' thine! Get out! Get out!'

He turned and reached for his spade, which was propped against the wall in one corner of the hut. I yelled at Hercules to follow me and ran.

He came after us, but we were too quick for him, my legs being longer and stronger; while Hercules, giving one last, defiant bark, outstripped me in the desire to save his hide. Finally, when I decided we were no longer being pursued, we eased up, trying, as we passed the cottages and duck pond, to look more like a man and his dog out for a late afternoon stroll.

I felt convinced in my own mind – but without a shred of proof – that the cloak had belonged to the missing page, and that there had been some link between him and the charcoal burner. But what that link was, I was no nearer knowing than before.

Supper was an awkward meal. Everyone avoided looking directly at any other person, and suspicion and unspoken accusations hung in the air, poisoning the atmosphere. Only the steward seemed unperturbed as he went about his official duties, attending to the comfort of both the household members and the guests – three pilgrims returning home to Southampton after visiting Glastonbury – who had begged sustenance and shelter for the night. Their presence was at once a blessing and a curse; the former because it ensured that we were all on our best behaviour, the latter because no one could discuss the topic uppermost in everyone's mind. The visitors had been informed that it was a house of mourning and were consequently very subdued, providing none of the merriment and anecdotes of the wider world that usually enlivened a stranger's visit. I noted that the Bignells were still with us, and, upon enquiry, Thomas informed me that they had decided to remain another night at Rose's urgent request.

'She's been having fits of the vapours all day,' he confided in a low voice, ladling another helping of pike in a galentyne sauce on to his plate and shovelling it into his mouth like a man whose appetite remained unaffected by sudden death or family problems. 'Maybe there was something in what Master Bellknapp wanted to tell me, after all.'

When the meal was finished and the three pilgrims had been shown to the guest chamber, I sought out Dame Audrea and again asked her permission to speak in turn to the other members of the household.

'I've already told you to do whatever you deem fit,' she said coldly. 'But don't forget young Master Attleborough.'

I promised that I would see him first, but warned the dame I thought it unlikely that he was the murderer.

'I think he would have run away by now. He had his chance when you sent him to fetch me back this morning.'

Nevertheless, I sought him out almost at once, George Applegarth having informed me Humphrey had retired to the chamber we had both shared, until sometime last night, with the murdered man. I found him sitting on the edge of his truckle-bed, his head propped despondently in his hands.

'What am I going to do now, Chapman?' he asked, tears welling up in his eyes. 'Here I am, far from my native county, robbed of my master and not likely to find another half as good anywhere else.'

I sat down facing him, on the big four-poster bed with its hangings depicting the story of Diana and Actaeon.

Not knowing the answer, I ignored this heartfelt plea and asked, 'When you fetched the all-night from the kitchen yesterday evening, your master was already here, in the bedchamber, when you arrived?'

Humphrey blinked stupidly at me for a moment or two, taken aback by the abrupt change of subject. Then he nodded.

'I think so ... Yes, he was. I remember now.

He was undressed, with his bed-robe over his night-rail.'

'Did he drink any of the wine?'

Again there was a pause while Humphrey thought – a distinctly slow process.

'Yes,' he said at last. 'He had a beaker almost straight away. He said he was thirsty. Then he had another one.'

'And after that? Did he touch the wine again?'

'I don't suppose so. He didn't usually drink as much as that before going to bed. Said too much wine gave him bad dreams. But last night, it was as if...'

'As if what?'

'I don't know. Nothing really. Just a stupid idea that came into my head at the time.'

'Go on!'

'Well...' Humphrey was reluctant to tell me. 'Is it important?'

'It might be. Anything might be important if you want to unmask the murderer.'

'All right. It just occurred to me that he was making up his mind to something he had to do. The wine was giving him courage.'

It was my turn to nod. 'And what were you doing while he was drinking the wine?'

'I stripped off, ready for bed.'

'So while you were undressing, you didn't have your eyes fixed on Master Bellknapp all the time?'

'I suppose not. Why?'

'So you might not have noticed if he'd slipped a sleeping potion into the jug? Poppy

295

and lettuce juice, for instance.'

'Why would he do that?'

'To make sure we both slept soundly and didn't wake when he left the bedchamber to meet Master Bignell. Did you have any of the wine?'

Humphrey nodded slowly, a frown creasing his brow.

'Yes … Yes, I did. One beakerful. I … I thought I felt strangely heavy when I woke up this morning, and although I couldn't remember them in detail, I knew I'd had peculiar dreams. I felt sick, too, and I'd over-slept. It was well past sunrise. But I never thought I might have been drugged. I just thought something I'd eaten at supper had disagreed with me. I'm still not sure I believe it.'

I recounted the symptoms I myself had suffered, and, after a while, he became convinced they were the same as the ones he had experienced.

'But I still don't understand why the master would have gone to all that trouble if all he wanted was to talk to Master Bignell. There was no harm in that. He could have told me. He could have told you. It was none of our business if he wanted to speak to the butcher. We wouldn't have spied on him.'

'Maybe he wasn't convinced of that,' I suggested. But I didn't really believe it. There was a mystery here that I had not as yet un-ravelled. I added, but without much hope of a positive answer, 'Is there anything you can recollect – anything at all – that your master did or said yesterday that struck you as odd?'

Much to my surprise, after a few seconds' hesitation, Humphrey once again nodded.

'Yes. It was sometime after Mass, but before dinner, I think. I can't remember exactly, but it doesn't really matter. But it must have been after you came back from your early morning jaunt to Croxcombe woods.'

'Why?' I enquired when he paused once more.

'Because I came across Master Bellknapp round by the stables with your cudgel in his hands. He was sort of weighing it, as though he was testing its strength or seeing how heavy it was.'

'Did you ask him what he was doing with it?'

'I didn't ask him exactly – he never encouraged me to be too forward – but he saw me looking and laughed a bit, like he was embarrassed. "A fine cudgel, this," he said. And I said, "It's Master Chapman's, isn't it?" and he said, "Yes. He left it in the hall this morning when he came in."'

I thought back to my return to Croxcombe woods. I had encountered the Bignells and accompanied them into the house before taking Hercules to the kitchens to be petted and made much of by the maids. I had a vague recollection of leaving my cudgel somewhere, and an even vaguer one of taking it with me when I returned to Croxcombe woods later in the afternoon.

'And did your master tell you what he was up to?' I asked.

Humphrey shrugged. 'Not really. He told me to take it and put it back by the door, where he'd found it. The one at the back of the dais that opens into the kitchen passageway. So I did. He went off to look for Master and Mistress Bignell.'

I said nothing, but sat staring thoughtfully out of the open window where the shadows were lengthening and the bright banners of the setting sun gilding the evening sky. Knowing what I did, that my cudgel had been the murder weapon that had struck Anthony Bellknapp the fatal blow before he was tumbled into the moat, I was even more confused than I had been before. Humphrey's information suggested that Anthony was the potential murderer, not the victim.

I thanked the lad and tried to cheer him up by advising him to apply to Dame Audrea for enough funds to see him safely home.

'But not until I've discovered the identity of her son's murderer for her. She won't let you leave until then.'

'Why not?' He was instantly alarmed. 'She doesn't suspect me, does she? Do you?'

'Not really,' I said, patting him soothingly on the shoulder. 'But the dame would prefer it to be you.'

He was no fool: he could work out why for himself and looked frightened. 'You will be able to prove it wasn't me, won't you?' I slid off the bed. 'Where are you going?'

'I'm going to talk to Thomas Bignell again. Meantime, stop worrying. No one can accuse you without proving that you had a reason to do away with your master.'

'I didn't!'

I smiled at him in what I hoped was an enigmatic way and left the room.

The Bignells had not yet retired to bed and were sitting with Rose and their son-in-law at the high table in the hall, watching in silence as the last of the day's rushes were cleared away by the servants and fresh ones laid down for the morning. Also of the party were Reginald Kilsby, the bailiff, whose dismissal seemed to have been rescinded in the wake of Anthony's death, and Jonathan Slye, the chamberlain. I pulled up a stool and forced myself in between Edward Micheldever and the butcher.

'What do you want?' the receiver grunted angrily. 'What's brought you back here, to Croxcombe?'

'Dame Audrea asked me to return,' I answered calmly. 'She wants to know which one of you villains killed her son.'

'I suppose you think that's funny,' growled the bailiff, half rising from his seat.

'No. Although I am known for my sense of humour. The sorry fact is that you and Master Slye and Master Micheldever here all had reason to wish Anthony Bellknapp dead.'

'That doesn't mean to say we murdered him,' the chamberlain protested.

'Not all of you, no. But one of you might have been goaded too far.'

But now *I* had gone too far. Edward Micheldever was on his feet, hands balled into fists, inviting me to step outside. He was a solidly built, pugnacious man. I declined his invitation.

'Sit down,' I said, trying to sound authoritative, 'and don't be a fool. I'm not accusing anyone. If you can tell me where you were last night, and prove it, I shall be satisfied. So will Dame Audrea.'

'I was in bed with Rose,' Edward answered promptly, 'and she'll tell you so. Rose!'

Rose smiled tremulously. 'It's true,' she concurred.

Well, she would, wouldn't she? It didn't really prove her husband's innocence, except that what little I knew of Rose had convinced me that she was not a good liar. And there was no faltering glance, no hesitation in the voice. 'It's true,' she emphasized, holding my gaze steadily.

I nodded my acceptance and turned my attention to the chamberlain. 'Master Slye?'

The thick neck turned red and he shifted his burly body in his chair so that he could fix me with his ice-cold stare more easily.

'I, too, was in bed, although I haven't a wife to prove it. But if you ask the little kitchen maid with the wart on her chin I'm sure she'll back up my story.' He grinned in a lascivious way that, for some reason, made me feel hot and uncomfortable, and I saw the bailiff

300

glance sideways at him with a contemptuous curl of his lip.

'I shall ask the young woman,' I said, 'but I feel sure that if she knows what's good for her, she will agree with what you've just told me.'

'It's true!' Jonathan Slye expostulated angrily, going an even darker shade of red.

I suspected that it was, but made no answer, turning my attention to Reginald Kilsby.

'I see you're still here, Master Bailiff. Are you able to account for your whereabouts last night?'

'Of course I'm still here,' he blustered. 'There was never any doubt that I would be.' I raised my eyebrows. 'Dame Audrea had no intention of permitting Anthony to dismiss me. She would have intervened.'

'Somebody most certainly intervened,' I said drily. 'So, what about last night? Were you also in bed?'

'Naturally. Where else should I have been?' He added nastily, 'And where were you, Master Chapman? And can you prove it? Why should we be subjected to your interrogation and not you to ours?'

He had me there, but when forced on to the defensive, the best thing to do is attack.

'I am acting on the authority of Dame Audrea,' I said with as much pomposity as I could manage. 'She wants to discover her son's killer, and she knows that I had no reason to wish him harm.'

I could see a retort hovering on the tip of

the bailiff's tongue, but he wisely left it to the receiver to voice it.

'And what about Dame Audrea herself?' Edward Micheldever demanded. 'And Master Simon?'

'Your mistress protests her innocence, like the rest of you. I haven't yet spoken to Simon.' I addressed the butcher. 'Master Bignell, it's still warm out of doors and not yet completely dark. I wonder if you'd take a walk with me. I could do with some fresh air.'

Mistress Bignell laid a hand on her husband's arm, looking uneasy. 'Don't go, my dear, if you don't want to.'

The butcher smiled and patted her hand. 'Why ever not? I'm quite safe with Master Chapman.' He got to his feet.

So did Ronan. 'I'll come, too,' he said. His tone was aggressive.

'You're more than welcome,' I told him. 'You can all come if you like. It's a balmy evening.'

I guessed that a general invitation was a certain way of discouraging the rest of the company, and I wasn't disappointed. Only the butcher and his son followed me out of the hall.

We strolled across the dew-damp grass to the edge of the moat, sulky and sluggish now in the waning light. Behind us, the windows of the house suddenly blossomed with candle flames as the servants went from room to room lighting the wicks. From the stables sounded the shifting of hooves and the neigh of a horse as the animals settled themselves for the approaching night. There was a burst of laughter, quickly suppressed, from the kitchen quarters. Somewhere a dog barked, swiftly answered by another and then another. A man's voice shouted and there was the thud of something being thrown; then all was silence.

'Well, Master Chapman,' the butcher said at last, 'what do you want to ask me that you don't want the others to hear? Because I don't flatter myself for a minute that you've invited me out here for the pleasure of my company.'

I laughed. 'You underestimate yourself, sir. But no, you're right. There is something I wish to ask you. When you kept your rendezvous with Anthony Bellknapp in the hall last night, did you notice if he had a cudgel with him?'

Seventeen

His answer was immediate and without prevarication.

'Oh yes! I didn't think anything of it at the time. But now you mention it, I suppose it was odd. Surely he wasn't afraid that I would attack him?'

'I don't know what he thought,' I said slowly. 'I'm not at all certain what he was up to. You ... You didn't happen to recognize the cudgel, I suppose?'

The butcher frowned. 'Well ... I've told you that I thought nothing of it then, but looking back ... Was it your cudgel by any chance? I've noticed yours is weighted at the base, as this one was. I can recall that when Master Bell-knapp swung it to and fro, it was rather like a pendulum swinging.'

'It could have been,' I agreed cautiously, not yet prepared to admit what I knew to be the truth. 'I had it in the bedchamber that I shared with Anthony and his man. It would have been a simple enough matter for him to take it with him when he went to meet you. But why he would have done so is another matter.'

The three of us continued our stroll as the

light dimmed still further, the wild flowers growing amid the tall grasses at the edge of the moat waving like pale flames in the dusk. The swans had long since gone to rest and the water gleamed grey and cold, like the steel of a naked sword. The trees stretched groping fingers towards the darkening sky and Ronan Bignell shivered suddenly.

'It was about here that Humphrey Attleborough found Master Bellknapp's body,' he said, pointing to a clump of bushes that formed a sort of sheltered arbour near the bank. 'He'd been out looking for his master and came running back into the house shouting that he was dead. Drowned, he said at first, and we all rushed out to see for ourselves. But when the steward turned the body over, we could see that it wasn't an accident, but murder.'

Thomas Bignell nodded. 'Someone had hit him a swingeing blow to the back of his head, then he'd either fallen or been pushed into the water.'

I held my breath, expecting the butcher to make the connection between the cudgel – my cudgel – that Anthony had been carrying and the weapon by which he had met his death. I was still confused as to why he had taken it in the first place if all he had wanted was a quiet talk with Master Bignell about the butcher's daughter and son-in-law, and why he had considered it necessary to drug both me and Humphrey. But a faint light was beginning to glimmer at the end of what appeared to be a long and very dark tunnel.

It was growing cold and, turning, I suggested that we start to retrace our steps.

'Is that all you wanted to ask me?' Master Bignell sounded disappointed. 'About the cudgel?' And Ronan muttered something about it not having been worthwhile to leave the comfort of the hall.

'Master Bignell,' I said, 'you told me once that you thought you might have recognized the horseman you saw near Croxcombe Manor on the night of Jenny Applegarth's murder. Do you know who it was?'

The butcher stared at me through the gloom, looking, as far as I could see, somewhat at a loss. But he was not as simple as he liked to make out and was quicker than his son on the uptake.

Ronan demanded, 'What's that to do with anything?'

But his father, after a brief pause, asked, 'Do you think that the two murders are connected?'

'They might be.' I spoke hesitantly as one catching at straws, not wishing to make a fool of myself by any firmer declaration. 'So, do you have any idea who the man could have been?'

The butcher sighed regretfully. 'If I said as much as that, then I'm sorry to have misled you. In my own defence, I have to say that there was a moment recently when I thought it could have been Master Simon, but it's all so long ago and the more I turn it over in my mind, the less certain I am that I saw any likeness to anyone. I must apologize again for raising your hopes. Does it matter?'

I shook my head, swallowing my disappointment, as we re-entered the candlelit hall. This was now deserted, except for Mistress Bignell, our other erstwhile companions having presumably taken themselves off to bed, a fact that the lady confirmed when asked.

'And it's time we were asleep, too, my love,' she said, taking her husband's arm. 'I've spoken to Dame Audrea while you were outside with the chapman, and she agrees that we may return home tomorrow, provided we agree to remain as quiet as possible for the present concerning the true circumstances of Master Bellknapp's death. She intends that Sir Henry shall conduct the funeral rites and the body be buried as soon as may be. The family vault in the church will be opened up in the morning and Master Anthony laid to rest by evening. She counts on our discretion. And,' Mistress Bignell added with more dryness than I would have thought her capable of, 'she suggests that we supply the manor with an additional two carcasses a week, preferably two young, tender porkers.'

Thomas Bignell gave no sign, not so much as by the flicker of an eyelid, that he recognized this offer for what it was, saying simply, 'That's very gracious of Dame Audrea and I shall tell her so before we take our leave of her tomorrow.' He turned to me, holding out his hand. 'In case we don't see one another again, Master Chapman, I'll say goodnight and goodbye. If you're ever in Wells, you must visit us.' He appealed to his wife. 'We shall expect it, shan't we, my dear?' Then without waiting for her assent, he went on, 'Now, we must go and find Rose and Ned and see if we can sort things out between them before we go. For my own part, I don't suspect there's anything seriously amiss. Nothing that recent events won't have remedied.'

This tactful way of referring to Anthony's death at first amused, but then made me uneasy. Was I overlooking the obvious? Was I naive in not being more suspicious of the butcher as the killer of the murdered man? He had both a motive (of sorts) and the opportunity. Furthermore, he was used to killing, no doubt slaughtering many of his own animals in order to ensure the freshness of his meat. But as I watched him quit the hall in search of his daughter, closely followed by his wife and son, I couldn't bring myself to think him guilty. There were other thoughts, other suspicions floating around in my mind like the pieces of flotsam they might well turn out to be, and in any case, I knew where to find the Bignells if I had cause to change my mind.

I went to look for Simon Bellknapp.

I was informed by the steward that he was already abed, but in spite of the lateness of the hour, he returned a grudging message by

George Applegarth – who had volunteered to be my messenger – that he would see me if he must.

His bedchamber was next to Dame Audrea's, an arrangement that I guessed had pertained since childhood; a small, stuffy room overburdened with furniture and with a row of wooden toys – horses, soldiers, cup-and-ball and even a tiny, jointed doll – arranged on a shelf alongside his bed. This was a large four-poster, far bigger than that needed by a solitary person, with dark red canopy and curtains and with numerous little drawers and cupboards let into the bedhead. (I had seen another like it some years before, in a house in Glastonbury, and presumed therefore that they were both the work of a local craftsman.)

Simon himself was sitting up, propped against the pillows. He was still very pale and his broken arm obviously continued to give him pain, a fact which might account for his unusually sour expression – sourer even than was customary for him – although I doubted this. He was not pleased to see me, and I suspected that he had been persuaded against his will by George Applegarth to give me audience. He was certainly on the defensive, as his opening remark clearly indicated.

'I didn't kill Anthony, so you can just go away and leave me alone. I'm master here again now, and I don't have to answer to you or anyone.'

I raised my eyebrows. 'Not even to your

lady mother? I think she'd argue with that, don't you? And I have her permission to question whomsoever I please.'

He snorted so vehemently that the flame of his bedside candle guttered in the draught, but I noted that he didn't contradict me. Instead, his eyes suddenly narrowed and he went on the attack.

'What about you?' he demanded nastily. 'How do I know – how do any of us know – that you're not my brother's murderer?'

'And why would I have wanted to kill Master Bellknapp?' I asked quietly.

He shrugged, pouting angrily. 'How can I tell? But I consider it very odd you turning up here the very same day that Anthony re-appeared after eight years' absence.'

'Coincidence,' I said. Or divine interference in my affairs. But I didn't risk saying that to Simon, lest he accuse me of blasphemy. And I was beginning to wonder myself if, in this case, it were true. I hadn't been able to save Anthony Bellknapp from a violent death, but maybe that had not been God's purpose.

Simon made no reply, but continued looking sulky and unconvinced. 'I still think it's strange,' he flung at me defiantly.

I ignored this. 'You, on the other hand,' I pointed out, 'had all the reason in the world to get rid of your brother. You made no secret of the fact that you wanted him dead from the moment of his return.'

The young man patted his broken arm. 'How could I have killed him with this?' he demanded truculently. 'Try not to be a bigger fool than you look, Chapman. Although that might be hard, I agree.'

I refused to let myself be riled.

'Your left arm,' I said. 'There's nothing wrong with your right. And you're right-handed.'

But even as I spoke, I silently acknowledged the fact that his injury would have proved a major difficulty to overcome. Whoever had wrested the cudgel from Anthony Bellknapp would have had to move swiftly to retain the element of surprise and to strike before the other man realized his intention. It would have needed two hands to swing my cudgel with the necessary force, and an accuracy of aim hardly achievable with the use of only one arm. Reluctantly, I relinquished the idea of Simon as his brother's murderer. Not that I was going to tell him that, at least not in so many words, although, if sharp enough, he might deduce it from the slight alteration in my manner.

So I abruptly changed the subject, a tactic I had often found disconcerted people and threw them off their guard.

'Do you remember any of the details of Jenny Applegarth's murder?' I asked.

'Wh-what?' he stuttered, blinking rapidly. 'Jenny Apple... No. I wasn't here. A-and what's that got to do with... ?' He tailed off, staring at me stupidly. Next moment, however, his native cunning and intelligence reasserted themselves. 'You think there's a link between them,' he accused me.

By now it was dark outside, the glimpse of sky beyond the still-open shutters a faded black, against which were sketched the inkier shadows of the distant trees. An owl hooted as it swooped past the window in search of prey. The shadows in the room were lengthening, inching forward until Simon Bellknapp and I were islanded in the pool of light thrown by the solitary candle.

'I was at Kewstoke Hall with my parents,' my companion continued, 'visiting my sister and brother-in-law.'

I nodded. 'And, as I understand it, all the household officers had accompanied your father and mother with the exception of the Applegarths and Dame Audrea's page.'

'Yes. John Jericho. I remember him.'

'What do you remember? Would you have thought him capable of robbery and murder?'

'I don't think I thought much about him at all. It must be all of six years ago. I wasn't much more than nine. He was just another servant.'

The sneering, dismissive tone angered me, but I was determined to hold on to my temper and not give rein to it.

'Then you can't help me,' I said, and turned to go. 'I'll wish you goodnight, Master Bellknapp, and pleasant dreams.'

'Wait!' His curiosity had been aroused, and now that I appeared to have abandoned the thornier subject of Anthony's murder, he was more willing to talk. 'It's perfectly true, I don't recall a lot about John Jericho – like many other people, I thought that a silly, made-up name – except that he was small and dark and was always disgustingly cheerful. I recollect that once, Mother had him quite severely beaten for some misdemeanour or another – I can't remember what – and he just laughed when it was over, as cocky as ever.'

'Who administered the beating? Can you remember?'

Simon shook his head. 'But it was probably Jenny Applegarth. She'd been our nurse, Anthony's and mine – I suppose she still was mine at the time, although Father declared I was growing too old for petticoat government – and she could always give a thrashing when she thought it was deserved.' He spoke with a certain venom, as if he hadn't shared his dead brother's affection for their former nurse. 'Mother could well have turned the page over to her for punishment.'

Here was something new to think about. 'Would he have resented it?' I asked.

'I told you, he didn't seem to. But who knows what people are feeling secretly?' Simon settled himself more comfortably against the banked-up pillows and eased his splinted arm into a different position, although not without a wince of pain. 'Perhaps that's why he killed her when he got the chance. When she caught him stealing the household plate and the jewels my mother had left behind, he couldn't resist the temptation to avenge his humiliation.'

An unplanned murder was how I had always visualized it, but until that moment, I had thought it was because the page could not risk leaving behind a witness to his guilt. Yet now I came to consider it more carefully, there never had been any doubt in anyone's mind as to who had committed the crime: John Jericho's flight had made that all too certain. And the killing of a woman, attempting to preserve her employers' property, had only made matters a thousand times worse for him. A moment of uncontrolled vindictiveness, however, offered a more reasonable solution.

All the same, 'You still haven't answered my question,' I said.

'What was that?'

'Would you have considered this John Jericho capable of robbery and murder?'

Simon curled his lip again. 'Who isn't, if pushed?' I watched him realize what he had said and he began to bluster. 'I mean ... well ... a low-born fellow like that, he's probably capable of anything.'

'You're sure he was low-born?'

Simon spluttered a laugh. 'Came out of nowhere, didn't he? Wandering about the countryside, sleeping rough. Mother took one of her inexplicable fancies to him. My father, the Applegarths, everyone told her she was mad. Courting trouble, I remember Father saying. But she wouldn't listen. She can be obstinate when she likes. And look what came of it!'

'You argue with hindsight,' I persisted. 'Think back to before the murder. Would you have considered John Jericho likely to turn thief, let alone killer, before it happened?'

'I've told you! I never thought about the man at all. I don't waste my time thinking of stable lads or kitchen maids or even Mistress Wychbold.' Again, he shrugged. 'Why should I? They're nothing to me.'

I could see that I was wasting my time, so I gave up. I didn't suppose Simon Bellknapp had ever seriously considered the thoughts and feelings of anyone except himself in the whole of his life. I detached myself from the bedpost against which I had been leaning, and gave a curt nod of my head. (I certainly wasn't prepared to give the little monster the courtesy of a bow, whatever the difference in our stations.)

'I'll wish you goodnight once more then, Master.'

'And don't come bothering me a second time,' he hissed viciously, jerking himself forward, away from the pillows, to emphasize his words.

For a moment, his head was haloed by the candlelight, and I was taken aback by his unexpected resemblance to his brother. The shadows had temporarily aged a face that was normally young and immature, giving it the same saturnine expression that I had occasionally noted on Anthony.

'What are you gawping at?' he demanded

ill-naturedly, irritated by my fixed, unblinking stare.

I ignored the question, briefly inclined my head again and left the room.

I judged it too late by then to interrogate any more of the household, most of whom would have already sought their beds, although it was possible that the maids had not yet retired to whatever corners they inhabited during the watches of the night. So I made my way to the kitchens and was rewarded by finding two of the girls still hard at work, one busy damping down the fire with sods of peat from a pile which stood at the side of the hearth, the other stacking bowls and plates on the table ready for use in the morning. And by a lucky chance, the first girl was the one I was looking for.

Both maids were plainly startled by my late appearance, but were immediately all smiles when they realized it was no one in authority come to spy on them.

'Goodness! You made me jump,' the fair-haired one complained, rising from her knees and brushing the residue of peat from her hands on the sides of her skirt. 'I thought you were Mistress Wychbold come to check on us. She does that sometimes.'

Her darker-haired companion agreed, nodding her head vigorously. 'The old dragon doesn't trust us. She suspects us of letting the stable lads in for a bit of you-know-what.' She giggled. 'She's never caught us at it yet, though. We're too clever for that.' The girl eyed me provocatively. 'Is that what you've come for? To try your luck?'

I grinned and gave her back look for look. 'Unfortunately, no. I don't think my wife would approve.'

'Oh, wives!' was the dismissive answer. 'What the eye doesn't see...'

'Bridget, behave yourself,' the first girl admonished her friend. 'What will Master Chapman think of you?' She glanced at me and asked shyly, 'Can we help you?'

'It's you I was hoping to see,' I answered.

'Your lucky night, Anne,' the girl called Bridget giggled.

Her friend blushed to the roots of her hair, but maintained a dignified silence, merely raising her eyebrows at me and waiting patiently to hear what I had to say.

'When we spoke at breakfast this morning,' I said, 'you told me that twice during the night you heard people moving about. I wondered if, by any chance, you knew who they were.'

She frowned a little in puzzlement, then her brow cleared.

'I remember. You were off your food and when I asked you why, you admitted to feeling queasy. And I thought it might have been something you ate at supper because I'd been woken by the noise of someone scuffling along the passageway. I usually sleep in the dairy in the summer,' she added by way of explanation. 'It's nice and cool in there.'

'And do you have any idea who it was?'

She shook her head regretfully. 'But it was a man. I heard him cough. That was the first time.'

'And the second?'

'It was just someone mounting the stairs to the bedchambers. The bottom two creak, and I remember thinking that perhaps now we had a new master, he'd get the treads replaced. Dame Audrea's been talking about doing it for ages, but so far nothing's happened.'

Bridget, irritated at being left out of the conversation, asked mockingly, 'You're sure you didn't dream all this, Annie? You're usually such a heavy sleeper.' She transferred her gaze to me. 'It takes me and another of the girls to wake her every morning.'

'I did hear it, just as I said,' Anne protested indignantly. 'If you don't believe me, you can ask Master Steward. He looked into the dairy a few minutes after I'd heard whoever it was go upstairs. He wanted to know if we were all right, as he'd heard someone creeping about, too. You wouldn't have known that, though,' she finished triumphantly. 'You were sound asleep and snoring!'

Honours now being even, the girls forgot their animosity and became firm friends again, both begging me to sit down and have a cup of ale.

'It's not very late yet,' Bridget urged.

'And no one's likely to come in and find you here,' Anne added. 'Mistress Wychbold said she was so worn out after the terrible events of the day, she didn't expect to stir all night.'

318

I declined their offer, tempting though it was, giving it as my opinion, based on experience, that it was when people were overtired and overwrought that their rest was most fitful. I wished them both a good night and pleasant dreams – although in the present unhappy circumstances this seemed like mere politeness – and returned for the second time that evening to the bedchamber I continued to share with Humphrey Attleborough. I was prepared to find him asleep, but he was still sitting just as I had left him, on the edge of his truckle-bed and fully clothed. He had not even bothered to light a candle, so, cursing, I fished in my pouch for my tinder box, made my way to the four-poster and lit the one standing on the chest beside the bed.

'For heaven's sake get undressed,' I said crossly.

'I'm not tired,' was his morose reply, whereupon I let rip with one of my more colourful oaths.

'Well, I am!' I roared, making him jump.

I was immediately contrite, particularly as he looked as if he might burst into tears.

'Shit! I'm sorry,' I said, going over to sit beside him. 'I know you're upset and worried, lad, but you ought to try to get some rest. You've important decisions to make tomorrow.' He still made no move, and I sighed wearily. 'Would it help to talk about Master Bellknapp? You seem to have been fond of him.'

Humphrey nodded and a tear trickled

down his cheek. 'He was kind to me. Mind you,' he added fair-mindedly, 'he wasn't kind to everybody. He could be very unpleasant to people he didn't like. In fact, more than just unpleasant. We were in an inn in Cambridge once, and a man annoyed him. I can't even recall now what the argument was about, but it grew very heated until the master lost his temper good and proper. The man had a dog with him, a thin, mangy-looking creature, but the man was obviously very fond of it. Kept pulling its ears and petting it. Master Bellknapp just picked up a knife off the nearest table and stuck it straight into the animal's throat. We had to get out of there in a hurry, I can tell you, or the other drinkers would have torn him limb from limb. In fact, we got out of Cambridge altogether for a while until we judged people wouldn't recognize us and it was safe to go back.' He must have seen the expression on my face, because he added apologetically, 'It was only a dog. A mangy cur. The master didn't kill a person.'

Even so, it struck me as a pretty ruthless thing to do, and I recollected Dame Audrea's statement – which I had dismissed at the time as a sign of her prejudice against Anthony – that her elder son had an evil streak in him. An uneasy suspicion was beginning to form in the back of my mind, only to be rejected as impossible. Or, then again, perhaps not...

'You say Master Bellknapp treated you well; fed you, clothed you as befitted the servant of a well-to-do man. Was he always wealthy, do you know?'

'As long as I've been with him, he seemed to want for nothing. But he had known lean times after he was first thrown out of home by his father. I've heard him say so.'

'I think I've asked you all this before, but if so, bear with me. How did he recoup his fortunes, have you any idea?'

Humphrey shrugged. 'Gambling mostly, I think. Though whenever I've watched him play at dice he's never had much luck. He must have had a winning streak at sometime or another, but it didn't last.'

'Were you conscious of the fact that money was becoming a problem to Master Bell-knapp?'

Humphrey nodded slowly. 'Now you mention it, yes. Looking back, I can see that there were economies; we'd begun to avoid certain inns and taverns that we used to patronize, as being too expensive, we'd started drinking cheaper wine, buying less costly garments and making them last longer.' (He was truly the devoted servant, identifying himself with his master in everything.) 'But it was very gradual, you understand. So gradual, in fact, that it happened almost without me noticing it. I suppose it wasn't really until we met that William Worcester, and the master suddenly learned that his father was dead and about the terms of the old man's will, that I realized how very relieved he was. Within a day, or two at the most, we were on our way to Crox-combe.'

'Master Bellknapp had no ties? No wife, mistress or children?'

'No. He told me once that he'd been put off women for life. His mother had never loved him, he said, and his nurse was treacherous, fondling him one minute and tanning his hide the next. Leave women well alone was his advice to me. Use them for your own purposes, but then let them be.'

Humphrey was at last beginning to yawn, his eyelids drooping. Talking had done the trick. I stooped and got hold of his legs, rolling him, still fully clothed, on to the hard straw mattress and throwing a blanket over him. He was snoring within a couple of minutes. Then I stripped off myself and clambered between the sheets of Anthony's bed, stretching my length and easing my tired limbs. But I knew there was little prospect of sleep coming quickly. Humphrey had given me too much to think about.

Eighteen

But that was where I was wrong. Sleep closed my eyelids almost immediately. I had reckoned without the trials and exhaustion of a very long day. And I might well have slept the whole night through had it not been for Humphrey riding the night mare. But then again, if he had not awakened us both with his violent tossing and turning until he fell out of bed, I would have slept even more soundly, never to wake again.

The August night was hot and stuffy, the darkness beyond the open casement almost impenetrable, when a heavy thump, accompanied by a huge snort and a muffled yell, brought me rudely to my senses.

I jerked upright in bed, reaching instinctively for my cudgel and demanding loudly of no one in particular, 'What was that?' For a second or two I wasn't even certain where I was and felt for the reassuring presence of Adela beside me before consciousness fully returned.

'It's all right,' Humphrey answered in a shaken voice. 'I was dreaming. A horrible dream.'

He hauled himself up from the floor while I

lit my bedside candle, and by its pale glow, I could see that he was shaking. I eased myself out of bed and poured him a beaker of ale from the all-night tray which had been left for us in the window embrasure.

'Here, drink this,' I advised, handing him the cup. 'You'll feel better. Do you want to tell me about it?'

He shuddered. 'I was pulling Master Bellknapp's body out of the moat, only his flesh was all white and shrivelled and eaten away. His head was just a skull, with gaping sockets and worms crawling in and out of them, all covered in blood.' A sound like a great sob was wrenched from him and he trembled so much that he spilled half his ale. He stared down at himself, bewildered. 'I'm still fully clothed.'

'Yes. I didn't have the heart to wake you when you finally did nod off, so I left you as you were. You can undress now if you want to. Do you feel any better?'

He began to shiver again. 'Not really. I don't think I shall be able to sleep any more tonight. Every time I close my eyes, I can see that ghastly ... that ghastly thing.'

'It was just a dream,' I told him soothingly. 'You had a nasty shock when you found your master in the water. It's only to be expected that the experience has left its mark on you. But you'll be all right now that you've purged yourself of its horror. Have another cup of ale and you'll find that you fall asleep again easily enough.'

Humphrey remained unconvinced.

'Will you share a bed with me for the rest of the night?' he asked. 'I think I might not be so frightened then.'

'With pleasure.' I jerked my head towards the four-poster. 'There's plenty of room for two.'

He looked appalled. 'Not there! I couldn't sleep in the master's bed. No!'

'Oh, sweet Virgin! Pull yourself together, lad!' I exclaimed impatiently. 'Very well! If you think it's going to call up the night mare from his stable again, I'll happily take Master Bellknapp's side of the bed and you can sleep in mine.'

But Humphrey shook his head vigorously. There was a wild expression in his eyes.

'No! No, I couldn't! I don't want to sleep in the same bed he slept in at all. I'm sorry. You must think me a fool, I know. But I can't help it. I'll dream of him again, I'm sure I shall. Don't make me.'

'I'm not making you. It's you who wanted to share a bed. So what do you suggest?'

He indicated the truckle-bed.

I laughed. 'I hope you're jesting! A couple of midgets would have trouble sleeping in such conditions, let alone a well set-up youth like you and a giant like me.'

'We could sleep toe-to-toe. You can put a pillow at the other end and then our feet and legs wouldn't take up so much room in the middle.' He turned huge, scared eyes on me. 'Please!' he urged. 'I know I shan't sleep a wink otherwise.'

I hesitated, then, very reluctantly, agreed. I could see that I wasn't going to get much rest either way. If I refused, I would most likely be kept awake by his muttering and moaning, or he might fall out of bed again in the grip of another bad dream. Or, worse still, he'd want to lie awake talking for what remained of the night.

'Just try not to move around too much,' I grumbled. 'I must be mad.'

He thanked me gratefully, then we both relieved ourselves in the piss-pot and, while he stripped down to his shirt, I fetched a pillow from the four-poster. And this was where God took a hand. I hadn't had a lot to say to Him lately; in fact, I wasn't even sure any more that He was really interested in what was happening at Croxcombe or had directed my footsteps there in the first place. So I had rather ignored Him, and told myself that at last I was in charge of my own affairs. But at the ripe old age of twenty-seven – less than two months short of twenty-eight – I ought to have known better.

As I picked up one of the pillows and put it under my arm, I suddenly remembered how, as a boy, when I sneaked out of my mother's cottage on warm summer nights to go prowling around the countryside in the mysterious dark, I always pushed my straw-filled bolster lengthwise under my blanket so that if, by some mischance, she woke up and glanced over towards my pallet, she would think I was still there. The memory was so vivid that for no sensible reason – except, of course, I can see now that God was jogging my elbow – I arranged the remaining pillows in the same way to represent my curled-up and sleeping body. Then, with a despairing chuckle at my own idiocy, I blew out the candle and returned to the truckle-bed where, after a few more dire warnings and threats of what I'd do to him if he didn't lie quietly, I settled down with Humphrey, our bare feet meeting in the middle and making cautious friends with one another.

'And no snoring!' was my final injunction as I prepared myself to endure what I was certain was going to be a sleepless few hours until daybreak.

But for the second time that night, the waters of Lethe closed over my head without me even knowing it, and doubtless (at least, if my dear wife was to be believed), I was the one disturbing the peace with his snores.

I have no idea how long I slept on this occasion, but it was still dark when an agonizing cramp in my left leg woke me yet again. I disentangled the afflicted limb from Humphrey's, flexed the muscles several times, reached under the blanket to rub my calf and was successful in ridding myself of the pain remarkably quickly. It was then I thought I heard the latch of the bedchamber door click. I sat up abruptly.

'Who's there?' I quavered, peering blindly through the almost total blackness.

Humphrey was awake on the instant. 'What's up? What's happened?' he demanded fretfully.

I whispered, 'I think someone may be in the room.'

I could hear his teeth chattering as I crept out of bed and groped my way across the bedchamber to the candle and my tinder box, which I had left beside it. After a few fumblings the flame blazed into life, searing the darkness, and the wick caught. I held the candlestick aloft, the light sending shadows scattering to the four corners of the room. Apart from Humphrey and myself there was no one else present.

But I saw, with a shock that jolted me from head to foot, that another person had indeed been there.

'What is it?' queried Humphrey's voice at my elbow. I could feel him shaking even though our bodies weren't touching.

Silently, I pointed to the bed and the curled-up shape of the pillows. Protruding from one of them, just about where my chest and heart would have been, was the handle of a long-bladed kitchen knife.

There was little sleep for either of us after that. I bolted the bedchamber door on the inside and closed the shutters, but even those precautions failed to reassure us until the first intimations of daylight began to seep into the room. By that time, stifled for air, our heads aching from bolstering our courage with the rest of the all-night ale, we were only too glad to put aside our fears and reopen the casement on a brightening world, where the stars were paling fast before being quite snuffed out. Birds, who had been cheeping gently on a sleepy, questioning note, suddenly shrilled into a full-throated chorus; and on the grass near the moat, I could see a cluster of astonished young rabbits, caught in the act of sitting up and washing their faces with front paws, wet with dew. I breathed in deeply. Normality had returned.

Well, for the time being, at least: I still had to face up to the fact that someone had tried to kill me during the night. And there was no clue as to the would-be murderer's identity to be gained from the knife.

'Taken from the kitchen,' I said to Humphrey as we examined it together.

'Do you think whoever it was realized that he hadn't killed you?' Humphrey asked in a nervous, unhappy voice.

'Bound to,' I said. 'There's no comparison between the feel of a blade slicing through flesh and one stabbing through feathers.'

'So' – my companion swallowed noisily – 'do you think he'll try again?'

Having thought about it, I shook my head. 'Not like that, at any rate. He'll know I'll be on my guard. It'll have to be something a good deal more subtle. A carefully arranged accident, perhaps.'

'Aren't you frightened?'

'Scared out of my wits,' I answered as

cheerfully as I could. 'But I shall make sure, at breakfast this morning, that everyone knows what's happened. That way, if anything untoward does befall me, they'll all know it's murder.'

'Do you suspect anyone?' Humphrey asked, but I refused to say.

'I might do. Then again, I might not,' was my deliberately ambiguous answer.

The truth was that I didn't know what I really thought myself. The worm of suspicion that had been wriggling around in my mind for a little while now, but largely ignored by me, was beginning to assume snake-like proportions. This was partly due to a dream that had troubled one of those brief interludes of sleep which had punctuated my almost continuous state of wakefulness since the discovery of the knife stuck in the pillow. In this dream, I had returned to the day of my arrival at Croxcombe, the previous Friday. Anthony Bellknapp and I were in George Applegarth's room and the former was questioning the steward about his wife's murder. It was all quite sane and sensible, without any of the inanities that normally distinguish a dream from reality, but I had woken with a sense of something missing; a conviction that something had not been asked that should have been asked in the light of what had happened later ... But then, I had not been constantly in Anthony Bellknapp's company, and the vital missing question could have been put during my absence.

Piqued by my refusal to say more, Humphrey dressed and, taking his razor, went off to hold his head under the pump before repairing to the kitchen to get hot water to shave in. I followed his example but at a slower pace, my thoughts making me pause every few moments while I tried to make coherent sense of what I knew and what I suspected. As a result, I was late for the start of breakfast and earned myself a pained look from Dame Audrea.

We were a reduced number at table, the Bignells having already departed, leaving the manor – or so I was informed by the chaplain – at first light, anxious to be home as early as possible. They had missed a whole day's trading and were keen to open their stall before the good women of Wells decided to take their custom elsewhere. The pilgrims who had sought shelter the preceding night had also gone on their way at a very early hour, and had charged George Applegarth with rendering thanks to their hostess.

I took a seat at one of the lower boards and waited for everyone present to finish their poached eel and oatmeal cakes before marching up to the dais and slapping down the kitchen knife under Dame Audrea's astonished gaze.

'Someone,' I announced baldly, 'tried to kill me with that last night. If you don't believe me, ask Master Attleborough there. He'll confirm what I say.'

There was silence, broken only by the

shuffle of feet as people left their places to crowd around the dais and stare with ghoulish fascination at the wicked, pointed blade, set in its black bone handle. Finally, Dame Audrea said, 'Someone tried to kill you, Master Chapman? This isn't some sort of jest?'

'Someone tried to kill me,' I repeated, ignoring the second question as being nothing more than a ploy on her part to stall for time. 'I've told you, Master Attleborough will back me up.' Humphrey nodded vigorously. 'We have a murderer in our midst, Madam, who doesn't want you to discover the identity of your elder son's killer.' I raised my voice slightly so that everyone present could hear. 'I tell you all this so that should any of you find me dead, however innocent-looking the circumstances, you will be on your guard against assuming that my death is natural. I would advise you most strongly, Dame Audrea, to make known the manner of Master Anthony's death to the proper authorities and let them instigate a hunt for his killer.'

'No.' The dame's answer was blunt and allowed of no argument. 'Croxcombe will keep its affairs to itself as it always has done. And if anyone here thinks of disobeying my orders, let me warn you that I have many friends and kinsmen in high places. I shall be believed, not you, and you might find life in the future very uncomfortable. So get on and exert these wonderful powers of yours, Master Chapman, that you have seen fit to boast about, and find the murderer. I shall know how to deal with him when you do.' She gave a curt nod as she rose from her seat and prepared to leave the dais. 'Anthony's funeral will take place at noon,' she added, 'in the chapel. I shall expect all of you to be present. Sir Henry, you have the key to the family vault. Please see that it is open and ready to receive my son's body by the appointed hour. That's all for now.' But as she turned to go, she flung at me over her shoulder, 'Remember our bargain!'

I wasn't likely to forget. She had the upper hand, and knew it. Now that Anthony was dead, Dame Audrea was once more sole ruler of her little kingdom. Whatever rumours and gossip might abound in the countryside at large concerning Master Bellknapp's death, no one would ever know the truth for certain. It would join the ever-increasing mythology of the district; just another of those stories endlessly discussed in taverns and alehouses, especially on winter nights when smoke from the fires wrapped the various taprooms in a ghostly pall, and the wind shrieked like a banshee through the hole in the roof.

After a short interval, I followed Sir Henry to the chapel and waited at the back, unnoticed, while he unlocked the door to the vault and disappeared inside, the pale flame of his lantern bobbing around like a ship on a stormy sea as he descended the flight of steps into its depths.

'Ah! Master Chaplain!' I said. At the sound

of my voice, he jumped like a startled fawn and dropped the lantern from nerveless fingers. With great dexterity, I caught it before it hit the floor. 'I'm sorry. Did I frighten you?'

'I – I didn't know you were there,' he stammered. Recovering himself, he went on petulantly, 'What do you want? I'm busy.'

The place smelled mustily of death and decay, of damp stone walls and mouldering bones. It was about twelve feet square and, by my reckoning, took up most of the space beneath the altar and the front half of the chapel. Each wall had three stone shelves, one above the other, on which were ranged the coffins of long-dead Bellknapps, including the pathetically small ones of children who had not survived infancy. Sudden tears sprang to my eyes as I remembered my own little daughter who had known less than four days of life. Angrily, I blinked them away and stepped back into the shadows so that the chaplain shouldn't be a witness to my unmanly emotion.

'I apologize for interrupting you,' I said, putting the lantern on a shelf. 'I simply want to ask you some questions.'

He had seized a besom from a corner of the vault and was busily sweeping the floor, the long broom twigs tied to their handle raising a great cloud of dust (making us both cough and sneeze) which then settled anew over everything. I forbore to point out what a singularly fruitless activity this was, and

334

waited for his response. After a moment or two, curiosity overcame annoyance and Sir Henry replaced the besom.

'What about?' he demanded, before adding hurriedly, 'If it concerns poor Anthony's death, I know nothing of that. Nor about the attack on you last night.'

'What do you recall about Jenny Applegarth's murder?' I asked.

His nervousness gave way to testiness. 'Jenny Applegarth's murder? Why, nothing! I wasn't here. I was at Kewstoke Hall along with the mistress and Master Simon.'

'I was thinking more of what happened when you all returned.'

'I don't understand. We were all deeply upset, naturally.'

'Naturally. But did you ever think it strange that this John Jericho should have done such a thing? Had you ever thought of him as a possible thief and murderer?'

'No, of course not! I'm a man of God. It's my duty to think the best of people.'

I found myself suppressing a smile at this ingenuous statement. It was not a belief shared by many priests of my acquaintance. (But then, I'm a cynic. Take no notice of my opinions.)

'George Applegarth,' I said. 'You must have had to minister to him. He must have been in an extremely distressed state of mind.'

'We-ell, yes,' the chaplain agreed doubtfully. 'But it was a couple of days before we came home that the murder had occurred. George

335

had despatched one of the stable lads to Kewstoke with a message the same morning as he discovered what had happened, but by the time Dame Audrea and the master had recovered from the shock, and by the time that the baggage waggons had been loaded, it was late the next evening before anyone arrived here. Master Steward had had time to overcome the worst of his grief, and he has never been a man who wears his heart on his sleeve.'

'You're saying he didn't seem as grief-stricken as you thought he should be?'

'No, no!' Sir Henry was flustered. 'He loved his wife. Of course he was upset. He blamed himself, I think, for not waking up when Jenny tried to rouse him.'

'Did he tell you so?' I asked.

'Yes. Yes, he did. I know it's a long time ago, six years, but I distinctly recollect him saying so.'

'You're implying that Master Applegarth was not in need of your comfort?'

'I've told you, George keeps his feelings to himself. And sorrow affects different people in different ways. He seemed numbed by what had happened. Everyone was saying dreadful things about the page, terrible things as you can imagine, but not George. The master rode into Wells and organized a posse, but George wasn't interested. Master Simon, as I recall, was urging him to ride with them, and I think we all expected him to go. Even I joined one of the bands, and I'm no horseman. But he just wouldn't bestir himself.'

'Did you ever hear him vilify the page later on?'

The chaplain scratched one ear. 'I've heard him swear a solemn oath to revenge himself on the person who did it.'

'But never on John Jericho by name?'

'Yes ... No ... Oh, really, I can't be certain after all this while. But of course everyone who heard him knew who he meant.'

I nodded. 'Well, thank you, Master Chaplain, you've been most helpful. I'll leave you in peace.'

He looked faintly surprised. 'If I've been of assistance, I'm glad, but I don't see how. Never mind! Never mind! I daresay you know what you're about. Will you attend the funeral Mass at noon?'

'Perhaps. Do you happen to know where I can find Master Bailiff?'

'At this time of day, he'll be around the demesne lands somewhere, talking to one of the stockmen. Try the swineherd. I think I heard him mention that a sow was almost ready to farrow.'

I thanked him again and took myself off to the pig sties, where Reginald Kilsby was indeed in consultation with the swineherd, a large, bald man with smooth, porcine features that made him appear almost like one of his charges.

As I approached, I heard him grunt, 'She ain't ready to drop 'em yet awhile, I reckon. No point in you stopping, Bailiff.'

'In that case,' I said, butting into the conversation and making them both jump, 'can I impose on your time, Master Kilsby? What I want to ask you won't take long, and Dame Audrea, as you know, has empowered me to ask what questions I deem necessary.'

I could tell that it was on the tip of the bailiff's tongue to refuse, but the mention of Dame Audrea's name changed his mind. In spite of anything the lady might have said to the contrary, he still hadn't given up all hope of marrying her now that the chief obstacle to his ambition had been removed.

'Very well,' he agreed brusquely. 'Make it short.' But he was nervous.

'I want to ask you about Jenny Applegarth's murder,' I said, watching with interest the expressions of astonishment and relief that chased one another across his handsome face.

'Jenny Applegarth? That was six years ago!' Then, making up his mind that I was serious, he laughed and replied, as the chaplain had done, 'I wasn't here. I was at Kewstoke Hall with the master and Dame Audrea.'

'Yes, I know,' I answered patiently. 'But did George Applegarth hold himself responsible, do you remember, for what had happened to his wife?'

'Of course not! How could he, when it was obvious that that evil little shit, John Jericho, had killed her?'

'Sir Henry seems to think that Master Steward blamed himself for not waking up

338

when Jenny tried to rouse him. Did you ever hear him say so?'

'Oh, that nonsense! We all told him not to be so foolish.'

'Who are "we"?'

The bailiff made an exasperated gesture. 'I don't know. It's all a long time ago. Ned Micheldever might have been present. What's this about? I thought you were investigating Master Anthony's death.'

I gave him a long, straight look and asked if the receiver was likely to be found in the counting-house at this time in the morning. He hesitated for a moment before giving an affirmative nod which sent me hurrying away to seek out Edward Micheldever.

I discovered Dame Audrea closeted with him, going through long columns of figures of various expenses incurred during the past four weeks; the number of meals supplied to guests and unexpected visitors, and the amount of hay consumed by their horses, flicking the beads on an abacus to and fro as they made their calculations.

'Well enough,' the dame announced when they had finished. 'Although I think we need to curb our hospitality a trifle. A little less generous with the animals' feed perhaps. And I'll tell them in the kitchens to serve slightly smaller portions. But that's nothing to do with you, Ned. Your work is meticulous, as always. I'm very pleased with you.' At last she deigned to notice my presence in the counting-house. 'Did you wish to speak to me,

Master Chapman? Have you anything to tell me?'

'I came to put a question to Master Receiver,' I answered, 'but now that you're here, Lady, I can ask you as well.'

I put to them, almost word for word, the same query as I had put to the bailiff. Dame Audrea shook her head.

'I don't recall much that anyone said. The place was in such turmoil and we were all so horrified by what had happened. If anyone blamed herself for anything, I did. I was the person who had been taken in by that rogue's pretty ways and flattering speeches. I was the one who, against all sane advice, had employed him to be my page. He had a golden tongue, that one. He had some Irish in him.' She nodded significantly at me. 'He still has.'

I took no notice of this. She had heard the faint Irish lilt in my half-brother's speech and memory had now transferred it to John Jericho.

I looked at the receiver.

'Do you have any recollection,' I asked him, 'of Master Steward blaming himself for his wife's death?'

'Why should I tell you?' The pugnacious jaw was thrust forward, the red hair seemed to catch fire in a shaft of sunlight that penetrated the dusty window panes.

'It's important.' I sounded equally belligerent.

'That'll do,' Dame Audrea intervened. 'Tell him what he wants to know, Ned.'

The receiver shrugged, but obeyed.

'Since you mention it, I do recall something of the sort being said,' he admitted.

'By Master Applegarth?'

'Of course! Who else could have said it? Most of us had accompanied Master Cornelius and Dame Audrea to Kewstoke Hall on a visit to Sir Damien and Lady Chauntermerle.'

'Let me understand this,' I said slowly. 'You, Master Micheldever, Sir Henry and Master Kilsby, all three tell the same tale. You all heard George Applegarth blame himself for not waking up when his wife tried to rouse him, presumably to inform him that the page, John Jericho, was stealing the silver. Am I right?'

The receiver frowned, puzzled.

'Yes. Well, I heard him and if the others say so, then they did, too. I must admit I'd forgotten the incident, but now you've jogged my memory, it comes back to me.'

'And, at the time, not one of you thought it a strange remark for Master Applegarth to make?'

'No. Should we have done?'

I didn't answer. I was looking at Dame Audrea, whose hand had stolen up to her mouth, her eyes, above it, narrowed in pain and shock.

'Oh, sweet Mother of God!' she murmured.

Nineteen

The receiver was still looking confused when a shaken Dame Audrea rose from her stool and bade me accompany her to her private solar. The boy who worked alongside Edward Micheldever in the counting-house was sent for the steward.

'Tell Master Applegarth to come to my chamber,' she instructed. 'Tell him it's urgent. Whatever he's doing, he must come at once.'

The upstairs room was just beginning to be warmed by the morning sun, but there was still a slight chill in the air and I couldn't help wishing that my hostess had decided to postpone this interview for at least another hour until after dinner had been served. Although I had eaten my usual hearty breakfast, my belly was already starting to grumble that it was in need of more sustenance.

The solar was a pleasant room with a deep window embrasure, two handsomely carved armchairs, a footstool covered in the same tapestry as adorned a luxurious day-bed and a number of velvet-covered cushions, which were scattered around with a liberal hand.

'Sit down,' Dame Audrea ordered brusquely, and waved a hand at the window-seat. She herself took one of the armchairs, drawing the footstool towards her and arranging her feet on it in a precise fashion, side by side. The scarlet leather of her expensive, half-revealed shoes looked like smears of blood against the dark green of the tapestry. She glanced at me again. 'Say nothing until I give you a sign.'

'Very well,' I nodded.

After that, we sat in silence. We did not, however, have long to wait before we heard footsteps in the passageway outside. There was a light, respectful tap on the door and, in answer to Dame Audrea's, 'Come in!' George Applegarth entered, his wand of office in his hand, looking mildly curious, but no more, at this unexpected summons. Then he noticed me, and I saw the first faint flicker of apprehension in those remarkable slate-grey eyes.

'You sent for me, Madam?' His voice was perfectly steady.

Dame Audrea kept him standing.

'Master Steward,' she said, her tone formal and without any of the warmth she normally employed when speaking to him, 'as you know, Master Chapman here has been authorized by me to make enquiries concerning the circumstances of Anthony's death. He has spoken to a number of people including, this morning, Sir Henry, Master Kilsby and Ned Micheldever. All three men have told him the same, rather curious tale concerning yourself.'

I watched the steward's apprehension deepen, then the eyes go blank, their colour intensifying and making him appear almost blind.

'About me, Dame Audrea? And what would that be?'

She fixed him with her own gimlet stare.

'I want you to think back, George' – the sudden, more intimate use of his given name took him off guard and he blinked several times in rapid succession – 'to the morning, six years ago, when Master Cornelius and I and the rest of the household returned from Kewstoke Hall to find Jenny murdered and the silver stolen. You told me and everyone else that you had been unaware of the events of the night until you got up in the morning to find Jenny dead, lying in her own blood, and the cupboards containing the family valuables ransacked. Was that true?'

There was no sign of confusion in his face; no indication that he found this reversion to an old murder at odds with my investigation into Anthony's death. He had missed an opportunity to be wily and did not realize it.

'Perfectly true.' His voice was even more expressionless than hitherto.

'You are saying,' Dame Audrea emphasized, 'that you knew nothing at all of what had happened until you discovered Jenny's body?'

The steward gave a little bow of assent. 'I had, most reprehensibly, drunk far more than I should have the previous evening. I was in a drunken stupor.'

'Which is no doubt why your wife was unable to rouse you when she came to you for help, to tell you that John Jericho was stealing the plate and my jewels.'

There was a sudden stillness about him, a wariness that meant he had scented a trap but could not yet see it.

'I don't know that Jenny tried to rouse me. I couldn't have.'

I was unable to hold my tongue any longer.

'Yet you informed Sir Henry, Master Kilsby and Master Micheldever that that had indeed been the case. They all three tell the same story.'

For the first time, the steward was shaken. 'If – If what you say is true, then all I must have meant was that that was what I presumed must have happened. It seems likely that she would have tried to wake me.'

I shook my head, ignoring Dame Audrea's look of silent reproach.

'That isn't the way your fellow officers tell the tale. According to Sir Henry and the other two they argued with you, exhorting you not to be so foolish, not to blame yourself. They understood you to mean that you knew Mistress Applegarth had sought your aid, but couldn't wake you. But as you've pointed out, there's no way you could be certain of that fact unless you know far more about the robbery than you are prepared – or ever have been prepared – to admit.'

'My friends mistook what I was trying to say,' he repeated doggedly. 'And anyway,' he continued, rallying, as though conscious that there was something he should have said earlier, 'what has all this to do with Master Anthony's death? My Jenny's been in her grave these six years past. It has nothing to do with present events.'

'It has everything to do with them,' I answered levelly, 'as no one knows better than yourself.'

'What do you mean by that?'

'You may recall, Master Applegarth, that I was in your room four days ago when you had your first encounter with Anthony Bellknapp after his return home. You and he talked about the circumstances of Mistress Applegarth's murder, but to the best of my recollection no mention was made of the reason you hadn't accompanied Dame Audrea and her husband to Kewstoke Hall. Later on, however, he referred to that broken arm of yours. Now I admit that may not be as significant as it sounds: someone might well have informed him of the fact. Or perhaps not. Maybe he had no need to ask. Perhaps he already knew.'

Dame Audrea twisted round in her chair. 'What is that supposed to mean?'

'It means, lady,' I answered steadily, 'that I don't believe your page, John Jericho, was the murderer of Jenny Applegarth. I think he was an innocent bystander who was also a victim of this crime.'

'What nonsense! If not John, who was the murderer, then?'

I took a deep breath. 'Your elder son, Master Anthony.'

There was a long silence broken only by Dame Audrea's gasp for breath. She looked ashen. I turned to the steward.

'Master Applegarth? Isn't that why you killed him? Because he murdered your wife.'

All his careful control suddenly left him. He buried his face in his hands.

'George?' Dame Audrea's voice rapped out, cracked and harsh. 'Tell Master Chapman his accusation isn't true. It can't be! Anthony wouldn't do such a thing!'

'Why should you be so astonished, Madam,' I demanded, 'when you yourself have been at great pains to tell me that there was a streak of evil in your elder son, on account of which you and your husband could never like him?'

She pressed a hand to her mouth for a second or two before replying in a shaken tone, 'But to rob his own parents and to murder his old nurse, of whom he was so fond, when she tried to prevent him, that's infamous. No! No! I can't accept it! George! For my sake – for all our sakes – refute this terrible allegation.'

The steward slowly lowered his hands, revealing a face ravaged by grief, but with his emotions now under control. He looked pityingly at the dame.

'I wish I could, Mistress,' he said. 'But things are even blacker than you imagine.

Blacker for me, that is. My Jenny didn't disturb Master Anthony as he robbed you.' He took a deep breath. 'She was his accomplice.'

Dame Audrea sprang to her feet, knocking over the footstool. 'You're lying! I refuse to believe it!'

The steward stooped and righted the stool before gently and respectfully pushing his mistress back into her chair.

'It's true, nonetheless. She told me so, herself.'

'She told you so! How could she, when she was dead?'

George Applegarth shook his head. 'She was still alive when I found her in the morning. Oh, she was dying. Nothing I tried to do could have saved her; she had lost too much blood. I was going to rouse the household – the maids and Mistress Wychbold – but she begged me not to. She had got what she deserved, she said, and even then – fool that I was not to have tumbled to it – she was giving that murdering rogue as much time as she could to get away.' He spat among the rushes. 'My Jenny always had a soft spot for Master Anthony.'

'But what about the page?' I asked angrily. 'What was his role in all this? Why did he run away?'

The steward sighed and lowered himself into the other armchair without waiting for, or being given, permission. He looked suddenly twice his years.

'It's better if I tell you the story as Jenny told it to me as she lay in my arms. Remember, this is a dying woman's testimony, Mistress. In such circumstances, on the brink of meeting her Maker, she wouldn't lie.'

Jenny Applegarth, visiting the market in Wells on a chilly summer's morning some six years previously, had been accosted by a seeming stranger, hat pulled down over his brows, cloak muffling the lower part of his face. (All right, I admit I am supplying some of these details myself, but only where they would seem to be feasible. Sometimes bare bones need fleshing out.) The stranger, when he had drawn Jenny aside into the shadows of the cathedral porch, had revealed himself to be her favourite, Anthony, down on his luck. His two-year exile from Croxcombe had left him almost destitute. He was also deeply embittered by what he saw as his unfair treatment by his parents.

Jenny, overwhelmed with delight at seeing him again, had revealed that his mother and father, together with Simon and most of the household officers, had gone on an extended visit to Sir Damien and Lady Chauntermerle at Kewstoke Hall, but that George had been forced to remain behind on account of a broken arm. To Anthony, penniless and desperate, this news must have appeared like an opportunity arranged by heaven. He had convinced Jenny that he had been shabbily used and that he was entitled to do something to put things right. If his parents were not prepared to treat him properly, according to his due, he would just have to rectify the situation for himself. And with Jenny's help, this was precisely what he intended to do.

How long it took Anthony to persuade Jenny to aid him can only be a matter of conjecture, but George, being brutally honest, thought not long. 'He could always twist her round his little finger,' he admitted sadly.

Jenny's part was to unlock the moat gate and to leave a door into the manor open that same night. She was also to lace her husband's all-night ale with a potion of either lettuce or poppy juice – or a combination of both – taken from the medicine chest, to make sure that he slept soundly with no chance of waking up. The other servants were obviously not considered to present a threat. But that was where both conspirators were mistaken.

Anthony left his horse tethered outside the moat gate and brought with him a large sack in which to load the family silver and pewter, together with anything else of value he could lay his hands on. All was going well when the page, John Jericho, who had also been left behind by Dame Audrea because he was suffering from toothache, and therefore sleeping badly, burst on the scene.

It was easy to imagine the shock and consternation his sudden appearance would have caused, but according to Jenny's dying confession to her husband, Anthony had been only momentarily daunted. Almost without a second's hesitation, he had drawn his dagger and stabbed the page in the chest. Horrified, she had cried out and caught at his arm, trying to wrest the dagger from him. Again without the slightest compunction, Anthony, tearing himself free of her clutches, had lunged at her, also, with every intention of silencing her for good. But in his hurry, his aim had been inaccurate, and although the blow eventually proved itself mortal, it was to be several hours before Jenny actually died; long enough for George to find her on waking and for her to tell him what had really happened.

'What became of the page?' I asked, as the steward's voice petered into silence and he sat staring into space with blank and empty eyes.

'The page?' He blinked and shook his head as though trying to get his thoughts in order.

'Yes, John Jericho! Dame Audrea's page! The poor lad who all this time has been wrongly accused of this dreadful crime.'

George passed his hand across his forehead. 'Jenny thought she recalled seeing Anthony throw the body over his shoulder. She was not fully conscious at the time, you understand, but the fact that he was nowhere to be found proves her recollection must have been correct. Anthony probably reckoned that if he took young Jericho's body with him and disposed of it somewhere where it wouldn't be found, the lad would be blamed both for the robbery and the murder. As, indeed, proved to be the case, while Anthony got clean away.'

'But you knew the truth!' It was with difficulty that I stopped myself from striking the man. One hand had already balled itself into a fist. 'Why, in the name of justice, didn't you speak out?'

'And what good would that have done?' the steward demanded angrily, suddenly galvanized into life and jumping to his feet. 'What good?' he repeated. 'It would have blackened my Jenny's name as an accomplice to robbery, and it would have tarnished the name of Bellknapp with robbery and a double murder combined. John Jericho was dead. What possible harm could it do him to be accused? A little nobody from nowhere! And I knew they'd never catch him because he wasn't alive to be caught. Even if his body was discovered somewhere, no one would ever get to the truth.'

Dame Audrea still said nothing, but her face was grey and she looked as though she might be sick.

I turned to George Applegarth once more, suddenly losing my temper, shoving him down into the chair with all my strength and standing over him, straddling his knees with my legs and lowering my head threateningly, like a bull about to charge.

'And when Dame Audrea accused my half-brother of being her page, you continued to hold your tongue, even though you knew he couldn't possibly be John Jericho because

352

John Jericho is dead.'

Some of the bravado drained out of the steward, but he raised his face to mine, his lower lip jutting.

'I denied that Master Wedmore was Jericho. I refused to identify him as such in spite of the fact that it would have been easier just to say nothing and give my tacit agreement to the accusation.'

'But Dame Audrea didn't admit of your objection. She had every intention of bribing Ned Micheldever to back her up because she was so certain that she'd found John Jericho after all these years. What did you intend to do if she had persisted in her prosecution?'

The slate-grey eyes went blank again and the adversarial gaze was lowered.

'I should have thought of something,' he mumbled.

'Would you at last have admitted the truth?'

He made no answer. I looked appealingly at Dame Audrea once again, willing her to say something, but although a tinge of colour had returned to her pallid cheeks, she shook her head at me as a sign that she was not yet ready to speak. I removed myself from the steward's vicinity and went back to the window-seat.

'So, let's come to recent events,' I said. 'Anthony's totally unexpected return last Friday finally gave you your opportunity for revenge. Your wife's murderer, who had no idea that you knew the truth, had come back to put himself in your power. It must have seemed like a gift from God.'

The steward smiled faintly. 'Don't mock! God moves in mysterious ways, Chapman. In faraway Cambridge, an unknown man with a sister in Bristol – a sister with whom he keeps up a regular correspondence – meets Master Anthony quite by chance, recognizes the name of Bellknapp and reveals to him the contents of his father's will. Could anything be more heaven-sent than that?'

And in Bristol, about the same time, or soon afterwards, Dame Audrea had been moved to pick out a stranger, with a passing resemblance to her long-dead page, as the missing John Jericho; a stranger who would prove to be my unknown and undreamt-of half-brother, so that I would come to Crox-combe to try to prove him innocent and, in the process, reveal the truth about the killing of Jenny Applegarth. Oh yes! There was no longer any doubt in my mind that God had been dabbling a Divine Finger in this particular pie and had once more availed Himself of my unwitting services. And not only me, but this William Botoner – or William of Worcester, or whatever he called himself – as well...

But then, suddenly, memory brought me up short; something Ronan Bignell had told me. On the night of the murder, he and his friends had seen the page staggering about in Croxcombe woods being sick and generally acting as though he were drunk. Did that mean, as with Jenny Applegarth, that

Anthony's aim had been faulty? That John Jericho might have survived, if only for a few hours? I tried to put myself in the murderer's shoes; to decide what I might have done with what I thought was a dead body, particularly one I didn't want found as he was to be presumed the killer. A grave in Croxcombe woods seemed to me the obvious answer, as no doubt it had done to Anthony. But he would have had nothing to dig a grave with and using bare hands would have been impossible.

Jenny Applegarth had told her husband that Anthony had had a horse tethered outside the moat gate, so, once he had made good his escape, he would have slung the body across the saddle, tied the sack of stolen goods to the pommel and walked the animal as deep into the woodlands as he could go until he or the horse or both were too tired to proceed further. On reflection, I reckoned this would not have been too far. Anthony must have been considerably shaken by the night's events, when what he had planned as a straightforward robbery had turned into the nightmare of a double killing. My guess was that he had reached Hangman's Oak and decided to abandon the page's body in the dense undergrowth that bordered the clearing. Not a very satisfactory conclusion, but it might well have been many months before the decaying corpse was found, and then only by Hamo Gough who coppiced that part of the woods to keep his fire alight for every new batch of charcoal that he made.

So, what had actually happened? John Jericho had recovered consciousness for a while, at least, when he had been seen by Ronan Bignell. What followed, I could only surmise. The page must have wandered deeper into the woods until loss of blood finally killed him. This would have delayed the discovery of his body by the charcoal burner or by anyone else; long enough at any rate for the woodland animals to have eaten away the body so that it was almost unrecognizable...

I realized that Dame Audrea was speaking to me and that I had been so engrossed in my own thoughts that I had been unaware of what she was saying.

'I – I'm sorry,' I stammered. 'I was miles away.'

'So it would seem.' But the reprimand was not delivered in the dame's usual high-handed manner. Her voice was subdued, her face still drawn. 'I was saying that I would give you a letter for delivery to the Sheriff of Bristol, completely exonerating Master John Wedmore of any wrongdoing and admitting that I was mistaken in his identity.' Judging by her pained expression, it obviously cost her a lot to admit to being mistaken in anything, but she knew she had no option in the circumstances but to do so. 'You may also tell Humphrey Attleborough that he is free to go and that I will give him his expenses for his journey. The horse he rode is presumably the rightful property of my ... of his master' – it was as though she could not bring herself even to mention Anthony's name, let alone refer to him as her son – 'but he may keep it.' This was generous: it was a good animal and valuable.

'And me, Mistress?' George Applegarth was still huddled in his chair. 'What do you intend for me? I shall, of course, leave your service, that goes without saying.'

'Nonsense!' A little colour was creeping back into the dame's face and she was beginning to regain something of her old self-confidence. 'I've no mind to lose a good steward. Nor do I wish to have to accustom myself to a stranger's ways. I won't say you have done nothing wrong, but I understand the motive for your secrecy all these years. You wanted to protect Jenny's and the Bellknapp family's good names. So I suggest we bury the past and breathe no word of the truth to any other person. Master Chapman, I rely on your discretion!'

But this was going too far and too fast for me. Besides, her peremptory tone annoyed me.

'I'm not sure about that,' I said. 'Apart from the fact that Master Applegarth's silence has blackened the name of an innocent man for the past six years, and will continue to do so, there's the trivial matter of the fact that he tried to kill me. I assume it was you, Master Steward, who stuck a knife into what you thought was my back but, through a fortunate circumstance, was really my pillow?'

He nodded. 'I can't deny it. I was growing desperate to prevent you discovering the truth.' He raised his head and looked me in the eyes for the first time since entering the solar. 'A sort of madness possessed me.' He sighed. 'I don't suppose you'll believe this – there's no reason why you should – but as I approached the bed, my heart had already failed me, and I was preparing to tiptoe out again when it struck me that the shape of the "body" was all wrong. Too soft, too lumpy. It was then I realized it was a pillow, so I stuck my knife in just to warn you off. Or, rather, in the hope of warning you off. If you considered your own life to be in danger, you might decide to abandon your search for the truth and leave. I should have known better.'

I wasn't certain whether he was telling the truth or not, but decided to give him the benefit of the doubt. I nodded. I felt some sympathy with him. It was, after all, his own stupidity that, in the end, had led to his undoing.

As though reading my thoughts, George Applegarth gave a short bark of laughter.

'For six years,' he said, 'that silly, unnecessary lie has been waiting to trip me up. At any moment, Ned Micheldever or Sir Henry or Master Kilsby could have reasoned out the truth if one of them had ever seriously thought about it.'

'They haven't the common sense!' Dame Audrea declared scornfully. Then her face changed and she added, as though a full understanding of the situation had only just suddenly hit her, 'You killed Anthony.'

The steward nodded. 'Yes. I killed him with the weapon he'd intended using on Master Bignell.'

'Master Bignell? But why?'

'Thomas told me he had seen a horseman near Croxcombe Manor on the night of my Jenny's murder, and that he thought there might have been something familiar about him. If he ever said that within Anthony's hearing, I suspect Anthony decided to do away with him before he had time to remember anything further. He arranged for the Bignells to remain here overnight, instead of returning to Wells as they'd intended, and persuaded Master Bignell to meet him after the rest of us had gone to bed, on the pretext of revealing something undesirable about Rose's marriage to Ned.

'I should say here, perhaps, that all this is so much guesswork on my part, but guesswork I believe to be as near the truth as we are ever likely to get. He took Master Chapman's cudgel from the room they shared. Indeed, I saw him come out of the chamber with it, and it made me suspicious, so I determined to keep an eye on him. I knew he had killed twice, and felt certain he would have no compunction in killing for a third time. I also had a fancy that, just as he used John Jericho as the scapegoat for him the first time, so he might be planning to lay the blame for Thomas Bignell's death on the chapman. I didn't doubt that he was growing nervous of our friend here, especially after you' – he glanced at me, faintly mocking – 'had boasted so openly of your past successes.'

I groaned and had the grace to blush.

'Fool!' I muttered to myself.

'Continue!' Dame Audrea commanded harshly.

The steward shrugged. 'There's little more to tell, Madam. After everyone else had retired for the night, I hung around outside the hall, waiting to see what would happen. I heard Master Anthony and the butcher talking, then Master Anthony came out, prowling around, looking to see that the coast was clear. I feel sure he intended to club Master Bignell over the head and push him into the moat.'

'Precisely as you did to him,' I interrupted.

George Applegarth nodded. 'It was the opportunity I'd been waiting for, for six long years. He was walking along the edge of the moat, looking for a sheltered spot in which to do the deed, and was totally unsuspecting of my presence. Almost before he had time to understand what was happening, I wrested the cudgel from his hand, swung it with all my might and knocked him into the water. Then I held him under until he drowned.'

Twenty

Hercules and I knew we were home as soon as I pushed open the door of the house in Small Street. The noise of Adam having a tantrum somewhere or other assailed our ears almost immediately, while the thunderous descent of the stairs heralded the arrival of my daughter and stepson, who had spotted our approach from an upper window. I did not delude myself, however, that they had missed me and were eagerly awaiting my return to ply me with hugs and kisses. Rather, their hands were at once searching my pockets and the scrip at my belt, at the same time demanding, 'What have you brought us?' To add insult to injury – or, in this case, injury to insult – I could hear Margaret Walker's voice uplifted in admonition to my longsuffering wife.

'You mustn't give in to him, Adela. Just let him scream.'

I walked into the kitchen where Adam, tied securely to his little chair, showed every intention of doing just that without any encouragement from my former mother-in-law, and dropped my pack and cudgel on to the table with a thump and a clatter that

361

surprised everyone into silence.

'Roger!' Adela exclaimed. 'You're home!' She left her cheese-making and hurried to greet me, slipping her arms around my neck and kissing me soundly. I returned the embrace with interest, having lived a celibate life for the past ten days.

'So you're back, are you?' Margaret said. 'And that's quite enough of that sort of behaviour, thank you.'

'Nuff that!' Adam screamed in support. 'Thank you!'

I untied the strips of cloth that bound him, picked him up bodily and tossed him into the air. He gurgled with delight, only threatening to resume his ear-piercing shrieks when I stopped. But I pacified him with a little wooden whistle that I had purchased from a fellow pedlar whom I had met during the leisurely three days it had taken me to walk home from Wells. I had refused all offers of rides in carts and proceeded quietly on foot, feeling that after the past few days, Hercules and I had earned time to ourselves before facing up once again to the strains and stresses of domestic life.

Declining to attend Anthony's funeral, I had quit Croxcombe Manor on the afternoon of the day we had discovered the truth (or as much of it as I presumed we should ever be able to piece together) about the murder, leaving behind me a situation fraught with tension, but one, I guessed, that would be quickly submerged by everyone's need to return to a normal, day-to-day existence. If George Applegarth had killed Anthony Bellknapp, then the latter had killed his wife, so it was impossible for either dame or steward to accuse the other without drawing attention to the crimes of their own kith and kin. It was a deadlock that I suspected neither wanted to break, or would ever allude to again. Rumour, gradually turning to legend, would surround the circumstances of Anthony's death and would add to the folklore of the surrounding countryside for all the generations still to come. John Jericho would continue to be blamed for a murder he didn't commit, but he was dead and it couldn't harm him. As far as I was concerned, all I had to do now was to take Dame Audrea's letter to the Sheriff of Bristol and ensure that my half-brother was released from prison.

Adela, generous woman, was almost as pleased as I was myself to learn of John Wedmore's innocence.

'You must bring him back here, Roger,' she insisted. 'Elizabeth can sleep with Nicholas and Master Wedmore can use her room for as long as he wishes to remain.'

'No news of Master Jay's expedition, then?' I enquired.

Both Adela and Margaret Walker shook their heads.

'They've been gone six weeks and more now and not a word of them being sighted anywhere,' the latter announced with a lugubrious shake of her head. 'Madness!

Folly! I always said so. The Isle of Brazil! Who has actually laid eyes on it? No one that I can discover. It's just a sailor's yarn, if you want my opinion, like men and women with fish-tails instead of legs. All nonsense! Ah, well,' she added, glancing around at our reunited family group, 'I'd better be getting back to Redcliffe, then, Adela. You won't want me hanging around, I daresay, now that your husband's back.' She wagged an admonitory finger at me. 'Look after her! She's worth her weight in gold.'

'Gold!' shouted Adam, unexpectedly adding his mite, and giving all our ears a momentary respite from his whistle-playing. 'Bad man,' he continued, jutting his lower lip in my direction and demonstrating that, although only two years old, he was perfectly capable of following the unspoken drift of adult conversation.

Margaret smiled grimly, picking up the stick she used nowadays to help her walking, and headed for the door.

'Perhaps I wouldn't go that far,' she grudgingly admitted. She ruffled my son's dark hair. 'But that father of yours does need keeping in order.'

Adam endorsed this by a blast on his whistle that speeded Margaret's departure, set Hercules barking furiously and hurriedly drove the rest of us from the kitchen. But, all in all, it was good to be home.

I'd missed it.

★ ★ ★

I took Dame Audrea's letter to Richard Manifold and gave him the honour of approaching such authority as he thought fit. It was a kindness on my part: he loved nothing better than to appear important and to bring himself to the attention of his superiors. And unlike his two henchmen, Jack Gload and Pete Littleman, he was efficient in whatever he undertook. My half-brother had been released from the bridewell by supper-time.

He looked paler and thinner than when I had seen him last and demonstrated a surprising lack of resentment for his unjust incarceration – to begin with, at least. He was too relieved for the present that his ordeal was over. Elation vied with despondency over the news that there was still no news concerning John Jay's ship. (The prevailing view in the city was that it had been lost with all hands.)

Adela welcomed her new-found brother-in-law with a shy kiss and, it being Friday, one of her fish stews for supper, her warmth and kindliness making up for the children's complete indifference. When I apologized for them, John merely laughed and said his younger brother, Colin, had always been the same with strangers. But mention of his brother plunged him once more into gloom and we finished supper in almost total silence on his part. This became so oppressive that, when the meal was over, Adela suggested that I take John to the Green Lattis, where a beaker or two – or even three – of their best ale might improve his mood.

Nothing loath, I walked my half-brother up Small Street in the sunshine of a warm August evening and found a favourite corner seat in the as yet deserted aleroom, secluded from the prying eyes of the dozens of after-supper drinkers who would soon be joining us.

John downed his first beaker very nearly in one gulp and, as Adela had foreseen, this considerably raised his spirits.

'You see,' he said, wiping his mouth with the back of his hand, 'I was right to trust you to clear my name.' He hesitated, then asked, 'Would you be willing to tell me all about it? How you managed it. What happened exactly?'

There was no reason, I felt, why he shouldn't be told the whole story. He had a right to know the fate of the young man whom he obviously resembled.

'Very well,' I agreed and fetched us another beaker of ale apiece. At the same time, I tried to persuade myself that I really wasn't interested in proving to my young half-brother just how clever I'd been. (And, indeed, when I came to think about things in detail, I wasn't so sure that I had been particularly clever in this instance.)

'Right,' I murmured, settling back on the bench beside him. 'It's complicated, so listen carefully.'

When I at last finished speaking, there was

a long silence between us. The aleroom had filled up, and all around us, the chattering of Bristol voices, with their familiar, hardedged, west country burr and Saxon diphthongs, was deafening. Still without speaking, John Wedmore signalled to a passing potboy to bring us another drink. And to my astonishment, we got it almost at once. (Potboys in the Green Lattis are often mysteriously afflicted with deafness and blindness when things get busy.)

'So,' my half-brother muttered at last, 'the truth's finally out. Anthony Bellknapp is exposed as the murderer he was and has been justly punished by George Applegarth.' He emitted a little snort of mirthless laughter.

I regarded him curiously. 'You sound as if you knew them,' I said. 'My powers of story-telling must be better than I thought.'

'Oh, it's not that,' John answered, without, I'm sure, meaning to be rude. 'The truth is, I *did* know them. Well, I knew the steward and his wife. But as for Anthony Bellknapp' – he spat vigorously into the rushes – 'I only had the misfortune of meeting him once.'

I digested this, sipping my ale, but quite unconscious of the fact as a suspicion slowly formed at the back of my mind.

'What do you mean? What are you saying? That ... that...?'

My half-brother nodded. 'Yes. I do mean what you think. Dame Audrea didn't make a mistake when she identified me as her page. I was John Jericho.'

・

It was now his turn to assume the mantle of storyteller while I listened, pushing aside my ale before my brain became too fuddled to understand what he was saying. I moved round to the other side of the table so that I could sit opposite him, occupying a stool just vacated by another customer.

'Go on,' I said.

'It was about two years after my mother had married Matthew O'Neill, and we'd gone to live in Ireland with him, that she told me who my real father had been; not Ralph Wedmore as I'd always thought, but your father, Roger Stonecarver. They'd been secret lovers and she said that whatever happened he'd promised to look after her. Perhaps he meant it. Masons and stone carvers have always been better paid than other trades, but in the end, whether he was sincere or not went for nothing. She was less than a month pregnant when he was killed. So she married my fa— She married her cousin, Ralph, who'd always been fond of her, and he brought me up as his own, although, looking back, I can see that he never really regarded me as his son. Especially not after Colin arrived, three years later.

'Anyway' – John paused to swallow a draught of ale – 'the news of my true paternity came as a shock to me. I also learned that I had an older half-brother, Roger. I was then about sixteen, a time of life when who you are seems very important. I immediately decided

368

to leave Ireland and return to Wells to try and find you. My mother pleaded with me not to go, Colin cried and begged me to stay, and even my stepfather – who rarely interfered in matters concerning us two boys – told me that he thought I was being over-hasty. He advised me to sleep on it, to consider my mother's feelings, but I wouldn't listen. I was too upset. I needed to get away.

'So I took ship at Waterford and arrived in Bristol that summer that the little Duke of York was born – I remember, because all the church bells were ringing in celebration – and from there I walked to Wells. But, of course, by then your mother was dead and I was told you were a novice at Glastonbury. But when I enquired for you at the abbey, one of the monks informed me that you'd never taken your vows and had left two years previously. No one could tell me where you were.'

'That year I was in Cornwall,' I said, thinking back to the affair at Trenowth and my subsequent, very reluctantly undertaken trip to Brittany. 'So what happened next? To you, I mean.'

John Wedmore shrugged. 'By that time I'd spent all my money. The monks at Glastonbury fed me and gave me a groat out of the poor fund to tide me on my way and I decided to go in search of my mother's family, the Actons. I made a few enquiries – there were two of them living between Wells and Wedmore – but before I got to visit them, I fell in with Dame Audrea.'

I laughed. 'How did you manage that? I wouldn't have thought her the sort of woman one just "fell in" with.'

My half-brother grinned, acknowledging the point. 'True, but miracles do happen. I just wandered into the kitchen at Croxcombe one day when she was there, and she took a fondness for me. Don't ask me why. I don't think even she knew the reason. She decided there and then to make me her page. Master Bellknapp tried to dissuade her, but she wouldn't be moved. In fact, the more he told her that she was being foolish, the more obstinate she became.'

I nodded. 'I can imagine that. A woman well set up in her own conceit was how she appeared to me. Not one to admit she was in the wrong.'

'No.' John's face grew sombre. 'And, indeed, in this instance she was proved right. I was a good and loyal servant to her until that night ... That night when her own son came back to rob her.'

'Tell me your version of events,' I said. 'I've heard George Applegarth's.'

He swallowed the dregs of his ale and placed both elbows on the table. 'I don't suppose my version differs much from his. As you already know, Dame Audrea, Master Bellknapp, young Simon and most of the household officers had gone on a visit to Kewstoke Hall, the home of the daughter, Lady Chauntermerle and her husband. I'd stayed behind because I was suffering from

370

toothache, and so had George Applegarth. He had broken his arm. The evening before the robbery, he was drinking fairly steadily in order to ease the pain, and at one point, I saw Jenny slip something into his ale, but attached no significance to it. Why should I? Like a good wife, she was giving him a potion to help him sleep. I nearly asked her for some myself. A pity I didn't. She'd probably still be alive today.

'I retired early. I had a truckle-bed in a passageway near the mistress's room. Usually I slept like the dead, but that night my toothache woke me up after an hour or two. I got up and went down to the hall, intending to get myself some clove paste from the medicine chest, but as I reached the bottom of the stairs, I saw Jenny and there was a man with her. He had a sack with him, and the door to the cupboard where the silver was kept was standing open. Even though my wits were befuddled with pain, I could see what was going on. Just before they became aware of my presence, I'd heard her call him Anthony, so I guessed he was the elder son people talked about. The one who'd been turned out of the house two years before.'

'Then they both saw you,' I said. 'And Anthony went for you with his knife.'

'Yes. I heard Jenny scream as the blade went into my chest, and just before I lost consciousness, I saw him turn on her, stabbing her just as he'd done me. My last thought was that both of us were dead.'

'But you weren't. So, how did you survive?'

'I couldn't have been wounded in a very vital spot. I lost a lot of blood, but I eventually recovered consciousness. I was as weak as a fledgling bird, but I wasn't dead, although I'd obviously been left as such. I was somewhere deep in Croxcombe woods, covered with leaves and branches, where, I suppose, I was meant to rot away until my flesh had been eaten off my bones by ants and animals. Until, if anyone found me, I was unrecognizable. I managed to get to my feet, although I could barely stand. I vaguely remember staggering about, sometimes falling over, but always picking myself up again. Then I was violently sick, but by that time, I was passing out once more. I can recall tripping over a tree root, but after that nothing ... until I came to my senses in Hamo Gough's hut.'

'You knew him?'

'Oh, yes. Not well, but by sight and to exchange the odd word with. He'd dressed my wound with cobwebs and bits of mouldy bread and bound my chest with a strip of linen, and as soon as I was sensible, he fed me slops of boiled oats and water ... I actually thanked him for looking after me and asked if he'd let them know at the manor that I was safe.' My half-brother laughed derisively. 'Of course, it was then he told me that I was a hunted criminal – that half the countryside was out searching for me – on a charge of robbery and murder.'

'You told him the truth?'

372

'Naturally, but I might as well have held my breath. He didn't believe me. He was sure, like everyone else, that I was the thief and murderer of Jenny Applegarth, and nothing I could say would convince him otherwise.'

'How did he think you got stabbed yourself?'

'I asked him that, and he said he supposed it was during a scuffle with Jenny. But I don't think he ever reasoned it out properly. He had only one object, and that was to persuade me to tell him where I'd buried the stolen goods. He said he'd keep me captive until I did, so in the end, I told him that when I recovered and was sufficiently strong to leave the hut, I'd take him to the place and we'd share them between us. I said I couldn't describe the spot exactly, but I'd know it again when I saw it.'

'Hoping to escape in the meantime?' I suggested.

John nodded. 'But I knew I'd have to get my strength back first, before I could do anything. Also, I needed a place to lie low until the immediate hue and cry died down. I was a marked man. Only Jenny Applegarth knew the truth, and she was dead. Somehow, I had to get to Bristol and find a ship to take me back to Ireland. For several weeks, I pretended to be weaker than I really was, putting off the day when I'd have to overpower Hamo. When he left the hut, he tied me to the bed and locked the door behind him. If anyone approached the hut, he knew I wouldn't call out for fear of being found and taken.'

'So?' I prompted as he stared sadly into his empty beaker. I hailed a potboy and ordered more ale.

'So,' my half-brother continued, perking up, 'the inevitable happened. Hamo forgot to lock the door, and that on a day when he'd failed to tie me very securely. He must have been in a hurry for some reason. I managed to free myself and went. And I had absolutely no compunction in really turning thief and filling my pockets from his store of money. I was penniless and I had to get back to Ireland somehow.'

'Weren't you afraid Hamo would tell the authorities when he discovered your escape?'

John took a swig of ale from his freshly filled beaker and shook his head.

'No. He'd have been forced to admit that he'd been sheltering me from the law, and would himself have fallen foul of it. All the same, I travelled by night and lay low by day until I reached Bristol, where I easily found a ship sailing to Waterford. And nothing,' he added violently, 'would have tempted me back to this part of the world had it not been for Colin's being a part of this fated expedition of Master Jay's. There's no news of the ship, I suppose?'

Gloomily, I had to admit that no sighting had as yet been reported. 'But you must stay with us,' I went on, 'until something definite is heard, or ... or until...'

'Or until it's plain that the ship and all her crew are lost,' he finished for me. 'It might be months. Are you sure your wife will want me?'

But when we returned to Small Street, Adela was at pains to assure her new-found brother-in-law that he would be more than welcome to remain with us if he had the strength to endure the curious attentions of three small children and the vagaries of an undisciplined dog. John grinned and said he thought he might manage it. So for the next couple of weeks, to keep himself busy and his mind from dwelling too often on the possible fate of his brother, he accompanied me on my expeditions in and around the city, learning the art of peddling and eventually getting so good at it that he thought he might try earning a living by the same means when he returned to Ireland. And it was one afternoon, as we were returning home for supper through Redcliffe, and as we approached Bristol Bridge, that we saw an elderly, grey-haired man pacing around, muttering busily to himself and making copious notes in a notebook.

'What's he doing?' John asked, breaking the miserable silence that had engulfed us ever since the Redcliffe gatekeeper had assured us that no news had been received during our absence of Master Jay and his crew.

I drew in my breath sharply. 'I believe I might know who he is,' I said.

As we approached the gentleman, I doffed my hat. 'Master Botoner?' I enquired.

He frowned. 'I prefer to be called William Worcester,' he corrected me. 'But how do you know who I am, Master?'

'Oh, your fame precedes you, sir,' I said. 'An acquaintance met you in Cambridge. You were able to give him some information regarding his family in Wells, learned from your sister, Mistress Jay.'

'I remember,' he answered shortly. 'The Bellknapps.' Fortunately, he seemed disinclined to pursue the subject further, merely waving his notebook in my face and asking, 'Do you know that this bridge is seventy-two yards long and five yards wide? That the Chapel of the Blessed Mary, in the middle, is twenty-five yards long and seven yards wide? That the Back to the west of it, where the River Frome flows, is two hundred and twenty steps, or three times sixty, plus forty?'

'Amazing,' I said inadequately, not knowing quite what else to say. 'Are you ... are you measuring the whole city, sir?'

He nodded briskly. 'That is my intention. You may like to see my calculations.'

I took the proffered book, but the closely written pages were written in a sort of dog-Latin that was almost impossible to read. I handed it back with a smile that suggested I'd understood every word.

'Mistress Jay must be worried about her brother-in-law. My kinsman, here, also has a brother on the voyage.'

Master Worcester nodded at John. 'Then you have my sympathy, young man. The Isle of Brazil, indeed!' He didn't say, 'What nonsense!' but he plainly thought it. 'Yes, it's a worrying time, Chapman, particularly as she has been recently widowed. I am here to sort out her affairs, but I shall stay now until there is some news. I shall keep myself occupied, as you see, writing the topography of Bristol and its environs in this year of Our Lord, 1480. Well, well! I must get on. There's much to do. Much to do.'

We were dismissed, but as we made to move on, I turned back and said, 'Let me recommend to you, Master Worcester, a talk with the ferryman at Rownham Passage. A veritable mine of information, sir.'

'Thank 'ee! Thank 'ee!' he exclaimed. 'I shall take your advice, young man. God bless you!'

Another week went by and September was already half done. It was still warm and one golden day succeeded another, the haze of late summer hanging over the thickly wooded hills and clouding the valleys in a shimmering veil. Only the faint yellowing of the leaves and a sudden sharp bite in the air, night and morning, hinted that autumn was not too far away. And then, three days before the feast of Saint Matthew, we were just sitting down to dinner when the clanging of the common bell arrested us with our spoons halfway to our mouths. Adam immediately bellowed in competition, furious that anything should be allowed to make more noise than he did.

Nicholas and Elizabeth screamed briefly in sympathy, then defied my strict instructions to remain where they were and, struggling down from their stools, beat me to the street door by a hairsbreadth. Adela and my half-brother followed so hot on my heels that they nearly managed to trip me up.

Small Street, like every other, was crowded with people, most interrupted in the middle of their meal, some still holding spoons and even bowls, all making as fast as possible for the High Cross at the junction of High Street, Wine Street, Broad Street and Corn Street. We pushed and jostled our way as close as we could to the crier, who, when the common bell at last stopped its insistent tolling, informed us that news had just come from Ireland that John Jay's ship and all his crew were safe and sound in Waterford. They had limped into port there early the previous morning and word had been carried urgently to Bristol on the next ship leaving harbour. The Isle of Brazil still remained, alas, an unrealized dream, but no lives had been lost and the ship was unharmed. Thanksgiving would be offered for God's great goodness at every church throughout the city, whose bells were already beginning to ring out in celebration, as no doubt they also were across the water, in Ireland.

The following day, I said goodbye to John Wedmore as he boarded the same ship that had brought the happy news to Bristol and was now returning home.

'Don't forget me,' he said, gripping my hands. 'Apart from the fact that I owe you more than I can ever repay, we are brothers. We share the same blood. If ever you should come to Waterford, ask for Matthew O'Neill. Everyone knows him in those parts. You'll be treated like a hero. If not, my mother will want to know why.'

We embraced and I watched him walk up the gangplank. At the top he turned and waved, grinning in the same way that I could just about remember my father grinning when I was a child. He was going home to his family, and I had a sneaking feeling that I would miss him more than he would miss me. The brother I had never known I had, and of whose existence I had only recently been made aware, was going out of my life before I had hardly got to know him.

I sighed and turned away from the quay. But then my pace quickened. I had my own family, waiting eagerly for my return. Well, Adela was, and that was all that really mattered.